The Taiheiki

Taiheiki. English

A CHRONICLE OF MEDIEVAL JAPAN

Translated, with an

Introduction and Notes

by Helen Craig McCullough

GREENWOOD PRESS, PUBLISHERS
WESTPORT, CONNECTICUT

Library of Congress Cataloging in Publication Data

Taiheiki. English.
 The Taiheiki : a chronicle of medieval Japan.

 Ascribed to Kojima Hōshi and others.
 Reprint of the 1959 ed. published by Columbia
University Press, New York, which was issued as no. 59 of
Records of civilization, sources and studies.
 1. Japan--History--Period of northern and southern
courts, 1336-1392--Fiction. 2. Godaigo, Emperor of
Japan, 1288-1338--Fiction. I. Kojima Hōshi, d. 1374.
II. McCullough, Helen Craig. III. Series: Records of
civilization, sources and studies ; no. 59.
[PL790.T3E5 1976]   895.6'3'2   75-31443
ISBN 0-8371-8510-6

The addition to the "Records of Civilization: Sources and Studies" of a group of translations of Oriental historical materials, of which this volume is one, was made possible by funds granted by Carnegie Corporation of New York. That Corporation is not, however, the author, owner, publisher, or proprietor of this publication, and is not to be understood as approving by virtue of its grant any of the statements made or views expressed therein.

Copyright © 1959 Columbia University Press, New York

All rights reserved

Originally published in 1959 by Columbia University Press, New York

Reprinted with the permission of Columbia University Press

Reprinted in 1976 by Greenwood Press,
a division of Williamhouse-Regency Inc.

Library of Congress Catalog Card Number 75-31443

ISBN 0-8371-8510-6

Printed in the United States of America

RECORDS OF CIVILIZATION
SOURCES AND STUDIES

EDITED UNDER THE AUSPICES OF THE
DEPARTMENT OF HISTORY, COLUMBIA UNIVERSITY

GENERAL EDITOR

JACQUES BARZUN
Professor of History

EDITORS EMERITI

JAMES T. SHOTWELL
Bryce Professor Emeritus of the History of International Relations

AUSTIN P. EVANS
Professor Emeritus of History

EDITOR: EUROPEAN RECORDS

JOHN H. MUNDY
Associate Professor of History

EDITORS: ORIENTAL RECORDS

C. MARTIN WILBUR
Professor of Chinese History

WM. THEODORE DE BARY
Associate Professor of Chinese and Japanese

CONSULTING EDITORS

SALO W. BARON
*Professor of Jewish History, Literature, and
  Institutions on the Miller Foundation
Director of the Center of Israeli Studies*

GILBERT HIGHET
Anthon Professor of the Latin Language and Literature

DONALD KEENE
Associate Professor of Japanese

PAUL O. KRISTELLER
Professor of Philosophy

GARRETT MATTINGLY
Professor of History

Preface

THIS TRANSLATION IS BASED primarily on the most widely current edition (*rufubon*) of the *Taiheiki*, which appears in many modern collectanea. (For the most part, I have used the text printed in Mozume Takakazu, *Shinshaku Nihon bungaku sōsho* [Tokyo, 1923–30; ser. 2, vol. 5].) Occasionally it has seemed preferable to follow one of two variant versions regarded as closer than the *rufubon* to the original *Taiheiki*: the *Saigen'inbon* (edited by Washio Junkei, Tokyo, 1936) and the *Kandabon* (edited by Shigeno An'eki, Kokusho Kankōkai, Tokyo, 1907). Numerous obvious errors and inconsistencies in the *rufubon* have also been corrected through reference to other versions collated in the *Sankō taiheiki* edited by Imai Kōsai (Kokusho Kankōkai, Tokyo, 1914). There is as yet no adequate commentary for the *Taiheiki* as a whole. Among modern studies of portions of the text, the most useful have been Ishida Kichisada, *Taiheiki shinshaku* (Tokyo, 1928) and Nagazumi Yasuaki, *Taiheiki* (*Zoku Nihon koten tokuhon* 5, Tokyo, 1948).

It is a pleasure to record my indebtedness for many kind suggestions and corrections to Professor Chen Shih-hsiang, Professor Ichiko Teiji, Professor Donald Keene, William McCullough, Sir George Sansom, and Professor Donald Shively. For financial support which enabled me to enjoy Professor Ichiko's generous assistance in Tokyo, I am grateful to the Fulbright program of the United States Government.

HELEN CRAIG MCCULLOUGH

※ Contents

PREFACE   vii
INTRODUCTION   xv

THE TAIHEIKI

ONE   3
The Reign of Go-Daigo Tenno and the Prosperity of the Military, 3; The Abolition of the Barriers, 6; The Nomination of a Consort and the Matter of Lady Sammi, 8; The Princes, 10; The Inner Princess Prays for a Safe Delivery; the Matter of Toshimoto's Feigned Seclusion, 12; The Band of Roisterers and Gen'e's Discourses on Literature, 14; Yorikazu Changes His Loyalty, 18; Suketomo and Toshimoto Go Down to the Kantō; the Imperial Message, 24.

TWO   28
The Imperial Journeys to the Southern Capital and the Northern Peak, 28; The Arrest of the Monks and Their Removal to Rokuhara; Tameakira's Poem, 31; The Three Monks Go Down to the Kantō, 33; Toshimoto no Ason Goes Back to the Kantō, 38; The Opinion of Nagasaki Shinsaemon-no-jō and the Matter of Master Kumawaka, 42; The Execution of Toshimoto and the Matter of Sukemitsu, 51; Marvelous Things in the Realm, 54; Morokata Climbs the Mountain; the Battle of Karasaki Beach, 57; The Highnesses of the Jimyōin Go to Rokuhara, 62; The Coming of the Supreme

Highness Is Found to Be a Deceit, Wherefore the Heart of the Mountain Gate Changes; Also, the Matter of Chi Hsin, 63.

THREE 67

The Dream of the Supreme Highness and the Matter of Kusunoki, 67; The Battle of Kasagi; How Suyama and Komiyama Attacked by Night, 70; The Supreme Highness Flees from Kasagi, 79; The Battle of Akasaka Castle, 85; Sakurayama's Suicide, 91.

FOUR 93

The Captives of Kasagi Are Put to Death or Sent into Exile; the Matter of Lord Fujifusa, 93; The Verse of the Seven-Year-Old Prince, 100; The Matter of the First Prince and the Prince of the Myōhōin, 101; Chün Ming-chi Visits the Palace, 103; The Grief of the Inner Princess, 104; The Former Sovereign Goes into Exile, 105; The Matter of Bingo no Saburō Takanori; the Fighting Between Wu and Yüeh, 107.

FIVE 127

The Enthronement of the Highness of the Jimyōin, 127; Lord Nobufusa Serves Two Masters, 128; The Extinction of the New Perpetual Lamp of the Central Hall, 130; The Sagami Lay Monk Amuses Himself with Field Music; the Matter of the Dog Fights, 131; How Tokimasa Shut Himself Up at Enoshima to Pray, 133; The Prince of the Great Pagoda Flees to Kumano, 135.

SIX 150

The Dream of Lady Mimbukyō, 150; Kusunoki Goes to the Tennōji; the Matter of Suda, Takahashi, and Utsunomiya, 152; Masashige Beholds the FORECAST of the Tennōji, 160; The Prince of the Great Pagoda Issues a Command to the Lay Monk Akamatsu Enshin, 162; A Host from the Kantō Goes Up to the Capital, 163; The Battle of Akasaka; How Hitomi and Homma Went before Others, 166.

Contents xi

SEVEN 175

The Battle of Yoshino Castle, 175; The Battle of Chihaya Castle, 181; Nitta Yoshisada Receives an Imperial Mandate, 188; The Rising of Akamatsu, 190; Doi and Tokunō Raise Their Banners, 191; The Former Sovereign Goes to Funanoe, 192; The Battle of Funanoe, 198.

EIGHT 201

The Battle of Maya, and the Battles of Sakabe and Segawa, 201; The Battle of the Twelfth Day of the Third Month, 205; The Highness of the Jimyōin Goes to Rokuhara, 209; The Sacred Rituals in the Palaces of the Emperor and the Retired Emperor; the Battle of Yamazaki, 214; The Soldier-Monks of the Enryakuji Invade the Capital, 217; The Battle of the Third Day of the Fourth Month, and the Valor of Mega Magosaburō, 221; The Supreme Highness Performs the Rites of the Golden Wheel; Lord Chigusa Fights in the Capital, 228; The Fire at the Tani-no-dō Temple, 235.

NINE 237

Lord Ashikaga Goes Up to the Capital, 237; The Attack on Yamazaki and the Battle of Koganawate, 240; Lord Ashikaga Crosses Beyond Ōe Mountain, 244; Lord Ashikaga Comes to Shinomura, Whereupon the Men of the Provinces Gallop to Join Him, 246; Takauji Offers Up a Petition at Shinomura Hachiman Shrine, 250; The Attack on Rokuhara, 253; The Flight of the Supreme Highness and the Former Emperors, 259; The Suicide of Nakatoki and His Warriors, 266; The Fifth Prince Captures the Supreme Highness and the Former Emperors; the Minister Sukena Renounces the World, 270; The Defeat of the Chihaya Attackers, 271.

TEN 273

Master Senjuō Flees from Ōkura Valley, 273; The Revolt of Nitta Yoshisada; How a Goblin Summoned the Armies of Echigo, 274; Miura Ōtawa Speaks of Warfare, 281; The Battle of Kamakura, 285; The Suicide of the Akahashi Governor of Sagami; Homma's Suicide, 287; A Beach Appears at

Inamura Cape, 289; War Fires in Kamakura; the Bravery of Nagasaki and His Son, 292; Daibutsu Sadanao and Kanazawa Sadamasa Die in Battle, 295; Shinnin Dies by His Own Hand, 296; The Suicide of Shioda and His Son, 297; The Suicide of the Shiaku Lay Monk, 298; The Suicide of the Andō Lay Monk; the Matter of Wang Ling of Han, 299; Master Kameju Flees to Shinano; Sakon-no-taifu Escapes in Disguise to Ōshū, 301; The Last Battle of Nagasaki Jirō Takashige, 305; Takatoki and His Kinsmen Kill Themselves at the Tōshōji Temple, 310.

ELEVEN 312

Godaiin Uemon Muneshige Deceives Sagami Tarō, 312; The Generals Send Couriers to Funanoe, 315; The Emperor Visits Shosha Mountain; Nitta's Report, 317; Masashige Comes to Hyōgo; the Emperor Returns to the Capital, 320; The Battle of Tsukushi, 322; The Surrender of the Military Governor of Nagato, 326; The Suicide of the Steward of Ushi-ga-hara in Echizen, 328; The Suicide of the Protector of Etchū; the Matter of the Unquiet Spirits, 330; The Punishment of the Besiegers of Mount Kongō; the Matter of Sakai Sadatoshi, 334.

TWELVE 340

The Court Governs Alone, 340; The Building of the Great Palace Enclosure; the Matter of the Shrine of Sugawara no Michizane, 346; The Rites for the Pacification of the State, and the Rewards Given to the Grand Marshals, 363; The Extravagance of Lord Chigusa and the Monk Reformer Monkan; the Matter of the Most Holy Gedatsu, 365; Hiroari Shoots a Strange Bird, 371; The Matter of the Garden of Divine Waters, 374; The Banishment of the Princely Minister of Military Affairs; the Matter of Lady Li, 379.

CHARACTER LIST 389

INDEX 393

LIST OF ILLUSTRATIONS

The Emperor Go-Daigo   Frontispiece

	Facing page
The Two Kings	30
Prince Morinaga (The Prince of the Great Pagoda)	31
Medieval Japanese House	62
Medieval Japanese Castle, Showing Tower	63
Soldier-Monks	222
Battle Scene	223
Warrior in Armor	254
Ashikaga Takauji	255

Introduction

THE *Taiheiki* BELONGS to the genre of Japanese literature known as *gunki monogatari,* or war tales. Because these stories celebrate martial adventures, they have sometimes been regarded as prose counterparts of the Homeric epics. Like the *Iliad* and the *Odyssey,* they have a strong tradition of oral recitation, and most of them seem to be the composite works of numerous anonymous authors. To cite an extreme example, there are eighty-eight extant versions of the *Heike monogatari* (*Tale of the Heike*), the best-known of these stories, which, sung for many generations by blind entertainers, was subjected to all the accretions and modifications which such a history implies. Again, like the Homeric epics, the war tales deal with historical events and personages, not denying a role to supernatural forces, but assigning great importance to gods, dreams, curses, and omens. The virtues they extol are warlike prowess, bravery, loyalty, filial piety, family pride, and reverence for gods and buddhas; they are filled with descriptions of heroism and cowardice, of subtle strategy and foolish blunders in battle, and of the weapons and armor of combatants.

Although additional resemblances could be cited, there remain fundamental differences. Even in the best of the war tales, one will not find the sonorous sweep of Homer's language, the wealth of his imagery, or the power and depth of his characterizations. Except for occasional poetic passages, they are written in simple and direct language, comparable perhaps to the Icelandic sagas at their best; flat and banal at their worst. If efforts to achieve distinction are made, they are likely to take the form of a somewhat monotonous use of parallelism, or of allusions to familiar Chinese and Japanese literary classics and historical events, some of which develop into lengthy digressions. Occasionally a minor character is brought to life by a revealing action, but for the most part their pages are filled with unsubstantial personages who never become much more than names, particularly since there are a great many of them. When one of these heroes falls in battle, we feel no particular sense of tragedy or personal involvement, as we do when we read of the death of Hector.

In short, the *gunki monogatari* are not great literature. But the best of them are worth reading, not only for what they have to tell about a society of great interest, but also because they are lively tales such as have found audiences everywhere in every age—first-rate entertainment of their kind.

There are five major war tales in existence today, all dating from the thirteenth and fourteenth centuries and relating events of the twelfth and fourteenth centuries: the *Hōgen monogatari* (*Tale of Hōgen*) and *Heiji monogatari* (*Tale of Heiji*), two short accounts of brief wars in 1156 and 1160, respectively; the *Heike monogatari,* which describes the downfall of a powerful military clan in the closing years of the twelfth century; the *Gempei seisuiki* (*Rise and Fall of the Minamoto and Taira*), a much longer version of the *Heike monogatari,* regarded as a separate work; and the *Taiheiki,* which deals with the civil wars of the first half of the fourteenth century.

The *Taiheiki,* the most recent of the five tales, and by far the longest except for the *Gempei seisuiki,* runs to two volumes in most printed editions. Of its forty chapters, more than two thirds are devoted to episodic, disorganized accounts of fighting in local areas; the sort of thing one finds in certain Icelandic sagas, where stories of particular interest to a certain family or other small group have been added haphazardly over the years, greatly to the detriment of the work as a whole. These episodes are not subordinated to a central unifying theme, and they are so similar to one another as to be dull reading for any but the specialist. When they are eliminated, however, a work remains which is still of respectable proportions.

Introduction

Moreover, there is a certain amount of evidence to indicate that it may include all of the original version of the *Taiheiki*. It is these remaining chapters of which the present translation consists: the first twelve, beginning more or less with the accession of the Emperor Go-Daigo in 1318, describing that sovereign's early unsuccessful attempts to overthrow the Kamakura shogunate, and ending with his triumphant return from exile in 1333, and the subsequent brief restoration of imperial power.

A good many sticks of Chinese ink have been consumed on behalf of theories of various kinds concerning the authorship of the *Taiheiki*, the date at which the present version was completed, and even the meaning of the title itself, apropos of which one sixteenth-century commentator plaintively inquired, "Since *taihei* is a word meaning peace in the realm, why should one say *taihei* when disturbances in the four seas are described?"[1] (The *ki* of *Taiheiki* means chronicle or record.) The obvious meaning of *taihei* is great peace or grand peace, and it is in this sense that the title has invariably been construed. But it is equally possible to interpret *taihei* as grand pacification, a term which appears more than once in the *Taiheiki* itself, referring to Go-Daigo's efforts to destroy, or "pacify," the shogunate. This seems to be an interpretation which is worth tentative adoption, at least; so let us say that *Taiheiki* means *Chronicle of Grand Pacification*.

As regards the *Taiheiki*'s authorship, enough is known about the successive stages of its growth to show fairly clearly that it has passed through many hands; a conclusion further supported by such internal evidence as factual contradictions and inconsistencies, differences of literary style, and varying attitudes toward the opposing sides. The one bit of specific evidence is an entry in the diary of Tōin Kinsada (1340–1399), a member of a prominent Kyoto family of courtiers and the author of a well-known and still valuable genealogical work, the *Sompi bummyaku*. Under date of the third day of the fifth month of 1374, Kinsada says:

I understand that the monk Kojima died on the twenty-eighth or twenty-ninth. He was the author of the *Taiheiki*, which is immensely

---

[1] Nisshō, *Taiheikishō* (Muromatsu Iwao, *Kokubun chūshaku zensho*, Tokyo, 1908–1910, vol. 8), p. 4. "The four seas," a term borrowed from the Chinese, means "the world" (i.e., Japan).

popular nowadays. Although of low degree, he was known as a man of great learning. His death is a pity.²

Although this is interesting, it tells us very little, since Kojima, as a man "of low degree," is not mentioned in genealogies or other records. It has been suggested that he was a monk of the Enryakuji Temple on Mount Hiei (Hieizan), since the *Taiheiki* shows a close acquaintance with the Hieizan monasteries, but it can as well be argued that he was a Zen monk, in view of the strong Zen coloration of some parts of the book. If we accept the theory that the *Taiheiki* is the work of more than one person, there is not much to be gained by such speculation.

Nor need we enter here into the complicated problem of dating. Almost the only thing that can be said with any degree of assurance is that the *Taiheiki* as a whole probably reached approximately its present form at some time during the sixth or seventh decade of the fourteenth century, and that the first twelve chapters undoubtedly go back to a much earlier period—some of them, perhaps, to before the fall of the Hōjō in 1333.

Until comparatively recent times, it was pretty much taken for granted by most people that the *Taiheiki* was a reliable work of history, written primarily for entertainment and edification, to be sure, but presenting an essentially accurate picture of events as they occurred. In the closing years of the nineteenth century, scholars began to look upon it more critically, pointing out discrepancies between its statements and those of family records, temple archives, and other documents of undisputed authenticity. A particularly devastating attack of this kind was delivered in 1891 by a famous historian, Kume Kunitake, in a series of articles uncompromisingly entitled, "The *Taiheiki* Is Worthless as a Historical Source," which, asserting that the *Taiheiki* was written to appeal to the lowest type of audience, exclaimed of Tōin Kinsada's diary entry, "One hesitates to call Kojima learned, but there is no doubt that he was of low degree!" ³

² *Tōin Kinsada nikki* (Tōkyō Teikoku Daigaku and Bunka Daigaku, *Bunka Daigaku shishi sōsho*, Tokyo, 1897–1908, vol. 48, pp. 1–41), p. 27b.
³ Kume Kunitake, "Taiheiki wa shigaku ni eki nashi." *Shigaku zasshi*, II (1891), 230–40, 279–92, 420–33, 487–501, 562–78. See p. 493 for the passage quoted.

Introduction

The impact of such castigations has been softened by more recent investigations, based in part on discoveries of new documents. Some of the *Taiheiki*'s most controversial statements have been corroborated, and there is probably no modern Japanese historian who would agree that it is useless as a historical source, or that it must be dismissed as a mere romance written to cater to the tastes of a credulous and ignorant public. At the same time, it is important to remember that it is not intended to be purely a history, and that the author's attitude toward such things as dates and numbers is extremely casual. Although there is probably relatively little outright invention of whole episodes, it is fairly clear that in some instances the author has not hesitated to offer a necessary explanation, or to supply a regrettable omission.[4] His attitude is somewhat similar to that of the learned ninth-century Italian biographer who wrote:

> Where I have not found any history of any of these bishops, and have not been able by conversation with aged men, or inspection of the monuments, or from any other authentic source, to obtain information concerning them, in such a case, in order that there might not be a break in the series, I have composed the life myself, with the help of God and the prayers of the brethren.[5]

Many inaccuracies and contradictions will be observed by all readers of this translation; many more will be apparent to students of Japanese history. It would be wearisome to deal with each of these in detail, and inconsistent with the basic intent of the *Taiheiki* itself. I propose rather to give some attention in the following pages to two broader subjects: the main course of events described in the first twelve chapters, and the general background upon which the story is superimposed.

Let us first examine the society of fourteenth-century Japan, which was made up of three major elements, the Kyoto court, the great Buddhist monasteries, and the provincial warriors. Of course, courtiers, monks, and warriors together constituted only a small minority of the total population, being far outnumbered by peas-

---

[4] For example, the appearance of Kusunoki Masashige to the emperor in a dream (Chapter Three), or the letter written by Prince Morinaga after his imprisonment (Chapter Twelve).

[5] Agnellus, Bishop of Ravenna. Quoted in G. G. Coulton, *Medieval Panorama* (Meridian Books edition, 1955; first published Cambridge Univ. Press, 1938). p. 439.

ants, artisans, and merchants. But, as Sir George Sansom has remarked, the peasants "merely did what they were told." [6] We glimpse some of them occasionally in the pages of the *Taiheiki*, carried off as laborers by armies on the march, having their wretched huts burned down to make beacon fires or torn apart for use in fortifications, or murdered wantonly by head-seeking warriors. Again we see them scavenging for spoils in the debris left behind by a defeated host, or, as outlaws, harassing and robbing those who flee. But for the most part they dwell in faceless obscurity, rice-machines serving their betters.

Of the people who mattered, the emperor and his courtiers mattered the most—albeit in a limited sense. As the source of coveted ranks, titles, and other honors, and as the guardian of the cultural heritage of the past, the court enjoyed an unrivaled prestige. Whatever the vicissitudes suffered by the throne, the reverence inspired by the divine ruler was something that always had to be taken into account by unruly subjects. Of the imperial line stretching back into antiquity, it was taught, "There is no land that is not the emperor's land, nor are there any folk that are not the emperor's folk." The great capital city of Heian was more than a cultural center. In spite of all that had happened since the glorious era celebrated by Murasaki Shikibu, it still contained virtually everything that counted of Japanese civilization, and those who lived elsewhere were *ipso facto* barbarians.

But never in Japanese history has there been a sovereign who could claim truthfully, "There is no land that is not the emperor's land, nor are there any folk that are not the emperor's folk." There have always been powerful subjects to circumscribe the ruler's freedom of action.[7] To understand the situation of the imperial court in the early years of the fourteenth century, it is necessary to go back for a moment to the history of some of those subjects.

Prior to modern times, there was one great attempt to establish a centralized imperial government, the Chinese-inspired Taika Re-

---

[6] *Japan: A Short Cultural History* (New York, Appleton-Century, rev. ed., 1943), p. 320.
[7] Some people have maintained that it is the very weakness of the Japanese throne that has preserved it for so many centuries, since ambitious subjects have always been able to use its prestige for their own ends.

Introduction

form of 645. All land was declared to be the property of the sovereign, to be redistributed among his subjects at regular intervals, and all local administration was to be put into the hands of officials appointed by the court. It was not really to the advantage of anyone except members of the imperial family that such a system should be made to work. In a rice economy where land was the source of wealth, it was much more profitable to establish one's own tax-free estates than to rely solely upon official stipends for income; and that is what was done by the great nobles, the imperial ministers of the Fujiwara family, who controlled the government from the Taika Reform until the end of the eleventh century.

During the centuries of Fujiwara domination, the public domain shrank steadily before the encroachment of private lands. We need not inquire into the details of the process. What is important is that no successful effort was ever made to combat it, so that by about 1150 all of Kyoto society, including the imperial household, was living upon the income from provincial estates, and the elaborate Chinese administrative hierarchy had long been dead of malnutrition, its offices mere empty honors. The incomes derived from private estates were sufficiently high to sustain a most luxurious standard of living, as readers of the *Tale of Genji* will recall, but of course the incomes continued only as long as the estates themselves remained unmolested by usurpers. In the absence of effective central military and administrative controls in the provinces, it was primarily the prestige of the court and the Fujiwara that safeguarded such properties from the depredations of land-hungry warriors.

Although the court had no armies of its own, it was not completely without military resources. During the centuries of Fujiwara rule, two great warrior clans grew up in the land, the Taira and the Minamoto (also called the Heike or Heishi and the Genji). These warriors considered it a supreme honor to be called upon by the throne to suppress local troublemakers, or to guard the capital against the incursions of soldier-monks from the monasteries of the Kyoto-Nara area, and they did not seem to mind being treated as servants and country bumpkins by the haughty aristocrats of the capital. It was natural, therefore, that the Taira and the Minamoto should have been summoned in 1156 and 1160, when rival court factions came to blows over the question of the imperial succession.[8] But after the fighting was over, the chief military supporter of the victorious side, Taira no Kiyomori, remained in the capital as *de facto* head of the government, ousting the Fujiwara, and completely dominating both the titular sovereign and the cloistered emperor.[9]

Kiyomori married his daughters into the imperial and Fujiwara families, assumed the title of Great Subject of the Grand Preceptorate (*dajō daijin*, the highest office in the ancient hierarchy), appointed his kinsmen to exalted positions, and in one way or another brought half the land of Japan into the possession of the Taira family. But although his dictatorial and high-handed actions gradually alienated the ex-emperor completely, there must have been many times after his death when the court wished to have him back. For he was not an innovator. He neither rejected the cultural values of the court nor sought to molest the existing land system. His successor, Minamoto no Yoritomo, was a man of quite a different stamp.

Yoritomo was the son and heir of the head of the Minamoto clan, Yoshitomo, who had been killed in the war of 1160. Sent by Kiyomori to the Kantō (eastern Japan) to live under the guardianship of a Taira clansman, Hōjō Tokimasa, he grew up as a man of forceful and sagacious nature, who soon attracted adherents in that region, the original home of the Minamoto. When at last he raised the standard of revolt, in 1180, even Hōjō Tokimasa supported him.

The Taira in Kyoto had alienated the warriors of the provinces, the courtiers, and the monasteries by their selfish and arrogant behavior. They were soon on the defensive before Yoritomo, who destroyed them decisively in 1185.[10]

After the Minamoto victory, Yoritomo retained his headquarters

---

[8] These two brief civil wars, known as the Disturbance of Hōgen and the Disturbance of Heiji, are the subjects of the *Tale of Hōgen* and the *Tale of Heiji*.

[9] Prior to this time, the Fujiwara had continued to hold all the important official titles at court, and their economic position was still very strong. Their political influence, however, had been fairly well destroyed some seventy-five years earlier, when an abdicated emperor first succeeded in displacing them and establishing his own administrative organs (known as cloister government). From then (1086) until the time of the Emperor Go-Daigo, such governmental powers as remained to the court were almost invariably exercised by a retired emperor.

[10] The battles of these years between the Taira and the Minamoto are described in the *Heike monogatari* and the *Gempei seisuiki*.

Introduction

at Kamakura in eastern Japan, whence in the name of military necessity he soon forced the court to agree to a measure which can be regarded as the beginning of the feudalization of Japanese society. This was the appointment of Minamoto vassals as protectors (*shugo*) and stewards (*jitō*) in the provinces. The protectors were somewhat like military governors, responsible for keeping the peace in their areas; the stewards were authorized to collect taxes for military purposes from all lands, including hitherto immune private estates. The effect of such innovations upon the Kyoto court may well be imagined from a contemporary entry in a noble Fujiwara's diary, which reads, "People say that the stewards will not stop at collecting commissariat rice, but will control the lands completely. It is unspeakable!" [11]

The extent of Yoritomo's interference in court affairs is suggested by another entry a month later in the same diary: "Although all of the many promotions and punishments suggested by Yoritomo are distasteful to His Majesty, whatever he desires must be done." But although Yoritomo was the undisputed political master of Japan, he treated the court with the outward forms of respect, providing generously for its economic needs. The same may be said of his two sons and successors in the office of shogun, Yoriie and Sanetomo.

After Sanetomo's death, the strength of the Kamakura shogunate appeared to waver slightly. It seemed to the ex-emperor Go-Toba, a clever and determined man, that this was a propitious time to attack the "eastern barbarians" and rid himself of their interfering protectors and stewards. On June 6, 1221, therefore, he issued a rescript calling for the chastisement of Hōjō Yoshitoki, Tokimasa's son, who by this time was the real head of the Kamakura government.[12] However, it was soon made abundantly clear that Go-Toba had miscalculated. Three large armies were dispatched promptly

---

[11] Entry of the twenty-eighth day of the eleventh month of 1185 in *Gyokuyō*, the diary of Fujiwara no Kanezane, a leading statesman of the period. (*Gyokuyō* [Kokusho Kankōkai, Tokyo, 1907], III, 119.)

[12] After the death of Yoritomo, his father-in-law Tokimasa, his widow Masako, and his brother-in-law Yoshitoki controlled the government which he had established. This was the beginning of many generations of Hōjō rule in Kamakura. No member of the family ever assumed the title of shogun, but as regents they occupied a position similar to that of the Fujiwara or retired emperors in relation to the emperors.

from Kamakura, and by July 6 the Disturbance of Shōkyū[13] had ended in the complete defeat of the court.

The full meaning of its loss of political independence was now brought home to the Kyoto court for the first time. Go-Toba was banished to the Oki Islands, his son and coconspirator Juntoku was exiled to Sado, and his son Tsuchimikado likewise was sent away from the capital (at his own desire, it is said), although he had not been implicated in the revolt. Henceforth the question of the imperial succession was decided not by the court itself but by the shogunate. The estates of the great nobles and others who had joined Go-Toba's conspiracy were confiscated, and the income of the imperial family was drastically reduced. It was at about this time, too, that the imperial palace enclosure, the extensive complex of buildings and courtyards that had housed the departments of state and the emperor, was abandoned permanently.[14] A fire in 1219 had destroyed the entire enclosure, and although a start at rebuilding was made, another fire in 1227 burned down the new buildings. Since the court was not able to bear the cost of reconstruction, the enclosure gradually fell into such complete ruin that it was used as a hunting ground. The emperors lived at various places in the capital and its environs, usually the residences of ministers of state.[15]

In the opening decades of the fourteenth century, the atmosphere in Kyoto was gloomy and pessimistic. Profoundly dissatisfied with the present, the courtiers looked back nostalgically to the days before the shogunate, when decisions of state were made in the capital, and the great civil and religious ceremonies and rituals of the four seasons were celebrated with suitable pomp and display. There was a general feeling that the world had entered the period of the

---

[13] A minor *gunki monogatari*, the *Shōkyūki*, deals with this brief war. (Shōkyū is an era name.)

[14] There is a somewhat garbled description of the enclosure in Chapter Twelve. The main buildings were the Daigokuden, or Great Hall of State, where coronations and other ceremonies of supreme importance were held; the Shishinden, used for ceremonies of slightly less moment; and the Seiryōden, the sovereign's habitual place of residence.

[15] Some of these were of considerable splendor, with buildings bearing the names of the main palace buildings. The "palace" of the *Taiheiki* was such an establishment.

Introduction

"latter end of the Law," a time of degeneration and wickedness heralding the extinction of the Buddhist teachings. A once-powerful noble who had fallen upon evil days did not seek an explanation for his misfortune in the objective circumstances in which he was placed, but blamed the times, or attributed his difficulties to an evil karma or the displeasure of a supernatural being. Again and again in the *Taiheiki* we find such remarks as the following, made by the warrior-guardian of an aristocratic prisoner:

By some karma-tie from an earlier life, this lay monk was chosen before all others to be your guardian. As though devoid of mercy, I must say to you that your time is at hand; but indeed a person like myself is without power. Many days have I delayed, awaiting tidings of your pardon, but now urgently from the Kantō there has come a command to destroy you. Please console yourself by remembering that all things are the results of the deeds of previous lives.

Closely related to these attitudes was the widely prevalent idea that change is the principle of life, and that the mighty must inevitably fall. This is a theme which recurs constantly in all the *gunki monogatari*, as in the famous opening lines of the *Heike monogatari*.

The sound of the bell of Gionshoja echoes the impermanence of all things. The hue of the flowers of the teak tree declares that they who flourish must be brought low. Yea, the proud ones are but for a moment, like an evening dream in springtime. The mighty are destroyed at the last, they are but as the dust before the wind.[16]

It was natural that all kinds of religious beliefs and superstitions should play a powerful role in such a society—Buddhism, Shinto, Chinese ideas of yin and yang, avoidance of inauspicious directions, belief in dreams, omens, and curses. It was also natural that in their desire to escape from reality many people believed fervently in the Pure Land Heaven of Amida Buddha, into which even the most unworthy could be reborn merely by reciting the name of Amida.

The avoidance of the present manifested itself also in the idealization of the past, in rigid adherence to precedent, and in the meticulous study and investigation of past ways of doing things. The men who were regarded as outstanding scholars were those who com-

[16] Translation by A. L. Sadler, "The Heike Monogatari," *Transactions of the Asiatic Society of Japan*, series 1, XLVI, part 2 (1918), 1.

piled lists of precedents and procedures from old diaries and other documents, or who jealously guarded and slavishly reproduced their ancestors' interpretations of the Chinese classics.

Virtual illiteracy was a commonplace among members of the nobility. The state university and the great private schools had long since been abandoned, and there was little incentive for most courtiers to seek an education, since family, rather than learning, had become the passport to office. The heads of the old scholar families guarded their stale secrets, while men in high place frowned upon upstarts who ventured to engage in studies inappropriate to their station in life.[17]

At Go-Daigo's court, this atmosphere of intellectual sterility was relieved somewhat by a keen interest in the newly imported Sung Confucianism, but the basic spirit of conservatism was very much present. In rebelling against the domination of Kamakura, Go-Daigo and his advisers had no desire to strike out in new directions, but sought only to restore the ancient order of things. This attitude (the same one that had actuated Go-Toba) is revealed very clearly in their slogan, "Back to Engi and Tenryaku!" [18]

Let us leave the court at Kyoto for a time, in order to give some attention to the Buddhist monasteries, the second of the three main elements of fourteenth-century society.

In the eyes of many men, the state of affairs in the great temples and monasteries was in itself ample proof that the world had entered the era of the extinction of the Buddhist Law. Of course, there were many devout and learned monks,[19] who provided the bulk of such substantial scholarly and literary activity as the period produced. Likewise, the teachings of the comparatively new Pure Land and Zen sects were a consolation and help to people of all

[17] Fujiwara no Teika, the leading poet of the day, is said to have protested strongly when a certain monk presented a commentary on the poems of the *Nihongi* to Go-Toba, on the ground that a man of low degree ought not to be allowed to express opinions concerning one of the classics of Japanese literature. Tanaka Kazuhiko, *Nihon bunkashi taikei* (Tokyo, 1938), VI, 164.

[18] Engi (901–923) and Tenryaku (947–957) actually were not very desirable eras to return to, since the growth of private estates was already well advanced, as were other processes inimical to the prosperity of the throne. But the emperors of those days escaped to some extent from Fujiwara domination, and life at court was elegant and amusing.

[19] One of the most notable of these was Gen'e, who figures in Chapter One.

classes. Despite glaring indications of corruption and worldliness, the efficacy of the prayers of the established institutions was perhaps never more highly regarded, nor the power of their curses more feared. In reporting the destruction of an ancient temple during the fighting in 1333, the *Taiheiki* reflects the superstitious awe in which the temples were held.

Now all the people spoke words of censure, saying:
"A shameless thing was the destruction of this auspicious and praiseworthy temple, a sign signifying the ruin of the Hōjō family."
How strange it was that the men of Rokuhara were struck down at Bamba within a very short while after, and all the Hōjō perished at Kamakura!

When every possible allowance is made, however, the fact remains that long before the fourteenth century, certain monasteries had become not so much centers of religion as political, military, and economic forces capable of standing up to the shogunate itself. The chief of these were the Tōdaiji and Kōfukuji in Nara (the "southern capital" of the *Taiheiki*), and the Enryakuji and Onjōji in the environs of Kyoto. The source of their strength was land, the source of all strength in ancient Japan. From the earliest times, they had been granted tax-free estates, which had been augmented steadily by new gifts, commendations, development of virgin territory, and other means. Their holdings came to occupy vast tracts in many parts of the country,[20] and their wealth increased correspondingly.

When the court became unable to preserve order in the provinces, these monasteries established their own fighting forces, at first recruited from their provincial estates and designed primarily for the defense thereof. It soon became apparent that such soldiers could serve a useful purpose in inter-temple disputes centering around estate boundaries, water rights, tax collections, and similar matters, as well as in descents upon the capital to protest against unpopular imperial appointments[21] or decisions affecting temple properties or

---

[20] The Kōfukuji at one time controlled almost all of the province of Yamato.

[21] The highest Buddhist prelates were all appointed by the emperor. Many of them appear in the *Taiheiki*, bearing such titles as Sign of the Law (*hōin*), Eye of the Law (*hōgen*), Bridge of the Law (*hokkyō*), monk reformer (*sōjō*), monk governor (*sōzu*), and teacher of discipline (*risshi*).

prerogatives. By the second half of the tenth century, there were already soldier-monks in residence at the Enryakuji and the monasteries of Nara.

If the *Taiheiki* is to be trusted, the monks of the Enryakuji rationalized this peculiar state of affairs in elegant language.

Now when the great teacher Dengyō first established this monastery, before the window of abstraction and contemplation we gazed upon the moon of permanent reality, which is the only illumination; but suddenly after the abbacy of the monk reformer Jie, we girded on the autumn frost of forged weapons over our garments of forbearance, that we might conquer interfering demons therewith. And thenceforth through the power of the Buddhist Law we expelled the evil that appeared in the realm, and through the strength of our god drove back treachery that disordered the state.

Their activities appeared in a somewhat different light to the harassed court, which they terrorized constantly during the last half of the eleventh century and the first half of the twelfth century, in particular. Indeed, it was primarily to protect itself against these incursions of thousands of hostile monks that the court called upon the military strength of the Minamoto and Taira, thereby preparing the way for the ascendancy of the warrior class.

The most troublesome monastery was the Enryakuji, of which the *Gempei seisuiki* reports:

It is related that the cloistered emperor Shirakawa used to say, "The waters of the Kamo River, the *sugoroku* dice, and the Mountain monks —these truly are things which refuse to obey the dictates of Our will." [22]

If the soldier-monks were formidable opponents, by the same token they were valuable allies. We shall see Go-Daigo courting them assiduously, and with a considerable degree of success, in his efforts to overthrow the shogunate. In particular, he went to very great lengths to win the allegiance of the Enryakuji, which figures so prominently in the *Taiheiki* that it will be useful to say a few words about it here.

The Enryakuji was founded in 788 on Mount Hiei, northeast of the capital, by the monk Saichō (Dengyō Daishi), who later introduced the teachings of the Tendai school of Buddhism into

[22] *Gempei seisuiki* (Teikoku Bunko, Tokyo, 1912), p. 89. The Enryakuji was popularly known as the Mountain, or the Mountain Gate.

Japan, making Mount Hiei the headquarters of the new sect. The original building erected by Saichō became the Central Hall, the focal point of the monastery, where the Healing Buddha Yakushi was worshiped. The general section of the mountain in which this hall was located was known as the East Pagoda. Similarly, there was a second main area called the West Pagoda, and a third called Yokawa. In addition to these three areas, which were subdivided into a total of sixteen valleys, there were two separate valleys, called Kurodani and Anrakudani. At the peak of the temple's prosperity, the whole mountain was covered with halls and cloisters, and there are said to have been three thousand monks in residence. Some of the cloisters were sufficiently important to be governed by imperial princes in holy orders, who alternated as abbots of the Tendai sect, with headquarters at the Great Pagoda in the heart of the mountain. There was also a very highly regarded Shinto shrine at the eastern base of Mount Hiei, the Hiyoshi Shrine, where a god called the King of the Mountain was worshiped. This shrine was an additional source of prestige to the monks, who periodically carried the god's sacred car down to the capital to reinforce a petition to the throne.

Let us turn our attention now to the warrior class, the third of the major elements in the society of the day. We have seen that there were two great military clans, the Taira and the Minamoto, and that the strength of the Taira was emasculated when they moved to the capital, adopted the effeminate and luxury-loving ways of the court nobility, and cut themselves off from their roots in the country. Aware of the dangers of such a course, Minamoto no Yoritomo established his government in the remote eastern town of Kamakura, prohibited free intercourse between his vassals and the capital, and strove by every means to keep the debilitating influence of Kyoto from making itself felt among the warrior class. The whole way of life of the court was the worst possible influence on a fighting man: the preoccupation with poetry contests, flower-viewing excursions, palace intrigues, elaborate rituals, ostentatious mansions, and costly dress. What was needed was to preserve intact the "way of bow and horse": bravery, skill in the military arts, a scrupulous regard for personal honor, simple and frugal living habits, filial piety, family pride, reverence for gods and buddhas, and, above all, willingness to die for one's lord.

There is a Nō play, set in the middle of the thirteenth century, in which a Hōjō vassal who has lost his lands speaks of his misfortunes. And yet not all is lost; for on the wall a tall spear still hangs, and armour with it; while in the stall a steed is tied. And if at any time there came from the City news of peril to our master—

> Then, broken though it be I would gird this armor on,
> And rusty though it be I would hold this tall spear,
> And lean-ribbed though he be I would mount my horse and ride
> Neck by neck with the swiftest,
> To write my name on the roll.
> And when the fight began
> Though the foe were many, yet would I be the first
> To cleave their ranks, to choose an adversary
> To fight with him and die.[23]

This is the spirit of loyalty in its purest manifestation, since the speaker, having been deprived of his lands, no longer derives material benefit from being a vassal. The true vassal is ready to give up his life for his lord on a moment's notice, with no questions. So in the *Taiheiki*, Utsunomiya Jibu-no-tayū sets forth without hesitation to attack a greatly superior enemy with a handful of men. "Nor did he return to his lodging place at all," says the chronicler, "for he could not cherish life, when alone he received the military's order to stand against a mighty enemy." In a sense, behavior of this kind is self-abnegation, but in another sense it springs from the highest possible regard for self—for one's own honor and the opinion of others. Quick to feel a slight dishonor, the Kamakura warrior was willing to kill himself to recover his good name. In Yoritomo's day, there was a warrior who renounced the world and became a monk because he failed to hit a deer while hunting with his lord.

Part of the explanation for this concern with honor lies in the strong family solidarity that was characteristic of warrior society. The individual was not a free agent. All of his actions reflected on the family and were conditioned by the approval of its head, whose authority was absolute. So, too, filial piety was an obligation as

---

[23] Arthur Waley, *The Nō Plays of Japan* (London, Allen and Unwin, 1950), p. 142.

Introduction

sacred as loyalty to one's lord.[24] When the *Taiheiki* tells of sons who kill the slayers of their fathers, or die with their parents "to accompany them on the road to hades," it is describing the behavior expected of offspring of warrior houses. At the destruction of Kamakura, a Hōjō retainer says of Takatoki's infant son:

Would it not be regrettable, were he to be sought out by the enemy, where like a hunted pheasant he hid in the grass; and with his young corpse dishonored the family name? Let him rather fall by the hand of His Lordship, and go together with him to the nether regions, that his filial piety may be remembered in generations to come.

Frugality and plain living were essential parts of this austere code. It is said that when a vassal entered Yoritomo's presence dressed in elaborate robes which would have done credit to a Kyoto aristocrat, Yoritomo seized a sword and slashed at the offending garments, sternly ordering their wearer to husband his resources for the support of retainers who could serve their lord in time of need.[25] The Hōjō regents also set an example of thrift in their own lives, as in the well-known incident when Tokiyori, seeking food to serve to a guest, could find nothing in the house but "some sauce at the bottom of a bowl and a little wine."[26]

As the history of the Kamakura shogunate progressed, these Spartan traits began to disappear. The story is told of how the regent Tokiyori attended a banquet given by the shogun in 1254, in the course of which he said, "It is most regrettable that of late the military arts have declined, and men seek to cultivate polite accomplishments instead of attending to their duties. Shall we not have a wrestling match here tonight?" Thereupon a number of guests left the hall precipitously, while those who remained made all manner of excuses. Only after repeated threats of disciplinary action did some ten men reluctantly agree to participate.[27]

Now that the men of Kamakura were the undisputed masters of the realm, there was less incentive to practice warlike accomplishments. At the same time, there were many temptations to lead a more pleasant life. The temptations arose chiefly from the fact that

---
[24] A conflict between these two duties often led to tragic consequences.
[25] *Azuma kagami* (*Zoku kokushi taikei*, Tokyo, 1903, vol. 4), p. 122.
[26] Sansom, p. 307.
[27] *Azuma kagami* (*Zoku kokushi taikei*, vol. 5), p. 497.

child shoguns,[28] imported from Kyoto after the extinction of Yoritomo's line in 1219, brought with them the culture of the capital. Snobbish officials, intricate ceremonies, luxurious habits, elegant diversions—everything that came was accepted unquestioningly because of the overwhelming prestige of Kyoto. Warfare became a novelty, rather than a way of life. Describing the dispatch of an army from Kamakura, the *Taiheiki* says:

Now since Shōkyū the storm winds of the east had sunk into slumber, and men were as though forgetful of the uses of bow and arrow. Wherefore were these sixty thousand warriors stirred up by the marvel of going forth to give battle, and rode out with haughty mien and splendid accoutrements. How glorious was the spectacle of their horses and armor and swords, all glittering and sparkling!

This is far from the professional spirit of Yoritomo's day. Nor would the Lord of Kamakura have approved of the siege described in Chapter Seven, where the besiegers called in prostitutes and poetry masters to relieve the tedium of camp life, and killed one another in quarrels over dice.

It is true that some of the influences from the capital were not incompatible with the old warrior code: for example, the vogue of Chu Hsi Confucianism, with its stress on loyalty and filial piety, or the teachings of Zen Buddhism, which were ideally suited to reinforce and appeal to the direct, self-reliant nature of the warrior. But in general the foreign influences encouraged idleness and extravagance. What is more significant, they added to the economic difficulties which the warrior class began to feel as its standard of living rose, its numbers increased, and its income remained stationary. These economic difficulties were of great importance to the fate of Go-Daigo's attack on the shogunate.

Probably the basic factor contributing to the strength of the Kamakura shogunate in the days of Yoritomo and the early Hōjō regents was its ability to satisfy the demands for land made by powerful local families. Most of the extensive properties confiscated after the fall of the Taira and the war of 1221 went to this end (although of course the shogun and the Hōjō themselves received considerable shares). As a result, personal vassals (housemen) of

---

[28] Fujiwara at first; imperial princes later.

Introduction

the Hōjō were settled in strategic places all over Japan, bound to their lords not only by the warrior code but also by ties of self-interest. To assure the continuation of this state of affairs, vassals were forbidden to sell or otherwise dispose of these "merit" lands, received as a reward for loyal service. Their economic security was vital to the security of the shogunate itself. As the generations passed, however, the size of vassals' families increased, their standard of living rose, and they fell into financial distress.

A potentially dangerous situation became critical as a result of the Mongol invasions of 1274 and 1281. The gigantic defense effort of the Japanese lasted for some fifty or sixty years, utterly exhausting the resources of the shogunate and the Hōjō family. Quite aside from military expenditures, huge outlays were made to temples and shrines, whose prayers were universally believed to have been the real cause of the nation's deliverance. Nevertheless, the recompense received did not satisfy the monks and priests, who thenceforth cherished a permanent grievance against the shogunate. Moreover, it was quite impossible to reward all of the warriors who submitted claims, since there were no confiscated lands to distribute. Hōjō justice, which had been swift and impartial in the early days, became temporizing and corrupt, and disaffection became widespread. Such developments emboldened the Emperor Go-Daigo and his advisers to think that they might succeed where Go-Toba had failed a hundred years earlier.

We are almost ready now to go on to a consideration of the events related in the first twelve chapters of the *Taiheiki*. Because of our story's preoccupation with battles and warfare, however, it will be convenient to end this discussion of the warrior class with a few words concerning the arms, armor, castles, and military tactics of the period.

Although some of the exaggerated figures of the *Taiheiki* produce a contrary impression, warfare in the Kamakura period (1185–1333) was not a matter of maneuvering large armies which acted as coordinated units under the command of their generals. It was a small-scale, disorganized, individualistic affair. In a typical case, a Hōjō vassal, receiving an order from Kamakura, would set out independently toward the enemy with all his retainers, who might number anywhere from one or two men to several hundred. The fighting force of an important vassal would include members of his family, mounted warriors of varying degrees of seniority (measured in terms of age, proficiency in the arts of war, and social status), and foot-soldiers of inferior rank. A fully accoutered warrior wore heavy armor made of cowhide, braided with colored cords. Below the skirt of the armor and beneath its wide, out-jutting sleeves, a costly two-piece garment of brocade or damask was visible, bloused and fastened below the knees and at the wrists. Special attachments fitted over vulnerable spots on the warrior's chest and sides, leggings and arm bands covered his limbs, and a helmet protected his head and neck. On his back he sometimes wore a billowing silk mantle, designed to check the impact of enemy arrows. At his waist he carried a sword, usually about three feet long, but occasionally more than twice that length, and a dagger, used for taking heads and committing suicide by disembowelment. His main weapons were his bow and arrow. The arrows, made of bamboo and feathers, were measured by handbreadths, from the tip of the thumb to the little finger. They varied in length from about three to three and three-quarters feet (twelve to fifteen handbreadths). As in the West, arrowheads of various types were used. The most interesting was the humming-bulb (also called turnip-head, from its shape), which, as the name implies, made an intimidating whistling sound in flight. Humming-bulb arrows were traditionally used to inaugurate a battle.

Although few areas in Japan are suitable for horse breeding, fine mounts were raised in the Kantō plain, and the eastern warriors were famous for their horsemanship and their prowess in individual combat.

The lightly armored foot-soldiers played an auxiliary role in the fighting, armed with halberds and grapnels. They also ran errands, carried enemy heads, and the like.

Usually a battle began with an exchange of arrows, developed into a combat between individual horsemen, and reached its climax with general hand-to-hand fighting. Here is a typical example of the most dramatic of the three stages, the second.

The defenders at Uchino were Suyama and Kōno, sent there with twenty thousand valiant chiefs. The imperial hosts could not gallop in

Introduction

easily, yet neither might the defenders gallop out easily. Wherefore both of these abode in their places, passing the time with shooting arrows. But soon from within the imperial army there emerged a single rider, wearing a lavender mantle over reddish-yellow armor shading to white toward the skirt. He galloped in front of the enemy, naming his name with a mighty shouting:

"Since I am a person of no consequence, it may be that no man of you will know my name. A retainer of Lord Ashikaga am I, Shidara Gorō Saemon-no-jō! If there is a retainer of the lords of Rokuhara that will fight against me, let him gallop forth to behold the degree of my skill."

So he spoke, and drew a sword three and a half feet long, raising it up in front of his helmet as a protection against arrows. And the two armies left off their fighting to gaze upon this man, whose warlike spirit was as that of one worthy to stand against a thousand.

Thereupon an old warrior of around fifty years advanced slowly from the army of Rokuhara, clad in black-threaded armor and a helmet with five flaps. He rode a pale chestnut horse, decked with blue tassels. And with a mighty shouting he named his name:

"Though I am a stupid man, for many years I served as a commissioner of the military government. And though I am of low degree, and may not be a worthy enemy in your eyes (for perhaps you scorn me, thinking, 'He is but a monk'), yet am I sprung from the house of the general Toshihito, a family that for many generations has followed the way of the warrior. Of the seventeenth of those generations am I, Saitō Genki the monk of Iyo! Why should I cherish life in today's battle, which decides the fate of our two armies? If there be those who are spared, let them speak to their sons and grandsons of my loyal fighting!"

As he spoke, these two galloped forward, and with clashing armor-sleeves grappled together furiously until they fell down. Being the stronger, Shidara got on top of Saitō and set about to cut off his head, but Saitō, nimble of limb, thrust upward and stabbed Shidara three times. Truly these were mighty men, that even in death did not relax their gripping hands, but pierced each one the other with their swords, and laid themselves down on the same pillow.

As used in the *Taiheiki*, the term castle is likely to be misleading to a Western reader, or to one acquainted with the warfare of later periods in Japanese history. Since the mounted archer had always been the mainstay of the fighting force, battles had traditionally been fought in open areas where horses could be maneuvered. Fortifications had been regarded as of secondary importance. Because of inferior numbers in general, and lack of mounted warriors in particular, Go-Daigo's adherents could not compete successfully under such conditions. They were forced to rely upon strongholds to which they could retreat to escape annihilation, and from which they could contain vastly superior attacking armies. Such a stronghold, or castle, was not an imposing bastion of the European type. It was primarily an area, a place easy to defend and hard to attack, such as the top of a steep mountain. The buildings in the area, if any, might be nothing more than the halls of a Shinto shrine or Buddhist temple, commandeered because of their strategic location. If time permitted, the defenders sowed the approaches with simple obstacles made from trees felled in the neighborhood, threw up wooden walls (sometimes plastered over with mud as a defense against fire arrows), dug ditches, and constructed flimsy towers which served as lookouts and vantage points for archers. In some cases, cliffs were substituted for walls.

The castle's boundaries were extremely flexible, since they were dictated by topographical considerations. Often there were several zones of defense, culminating in a last retreat at the top of a peak or in some other advantageous location. In the rare case where the land was flat, the castle would ordinarily be partially surrounded by a swamp or stream, or by a ditch which might be either dry or filled with water.

Now at last we are prepared to consider the events and personages of the *Taiheiki* itself. First let us meet the villain, Hōjō Takatoki. In 1316, two years before the Emperor Go-Daigo's accession to the throne, Takatoki assumed the office of regent. Of this event the *Taiheiki* says:

But then came the day of the lay monk Taira no Takatoki Sōkan, the former governor of Sagami, a descendant of Tokimasa in the ninth generation. Then indeed was change close at hand in the mandate of heaven and earth! The deeds that Takatoki did were exceedingly base, and he was unashamed before the scorn of others. Without righteousness did he govern, not heeding the people's despair. By day and by night, with wanton acts he dishonored his glorious ancestors under the ground; in the morning and in the evening, with vain merriment he invited ruin in his lifetime. . . . Those who saw knit their eyebrows, and those who heard uttered condemnations.

Introduction

Takatoki held office only until 1326, when ill health caused him to resign and take religious vows, but thereafter he continued to be regarded as the *de facto* regent. He is a convenient whipping boy for the hostile author of the *Taiheiki*, who dwells indignantly on his unnatural fondness for dogfights, dancing, and other unsuitable pastimes. We have already seen, however, that the stability of the Kamakura shogunate was seriously threatened by fundamental weaknesses which developed long before Takatoki's time, and which probably were beyond the power of any individual to correct. Moreover, in 1316 Takatoki was a feeble-minded youth of thirteen, qualified for his exalted position only by the accident of birth. Just as the shogun had long been a puppet manipulated by the Hōjō regents, so Takatoki himself was a mere figurehead. The real power rested with Nagasaki Enki, the steward of the Hōjō family; Adachi Tokiaki, Takatoki's maternal grandfather; and (somewhat later) Nagasaki Takasuke, Enki's son. All three of these men were dishonest and self-seeking, and Takasuke in particular was notoriously susceptible to bribes. Encouraging Takatoki to devote himself to simple-minded pleasures, they administered the government so corruptly and unjustly that only fear of the shogunate's military strength prevented active revolts in many quarters. Even this deterrent was removed in the spring of 1322, when the government failed miserably in a punitive expedition against a contumacious family in eastern Japan, the Andō.

The course of affairs in Kamakura was observed with pleasure by the new emperor Go-Daigo and his courtiers. Go-Daigo was a vigorous man of thirty when he ascended the throne. This was a distinct oddity in a political system which for centuries had been based on the control of a child ruler by a maternal (Fujiwara) or paternal (retired emperor) relative. Moreover, after he had reigned for three years, his father Go-Uda voluntarily dissolved his cloister government and returned all the imperial prerogatives to the throne, thus permitting Go-Daigo to rule personally, the first emperor for whom this had been possible since the establishment of the system of cloister government more than two hundred years earlier.

It is not easy to arrive at a fair evaluation of Go-Daigo's character. Although leading Japanese historians have called him one of the nation's greatest sovereigns, the evidence of the sympathetic *Taiheiki* itself shows him to have been devious, arrogant, callous, and cowardly. It is true that he ruled during an era in which emperors sacrificed loyal subjects as a matter of course, but even so it is difficult to excuse his ruthless betrayal of two of his most able and devoted advisers, and later of his son, Prince Morinaga, in order to salvage his own position. As a politician, he was cunning, rather than statesmanlike. He was vain and stubborn, and his obstinate concern for the dignity of the throne frequently blinded him to realities, resulting in such misguided ventures as the costly attempt to rebuild the great palace enclosure immediately after his restoration to power. Yet he was by no means a stupid or ignorant man. He was intimately acquainted with the Chinese and Japanese classics, well-read in the doctrines of Shingon and Zen Buddhism, deeply interested in the newly imported Confucianism of Chu Hsi, and versed in the ancient law codes, precedents, and usages. Likewise, although in many respects a product of his conservative environment, he possessed an independence of spirit that was not common in fourteenth-century Kyoto.[29] Soon after the government was returned to his hands, he selected the ablest men in the capital to be his advisers. Some of these had already served Go-Uda well, notably the "three Fusa," Madenokōji Nobufusa, Yoshida Sadafusa, and Kitabatake Chikafusa. Two others, Hino Suketomo and Hino Toshimoto, were obscure members of an unimportant family, a house which had the further disadvantage of being known as a supporter of the rival Jimyōin line of the imperial family. When Go-Daigo suddenly raised Suketomo and Toshimoto to relatively high office, there was a good deal of adverse comment in the tradition-minded capital. It is interesting, however, that the emperor's action was praised by no less a personage than the ex-emperor Hanazono, who had been pushed off the throne to make room for Go-Daigo. Hanazono had no reason to look kindly upon Go-Daigo, but he wrote in his diary:

[29] Perhaps this was due in part, at least, to the influence of his father and grandfather, the emperors Go-Uda and Kameyama, who were both unusually gifted and well-educated men.

Introduction

It is most admirable of His Majesty to have promoted men of ability. It is a sign of the degeneracy of the times, and a result of ignorance of fundamental moral principles, that he is censured for doing such a thing. How regrettable it is![30]

Surrounding himself with such men, Go-Daigo seems to have labored diligently to make himself a virtuous Confucian ruler. We know very little concerning the details of his early administration, but it is certain that he reconstituted the Records Office, an imperial court of law that had virtually disappeared during the centuries of cloister rule, and spent long hours hearing suits—as the *Taiheiki* says, "fearful lest the condition of those below be unknown to those above." And in Hanazono's diary we read, "The government is much reformed of late. Truly His Majesty is a most excellent sovereign."[31]

In the final analysis, however, the policies adopted by the court had little effect upon the country at large, nor did the jurisdiction of the Records Office extend far beyond a few nobles, temples, and shrines. Because Go-Daigo was a proud and ambitious man, this was an unbearably galling situation for him. Moreover, the state of affairs within the imperial family was such that the continued existence of the Kamakura shogunate was a grave threat to his position as emperor.

Since the time of the Emperor Go-Saga (reigned 1242–1246), the imperial family had been split into two rival factions, the Jimyōin line and the Daikakuji line,[32] descended from Go-Saga's elder son Go-Fukakusa and his younger son Kameyama, respectively. When an emperor from one of these factions sat upon the throne, the members of the other faction worked tirelessly to persuade Kamakura to force him to abdicate in favor of a candidate of their own. Go-Daigo himself owed his elevation to the persistent representations of Go-Uda and Kameyama, who were finally successful in ousting the Jimyōin incumbent, Hanazono, in 1318. But Go-Daigo's accession was secured only at the price of a com-

---

[30] *Hanazono tennō shinki* (Ressei Zenshū Hensankai, *Ressei zenshū*, Tokyo, 1915–17, vol. 21), p. 427.
[31] *Ibid.*, p. 434.
[32] So called from the places of retirement of Go-Fukakusa and Go-Uda (Kameyama's son).

promise which forced a hostile crown prince upon him, putting him into a position very similar to the one which had just cost Hanazono the throne.[33]

It is impossible to tell precisely how early Go-Daigo began to think of overthrowing the shogunate. His father and grandfather seem to have been more antagonistic to the rule of Kamakura than the sovereigns of the Jimyōin line, and it may be that he harbored some such design even before he ascended the throne. At any rate, on the very day of his accession (the twenty-sixth day of the second month of 1318), he sent his oldest son, Prince Morinaga, to be a monk in one of the cloisters of the Enryakuji Temple, and in 1328 he made the prince the supreme head of the Tendai sect. Morinaga was nineteen when he became the Tendai abbot, a brave, warlike youth with no discernible religious inclinations. It is hard to understand why Go-Daigo should have cut him off from political life in this way, unless from the start he intended to use him to gain the support of the soldier-monks of Mount Hiei.

Meanwhile, the emperor's advisers were urging him to rise against the shogunate. Evidence from Hanazono's diary and other sources bears out the substance of the *Taiheiki*'s account of the progress of the conspiracy: the meetings held on various pretexts, and the efforts to locate military support. Hino Suketomo traveled to the Kantō to seek adherents, disguised as a wandering monk, while Toshimoto looked for support in Yamato and Kawachi. The immediate results of these excursions were not impressive, since the only warriors recruited were Tajimi Kuninaga and Toki Yorisada, two men who lived on imperial estates. It seems likely, however, that Toshimoto was responsible for the later adherence of Kusunoki Masashige, whose contribution to the court's ultimate victory can hardly be overestimated.

In the ninth month of 1324, the anti-shogunate plot came to light.

---

[33] This is an oversimplification. The Daikakuji line was itself split in two, and Go-Daigo's first crown prince was Kuninaga, the candidate of the other group. A prince of the Jimyōin line, Tokihito, was designated as Kuninaga's future crown prince. Kuninaga died suddenly in 1326, whereupon Go-Daigo claimed that another prince of the Daikakuji line ought to be appointed to replace him (namely, one of his own sons). In the end the shogunate obliged him to accept Tokihito, most unwillingly.

Introduction

Toki and Tajimi were promptly exterminated, and Suketomo and Toshimoto were sent to Kamakura for questioning. The emperor made haste to write a letter disclaiming knowledge of the plot, which he sent to Takatoki by the hand of Madenokōji Nobufusa. The shogunate accepted the explanations offered by Nobufusa, who was then a man of sixty-six with enormous personal prestige, and the envoy returned to the capital to enjoy a well-earned promotion. In the end, the release of Toshimoto (1325) left Suketomo as the sole victim. He was exiled to Sado.

The exposure of Go-Daigo's plot was highly encouraging to those elements in Kyoto who hoped to bring about his early abdication. As their intrigues grew more frenzied, relations between them and Go-Daigo became increasingly strained. Meanwhile, in 1326, a series of elaborate Buddhist rituals had been inaugurated in the palace, avowedly to pray for the safe delivery of the imperial consort. When no child appeared after two years, it began to be rumored that these ceremonies were really exorcism rituals directed against the Hōjō, and Go-Daigo was at last obliged to send a new letter of disclaimer to Kamakura.

In 1328, as we have seen, Prince Morinaga became the head of the Tendai sect. In 1330, the emperor personally presented generous offerings to the religious institutions whose military support would be most valuable to him—Kasuga Shrine, the Tōdaiji, the Kōfukuji, and the Enryakuji. Around the same time, he also made substantial gifts to the Onjōji. The necessity of these overtures, of course, derived from the fact that the Hōjō, although weakened, still controlled most of the land in Japan,[34] so that Go-Daigo's only potential supporters in the initial stages of a revolt were either warriors from estates owned by the imperial family, shrines, and temples, or soldier-monks from the great religious institutions. Shortly after Go-Daigo's visit to Mount Hiei, his fourth son, Prince Munenaga (Sonchō), replaced Prince Morinaga (Son'un) as Tendai abbot. Morinaga remained on the mountain, devoting all of his time to military preparations.

In the fourth month of 1331, these new plottings were abruptly

---

[34] In 1333, the protectors of more than half the provinces (including the most strategic ones) were Hōjō kinsmen.

revealed to the shogunate. Toshimoto, who was named as the ringleader, sought refuge in the palace, where he was unceremoniously sought out and arrested by a disorderly troupe of warriors. Go-Daigo hastily made plans to summon fighting men and Hiei monks for an attack on Rokuhara, the Hōjō headquarters in Kyoto, under cover of which he hoped to escape to the Enryakuji to establish a base of operations in conjunction with his two sons. Late in the eighth month, however, word came that the shogunate was about to surround the palace, and he was obliged to flee with the imperial regalia. He went first to the Southeast Cloister of the Tōdaiji in Nara, whose abbot Shōjin was a reliable supporter, but Shōjin advised him not to remain there, since the soldier-monks of another cloister of the temple, at odds with his monks, showed signs of hostility to the emperor.

On the following day the emperor left Nara, accompanied by Shōjin and some of his monks. After stopping briefly at a temple on Mount Jubu, he sought refuge at Kasagi Temple. There was a considerable number of soldier-monks at this temple, which was a subsidiary of the Tōdaiji, presided over in absentia by Shōjin himself. Kasagi Mountain was only about six hundred feet high, but it was strategically situated in rough terrain beside the Kozu River. The emperor at once issued a call for warriors, while the monks set to work on some hasty fortifications.

Meanwhile the shogunate representatives at Rokuhara attacked the soldier-monks of Mount Hiei, deceived by the ruse described in Chapter Two of the *Taiheiki*, whereby a courtier wearing the imperial robes had ostentatiously fled to the mountain. An envoy arrived from Kamakura on the fifth day of the ninth month with orders to enthrone Prince Tokihito, who performed the accession ceremony on the twentieth day.[35]

It is at about this time that we first hear of Kusunoki Masashige, the warrior who has been revered by generations of Japanese as the classic example of a loyal subject. Little is known of the Kusunoki ancestors, who were obscure warriors in the province of Kawachi. Masashige himself, who apparently had nothing to gain

---

[35] This was the emperor later known as Kōgon-in. His foster father, Hanazono, established a cloister government.

Introduction xliii

by adhering to the imperial cause, seems to have been actuated solely by loyalty to the throne. Although the *Taiheiki*'s eulogies of him are somewhat overdone, he is an attractive figure, and his conduct is a pleasant contrast to that of the other major imperialist warriors, who were all actuated by self-interest.

In the middle of the ninth month, Kusunoki established a stronghold at Akasaka in Kawachi, where he made ready to shelter the emperor in case of necessity. Warriors from Rokuhara had already laid siege to Kasagi, which was so poorly manned that the defenders were compelled to rely almost entirely on the terrain. The castle fell on the twenty-eighth day of the ninth month. The emperor, attempting to escape to Kusunoki's castle, was captured and taken first to the Byōdōin Cloister at Uji and later to Rokuhara (tenth month, third day).

Shortly before the fall of Kasagi, Prince Morinaga made his way to Akasaka. He had originally remained on Mount Hiei with his brother the abbot, rallying the monks to battle against the Rokuhara warriors. When the monks learned of the deception practiced upon them, they refused to fight longer, and Morinaga and his brother went to Kasagi to join the emperor. The prince's stay at Akasaka was brief, since a large army sent down from the Kantō attacked and captured it in less than a week (fifteenth to twenty-first days of the tenth month).

Kusunoki and Prince Morinaga disappeared after the fall of Akasaka. It is likely that they remained in the vicinity of the capital for a time, seeking a means of rescuing Go-Daigo from his captivity at Rokuhara. Some such plan seems to have been afoot; and on one occasion the emperor actually eluded his jailers for a few hours before being recaptured. The prince's activities in the Yoshino area, described in Chapter Five, probably began after Go-Daigo was sent into exile in the third month of the following year, 1332.

The fall of Akasaka ended the first phase of the Disturbance of Genkō, so called from the name of the era during which these events took place. Go-Daigo was banished to Oki, while the chief of his noble advisers were decapitated—Suketomo, Toshimoto, and others. The latent discontent of the members of the warrior class had been aroused, however, and many of them began to consider the advisability of taking up arms against the Hōjō. Meanwhile, from his base in Yoshino, Prince Morinaga (who had returned to lay life) sent out calls to warriors and temples all over the country, receiving a number of favorable responses.[36] He also kept in close touch with Masashige, who built a new stronghold at Akasaka, higher in the mountains than the first one, and early in 1332 defeated Hōjō armies repeatedly in the vicinity of the Tennōji Temple. The activities of these two men became so troublesome to the Hōjō that before the end of 1332 the shogunate issued orders for their execution, rescinding previous orders which had merely called for their capture.

Early in 1333 three large armies left the east, determined to crush Prince Morinaga and Kusunoki Masashige once and for all. At this time the prince was entrenched in a monastery in Yoshino with a defensive force of soldier-monks, while Masashige had established two bases, one at Akasaka and another at Chihaya on Mount Kongō. Since neither Yoshino nor Akasaka was very strong, both soon fell. All three attacking armies then converged upon Kusunoki at Chihaya—a million men, according to the *Taiheiki*. This figure need not be accepted, but it is clear that the whole strength of the shogunate in the capital area was committed. Nevertheless, the castle held out so stubbornly that it was never breached. It is difficult to exaggerate the importance of Kusunoki's contribution to the eventual success of the imperial arms. By containing the entire strength of the Hōjō, he not only encouraged other rebels to rise, but also prepared the way for the loyalist capture of the virtually undefended capital.

Meanwhile the exiled Go-Daigo, refusing to give up hope, sent vows to temples and shrines, performed mystic rites, and otherwise sought to assure his return to the capital. He received occasional news of events in the outside world from Prince Morinaga, who utilized fishermen as messengers. By the end of the second month of 1333, the prince was able to suggest that his father flee from Oki, which Go-Daigo proceeded to do, with the help of a friendly

---

[36] Akamatsu, Doi, and Tokunō, whose activities are described in the *Taiheiki*, were among the first to answer the summons.

Introduction

guard. Probably in accordance with arrangements previously made by the prince, the emperor went directly to the home of Nawa Nagatoshi, a warrior in the province of Hōki, where he issued a call for support.

The researches of Japanese scholars have shown that the events of the succeeding weeks were almost entirely the result of long and careful planning on the part of Prince Morinaga. On the seventh day of the fifth month, a concerted attack by many armies reduced the capital; on the twenty-first day of the same month, Kamakura was captured by forces which converged from all over Japan, led by Nitta Yoshisada; on the twenty-fourth day Hōjō Hidetoki, the military governor of Kyushu, was destroyed by rebellious local families.[37]

It is useful to remember that Prince Morinaga's secret orders were primarily responsible for the fall of Kyoto, because one of the attackers, Ashikaga Takauji, was a shrewd and ambitious man who managed to claim the credit for himself. Throughout the period of the Kamakura shogunate, the Ashikaga were one of the most powerful families in eastern Japan, holding high positions in the military government and intermarrying with the Hōjō. But as direct descendants of the great Genji chieftains, they had long chafed under Taira domination,[38] hungry for an opportunity to regain the power which had passed from Minamoto hands with the extinction of Yoritomo's line. This was the motive underlying Takauji's defection, as the *Taiheiki* says.

Takauji arrived in the capital on the sixteenth day of the fourth month of 1333, ostensibly to join in an attack on Nawa Nagatoshi in Hōki. On the twenty-ninth day he publicly announced his support of the imperial cause, calling upon warriors all over the country to follow him. By that time, it was clear that the Hōjō were in

---

[37] All of these loyalist warriors hoped to better their fortunes by joining the imperial side, and some of them had specific grievances to redress. For example, the Shōni and Ōtomo families in Kyushu had monopolized the highest offices in the island for generations after Yoritomo, until they were displaced by Hōjō kinsmen. Similarly, Nitta Yoshisada hoped to restore the ancient prosperity of his house, which, he claimed, was the senior branch of the Minamoto. Because their ancestors had refused to join Yoritomo promptly in the early days of the war against the Heike, the Nitta were never given important posts in the Kamakura government, and were far inferior socially and militarily to the Ashikaga.

[38] As previously noted, the Hōjō belonged to the Taira clan.

serious trouble, a fact which combined with the prestige of the Ashikaga name to assure an impressive response. It is not surprising, therefore, that many people at that time and later believed that Takauji had recruited all of the warriors who captured the capital. After the fall of Kyoto, Takauji promptly established a temporary government in the capital, where he accepted the personal allegiance of the bulk of the Hōjō warriors who had participated in the siege of Chihaya. He also saw to it that his three-year-old son Yoshiakira "led" a force in the attack on Kamakura, seeking successfully in this way to share the credit for that city's reduction.

Go-Daigo returned to the capital on the fifth day of the sixth month of 1333. Since he had never admitted that he had ceased to be the emperor, he did not go through a new accession ceremony, but behaved as though returning from a journey. All the changes made by Kōgon were ignored—his new era name, his promotions and appointments and the like—and in all possible ways the old order was restored.

Two days after Go-Daigo's return, he generously confirmed the titles of estates held by members of the Jimyōin line, and assigned the province of Harima for the support of the deposed Kōgon. His next step was to guarantee the holdings of his favorite temples, notably the Shingon Eastern Temple (Tōji) and the Zen Tōfukuji. Then rewards were conferred on the leading generals, substantially as reported in the *Taiheiki*.

Two organs of government were established soon afterward, the Records Office and a lower court, divided into eight sections, which dealt with less important cases. Kusunoki and Nawa were among the members of the lower court, but it is worth noticing that Ashikaga Takauji was not appointed to either body. Both the emperor and Prince Morinaga distrusted Takauji from the start, as did the other generals.

A special board was also established to deal with the problem of rewards to loyalist warriors. The *Taiheiki*'s description of the government's difficulties and ultimate failure in this all-important area seems to be essentially accurate. The capital was filled with reward-seekers, who invaded the palace, bribed influential men, and pressed their cases in every possible way. Shrines and temples also

Introduction

claimed recompense for prayers, provision of military supplies, and participation in the fighting. Court nobles and undeserving claimants who gained the ear of Lady Sammi or other imperial favorites were handsomely treated, while others with legitimate demands received nothing, or found that they had been given titles to lands which had already been granted to other men. Rewards once given were frequently revoked, and forged imperial edicts began to circulate.

Such unfair and uncertain decisions robbed the warrior class of its security, causing many of its members to regret their defection from the Hōjō. Their dissatisfaction was aggravated by the arrogant behavior of the newly prosperous nobility, who seemed to think that they could turn back the clock to the days when the military were the humble lackeys of the Fujiwara aristocrats. Go-Daigo himself apparently did not share this view, but rather sought to govern the two classes on terms of equality. Through sumptuary legislation he tried to check the ostentatious behavior of the courtiers, but with little success. His own ill-advised attempt to rebuild the imperial palace enclosure contributed to popular disaffection by imposing a financial strain which the country was in no position to bear.

Perhaps the basic difficulty was that Go-Daigo did not clearly understand the reasons which had impelled the warrior class to turn against the Hōjō. He seems to have felt that they had been actuated solely by loyalty to the throne, and that they would continue to support him under all circumstances. As one writer has said, he thought that an imperial order could turn stone to gold.[39] Ashikaga Takauji, who knew better, skillfully gave people to understand that he was a man who could satisfy the land hunger of local warriors and restore the security of the early Hōjō regime. In the end, partly because of the groundwork that he had laid earlier, he was able to force Go-Daigo off the throne and plunge the nation into civil war.

These events are beyond the scope of our inquiry, which must close, as does the twelfth chapter of the *Taiheiki,* with a discussion of the manner in which Takauji rid himself of a dangerous enemy,

---

[39] Takekoshi Yosaburo, *The Economic Aspects of the History of the Civilization of Japan* (London, 1930), I, 205.

Prince Morinaga. As has been mentioned, the prince was not alone in fearing and distrusting Takauji. Nitta, Kusunoki, and Nawa all agreed that he was a danger, and the emperor seems to have invested the prince with the title of shogun in considerable haste, so that he might forestall a request for the appointment from Takauji. Not long after the success of the imperial arms, the atmosphere in the capital became charged with hostility and suspicion. It was rumored that the prince was preparing to attack Takauji, who guarded his residence with armed warriors. In actual fact, the prince, Yoshisada, Masashige, and Nagatoshi had received an imperial mandate to destroy Ashikaga, but Takauji himself went to the palace before they could find an opportunity to strike, complaining that the prince was conspiring to kill him. The emperor, who did not feel strong enough to risk a showdown, protested surprise and arrested the prince. Like Suketomo nine years before, the prince became the scapegoat. He was sent away to prison in Kamakura,[40] never to return. "And at last when the life of the Prince of the Great Pagoda was ended," says the *Taiheiki*, "all the realm entered swiftly upon the age of the generals' rule."

THE HOURS OF THE DAY

Hour of the Rat	12:00 midnight to 2:00 A.M.
Hour of the Ox	2:00 A.M. to 4:00 A.M.
Hour of the Tiger	4:00 A.M. to 6:00 A.M.
Hour of the Hare	6:00 A.M. to 8:00 A.M.
Hour of the Dragon	8:00 A.M. to 10:00 A.M.
Hour of the Snake	10:00 A.M. to 12:00 noon
Hour of the Horse	12:00 noon to 2:00 P.M.
Hour of the Sheep	2:00 P.M. to 4:00 P.M.
Hour of the Monkey	4:00 P.M. to 6:00 P.M.
Hour of the Cock	6:00 P.M. to 8:00 P.M.
Hour of the Dog	8:00 P.M. to 10:00 P.M.
Hour of the Boar	10:00 P.M. to 12:00 midnight

[40] Not in a cave, as the *Taiheiki* has it, but in a temple.

WESTERN EQUIVALENTS OF ERA NAMES APPEARING IN THE TEXT

Angen	1175–1177	Jōgan	859–877		
Bumpō	1317–1319	Juei	1182–1185		
Bunji	1185–1190	Kampyō	889–898		
Einin	1293–1299	Karyaku	1326–1329		
Enchō	923–931	Kemmu	1334–1336		
Engi	901–923	Kempō	1213–1219		
Enkyū	1069–1074	Ninna	885–889		
Enryaku	782–805	Shōgyō	1332		
Genkō	1331–1334	Shōkyū	1219–1222		
Genkyō	1321–1324	Shōtai	898–901		
Genryaku	1184–1185	Tengen	978–983		
Gentoku	1329–1331	Tengyō	938–947		
Heiji	1159–1160	Tenryaku	947–957		
Hōgen	1156–1159	Tentoku	957–961		
Jiryaku	1065–1069	T'ien-pao (Chinese)	742–755		

The Taiheiki

A CHRONICLE OF
MEDIEVAL JAPAN

1

The Reign of Go-Daigo Tenno and the Prosperity of the Military

Now IN THE REIGN OF THE Emperor Go-Daigo, there lived a warrior known to men as Taira no Takatoki the governor of Sagami, even in the days of Go-Daigo Tenno, the ninety-fifth of mortal sovereigns in our land. Takatoki turned away his face from the virtue of the emperor, holding his subject's duty as nothing. Wherefore has it come to pass, that since his time the four seas[1] are disordered utterly, and no man's heart is easy within him. For more than forty years have beacon fires veiled the skies, and warring shouts made the earth to tremble. No man amasses springs and autumns in rich abundance,[2] nor is there a haven to shelter the myriad folk.

Rightly considered, these things are not the fruit of a day or night. For in the years of Genryaku, Lord Yoritomo, the Kamakura Grand Marshal of the Right, achieved merit by chastising the house of Taira. And Go-Shirakawa-in rejoiced greatly thereat, appointing Yoritomo to be constable-general of the sixty-six provinces. Then for the first time the military named protectors in the provinces, and established stewards in the estates. Later Yoritomo's eldest and second sons were made barbarian-subduing shoguns after him, each in his turn; Yoriie the Chief of the Left Gate Guards, and Lord Sanetomo the Great Subject of the Right. Wherefore indeed do men call these the three generations of

[1] See note 1, Introduction.
[2] I.e., grows old.

shoguns. Yet, because Lord Yoriie was struck down by Sanetomo, and Sanetomo by Yoriie's son, the evil meditation teacher Kugyō,[3] therefore did father and sons together endure but forty-two years. The power in the realm passed to Yoshitoki, the former governor of Mutsu, a son of Lord Yoritomo's father-in-law, Taira no Tokimasa, the governor of Tōtōmi. And Yoshitoki sought to rule over all the four seas.

Now Go-Toba-in, the retired emperor of the day, was moved to strike down Yoshitoki, for it was hateful to his heart that the government of the court was set aside by the power of the military. And thereupon the Disturbance of Shōkyū began, utterly disordering the realm. But when at last the two hosts contended together at Uji and Seta, with banners dimming the sun, then quickly the imperial armies fled away defeated before a day of fighting was ended. Go-Toba-in was sent away to exile in the land of Oki, and Yoshitoki held the realm in his hand.

For six generations the government issued from this family of the Hōjō, that ministered to the needs of the distressed folk: Yasutoki the governor of Musashi, Tokiuji the assistant chief of the Palace Construction Office, Tsunetoki the governor of Musashi, Tokiyori the governor of Sagami, Tokimune the acting chief of the Stables of the Left, and Sadatoki the governor of Sagami. But although their power extended over all men, yet were they content to receive the fourth court rank. They lived modestly, dispensed benevolence, castigated their own faults, and observed the proprieties. "Though highly placed, they were not dangerous; though the cup of their power was full, it did not overflow." [4]

From Shōkyū on, a person of noble blood was brought down to Kamakura to be the barbarian-subduing shogun, such a scion of a princely or regent family as might bring order to the land and peace to the people; and all the military subjects bore themselves toward him with careful ceremony. Moreover, in the third year of Shōkyū, two Hōjō kinsmen were appointed to dwell in the capital, to govern

---

[3] A meditation teacher (*zenji*) was a Buddhist monk who specialized in meditative exercises. *Akuzenji*, a name applied to ill-behaved monks in general, is best known as the sobriquet of Kugyō, who was a monk at the Tsurugaoka Hachiman Shrine in Kamakura.

[4] Paraphrased from the *Classic of Filial Piety*.

the western provinces and protect the city, those whom men called the two Rokuharas.[5] And from the beginning of Einin on, a military governor was established in Chinzei,[6] to govern the land of Kyushu and guard straitly against invasions of foreign bandits. There was no place in the realm but obeyed the orders of the military, nor was there a man that did not bow before their power, though he were beyond the bounds of the four seas.

It is the way of the morning sun that without evil intent it robs the lingering stars of their radiance. Even so was it in the estates of the land, where stewards grew strong and landholders grew weak, although the military in no wise sought to dishonor the court. Likewise in the provinces the protectors were respected, but the governors were held lightly. Year by year the court declined; day by day the military flourished.

The generations of emperors thought always, "Would that the eastern barbarians might be struck down!" For it was in their hearts to comfort the spirit of the imperial exile of Shōkyū; likewise, they sorrowed to think upon the court's power, how it wasted and became as nothing. Yet they abode in silence, troubled that the design was beyond their compass or the time was not fitting. But then came the day of the lay monk Taira no Takatoki Sōkan, the former governor of Sagami, a descendant of Tokimasa in the ninth generation. Then indeed was change close at hand in the mandate of heaven and earth! The deeds that Takatoki did were exceedingly base, and he was unashamed before the scorn of others. Without righteousness did he govern, not heeding the people's despair. By day and by night, with wanton acts he dishonored his glorious ancestors under the ground; in the morning and in the evening, with vain merriment he invited ruin in his lifetime. Fleeting indeed was his pleasure, even as the pleasure of Duke I of Wei who carried cranes; near at hand was his regret, even as the regret of dog-lead-

---

[5] Rokuhara, Taira no Kiyomori's old residence east of the Kamo River, had been rebuilt by Yoritomo after its destruction by fire in 1183. In the third year of Shōkyū (1221), it became the headquarters of Hōjō Yasutoki and Hōjō Tokifusa, who occupied areas north and south of Yoritomo's house, respectively. They and their successors were known as the two Rokuharas, or the Rokuhara of the North and the Rokuhara of the South.

[6] Another name for Kyushu.

ing Li Ssu of Ch'in![7] Those who saw knit their eyebrows, and those who heard uttered condemnations.

The emperor of that time, who came forth from the womb of Dattemmon'in, was Go-Daigo, the second princely son of Go-Uda-in, set upon the throne in his thirty-first year by design of the governor of Sagami. In his reign this emperor obeyed the way of the Duke of Chou and of Confucius, properly observing the three relationships and five virtues; nor was he neglectful of the myriad affairs and hundred offices of his government, but followed the uses of Engi and Tenryaku. Hopefully the four seas gazed upon his aspect; with joyful hearts the myriad folk bowed before his virtue. In truth he revived forgotten things and rewarded all that was good, so that shrines and temples flourished, and Zen and Ritsu,[8] and fulfillment blessed the great teachers of the revealed and secret ways of Buddhism and the truths of Confucius. There was no man but praised his virtue and exulted in his goodness, saying, "Surely this is a heaven-endowed emperor, an earth-ruling sovereign."

The Abolition of the Barriers

The barriers in the four directions and seven circuits were places where the great prohibitions touching the provinces were made known, and where warnings were issued in extraordinary times, yet now the emperor closed all the barriers of all the regions, save Ōtsu and Kuzuha alone. For it had come about that they impeded the bringing of the annual tribute, and by enjoyment of exclusive controls they caused expense to merchants in their travels.

In the summer of the first year of Genkyō,[9] a terrible drought dried up the earth, withering the land of the home provinces, where

---

[7] Allusions to Chinese history. Duke I alienated his subjects by an excessive fondness for cranes, which he allowed to ride in officers' carriages. Li Ssu, a prime minister in the third century B.C., fell from favor and was put to death. When parting from his son for the last time, he said, "I wish I could go with you once more out of the eastern gate of Shang-ts'ai, that we might hunt rabbits with a brown dog."

[8] Buddhist sects.

[9] Properly Genkō (1321–1324). *Kyō*, an alternative reading of the second character, has been adopted in this translation to avoid confusion with Genkō (1331–1334). See Character List.

the young green shoots were wont to grow. The fields overflowed with the bodies of those who starved, and men fell down to the ground from hunger. It was in that year that people gave three hundred coins for half a bushel of millet.

Hearing of the famine in the realm, the emperor spoke, saying: "Let heaven's punishment be visited upon Us alone, if We are lacking in virtue. What is the fault of the myriad folk, that they meet with this calamity?"

So he spoke, grieved that the imperial virtue offended against heaven, and graciously gave over his morning meal to be a charity to those who hungered and suffered want. Likewise he summoned the chief of the police commissioners (for he thought in his heart, "Not by this charity alone may the hunger of the myriad folk be assuaged"). And he caused him to inspect the cereals hoarded for manifold gain by the rich men of the time, and to build market buildings in the Second Ward, where inspectors weighed and determined prices for the selling thereof. Thus indeed did the merchants enjoy their profit, while all the people were as though possessed of a nine-year store of goods.

When there were suits at law, the emperor went forth to the Records Office to hear complaints and determine merits, fearful lest the condition of those below be unknown to those above. Contentious men left off their disputing, shamed by his virtue in an instant. The punishment whips crumbled away, nor did any strike the admonitory drum.[10]

Truly was this Go-Daigo Tenno an illustrious and sage emperor; even such a one as might bring justice to the state and peace to the folk. Alas, that even a little he resembled Huan of Ch'i and the prince of Ch'u who lost his bow![11] Although he grasped the realm in his hand, because of this he endured for three years only.

---

[10] Yao, a legendary Chinese sage-ruler, put up a drum for the convenience of subjects who wished to call him to admonish him. The reader is probably intended to recall an old poem in the *Wakan rōeishū*:

    The punishment whips and cattails are rotted . . .
    On the admonitory drum the moss is deep
    And the birds are not disturbed.

[11] Duke Huan was arbitrary and dictatorial; the prince of Ch'u was criticized by Confucius for being small-minded.

The Nomination of a Consort and the Matter of Lady Sammi

On the third day of the eighth month of the second year of Bumpō, it came to pass that a lady was honored with the degree of imperial consort and brought into the Kōkiden;[12] even she who was the gracious daughter of Lord Sanekane, the Later Saionji Great Subject of the Grand Preceptorate. Already for five reigns had imperial handmaidens been chosen from this house of Saionji, that since Shōkyū had amazed the eyes and ears of the realm with its flourishing, since it had found favor in the eyes of the generations of the family of the Governor of Sagami. May not the emperor have held it in his mind to give pleasure to the men of the Kantō, when by edict he singled out this lady to be his consort?

She was in the sixteenth year of her life, when first she came to be served beside the golden pheasant doors within the lofty palace halls. Well might Mao Ch'iang and Hsi Shih have felt shame for their faces, or Chiang Shu and Ch'ing Ch'in covered their mirrors, so like was this lady to a tender peach blossom opening in spring, or a drooping willow, breeze-laden![13] Assuredly did it seem that she would enjoy the sovereign's gracious regard beyond all others; yet her life was spent in vain waiting, nor ever did she draw near to the august countenance, for the favor of an emperor is more fragile than a leaf. Inside the deep-receding palace she mourned the slow-ending spring days and the long sadness of autumn nights. When none remained with her in the rich chambers, she wept where the bright night lamp patterned the wall, while scent vanished from the bronze censers and the night rain tapped drearily at the windows. The words of Po Lo-t'ien[14] bit into her heart:

> Do not be born a woman in this life,
> Lest the joys and griefs of your hundred years
> Wait upon the pleasure of another.

---

[12] The palace building set aside for the use of the emperor's principal consort.
[13] Mao Ch'iang, Hsi Shih, Chiang Shu, and Ch'ing Ch'in were Chinese beauties.
[14] Po Chü-i, the celebrated T'ang poet.

Chapter 1

Now around that time the emperor beheld the daughter of Kinkado, the Ano Middle Marshal, she who was called Lady Sammi and served as a lady in waiting to the Inner Princess.[15] Because this lady found favor in his sight beyond all others, upon her alone he lavished his wide-ranging imperial favors, blanching the exquisitely painted faces of the six palaces. Not by the three legitimate spouses could the heart of the Son of Heaven be won, nor by the nine princesses, nor the twenty-seven concubines, nor the eighty-one imperial handmaidens,[16] nor even by the beauties of the rear palace or the dancing girls of the Music Office. For not alone by her pearllike fairness did the lady captivate him, but by her words that were adroit and cajoling, and by knowing his will beforehand, and proposing novel things. Whether to spring entertainments under the cherry blossoms or to autumn banquets facing the harvest moon, her hand-drawn carriage was in attendance when he rode forth; and she took what seat she desired when he traveled over the water. Thenceforward the sovereign did not concern himself with affairs of state in the morning.

Soon the emperor handed down an edict, one such as would make Lady Sammi an empress's peer; and all men thought of her as the true empress. Upon her kinsmen glory descended, most amazingly, so that the people of the realm were scornful of a man-child, thinking only of baby girls. Were it but said, "The empress has an interest," even the head of the Records Office would bestow a reward where merit was lacking, or a magistrate call right wrong.

"In the Kuan-chü, there is enjoyment without wantonness and grief without morbidity." [17] So spoke the poet concerning the virtue of an empress. Alas! How shameful it is, that because of a beautiful woman we suffer the bitter disturbances of our times!

They who lived in the palace were even as close-dwelling locusts,

---

[15] *Chūgū*, the imperial consort, Sanekane's daughter. The *chūgū* ranked above the concubines and below the empress (*kōgō*). (There was no empress during Go-Daigo's reign.)

[16] This hierarchy is not Japanese but Chinese. It was probably suggested to the author by a commentary on the "Song of Everlasting Sorrow," Po Chü-i's well-known poem, which is the source of many of the phrases in this passage, such as the reference to the "six palaces," nonexistent in Japan.

[17] From the *Analects*. The Kuan-chü is the first poem in the *Book of Odes* (*Shih ching*).

The Princes

harmonious and free of envy.[18] Because the sovereign's favors were not conferred upon the imperial consort alone, but also upon court ladies in numbers exceedingly great, therefore were sixteen princely sons born to him, the one after the other. The first among these was Prince Sonryō, that came forth from the womb of Tameko of posthumous junior third rank,[19] a daughter of Lord Tameyo, the Great Counselor of the Princely Left; Sonryō, the foster child of Lord Sadafusa, the Yoshida Great Subject of the Interior. This prince was one who from his fifteenth year was skilled in the six poetic principles, scooping up the clear waters of the Tominoo River,[20] treading on the ancient ruins of Asaka Mountain, and worrying his head with crying out to the wind and admiring the moon.

Likewise the second prince was born of the same womb. While yet his hair was dressed in a child's braid, this prince entered the Myōhōin Cloister to receive the teachings of the Buddha and study the three mysteries of Yoga. In moments of leisure he gladdened his heart with writing verses, surpassing the elegance of the Most Reverend Jichin, and unashamed before the poems of the Great Teacher Dengyō.

The third prince[21] came forth from the womb of one who was called Lady Mimbukyō of third rank. Within the emperor's heart the desire was strong to entrust the realm to this son, since from childhood he was acute and quick of mind; yet in the end a personage of the Jimyōin line was granted the estate of crown prince. For in the days of Go-Saga-in had it been laid down that the lords of the Daikakuji and the lords of the Jimyōin should succeed in turn to the imperial throne. Truly all matters in the realm were

---

[18] In ancient China, locusts were thought to reproduce prolifically because they lived together peacefully.

[19] This means that the lady was posthumously elevated to the third court rank, junior grade (first rank, senior grade, being the highest).

[20] This phrase and the one which follows are euphemisms for the study of poetry, because the Tominoo River and Asaka Mountain are the subjects of two famous old verses.

[21] Prince Morinaga.

made the business of the Kantō, great and small alike; nothing whatever was left to the imperial will! Because of this, the third prince entered the Nashimoto monastery to become the disciple of Prince Shōchin.

When this prince saw one thing, he understood ten, so great was his native genius, without equal in the world. Through him were the breezes of Ching-ch'i perfumed by the flower of One Reality and Instant Buddhahood through Perfect Merit; through him the waters of Yü-ch'üan were infused with the moonlight of the three dogmas' inseparability. The whole mountain joined its palms joyously, and the nine cloisters inclined their heads respectfully, saying, "Surely in the day of this abbot will the flickering lamp of the Law be raised aloft, and the failing pulse of Buddhism revive!" [22]

The fourth prince, who indeed sprang from the same womb, became the disciple of the prince of the second rank of the Shōgoin Cloister, dipping the waters of the Buddha-truth from the flow of the Three Wells, and anticipating his reward in Maitreya's dawn.[23]

For the rest, the selection of future sovereigns and the furnishing of bamboo gardens and pepper courts caused men to think in their hearts, "Surely the time is come when the imperial dignity will again prevail, and a foundation will be laid for the eternal prosperity of the throne." [24]

[22] The Nashimoto monastery was a subsidiary of the Enryakuji Temple, the headquarters of the Tendai sect. Ching-ch'i and Yü-ch'üan are places in China made famous by patriarchs of the parent T'ien-t'ai school. One Reality and Instant Buddhahood through Perfect Merit are Tendai teachings, as is the inseparability of the three dogmas (the doctrine of immateriality, the doctrine of empiricism, and the doctrine of the mean). "The whole mountain" and "the nine cloisters" are two ways of referring to the Enryakuji.

[23] "The flow of the Three Wells" is a play on Miidera (the Temple of the Three Wells; also called the Onjōji), which was customarily governed by the monk-prince residing at the Shōgoin. "Maitreya's dawn" refers to the coming of Maitreya Buddha, destined to descend to earth 5,670,000,000 years after Śākyamuni's entrance into Nirvana.

[24] Because there were many princes available to bolster the sovereign's position. "Bamboo gardens" and "pepper courts" are elegant Chinese names for princes' quarters and women's apartments.

The Inner Princess Prays for a Safe Delivery; the Matter of Toshimoto's Feigned Seclusion

Around the spring of the second year of Genkyō, the emperor laid down a command to revered monks of divers temples and monasteries, charging them to practice mystic rites of many kinds, that the Inner Princess might pray for the child in her womb. By special decree, the Most Holy Enkan of the Hosshōji Temple and the monk reformer Monkan built a fire altar inside the forbidden gate, drew near to the august presence of the princess, and prayed mightily, performing the Buddha-eye, golden wheel and five-altar rites, reciting the fivefold character-repeating *Peacock Monarch Sutra,* and invoking the seven healing buddhas, Shijōkō, male-producing Ususama, and the five great treasury-of-emptiness bodhisattvas. Likewise, they performed the six-Kannon six-word river-facing and Kariteimo rites, recited the eight-word Monjū formula and Fugen longevity prayers, and invoked Kongō Dōji.[25] Smoke from their sacred fires filled the Inner Princess's garden, and the sound of their hand bells reverberated through the women's apartments. In no wise did it appear that any demon or vengeful ghost could possibly intervene. Yet by the coming of the third year of

[25] All rites of esoteric Buddhism. The Buddha-eye rite celebrated the eye of the Buddha, the symbol of his omniscience. The golden wheel rite called for protection upon the Gold Wheel Cakravartin, one of four kinds of universal buddhas, conceived of as rulers whose chariot wheels rolled unobstructed everywhere. The five-altar rite, a prayer to avert calamity, employed five altars holding large statues of the Five Great Holy Bright Monarchs (*godai sommyōō*), with Fudō (Skt. Aryaacalanātha) as the central deity of the group. The Shijōkō services were calamity-averting rituals to which great effectiveness was ascribed. The object of worship was the buddha Shijōkō, said to radiate light from every pore. Ususama, a deity noted as a purifier of the unclean, was thought to be able to change a female foetus into a male. The five treasury-of-emptiness bodhisattvas were the five forms of Kokuzō (Skt. Ākāśagarbha), whose name derived from his emphasis upon the vanity of all worldly things, including such virtues as wisdom and compassion, which he compared to a treasury of emptiness. The six-Kannon six-word river-facing rites, which were prayers for health and the conquest of enemies, stressed the repetition of six magic words and were addressed to Kannon (Kanzeon, Skt. Avalokiteśvara) in six of the many forms in which that deity is represented. Kariteimo (Skt. Hāriti) was worshiped as a protector of women and children. Monjū (Skt. Manjuśrī) and Fugen (Skt. Samantabhadra) were called upon because they were bodhisattvas of great efficacy. Kongō Dōji (Skt. Vajrakumāra), a divine messenger, was the principal deity invoked in several calamity-averting rituals.

Chapter 1

Genkyō the child was still unborn, though day by day the Inner Princess accumulated merit in this way, praying with all her strength. Later it became known that the confinement of the princess was but a pretext, and the true design of those prayers was to exorcise the wickedness of the Kantō.

For it came to pass at this time that thoughts of striking down the military weighed upon the spirit of the emperor. And the desire was strong within him to seek the counsel of his ministers. Yet he uttered no word to those close about him, nor to his prudent and wise courtiers; for fearfully he thought, "If those who learn of the matter are many, assuredly tidings thereof will be borne to the military." In secret he spoke together with the Hino Middle Counselor Suketomo, the Archivist and Lesser Controller of the Right Toshimoto, the Shijō Middle Counselor Takasuke, the Regulator and Great Counselor Morokata, and the Taira magistrate Narisuke, seeking through these to bring together men of war. Yet there was none that responded to the imperial will, save only Nishigori Hōgandai, Asuke Jirō Shigenori, and the soldier-monks of the southern capital and northern peak.[26]

Now the emperor had tendered high place to this Toshimoto, a man of rare and excellent learning sprung from many generations of Confucian scholars, raising him up to the Orchid Dais[27] and making him an archivist. Wherefore so great was the multitude of Toshimoto's charges that there was no hour wherein he might devise stratagems against the Hōjō.

"In some way I must keep apart for awhile," he thought, "that I may consider plans for the revolt."

Just at that time, it chanced that soldier-monks came from the Mountain Gate[28] and Yokawa, appealing to the court with an earnest petition. And when Toshimoto opened that petition to read it aloud in the court, as though mistakenly he read "Mangon'in" where it was written "Ryōgon'in."

All the ministers looked at one another gleefully.

"Whether one considers the left side of the character or the right

---

[26] Nara and Mount Hiei.
[27] A Chinese name for the office of controller.
[28] The Enryakuji.

side, *sō* ought to be pronounced *moku!*"²⁹ they said, striking their palms together.

And Toshimoto took his way out of the hall red-faced, as one humiliated sorely.

Then Toshimoto made it known that because of his dishonor he would remain apart from men, nor for fully half a year did he come forth to perform the duties of his offices. But in the guise of a wandering monk he in fact journeyed to Yamato and Kawachi to find out places where castles might be built, and went down to the east and west to observe the temper of the provinces and look upon the aspect of the warriors of the land.

The Band of Roisterers and Gen'e's Discourses on Literature

There were two residents of the province of Mino called Toki Hōki no Jūrō Yorisada and Tajimi Shirōjirō Kuninaga, seed of the Seiwa Genji, renowned for valor. In divers ways Lord Suketomo drew near to these, until the bonds of his friendship with them waxed strong. And it came to pass that Suketomo made a group, called by the name of the Band of Roisterers, thinking thereby to search their hearts to the bottom (since not lightly could his great trust be made known). Those whom he gathered together were the Regulator and Great Counselor Morokata, the Shijō Middle Counselor Takasuke, the Tōin Chief of the Left Gate Guards Saneyo, the Archivist and Lesser Controller of the Right Toshimoto, Date Sammibō Yūga, the Eye of the Law Genki of the Shōgoin Cloister, Asuke Jirō Shigenori, and Tajimi Shirōjirō Kuninaga.

Most amazing was the aspect of those men's parties and meetings! In offering wine, they made no distinction of degree between the high and the low. Likewise, men cast off their caps and loosened their top hair, while monks showed their persons in white undergarments without their gowns. The wine was served by more than twenty maidens of sixteen or seventeen years, clear-skinned and

---

²⁹ The Ryōgon'in was the main building at Yokawa. Toshimoto acted as though he did not recognize the initial character of its name, reading it *man* because it contained the phonetic element *hō*, which he pretended to confuse with the similar *man*. Either of the two component elements of *sō* can be read *moku* when standing alone. See Character List.

superior in face and figure, through whose unlined robes of raw silk the snowy skin gleamed fresh as lotus blossoms newly risen from the waters of T'ai-i.[30] Suketomo brought forth many curious foods from mountain and sea, with excellent wine free-flowing as spring-water, and the guests sported and danced and recited verses. Yet all the while they took counsel together, how they might strike down the eastern barbarians.

Now these conspirators thought in their hearts, "May it not attract the eyes of others, to be assembling together constantly without a purpose?" Wherefore they petitioned the scholar called the Sign of the Law Gen'e, renowned for learning beyond all men of the age, and caused him to speak before them of the *Collected Works* of Ch'ang-li,[31] that their meetings might be thought to be literary arguments. Even in his dreams, this Sign of the Law knew nothing of the rebellious plan, but faced his hearers on every meeting day to expound mysteries and reveal principles.

There was contained within those *Collected Works* a long passage, "Ch'ang-li Goes Forth to Exile in Ch'ao-chou." Coming upon it, those who were listening to the lectures spoke among themselves, saying:

"All that is written here is inauspicious. The authors of the *Wu-tzu, Sun-tzu, Lu-t'ao,* and *San-lüeh*[32] are indeed the right men of letters for our present needs!"

So they spoke, and gave up the discourses on Ch'ang-li's works.

[*One of the* Taiheiki's *authors has taken advantage of this opportunity to insert the following anecdote concerning Han Yü (Ch'ang-li).*]

He who was called Han Ch'ang-li came forth at the end of T'ang, a man excellent in literary attainments. Not inferior were his poems to the poems of Tu Tzu-mei and Li T'ai-po;[33] and his prose was superior to the prose of Han, Wei, Chin, and Sung. Among his nephews was one called Han Hsiang, a person without taste

---

[30] A pond created by order of the Chinese emperor Han Wu Ti (156–87 B.C.).
[31] Ch'ang-li was the style (*hao*) of the distinguished T'ang writer Han Yü (768–825).
[32] Ancient Chinese military treatises.
[33] Better known in the West as Tu Fu and Li Po.

for letters or interest in poetry, who studied the arts of the Taoists to the exclusion of all else, making nonaction his business and lack of occupation his occupation. And once it fell out that Ch'ang-li admonished Han Hsiang, saying to him:

"In appearing in the world in diverse forms, you stray beyond the bounds of benevolence and righteousness. This is the shame of the gentleman, and the invariable practice of the ignoble man. I regret it deeply for your sake."

Han Hsiang answered with a loud and scornful laugh, saying:

"Benevolence and righteousness emerge where the Great Way has been discarded; learning flourishes when the Great Hypocrisy arises. I take my leisure within the confines of nonaction, and find satisfaction outside right and wrong. Thus do I hold the elbow of the True Ruler, conceal heaven and earth within a jar, take possession of the skills of creation, and tower above mountains and seas inside a mandarin orange seed. The regrettable thing is rather that you, my lord, in merely following after old masters, have devoted your life vainly to trivial things." [34]

Then Ch'ang-li spoke to him again, asking:

"Not yet can I believe in your words. Can you take possession of the skills of creation now?"

In silence Han Hsiang turned over a lapis lazuli tray, one which was lying before him, and rapidly turned it back again; and suddenly it bore a graceful branch of jasper peony blossoms. Seized with amazement, Ch'ang-li beheld a distich among the flowers, written in characters of gold.

> Clouds lie athwart Ch'in-ling; where is my home?
> Snow embraces Lan-kuan; the horse will not advance.

Ch'ang-li read it, marveling, and his heart filled with awe; yet then he perceived that the elegance and profundity of the phrases were but form, without discernible design or conclusion. When he took the tray in his hand to look at them, suddenly they disappeared. But thenceforward indeed was it known to the men of the realm that Han Hsiang had acquired the way of the supernatural arts.

---

[34] Han Hsiang is defending Taoism (the Great Way, the True Ruler) and attacking Confucianism (the Great Hypocrisy). His references to supernatural exploits are too involved to explain here.

Chapter 1

At a later time Ch'ang-li was traveling to exile in Ch'ao-chou; for he had disdained the Buddhist Law, and had offensively offered up a memorial asking reverence for the teachings of Confucius. As the day darkened, weariness seized the limbs of his horse, and the way ahead was long. When he gazed back toward his native place, there were clouds across the Ch'in-ling mountains, hiding the road behind him; when with lamentations he sought to climb the towering heights, there was snow enveloping the Lan-kuan barrier, covering the road ahead. But then with his horse's feet stopped from going forward or backward, he turned his head to behold Han Hsiang, come suddenly to his side from an unknown place.

Ch'ang-li's heart was joyful within him. He got down from his horse, pulled at Han Hsiang's sleeve, and spoke to him tearfully, saying:

"By means of the distich among the jasper flowers in a bygone year, you informed me beforehand of the sorrow of my demotion. Since you are come here now, I know that I shall never be able to return home, but shall perish grievously in exile."

Again Ch'ang-li thought:

"Oh heavy sorrow! There will be no further meeting between us, for this is our final parting."

He added to the distich, and made it into an eight-line poem for Han Hsiang.

> In the morning, I presented a memorial to the ninefold heaven;[35]
> In the evening, I was exiled to Ch'ao-yang, eight thousand leagues away.
> For the sake of the throne I wished to cast out evil things.
> Being enfeebled and decayed, why should I grieve for my remaining years?
> Clouds lie athwart Ch'in-ling; where is my home?
> Snow embraces Lan-kuan; the horse will not advance.
> I know that you come from afar and must have kindly intentions.
> Your purpose is to gather up my bones beside the Miasmic River.[36]

Then Han Hsiang put the poem in his sleeve, and they parted weeping, the one to the east and the one to the west.

[End of anecdote]

---

[35] The court.
[36] The Han River in Kwantung Province, to which Han Yü was exiled.

Truly, is it not well said, "Do not discuss a dream in front of a fool"? Stupid indeed were the superstitious fears of those who heard this lecture!

Yorikazu Changes His Loyalty

Among the conspirators there was a person called the Toki Archivist and Left Proximate Guard Yorikazu, who was wed to the daughter of a Rokuhara magistrate, Saitō Tarō Toshiyuki Saemon-no-jō. Yorikazu feared the coming parting with his beloved wife, saying to himself, "Not by one chance in a thousand may I escape death, when disturbance afflicts the realm and the hosts clash in battle." So it came about on a certain night, when after sleep they two awakened to talk, that suddenly he entreated his wife with flowing tears, saying:

"Even when people take shelter together under the same tree or dip water from a single stream, it is because strong karma-ties from many lives bind them together. Close indeed must be your union with me, who have cherished you tenderly for more than three years! I have shown my love's degree in my face, and I think that even on very casual occasions you have been aware of it. Yet uncertainty is the lot of mankind. Since we two share an eternal vow, let your woman's heart remain chaste to the end if you should hear that my body has passed into nothingness, and perform holy rites for my sake in the after-existence. If I return to humanity I shall renew our vows of husband and wife, and if I am born in the Pure Land [37] I shall await you, making a seat for two on a single lotus calyx."

Thereupon his attentive wife wept sadly, saying:

"What is the matter, that you speak so strangely? Though I know that this is a world wherein no pledge endures until tomorrow, yet in speaking of the next life you seem to be saying that our vows will be broken soon. If it were not so, I do not believe that you would behave in this way."

So she spoke, and the shallow-minded man spoke to her again, saying:

---

[37] Amida's paradise, the goal of the Jōdo sect of Buddhism.

Chapter 1

"Know then that the emperor has favored me with such a command as I did not dream of, and places his trust in me. Thus I have become party to an imperial revolt, for there is no way to draw back; yet not by one chance in a thousand may I escape death. With heavy heart I spoke to you just now, made sorrowful by the parting that is soon to come. But this is a most serious matter; do not let anyone learn of it."

Although he pressed her strongly to guard the secret, the quick-minded woman rose up early, thinking:

"When one considers the matter carefully, if the imperial revolt is brought to nothing, then instantly the military will mete out death to my husband, in whom the emperor has placed his trust. Yet if ruin is visited upon the military, who among my kinsmen will be spared? Let me rather speak of this thing to my father Toshiyuki, setting it forth that Yorikazu has transferred his loyalty, that in this way I may aid my husband and my kinsmen equally."

And Yorikazu's wife hastened to her father's side, and spoke secretly of the matter exactly as it was.

Seized with amazement, Saitō made speed to summon Yorikazu.

"Is there truth in this marvel that I have heard? Even as a man who steps into a deep pool bearing a stone in his arms, so is one who plans such a thing in today's world. If you are willing, I will go in haste to say to the lords of Rokuhara all that I have learned from you, so that both of us may escape the blame; for death will be the portion of all, even my own, if another mouth tells the story."

So he spoke, nor could dread fear fail to take hold of the heart which had discovered to a woman such a matter as this.

"I agreed because of the urging of Yorisada, whose surname is the same as mine, and of Tajimi Shirōjirō," said Yorikazu. "Please devise a plan to save me from blame."

Then before the night lightened Saitō took his way quickly to Rokuhara, where he spoke concerning all these things. At once the lords of Rokuhara sent off a swift messenger to Kamakura, and issued orders to the warriors of the capital, and to men outside the city, that they might assemble together at Rokuhara. And the names of those who responded were set down in a register, each in the order of his coming.

Just at that time there was fighting in the province of Settsu at the estate called Kuzuha, where warriors rose up against the steward's deputy. Wherefore it was heralded abroad that the assembling of the watchmen of the forty-eight places[38] and the warriors of the capital was to place the master's agent in the estate office, according to the will of Rokuhara. (This was a stratagem, that the conspirators might not run away.) And with tranquil hearts Toki and Tajimi made ready to go forth toward Kuzuha on the morrow, each in his own dwelling place.

Like clouds or mist[39] the hosts galloped to Rokuhara at the hour of the hare on the next day, which is to say the nineteenth day of the ninth month of the first year of Gentoku. Crested banners were handed to the attackers' grand marshals, Kogushi Saburō Saemon-no-jō Noriyuki and Yamamoto Kurō Tokitsuna, who took their way to the Sixth Ward river bed and divided their three thousand horsemen into two parties, to advance against Tajimi's dwelling place at Nishiki-no-kōji Takakura and Toki Jūrō's dwelling place at Sanjō Horikawa.

Leaving behind the great numbers of his warriors at the Third Ward river bed, Tokitsuna rode by stealth toward Toki's house, with none but two foot-soldiers bearing halberds. Doubtless he thought, "If a clamorous host draws near, may not the prized enemy escape in some way?"

When he came to the portal, he got down from his horse and went in quickly by the small side gate. At the middle gate he beheld the night watch, snoring lustily, with swords and pieces of armor scattered round about their pillows. And when he sought behind the stables lest there be a way to leave—behold: in the rear stood an earthen wall, so that no man might go forth except by the gate.

Thereupon with tranquil heart Tokitsuna pulled open the door of the small chamber rearward of the guest hall and came in to where Toki Jūrō stood combing and arranging his side hair, even as one newly arisen from his bed.

---

[38] Check points in the capital, manned by warriors from the neighboring provinces (home provinces), who acted as night watchmen and lit signal fires when necessary.

[39] I.e., they were so numerous that they resembled clouds or mist.

Chapter 1

Toki cried out when he beheld Yamamoto Kurō, caught up his sword swiftly, and sprang through a door panel into the guest hall. Furiously he slashed at Tokitsuna like a reaper mowing grain, taking care that his sword might not strike into the ceiling. But Tokitsuna thrust and gave back, and pressed and jumped away, since it was in his mind to draw this enemy forth into the courtyard, the better to take him alive.

As they two fought all alone, Tokitsuna looked backward upon the great numbers of his rear guard, more than a thousand horsemen, sweeping through the second gate with a mighty battle cry. And then perhaps Toki Jūrō feared to fight longer lest he be taken alive, for he hastened back into his sleeping chamber, cut open his belly in the shape of a cross, and perished.

All of Toki's retainers who had been sleeping in interior apartments also met death, each in his own way. And Yamamoto Kurō's men galloped back to Rokuhara with the heads of the slain affixed to their sword points.

Meanwhile, two thousand horsemen advanced against the dwelling place of Tajimi, led by Kogushi Saburō Saemon-no-jō Noriyuki. Their battle cries affrighted Tajimi, where he slept with senses confused by a night's drinking, and he cried out alarmed. But the woman of the town at his side, wise in the ways of the world, took up the armor by his pillow, dressed him in it, tightened his belt, and roused others who slumbered.

One man thus awakened, Ogasawara Magoroku by name, seized his sword and ran out to the middle gate. Rubbing his eyes and gazing sharply in the four directions, Magoroku beheld above the earthen wall a banner bearing a crest fashioned after the manner of a carriage wheel.[40] And he returned within, shouting to the others in a great voice:

"Assuredly is the imperial design laid bare, for attackers from Rokuhara stand against us. Arise, warriors! Let each man fight until the very hilt ornaments of his sword give way; and let each cut open his belly at the last!"

With a corselet slung across his body, he ran up to the gate tower, carrying a closely wound rattan bow and a twenty-four-arrow

[40] Used by the Hōjō family.

war quiver,[41] drew forth an arrow from the middle of the quiver, fitted it along the string, and opened the boards of a window to make a peaked hole. And shouting down he spoke a word to the enemy.

"Soon will you know the degree of our skill, pretentious host! Who may your grand marshal be? Let him approach to receive one of my arrows!"

Speaking, he pulled back the bowstring, full and slow, until with a singing sound the arrow flew away, that measured twelve hands and the breadth of three fingers. Its arrowhead hit square in the middle of the foremost rider's helmet and drove through cleanly to the first neck plate, so that he fell headlong from off his horse: Kinuzuri Sukefusa, a retainer of Kanō Shimotsuke-no-zenji.

Thereafter Magoroku shot rapidly, striking as he willed, whether in the armor sleeve, the skirt, or the helmet bowl, until twenty-four warriors were stricken by his arrows. When but one arrow remained in his quiver, he drew it forth and sent the quiver falling down lightly from the tower, saying, "This single arrow do I retain to guard my journey to the nether world!" Then he put the arrow into his belt, and called out in a mighty voice, saying, "Look well, that you may tell others how the bravest man in Japan kills himself after joining a conspiracy!" And he sprang down headfirst from the tower with the point of his sword in his mouth, so that the sword bit into him and killed him.

In the meantime Tajimi and his kinsmen and retainers leapt into the courtyard, girt in all their armor: twenty men, waiting for the attackers, with a wooden bar laid across the gate. Yet of those others like clouds or mist, none would willingly cut his way inside, for terror seized them when they thought of the resolute defenders, shut up with desperation in their hearts.

At last four men crawled through a small broken place in the door of the gate: Itō Hikojirō with his son and two brothers. To be

[41] Although a "twenty-four-arrow quiver" actually contained twenty-five arrows, an ancient warrior tradition forbade the use of the last one. The origin of this curious prohibition is uncertain, but Magoroku's speech below suggests that the arrow thus preserved was believed to possess the power of safeguarding its owner after death.

sure, the hearts of these four were valorous, yet all perished beside the gate when they reached the waiting enemy, before they might even cut at them with their swords. And when the attackers had seen these things, there was none that would draw near willingly.

Thereupon the defenders pushed open the door of the gate from within to shame the attackers.

"Can anyone be so base as people who agree to make up a punitive party?" they said. "Enter quickly, that we may give you our heads as farewell presents!"

When the attackers were thus dishonored utterly by the foe, five hundred of the foremost sprang down from their horses to charge into the courtyard, screaming aloud. Yet the resolute warriors inside would not fall back so much as a foot. Without a sideward glance, those twenty rushed into the middle of the great force, slashing at them with their swords until the five hundred ran back outside the gate, beaten down terribly.

Now when the first warriors drew away, a second line rushed in clamorously, so great were the numbers of the attackers. Rushing in, they were beaten back; beaten back, they rushed in again. And with scattering sparks of fire the fighting continued, from the beginning of the hour of the dragon until the end of the hour of the horse.

By reason that the battle raged furiously in front, a thousand of Sasaki Hōgan's followers went around to the rear to break in from Nishiki-no-kōji by destroying the commoners' houses. And then perhaps Tajimi and his warriors became disheartened; for these twenty-two men stabbed one another again and again, lined up at the middle gate, until they lay like scattered divining sticks. The warriors at the main gate smashed through, the host from the rear poured in, and all the attackers galloped back to Rokuhara with the heads of the defenders. Although the fighting had endured for four hours only, those who were killed or wounded were two hundred and seventy-three men.

Suketomo and Toshimoto Go Down to the Kantō; the Imperial Message

After Toki and Tajimi were struck down, step by step the imperial plot was made known. Two eastern messengers came up to the capital, Nagasaki Shirō Saemon Yasumitsu and Nanjō Jirō Saemon Munenao; and these laid hands on Suketomo and Toshimoto on the tenth day of the fifth month.

Suketomo and Toshimoto had thought, "It cannot be that a confession has been made, since no man suffered capture when Toki died. Surely our part will not become known." Wherefore they had not made ready for untoward happenings, neglectful because of a vain hope. But now their wives and children fled bewildered to the east and west, finding no hiding place; their precious goods were scattered over the highroads, becoming dust under horses' feet.

Lord Suketomo of the Hino was one who beyond other men had found favor in the imperial eyes and had brought prosperity to his house; for he had received honor as chief of the police commissioners and had risen to be a middle counselor. Likewise Toshimoto no Ason came forth from a scholar family, and by virtue of illustrious deeds had received high office, so that men of equal rank followed eagerly after the dust of his fat horses, and his seniors drank gladly of the cold dregs from his emptied wine cup.[42] Well is it said, "If righteousness be lacking, then are wealth and honor but as a floating cloud in my eyes." Since these are the excellent words of Confucius, recorded in the *Analects* of Lu, how can the truth be otherwise?[43] The dream of their happiness was transformed instantly into bitter sorrow. Of all who saw or heard, there was none but understood that the prosperous must decline; nor was there any whose sleeve remained dry.[44]

On the twenty-seventh day of the same month, the two eastern messengers came back again to Kamakura with Suketomo and Toshimoto. Truly it seemed that these nobles, leaders of the plot,

---

[42] The last two phrases are from a poem by Tu Fu.

[43] This is not a very pertinent quotation, since the author has not suggested that Toshimoto and Suketomo obtained their honors by questionable methods.

[44] I.e., there was none who did not wipe away tears with his sleeve.

Chapter 1

would meet death soon. Yet after all the military were fearful of the censure of the realm and the anger of the sovereign, since Suketomo and Toshimoto were men close to the emperor's heart, distinguished in learning and talents. They stayed their hand, nor so much as tortured them, but only kept them in the charge of the Samurai Office as though they had been ordinary persons under confinement.

So with the passing of time came the night of the seventh day of the seventh month, when the herdsman and the weaver-maid cross the raven bridge, freed of the yearlong restraint upon their desire. It was ever the custom on this night, that in celebration of the skill-beseeching festival the palace ladies would attach petition-threads to bamboo wands and arrange auspicious fruits in the garden.[45] But in this year no poets offered up verses in Chinese and Japanese, nor were there musicians to play upon strings and reeds; for it was a time of disorder in the realm. The great nobles and courtiers who chanced to be serving at night knit their brows and lowered their heads, for it was a time when men's spirits faltered, cold terror gripped them, and they asked themselves, "Who will be the next to suffer from the disturbances in the world?"

When the night was far advanced the emperor spoke, saying, "Who is on duty?" And the Yoshida Middle Counselor Fuyufusa came into the august presence to serve.

The supreme highness caused Fuyufusa to draw near, saying:

"The capital is in dire peril, for never since the taking of Suketomo and Toshimoto has the eastern tempest ceased to rage. Ever is Our spirit troubled, lest the men of Kamakura be devising new things. Is there no plan that will tranquillize the eastern barbarians?"

So he questioned him, and respectfully Fuyufusa spoke, saying:

"It is in my mind that the Hōjō will do no more, because I have not heard of any confession that Suketomo and Toshimoto have

[45] This festival is based on a legend about the marriage of two stars, the weaver-maid (Vega) and the herdsman (Altair), who meet once a year when a raven spreads his wings across the Milky Way to make a bridge. It is celebrated especially by young girls, who ask to be made as skillful at their work as the weaver-maid.

made. Yet there ought to be no remissness, so rash and hasty are the eastern barbarians of late. It would be well for His Majesty to vouchsafe an imperial message to still the wrath of the Sagami lay monk." [46]

Perhaps the supreme highness thought in his heart that it ought to be so, for he said to him again, "Let Fuyufusa make speed to write a message."

Then Fuyufusa wrote a message in the imperial presence and offered it up. The sovereign wept fluttering tears, that he wiped away with his sleeves; and all the great lords sorrowed to behold him.

Soon the Madenokōji Great Counselor Lord Nobufusa, named to be an imperial commissioner, took his way with that message to Kamakura, where the Sagami lay monk received it through Akita Jō-no-suke. As the lay monk made ready to hear it read, Nikaidō Dōun the lay monk of Dewa admonished him, saying:

"Never has a Son of Heaven deigned to grant a message directly to a military subject, either in another country or in our own. Will there not be danger from watching gods and buddhas, if heedlessly you open and read it? Would it not be proper simply to return it to the imperial commissioner, not opening the box?"

So he spoke over and over. But the Sagami lay monk, saying, "What is there to fear?" commanded Saitō Tarō Saemon Toshiyuki to read.

When Toshiyuki read where it was written, "Let the Sun Goddess be the witness that the imperial heart is not false," suddenly his eyes were blinded, blood dripped from his nose, and he withdrew without reading the rest. From that day forth a swelling came out at the base of Toshiyuki's throat, so that within seven days he died, spitting up blood. Not one of the people who heard of it but trembled with fear, saying, "Although we live in the era of depravity, yet is divine retribution still the lot of those who abandon a subject's rightful course!"

Now at first the military decided in consultation together:

"Let no faith be placed in the imperial message, since it was surely from the sovereign's mind itself that the plot of Suketomo

---

[46] Hōjō Takatoki (so called because he held the title of governor of Sagami).

and Toshiyuki came forth. The supreme highness must be exiled to a far-off province."

So they resolved; yet Lord Nobufusa the imperial commissioner spoke to them persuasively; and likewise all were made dumb with fear when suddenly Toshiyuki spat blood and died, he who had read the august message. And perhaps the Sagami lay monk himself looked up to the Son of Heaven with awe, for he sent back the august message, saying, "Decisions in political matters rest with the court. It is not proper for the military to meddle."

When Lord Nobufusa went back to the capital to report these things to the throne, then indeed was the imperial heart at ease for the first time, and color returned to the faces of the courtiers. The military granted freedom to Toshimoto no Ason, since his guilt was doubtful in their eyes; and Lord Suketomo they banished to the land of Sado, making his death sentence one degree easier.

2

The Imperial Journeys to the Southern Capital and Northern Peak

ON THE FOURTH DAY of the second month of the second year of Gentoku, the sovereign summoned his master of ceremonial, the Madenokōji Middle Counselor Lord Fujifusa, saying:

"We shall travel to the Tōdaiji on the eighth day of next month, and to the Kōfukuji. Let instructions be given quickly to those who will go together with Us."

Fujifusa settled upon the traveling dresses of the attendants, heedful of custom and mindful of precedent, and laid down the order of the procession. As chief of the guards, the Sasaki governor of Bitchū made bridges, and the watchmen of the forty-eight places defended the crossroads in helmets and armor. With splendid and solemn ceremony the lords and dignitaries journeyed forth, and the hundred officials and thousand functionaries.

The Tōdaiji was built by a vow of Shōmu Tennō to enshrine the largest Vairocana Buddha in this transient world;[1] and the Kōfukuji was a great monastery honoring the ancestors of the Fujiwara house, built by a vow of Lord Tankai.[2] It was the desire of all the generations of sage rulers to be bound by close ties to these holy

---

[1] This colossal statue, dedicated in 752, is still one of the famous sights of Japan, although little of the original remains.
[2] Fujiwara no Fubito (659–720), the son of the founder of the house of Fujiwara.

places, yet not for many years had a sovereign journeyed thereto, since not lightly may the first person under heaven go forth. But because this reign resumed what was discontinued and revived what was abandoned, the turning wheels of the phoenix carriage caused the soldier-monks to join together rejoicing palms, and the miraculous buddhas to diffuse the light of their divine virtue.

Likewise on the twenty-seventh day of the same month, the emperor went forth to Mount Hiei to make an offering in the Great Lecture Hall. This Great Lecture Hall was a votive hall of Fukakusa Tenno,[3] consecrated to the worship of Dainichi Henjō,[4] yet for long had it remained undedicated, since the building of it was not finished. For many years had frosts fallen, and for many years had the Wood Star[5] turned in the sky, while all the mountain lamented.

> Through broken tiles the fog's eternal incense smoked;
> Through ruined doors the moon hung up its constant lamp.

Now all the monastery rejoiced, and the nine cloisters bowed their heads, that suddenly this emperor took up the great work of building and quickly made ready for the dedication.

At the dedication ceremony the chief of the priests was the Canonical Prince of the Blood Sonchō of the Myōhōin Cloister, and the offertory prayers were written by the Tendai abbot of that time, the Canonical Prince of the Blood Son'un of the Great Pagoda. More fragrant than the flowers of Vulture Peak was their incense, burned to glorify the Buddha;[6] from Yü-shan itself the wind brought back the echo of their pious hymns.[7] When the musicians played their cloud-arresting melodies and the child

---

[3] The Emperor Nimmyō (810–850), so called after Fukakusa, his burial place in the province of Kii.
[4] One of the names of Vairocana Buddha, the principal object of worship of the Tendai sect.
[5] Jupiter.
[6] Vulture Peak, near Rājagṛha, is celebrated as the place at which Śākyamuni revealed the teachings of the *Lotus Sutra* to a multitude who showered him with flowers.
[7] The Chinese poet Ts'ao Chih (192–232) is said to have composed a Buddhist hymn in imitation of the sound of the voice of Brahma, heard by him at Yü-shan (northwest of Tung-o in modern Shantung Province).

and himself received imperial commands concerning the dedication of the Mountain Gate's Lecture Hall and divers other things, therefore did they lay hands upon him, thinking, "He will not fail to know of the plan to appeal to the soldier-monks." The monks Chikyō and Kyōen also were summoned from the southern capital, that they might present themselves at Rokuhara.

Now the Nijō Middle Marshal, Lord Tameakira, was a person skilled in the art of poetry, one who was called to join imperial poetry contests on moonlit nights and snowy mornings, and who ministered constantly to the sovereign at banquets. The men of Rokuhara seized this Tameakira and placed him in the custody of a certain Saitō, not charging him with guilt, but thinking to know the emperor's mind by asking of him. And although the five monks were not examined closely at Rokuhara (since from the beginning these were summoned to be judged in Kamakura), yet Lord Tameakira was given over to the inquisitors for torture. For of him it was ordered, "Let there be questioning in the capital, and let the Kantō know it if a confession be made."

Charcoal was set to blazing in the north compound of Rokuhara, most like to a fiery hell-furnace, with split pieces of green bamboo on top, and fierce flames belching up terribly through the cracks. Two soldiers of low degree stood on either side, to stretch out Tameakira's arms and cause him to walk over the top. It was a sight to make men faint with terror, thinking, "Surely it is even so when a sinner is consumed by the flames of the burning hells, or is tortured by demons with the heads of oxen and horses!"

Lord Tameakira called for an inkstone; and they gave it him with paper, thinking in their hearts that he would make a confession. Yet it was not a confession that he wrote, but a poem, saying, "Did I believe it?—that I would be questioned, not concerning our Shikishima Way,[14] but about things of the transient world!"

The Tokiwa governor of Suruga[15] was struck with admiration,

---

[14] The art of Japanese verse. Shikishima is a poetic name for Japan.
[15] Tokiwa Norisada, a Hōjō kinsman who was the head of the northern Rokuhara office.

The Two Kings

Prince Morinaga (The Prince of the Great Pagoda)

dred and more generations since the Harmonious Reverence Gishin was first made head of the Tendai faith! Later, men understood the reason thereof: that thinking to strike down the eastern barbarians he trained his body in the military arts.

The Arrest of the Monks and Their Removal to Rokuhara; Tameakira's Poem

Now to the Kantō came word of the conduct of the Prince of the Great Pagoda, and of the exorcism rituals in the palace, for these were easily discovered things, inviting disaster. The Sagami lay monk waxed exceeding wroth, saying:

"No, no! Never will the realm be tranquil while this emperor sits upon the throne! He shall be removed to a distant province, according to the precedent of Shōkyū; and the Prince of the Great Pagoda shall be killed. But first we must lay hands upon the Most Holy Enkan of the Hosshōji Temple to examine him, and likewise on the monk reformer Monkan of Ono, on Chikyō and Kyōen of the southern capital, and on the monk reformer Chūen of the Jōdoji Temple. All these have waited closely upon the dragon countenance[11] of late, calling down curses upon our house."

Thereupon Nikaidō Shimotsuke Hōgan and the Nagai governor of Tōtōmi[12] went up from the Kantō to the capital.

When these two messengers were come into the city, the spirit of the supreme highness was sore afflicted, by reason that he feared evil things from them. And truly it came to pass that at dawn on the eleventh day of the fifth month these sent forth one Saiga Hayato-no-suke, who laid hands on the Most Holy Enkan of the Hosshōji, the monk reformer Monkan of Ono, and the monk reformer Chūen of the Jōdoji, and fetched them to Rokuhara.

The monk reformer Chūen was not one of those who had performed the rites of exorcism, but was a virtuous apostle of the revealed Law.[13] Yet because he waited closely upon the emperor,

---

[11] The emperor; an expression borrowed from the Chinese.
[12] Provincial governorships were customarily awarded to military men. The author supplies Nagai's surname in order to distinguish him from other holders of the same title.
[13] That is, he belonged to one of the exoteric sects of Buddhism, rather than to a magic-working esoteric sect.

and himself received imperial commands concerning the dedication of the Mountain Gate's Lecture Hall and divers other things, therefore did they lay hands upon him, thinking, "He will not fail to know of the plan to appeal to the soldier-monks." The monks Chikyō and Kyōen also were summoned from the southern capital, that they might present themselves at Rokuhara.

Now the Nijō Middle Marshal, Lord Tameakira, was a person skilled in the art of poetry, one who was called to join imperial poetry contests on moonlit nights and snowy mornings, and who ministered constantly to the sovereign at banquets. The men of Rokuhara seized this Tameakira and placed him in the custody of a certain Saitō, not charging him with guilt, but thinking to know the emperor's mind by asking of him. And although the five monks were not examined closely at Rokuhara (since from the beginning these were summoned to be judged in Kamakura), yet Lord Tameakira was given over to the inquisitors for torture. For of him it was ordered, "Let there be questioning in the capital, and let the Kantō know it if a confession be made."

Charcoal was set to blazing in the north compound of Rokuhara, most like to a fiery hell-furnace, with split pieces of green bamboo on top, and fierce flames belching up terribly through the cracks. Two soldiers of low degree stood on either side, to stretch out Tameakira's arms and cause him to walk over the top. It was a sight to make men faint with terror, thinking, "Surely it is even so when a sinner is consumed by the flames of the burning hells, or is tortured by demons with the heads of oxen and horses!"

Lord Tameakira called for an inkstone; and they gave it him with paper, thinking in their hearts that he would make a confession. Yet it was not a confession that he wrote, but a poem, saying, "Did I believe it?—that I would be questioned, not concerning our Shikishima Way,[14] but about things of the transient world!"

The Tokiwa governor of Suruga[15] was struck with admiration,

---

[14] The art of Japanese verse. Shikishima is a poetic name for Japan.
[15] Tokiwa Norisada, a Hōjō kinsman who was the head of the northern Rokuhara office.

bowing down tearfully before Tameakira's righteousness. Likewise the two eastern messengers drenched their sleeves when they read it. And in this manner Tameakira escaped the ordeal and was adjudged guiltless.

The arts of poetry weighed little with the military, since their attachment was to bow and horse, even as the court took pleasure in Chinese and Japanese verse. Yet because it is the way of the world for one thing to act upon another, therefore by a single poem Tameakira's ordeal was forestalled, and the hearts of the eastern barbarians were gentled. Surely with reason did Ki no Tsurayuki write in the *Kokinshū* preface, "By poetry are heaven and earth swayed effortlessly, and invisible demons and gods are moved to compassion. Poetry brings harmony between men and women; it soothes the violent warrior's heart." [16]

The Three Monks Go Down to the Kantō

The eastern messengers went forth toward the Kantō on the eighth day of the sixth month, and with them the three monks.

The monk reformer Chūen was a disciple of the monk reformer Jishō of the Jōdoji, a man excellent in judging arguments, learned beyond others of his monastery. The monk reformer Monkan dwelt at the Hokkeji in Harima province, and in the vigorous days of his young manhood removed to the Daigoji. A great deacon of the Shingon faith, he served as abbot of the Tōji and the Daigoji, and was a pillar supporting the four mandalas and three mysteries. And in the beginning the Most Holy Enkan was a monk of the Enryakuji, surpassingly skilled in revealed and secret doctrines. The whole mountain marveled and counted him as specially blessed; the temple buildings were as though empty of others because of the renown of his wisdom and austerities. But in his heart Enkan thought:

"If in these degenerate times I follow the uses of the Mountain Gate, then surely I will wax arrogant and fall into the hands of

---

[16] Tsurayuki (883–946), a leading poet and prose stylist of the early Heian period, was the principal compiler of the *Kokinshū* (905), the first official poetic anthology.

Deva Māra.¹⁷ Let me rather cast off the glory of preaching in high places and return to the ancient rules of the great teacher Dengyō."

Ridding himself of the bridle of renown and profit, for a long time he locked the mossy door of solitude in the place called Saitō no Kurodani, laying down his few garments on frosty lotus leaves and entrusting his single food bowl to the morning breeze from the pine flowers. But "virtue is not left to stand alone. He who practices it will have neighbors." ¹⁸ Since a great light cannot hide its radiance, at last Enkan became the religious teacher of five rulers, and the father of the three cumulative commandments.¹⁹

How strange it was that such wise and upright monk-saints were forced to wander beneath a travel-hostel moon, the prisoners of distant barbarians! Was it because not even these might escape the calamities of the times? Or was it perhaps the karma of a previous existence?

The Most Holy Enkan was accompanied by three faithful disciples, Sōin, Enshō, and Dōshō, serving before and behind his litter, but the monk reformer Monkan and the monk reformer Chūen rode unattended upon sorry relay hacks. How pitiful were they who in the darkness of night went forth toward the eastland of calling birds, compassed about with unaccustomed warriors! Their spirits fainted utterly while yet their dew lives endured, for there were men that said, "Never will they come to Kamakura, since death will overtake them on the way." At every post station they thought, "The final moment is come"; at every mountain resting place, "This is the end."

Yet slowly they went forward, day after day, until in the fullness of time they came to Kamakura, on the twenty-fourth day of the sixth month.

The Most Holy Enkan was placed in the charge of the Sakai gov-

---

¹⁷ An interfering demon who seeks to destroy the Buddhist Law.
¹⁸ From the *Analects*.
¹⁹ *Sanju jōkai* (Skt. *tri-vidhāni śīlāni*), defined as "(a) the formal 5, 8 or 10, and the rest; (b) whatever works for goodness; (c) whatever works for the welfare or salvation of living, sentient beings." W. E. Soothill and Lewis Hodous, *A Dictionary of Chinese Buddhist Terms* (London, Kegan Paul, Trench, Trubner and Company, 1937), p. 74b.

ernor of Echizen, the monk reformer Monkan was placed in the charge of the Sakai governor of Tōtōmi, and the monk reformer Chūen was placed in the charge of the Ashikaga governor of Sanuki.

The two returned messengers drew pictures of the principal images and burnt-offering altars employed by those monks; and the monk reformer Raizen of Sasame was called forth to behold them, since they were things not understood by secular men.

"Beyond doubt rituals of exorcism were performed," said Raizen.

And thereupon the monks were given over to the Samurai Office to be tortured with fire and water.

For a time Monkan would not yield before the questioning. But being tortured grievously by water, with weakened body and fainting spirit he uttered words of confession, saying, "I did indeed perform rituals of exorcism, according to the imperial command."

Next they made ready for the torture of Chūen, but this monk reformer, timid by nature, set down all things without omission in a scroll of confession, not waiting for the ordeal. He spoke of the supreme highness's dealings with the Mountain Gate, of the actions of the Prince of the Great Pagoda, of Toshimoto's devisings, and even of things which were not true.

Thereupon the men of Kamakura agreed together, saying, "Although there can be no further doubt, we must examine the Most Holy Enkan on the morrow, for being equal in guilt he cannot be spared." But in a dream that night the Sagami lay monk beheld two thousand monkeys, or perhaps three thousand, that came forth in a great multitude from the eastern base of Mount Hiei, and lined up as though to protect this holy man. And therefore he ordered a messenger to be sent out to the warder before dawn, that he might defer Enkan's torture awhile, for the import of the dream was heavy in his mind.

Just at that time the warder himself took his way to the abiding place of the Sagami lay monk, saying:

"Because the holy man was to be tortured at dawn today, I went in to him, where he meditated on the sacred truth in front of a lamp. When I beheld his shadow on the door, truly it was even as the image of the Bright Monarch Fudō![20] And therefore am I come to speak of this thing, since it is most strange."

Then indeed were the torture preparations laid aside, for from the dream and apparition it was known that this was no ordinary man.

On the thirteenth day of the seventh month, the names of the places of exile were laid down, whereto these three monks were banished. The monk reformer Monkan was banished to Iō-ga-jima, and the monk reformer Chūen was banished to the province of Echigo. As regards the Most Holy Enkan, although his punishment alone was not called distant banishment, he was sent on a long journey to the province of Mutsu, to be in the charge of the Yūki lay monk of Kōzuke. Truly it was in name only that his punishment was made light, for he went to a far place among distant barbarians, and the days of his journeying were many. Sadly at the crossing of the Natori River he wrote a verse, saying, "In the approaching flow of Michinoku's melancholy Natori River, it will doubtless sink completely—the fossil-wood of the shoals."[21] May it be that not even a holy living buddha could find deliverance from the calamities of the times?

[*The author now attempts to explain Enkan's ill fortune by means of the following story, intended to illustrate the manner in which the events of one lifetime determine a man's fate in a future reincarnation.*]

Long ago in the Indian state of Vārānsī, there lived a sramana versed in the three learnings, which are discipline, meditation, and wisdom. And it came about that this sramana was appointed to be the religious mentor of the state, whose people turned to him as to a living buddha.

---

[20] The chief of the "terrible deities" of Japanese Buddhism, particularly important in the Shingon sect. He carries a sword to cut away ignorance and a rope to bind the forces of evil.

[21] Fossil-wood is prized in Japan as a source of fine articles for the table. The word also has the figurative meaning "living in obscurity." *Shizumu*, "to sink," also means "to be downcast." Enkan compares himself to this neglected, though potentially valuable, object.

Chapter 2

On a certain occasion, the great monarch of the nation thought to convoke a Buddhist gathering, whereat this sramana would expound the discipline. And the sramana took his way to the palace according to the royal command.

When the royal page reported the sramana's coming, it chanced that the king was taking his pleasure at checkers. The king heard nothing of the page's words, his mind being filled with the game; but thinking of the game the king spoke, saying, "Cut!"

The page mistook the king's words, which fell upon his ears as a command to kill the sramana. Wherefore he took the sramana out of the palace and struck off his head.

When the king's game was ended, he called for the sramana to be brought before him. But thereupon an officer of the prison reported to him, saying, "His head is cut off, according to the royal command."

Greatly angered, the king said:

"It is said, 'Report for instructions three times when a man has been sentenced to death.' In doing what is wrong because of a single word, this man treasonably deprives Us of virtue."

And he summoned the page and punished him and his family.

The king marveled that this guiltless sramana had been put to death, thinking in his heart that it was the karma of a former life. He questioned an arhat, that he might learn the truth thereof, and for seven days that arhat remained in a trance, achieving buddha-knowledge of all previous existences, and beholding the past and present. It was revealed to him that the sramana had been a farmer tilling the soil, and the king had been a frog dwelling in the water. By chance the farmer, turning the soil of a mountain field in the spring, had cut off the head of the frog with the tip of his plow. How pitiful it was! Because of this karma the peasant was born a sramana, and the frog was born the great monarch of Vārānsī, that another mistaken killing might come to pass.

[*End of story*]

Likewise as regards the Most Holy Enkan, through what workings of cause and effect did he suffer this unforeseen punishment? How strange it was!

Toshimoto no Ason Goes Back to the Kantō

Once in a bygone year had Toshimoto no Ason gone down in captivity to Kamakura, even after the chastisement of Toki Jūrō Yorisada, when with explanations of divers kinds he had won deliverance. Now again on the eleventh day of the seventh month he was brought to Rokuhara to be sent to the Kantō, since in the confessions it was set forth, "Toshimoto was the leader of the rebellion." And because the law does not suffer a second crime to be forgiven, in no wise might he be pardoned. Going forth, he thought in his heart, "Assuredly I must either perish on the way or be struck down in Kamakura. How may it be otherwise?"

> Ever sad is a traveler's sleep,[22]
> Though his journeying endure for but a night,
> To wander through Katano's snow
> Of falling flowers in spring,
> Or from Storm Mountain come home again,
> Robed in autumn's maple-leaf brocade.
> But piteous was Toshimoto's heart
> (O journey unforeseen!),
> That left behind his wife and child,
> Well-loved, whose fate he would not know,
> And to the fair familiar capital
> Said his last goodbye.
> First in the lucent waters of Ōsaka[23]
> (No barrier to grief),
> He drenched his tear-wet sleeves;
> Then traversed mountain paths to Uchide beach,
> Whence on Biwa's saltless sea
> He watched the rowing boats that rose and fell,

---

[22] Here begins one of the best-known passages in the *Taiheiki*, Toshimoto's *michiyuki* (journey), in which the names of places between Kyoto and Kamakura are woven into the account of the journey in a long series of poetic allusions and plays on words. Its elegant language, softly dissolving images and rhythmic five-seven cadence make this *michiyuki* a fine representative of the tradition in Japanese literature which later produced the *michiyuki* of the Nō and Chikamatsu. (Explanations of the allusions and puns, which are too complicated to be undertaken here, are available in the translator's *A Study of the Taiheiki, a Medieval Japanese Chronicle*, unpublished Ph.D. dissertation, University of California, 1955.)

[23] A well-known barrier near the capital.

Chapter 2

Rose and fell, like his unhappy star.
Across the tedious Seta Bridge the horses' hoofs beat loud;
Along the Ōmi road the goodfolk came and went;
At Une Moor a calling crane—
"Mourning perchance an absent child"—
How pitiful his thoughts!
Now on the trees of Forest Hill
The autumn rain beat hard,
That dripping soaked his tear-wet sleeves;
And from Bamboo Field of wind-swept dew,
He passed along the bamboo-cleaving path,
Yet knew not Mirror Mountain,
That was as cloud-enfolded from his tears.
Again in the grass of Oiso wood
While the horses stopped he turned his gaze
Backward, where clouds concealed his home.
Past Bamba, Samegai and Kashiwabara
To Fuwa barrier-hut,
That ruined lay, with autumn rain for guard.
Alas, that soon he must take leave of life!
Quickly then he bowed before
The sacred sword of Owari Atsuta,
And passed the beach of Narumi
Beneath a sinking moon, when the tide ran low.
Was there no end to this long road,
Followed day and night?
At Hamana Bridge in Tōtōmi,
A derelict boat on the evening tide
Drifted like his friendless self.
Was there none to call it pitiful?
When the sunset bell had tolled he came
To lodge the night at Ikeda,
Where stopped the Middle Marshal long ago
(Was it the first year of Genryaku?),
Shigehira, a captive of the eastern barbarians,
And the hostler's daughter wrote:
"In the squalor of this wretched hut
On the Eastern Road,
How sorely you must long for home!"
Weeping, he knew the sadness of the ancient tale.
Now when the hostel's lights grew dim
And cocks proclaimed the dawn,
The horses neighing in the wind
Crossed the River of the Celestial Dragon.

Again at dusk he trod the hills
Of Sayo no Nakayama;
While ashen clouds came burying
The path, where lost he bent his gaze
Back toward the skies of home,
And thought with envious heart how long ago
The holy Saigyō[24] crossed there twice,
Singing, "It was my fate."
But when the hours had sped,
Till on the meridian rode the sun,
There was a courtyard where his litter stopped,
That he might eat a travel meal.

Lord Toshimoto summoned the warriors of his guard, rapping on the shafts of the litter, and asked them, "What is the name of this station?" And they answered, "It is called Kikugawa," which is to say Chrysanthemum River.

At the time of the fighting of Shōkyū, a certain Lord Mitsuchika was called down to the Kantō, by reason that he had composed a proclamation issued by the former emperor, and at this relay station Mitsuchika was struck down. Likewise it was at this place that he wrote:

O ancient Chrysanthemum Stream
Of Nan-yang-hsien—
By drinking of your lower course
Once men prolonged their days.
But you, Chrysanthemum River
Of the Eastern Sea Road—
Lodging on your western bank
I bid farewell to life.

Then painfully Toshimoto felt
The sadness of the ancient tale
(For even so his fate must be);
And on the hostel pillar wrote:
"Shall I too sink beneath the stream
Of the Chrysanthemum River,
Where such things happened long ago?"
Now when he passed the Ōi River,[25]

---

[24] One of the most celebrated of Japanese poets, who lived in the twelfth century. The reference is to his verse, "Did I think, borne down with years, to cross another time? It was my fate . . . Sayo no Nakayama."

[25] On the border between the provinces of Tōtōmi and Suruga. There is a river of the same name near Kyoto.

Its name brought memories of home:
How the emperor went to Tortoise Mountain Hall
To gaze upon Storm Mountain's flowers in bloom;
And riding in the imperial boat,
With dragonhead or waterfowl prow,
He too attended at the banqueting,
At verse and song, at music of reeds and strings.
Even as a night's dream were those things now,
Not to be seen again.
Past Shimada and Fujieda, and beyond Okabe,
Where on the slopes the withered *kuzu* clung. . . .
And in the melancholy dusk
He crossed the Utsu hills,
Whose maple trees and ivy vines
Covered the road with abundant green.
"Was it not so when the Middle Marshal long ago
Went down to the east in search of a home,
Lord Narihira, who wrote a verse:
'I met no man, nor even in a dream
Beheld my beloved'?"
At Clearview Beach, where once a barrier stood,
Like barrier guards the noisy waves
Suffered no passage to his dreams
That sought to turn back to the capital,
And brought the bitter tears.
But now ahead the Cape of Miho lay;
And passing Okitsu and Kambara he saw
Mount Fuji's lofty peak, where high from the snow
The smoke rose heavenward,
Unrivaled as his own deep grief.
And as the melting morning mist
Revealed the spreading pines,
He traversed Floating Island Moor.
At low tide in Peasant Bay
A peasant toiled beside a boat,
Care-burdened in this transient world
As the one who sadly voyaged on
To Kurumagaeshi of turning carriage wheels.
Distressfully from Takenoshita he trod
A road beneath bamboo
To Ashigara's mountain pass, where gazing down
He saw the Greater Beach and Lesser;
And soon by chiding waves his sleeves were wet
On Koyurugi shore.

Not hastily did Toshimoto travel forward; yet day was joined to day, until on the twenty-sixth day of the seventh month he came to Kamakura in the twilight. Quickly on that day Nanjō Saemon Takanao received him, and delivered him over into the charge of Suwa Saemon, who put him into a tiny cell stoutly barred on every side. Surely it is thus with sinners in hell, who go pilloried and manacled to the Ten Monarchs[26] for judgment!

The Opinion of Nagasaki Shinsaemon-no-jō and the Matter of Master Kumawaka

When Go-Daigo Tennō's devisings were found out, the people of the Jimyōin rejoiced exceedingly—the intimate attendants, and even the youngest palace ladies, saying, "Assuredly His Highness of the Jimyōin will sit upon the throne very soon." But the military abode in silence after Toki's chastisement, nor yet after Toshimoto's arrest did they proclaim an order touching the throne.

In disappointment the courtiers of the Jimyōin fell to complaining; and it may be that some among them prevailed upon their lord with divers arguments. For it came about that a messenger was sent down secretly to the Kantō from this highness, saying:

"Most dangerous of late are the sovereign's rebellious plottings. Let the military make inquiry quickly, lest disorder afflict the realm."

Then in alarm the Sagami lay monk assembled together his important kinsmen and chief councilors, that each might offer up his opinion. At first all of these forbore to speak, whether from deference to others, or from heedfulness of their own well-being. But then Shinsaemon-no-jō Takasuke,[27] the son of the Nagasaki steward, came forward and spoke all that was in his heart fully, saying:

"When in a former year Toki Jūrō was chastised, then had it been fitting that this emperor should no longer sit upon the throne. Yet we wavered through fear of the court's power, and still the matter is not settled. It is the duty of men of war to put down disturbances, that the realm may be governed tranquilly. I do not

---

[26] The rulers of the ten Buddhist purgatories.
[27] Takasuke held the real power in Kamakura during most of Takatoki's tenure.

believe we can do other than remove the sovereign to a distant land, banish the Prince of the Great Pagoda to a place whence there can be no return, and strike down Toshimoto, Suketomo, and every other rebellious subject."

Then considering awhile, Nikaidō Dōun, the lay monk of Dewa, spoke a word, saying:

"These words are persuasive; yet how is it that for one hundred and sixty years the military have held the realm in their hand? How has their might extended over the four seas, and fortune smiled upon their successive generations? Is it not because they have revered the emperor with loyalty and selflessness, and have cherished the common folk with benevolent government? It must be called a grievous fault, that now they have laid hands upon two of the sovereign's trusted courtiers and banished three holy monks who were his religious guides. If, moreover, they remove the supreme highness to a remote place and send the Tendai abbot into distant banishment, then indeed will heaven abhor their arrogance, and the Mountain Gate unloose its wrath. When gods are angry and men rebel, how shall the military be delivered from their peril? 'Though the ruler be not a true ruler, let the subject be a true subject.'[28]

"Now as regards the revolt, there will be none to aid the sovereign, whatever he may devise, so mighty is the hand of the military. And if we bow respectfully before his commands, may not his august heart alter its design? Thus indeed will peace bless the land and fortune sustain the Hōjō family. What do you others think of this?"

Then, greatly angered, Nagasaki Shinsaemon-no-jō spoke again, not waiting for the opinions of others.

"The civil and the military follow both the same Way; yet according to the times is one used, and the other not so. When the world is at peace the civil governs; when disorder threatens, then quickly the military restores order. Just as the teachings of Confucius and Mencius were unable to prevail in the Era of Warring States, so weapons are not required in a tranquil world. Therefore, in this hour of danger the military must restore order.

[28] A quotation from Kung An-kuo's preface to the *Classic of Filial Piety*.

"In another country, the subjects Wen Wang and Wu Wang chastised a ruler lacking in virtue, while in our country Yoshitoki and Yasutoki banished unrighteous sovereigns; and the world saw that it was good.[29] So the classic says, 'When the ruler looks upon his subjects as dirt and weeds, the subjects look upon the ruler as a highwayman and an enemy.' [30] If, while we hesitate, the emperor issues a command for our chastisement, then it will be too late to feel regret. We cannot do other than remove the sovereign to a distant land at once, banish the Prince of the Great Pagoda to Iō-gajima, and strike down the plotting and rebellious subjects Suketomo and Toshimoto; for only thus can our peace endure for a myriad generations. Such indeed is my belief."

So he spoke, drawing up his shoulders wrathfully, and all the chief councilors that were gathered together supported him, whether from obsequiousness to one in power or from agreement with his foolish devisings. But Dōun departed troubled, not repeating his loyal words.

Thereupon the men of Kamakura decided firmly:

"Those who encouraged the sovereign's conspiracy were the Minamoto Middle Counselor Tomoyuki, the Lesser Controller of the Right Toshimoto, and the Hino Middle Counselor Suketomo. They shall all die."

They sent an order to the lay monk Homma of Yamashiro, the protector of the land of Sado, saying, "Let Lord Suketomo be struck down, he who has dwelt in the land of Sado since his exile in a previous year."

Now soon it was noised abroad in the capital that Suketomo would die. And tidings thereof came to the ears of Suketomo's son, the Middle Counselor Kunimitsu, abiding in stealth hard by the Ninnaji Temple, because of the arrest of the lord his father. In those days Kunimitsu was called Master Kumawaka, being but in his thirteenth year.

---

[29] It was actually Wen Wang's son, Wu Wang, who overthrew the last Shang (Yin) ruler in China and established the Chou dynasty (ca. 1027 B.C.–256 B.C.). Hōjō Yoshitoki and Hōjō Yasutoki banished the emperors Go-Toba, Juntoku, and Tsuchimikado after the Disturbance of Shōkyū.

[30] From *Mencius*.

Chapter 2

Hearing that his father would be killed, Kumawaka went to take leave of his mother, saying:

"Why should I prize life? Let me perish together with my father, that I may share his journey to the nether regions and see him as he appears at the end."

His mother admonished him sternly, saying:

"Indeed I have heard that Sado is a dreadful island, unfrequented by human beings. How do you propose to go there, since the road is one which consumes many days? If I am parted from you, too, I do not feel that I can live for an instant."

So she detained him, weeping and lamenting. But Kumawaka spoke to her again, saying, "Well, then, if there is none to accompany me, I shall fling my body into a river to drown!"

By these words the heart of the mother was stricken with fear, lest through zealously detaining him she might suffer a bitter parting, wherefore she sent him away toward the far-off land of Sado with the single manservant who had ministered to her wants.

Brushing aside the dew, Master Kumawaka made his way into the northern land, with unaccustomed straw sandals on his feet and a tilted sedge hat on his head. (There was no horse that he might ride, although the road was exceedingly long. How pitiful it was!) When he had gone more than ten days' journey from the capital, he came to the harbor of Tsuruga in Echizen, took passage aboard a merchant boat, quickly reached the land of Sado, and went to Homma's dwelling place himself, since there was no other to speak for him.

As Master Kumawaka stood in front of Homma's middle gate, a monk came forth from within.

"Do you have business within, that you stand here?" he asked. "What is your business?"

Weeping bitterly, Master Kumawaka answered him:

"I am the son of the Hino Middle Counselor, come from the distant capital to be with my father at the last. It is said that he will be struck down very soon."

Without hesitating, the kindly monk bore these tidings to Homma. Perhaps Homma's heart was moved within him, since he was not made of stone or wood; for at once he caused the monk to fetch Master Kumawaka in to the Personal Buddha Hall,[31] and to draw off his footgear and leggings and bathe his feet, and he treated him with great consideration.

Master Kumawaka rejoiced thereat, and begged to see the lord his father. But Homma would not suffer parent and child to meet.

"Rather would death be harder to bear, were I to show the boy to this man who will be struck down today or tomorrow," he said. "And how would it be, were tidings thereof to reach the Kantō?"

Since they two were lodged but five or six hundred yards apart, the noble father learned of Master Kumawaka's coming. His affliction increased, and was greater than before, when in his heart he had thought, "How is the boy getting on, there in the capital which these eyes will not behold again?"

And looking out toward his father, Master Kumawaka could not dry his sleeves, but thought, "How inconsequential were my tears when I but pictured the wild dwelling place far away across the waves!"

Master Kumawaka knew that the Middle Counselor was imprisoned in a place overgrown with a bamboo thicket, encompassed about by a moat and wall, where few men came and went. How cold was Homma's heart! Since the father was a prisoner and the son but a child, why was it dangerous to place them together? Even as though born in separate lives while yet dwelling in the same world, so were these two that were not suffered to meet. "Only when we lie dead under the moss may we gaze upon one another," they thought, "save in the dreams that follow sad thoughts." Pitiful indeed was the sorrowing love of father and son!

On the evening of the twenty-ninth day of the fifth month, men came to fetch Lord Suketomo from his prison, saying:

"You have not had a bath for a long time. Please cleanse yourself."

It came to Suketomo that soon he would be struck down. Yet he said merely, "Alas, how hard it is to die without a glimpse of my child, who has come seeking afar to look upon me at the end!" Thenceforth he spoke no word, but thought only of attaining enlightenment, as though removed utterly from worldly things, al-

[31] A hall enshrining the buddha regarded by a man as his special protector.

though until that morning he had forever been wiping away tears of dejection.

At nightfall men came bearing a litter for Suketomo, took him away to a river beach a thousand yards distant, and set him down. Yet in no wise was Suketomo's countenance affrighted. Seated upright on an animal skin,[32] he wrote a farewell poem in praise of the Buddhist Law.

> The five skandhas have formed this transient shape
> Whose four elements return now to true being;
> I hold my neck against the naked blade—
> The cutting is like a gust of wind.

When he had written the date, with his name below, and had laid aside the brush, the executioner came around behind him. And Suketomo's noble head fell onto the animal skin while yet his body sat up straight.

Then there came forward a monk, Suketomo's teacher in religious matters, who cremated the body according to form, and picked up the lifeless bones to take to Kumawaka. When Kumawaka beheld them, his welcoming hands grew limp, and he fell prostrate. It was indeed natural that he mourned tearfully:

"Unable in the end to meet him in this life, I behold him now, changed into charred bones."

Although Kumawaka was young, his spirit was that of a man. He entrusted his father's remains to his single manservant, whom he sent back toward the capital, saying, "Go before me to Mount Kōya, and inter them in the Inner Cloister or a like place." But he himself abode in Homma's dwelling place, feigning to be stricken of a disease. For it was in his mind to requite Homma's heartlessness, that had not suffered him to meet with his father in this world.

For four or five days Kumawaka lay in bed, as one afflicted in all his members. Yet secretly at night he stole forth to learn the place where Homma slept, thinking, "If there is a chance, I will stab Homma or his son and rip open my belly."

There came a night of violent rain and wind, when all the re-

---

[32] Used by the military on campaigns, during archery practice, and, as here, for decapitations. Usually a deerskin.

tainers on duty slept inside the guard quarters beyond the courtyard. And on that night Kumawaka took his way in stealth to Homma's sleeping apartment, thinking, "This assuredly is the good fortune I have awaited!"

Was not Homma's luck strong? He was gone away from his accustomed sleeping place; nor in any wise might Kumawaka find him out. Kumawaka beheld a lamp burning in a small room, and stole inside, thinking, "If the lay monk's son is within, I shall take my vengeance by striking him down." Yet after all it was not the son, but the person called Homma Saburō, sleeping alone, even he who had struck off the head of His Lordship the Middle Counselor.

"Very well!" thought Kumawaka. "He too may be called my father's enemy, equally with the lay monk of Yamashiro."

He made ready to rush upon Homma Saburō. Yet again he hesitated, thinking disquieted:

"Having no sword or dagger of my own, I must take possession of his. The light is exceedingly bright. Will he not awaken when I draw near?"

So he thought, and stood perplexed, when gazing toward the lamp he beheld a multitude of moths clinging to the clear sliding doors (the season being summer). Thereupon he set a door ajar, so that the insects entered in swarms, quickly putting out the light.

"Now I shall succeed!" he rejoiced.

Going up to Homma Saburō, where he slept deeply, Kumawaka beheld a sword and dagger beside the pillow. He put the dagger into his belt, drew forth the sword from its sheath, touched it to Homma's breast, and kicked the pillow, thinking, "To kill a sleeping man is no different from stabbing a corpse." And when Homma awoke, steadily Kumawaka drove in the sword above his navel, all the way to the floor mat, and thrust it again into his glottis. Then, in no wise affrighted, he hid himself in a bamboo thicket to the rear.

Having heard Homma Saburō cry out when the sword drove into his breast, the guards fell to rushing about clamorously. And when they had made a light, they beheld small bloody footprints.

"Master Kumawaka has done it!" they said. "By no means has

Chapter 2

he passed outside the gate, for the waters of the moat are exceedingly deep. Let us seek him out and kill him!"

Kindling pine torches to carry, they searched everywhere, even under trees and in the shadows of plants.

In the bamboo thicket, Kumawaka thought:

"Where shall I flee now? It will be better to destroy myself than to fall into the hands of others."

But again he considered, thinking:

"I have killed the detested enemy of my father. If now I can preserve my life in some way, may I not assist the emperor as well, and accomplish my father's desire of many years? Then indeed shall I be a loyal subject and filial son! If it is possible, why should I not seek to flee secretly?"

He thought to jump across the moat; yet in no wise might he do it, for it was six yards wide and more than ten feet deep. But then he climbed nimbly to the top of a black bamboo growing above the water, saying, "I will cross by making a bridge of this." And the tip thereof bent down to the other side, so that he crossed over easily.

With faltering feet Kumawaka took his way toward the harbor, thinking, "Since it is yet dark I will go toward the harbor, that I may seek passage on a boat to the mainland." But when the night lightened, he hid his body; and all through the day he hid; for there was no way whereby he might travel unobserved.

While he lay in a growth of hemp and mugwort, a hundred and forty or fifty horsemen bearing the guise of pursuers galloped around on all sides, and as they departed he heard them calling out to every passer-by, saying, "Has a child of eleven or twelve years come this way?"

So Kumawaka passed that day in the hemp, and with the falling of darkness set forth aimlessly to search for the harbor. May it not be that the buddhas and gods cast protective eyes upon him, moved by his filial resolution? For he came upon an aged wandering monk, who looked at this child with compassion, asking him, "Whence are you come, and whither would you go?" And Kumawaka told him everything truthfully.

When the monk had heard Kumawaka's story, he thought, "If I do not help this person, very soon he will meet a pitiful fate." He spoke to him, saying:

"Be of good cheer! There will be many merchant boats in the harbor. I will put you on one of them and go with you to Echigo or Etchū."

Then, because Kumawaka's feet were tired, the monk carried him on his back, and quickly brought him to the harbor.

When the night lightened, the monk sought a vessel, yet just at that time there was no boat inside the harbor. But while he stood perplexed, a large boat riding in the offing put up its mast and rolled up its rush matting,[33] rejoicing in the fair wind.

The monk raised his arms, shouting:

"Over here, boat! We are seeking passage!"

Yet the boatmen would not listen, but rowed away from the harbor, raising their voices aloud.

Greatly enraged, the monk tied back the sleeves of his persimmon-colored robe, faced the boat heading out toward the sea, clicked his angular prayer-beads, and intoned the words of a chant.

> Through life on life Fudō protects
> Who speaks but once his secret charm;
> And as a buddha's is the power
> He gives his holy ministrants.

How might the many years of this monk's devout works be of no avail?

Again he prayed mightily, and leapt up and down, saying, "If there be no error in the Original Vow of the Bright Monarch Fudō, then hearken, divine Kongō Dōji, and ye heavenly monarchs and nagas and yakshas, and ye eight naga monarchs, that ye may cause the vessel to row back toward this place!"

Perhaps this prayer fell upon the divine ear of the Bright Monarch, who was graciously pleased to grant his protection. For suddenly the boat made as if to overturn, by reason of an ill wind blowing in from the sea. The frightened boatmen knelt with folded hands, crying, "Save us, good monk!" and rowed the boat back with

---

[33] Used as a temporary roof at night; also employed for protection against the elements.

all their might. When they drew near to the beach, the head boatman jumped down, took the child onto his shoulder, and drew the monk by the hand into the cabin. And thereupon the wind changed and became as before, so that the boat went forth from the harbor.

Thereafter a hundred and forty or fifty pursuers came galloping into the shallow water, whence they signed to the boat to stop. But the boatmen then hoisted their sail in the fair wind, feigning not to see them, and brought their craft to the government seat of Echigo at the end of the day.

Most assuredly was it through the Bright Monarch's divine protection that Kumawaka, aided by the wandering monk, came forth alive from the crocodile's mouth!

The Execution of Toshimoto and the Matter of Sukemitsu

Of Toshimoto no Ason it was decided, "Since he was the leader of the plot, he may not be sent away to a distant land, but must be struck down quickly in Kamakura." Now Toshimoto had made a vow many years before, vowing to read aloud the *Lotus Sutra* six hundred times, and of the six hundred readings, two hundred were not yet accomplished. Wherefore earnestly he entreated the men of Kamakura, saying, "Please spare my life until the six hundred readings are done, and then do what you will." And they granted it him, and waited the few days until the two hundred were finished, thinking, "Truly it would be a sin to prevent the accomplishment of so great a vow." How pitiful was the extent of his life!

There was a person called Gotō Saemon-no-jō Sukemitsu, a young attendant who had ministered to Toshimoto since times gone by. When his master was taken away, Sukemitsu went with Toshimoto's wife to hide in Saga. The lady lamented and mourned bitterly because Toshimoto was summoned to the Kantō, and Sukemitsu likewise sorrowed grievously to behold her. And it came to pass in a little while that Sukemitsu went forth in stealth toward Kamakura, bearing a letter from the lady.

Rapidly Sukemitsu took his way to Kamakura, asking tidings of wayfarers, lest already his master be struck down (since the day of

Toshimoto's death was close at hand). And arriving in the east he lodged hard upon the prison of the Lesser Controller of the Right Toshimoto, and sought earnestly to tell him of the lady his wife, yet in no wise might he find the means thereof.

When some days had passed, Sukemitsu heard men saying:
"The prisoner from the capital will die today. How pitiful it is!"

Sore perplexed, Sukemitsu stood here and there to look and listen. He saw that Toshimoto rode toward the Kewaizaka hills in a covered litter, and that Kudō Saemon-no-jō Jirō met Toshimoto, and that Toshimoto sat on an animal skin where a great curtain was put up, even at the base of the high land called Kuzuhara-ga-oka. Who can speak of the feelings in Sukemitsu's breast! His eyes darkened, his legs failed, and his spirit fainted within him. Weeping, he advanced into Kudō's presence, saying:

"I am a person in the service of His Lordship the Lesser Controller of the Right, come from afar to behold his final moments. If it be fitting, grant that I may go in to him with this letter from the lady his wife."

Nor might Kudō hold back his quick tears of sympathy, but consented, saying:
"There will be no difficulty. Go inside the curtain at once."

Sukemitsu went inside the curtain and fell down on his knees in front of his master. But Toshimoto said merely, "How now!" by reason of the tears that filled his throat.

"I have come bearing a letter from her ladyship."

Sukemitsu placed it in front of him, and wept with bowed head, unable to see by reason of his tears.

When for awhile they had remained thus, Toshimoto wiped away his tears to look upon the letter. With love too deep to express in words, the lady had written in excessively black ink:

"I know that there is no hope for the transient existence about to be extinguished; yet only imperfectly can you surmise my despairing grief, as I wonder on what evening I shall learn that we are not to meet again in this life."

Toshimoto read no more, for tears darkened his eyes. Nor did any of those who watched fail to moisten his sleeve.

Now Toshimoto called for an ink stone; and when they placed

Chapter 2

it before him, he cut off a lock of his side hair with a penknife, rolled it up in the letter from his wife, and wrote a message on the back of the paper, that he put into Sukemitsu's hand. And weeping grievously, Sukemitsu placed it in his bosom.

Then Kudō Saemon-no-jō came inside the curtain, saying, "Too much time is passing."

Toshimoto drew out a paper handkerchief to wipe his neck, opened it, and wrote a farewell poem in praise of the Buddhist Law.

> Since ancient times has it been said,
> "There is no death; there is no life."
> Yet as a cloudless sky is welcome death,
> As a mighty river, flowing clear.

When he had laid aside the brush and was smoothing his side hair, then indeed the sword flashed behind him, his head dropped forward, and his body fell prostrate thereon. How is one to speak of Sukemitsu's feelings!

Tearfully Sukemitsu cremated the corpse, and tearfully he went up to the capital with the lifeless ashes hung around his neck. The lady came out from behind her screens to meet him, not heedful of the eyes of others, but rejoicing to have tidings of her lord.

"How is it?" she said. "When does His Lordship the Controller reply that he will come up to the capital?"

As falling rain were the tears that Sukemitsu wept, when he answered her, saying:

"Already they have struck him down. Here indeed is the reply of his last hour."

Weeping aloud, he gave her the lock of hair and the message. And when the lady beheld the keepsake and ashes, she did not go within, but fell prostrate on the veranda as though dead.

There is sadness even in the parting of two strangers who but shelter beneath the same tree or drink of a single stream. How then must be the leave-taking of those bound for more than ten years by sacred conjugal vows! It was entirely natural that the lady should faint with grief when she heard that they two must part forever in this world, never to meet again save in dreams.

After Buddhist services were held according to form on the forty-ninth day,³⁴ the lady put on the deep black robes of a nun, that early and late behind the brushwood door of a rustic retreat she might pray for the enlightenment of her dead husband. Likewise Sukemitsu shaved his head and shut himself up on Mount Kōya to pray for his master's enlightenment in a later life. Not even death could break the vow between husband and wife, or sever the bond between master and servant. How touching it was!

Marvelous Things in the Realm

Around the spring of the second year of Karyaku in the southern capital, the meditation teachers of the Daijōin Cloister disputed with the monks of the monasteries tributary to the Kōfukuji Temple, and strove against them in battle. And the fires of war spread, so that instantly the Golden Hall and Lecture Hall became ashes, and likewise the South Perfection Hall and West Golden Hall, all great buildings of the Kōfukuji.

Again, in the first year of Genkō, a fire came forth from the Northern Valley of the East Pagoda of the Mountain Gate, instantly destroying the Cloister of the Four Kings, the Longevity Cloister, the Great Lecture Hall, the Lotus Hall, and the Amida Hall. Wherefore the spirits of men were chilled within them, and they thought, "Surely these are omens of disaster in the realm."

Moreover, on the third day of the seventh month of the same year of Genkō, a great earthquake suddenly dried up the tidal beach at Senri-ga-hama in Kii for more than two thousand yards. And at the hour of the cock on the seventh day of that month, an earthquake crumbled the summit of Mount Fuji for five thousand feet.

Then did Urabe no Sukune divine by roasting a large tortoise shell, and the yin-yang doctors elucidated the divination texts. The omens said, "The sovereign's estate will change; the great ministers will encounter calamity." Wherefore secretly the diviners offered up an unquiet opinion to the throne, saying, "In all things let the emperor be prudent." And with anxious hearts men thought, "These

---

³⁴ According to Buddhist doctrine, on the forty-ninth day after an individual's death his future lot is determined, and he leaves the "intermediate shade" in which he has been dwelling. The purpose of the forty-ninth day ceremonies is to make his new life auspicious.

fires at temples are not commonplace occurrences, nor the earthquakes in divers places. Untoward happenings are close at hand."

Without fail, two eastern messengers came up to the capital with three thousand horsemen, on the twenty-second day of the eighth month. The warriors of nearby provinces came galloping to assemble there, saying, "What is it? What can be happening in the capital?" And a great clamor arose within the city.

The two messengers having reached the capital, in some manner tidings were borne abroad while yet their dispatch box remained unopened, so that at the Mountain Gate men said, "These eastern messengers are come to remove the supreme highness to a distant province and kill the Prince of the Great Pagoda."

In stealth the Prince of the Great Pagoda sent a messenger to the supreme highness on the night of the twenty-fourth day, saying:

"From words spoken secretly have I learned a thing concerning the coming of the eastern messengers to the capital: that they will send away His Majesty to a distant province and strike me down. His Majesty must make speed tonight toward the southern capital to hide. If men of evil heart approach him while our castles remain unbuilt and our hosts unassembled, how shall we prevail against them?

"Now to cut off the enemy in the capital, and likewise to search the hearts of the monks, let one of His Majesty's trusted ministers be called the Son of Heaven. Let him be sent to the Mountain Gate, and let the tidings of his journey be proclaimed abroad. Assuredly the enemy warriors will go forth toward Mount Hiei to give battle, whereupon, jealous of their mountain, the monks will stand against them, heedless of life and limb. When those evil men are tired by five or six days of fighting, we shall attack the capital with loyal warriors of Iga, Ise, Yamato, and Kawachi, that quickly they may be destroyed. In these hours the nation's future will be decided."

Greatly astonished, the supreme highness summoned those who were serving at night in the palace: the Great Counselor Morokata, the Madenokōji Middle Counselor Fujifusa, and Suefusa, the younger brother of Fujifusa, to question them concerning these things. And coming forward, Lord Fujifusa spoke a word, saying:

"When traitors threaten the sovereign, there are auspicious precedents for avoiding calamity awhile, that the state may be preserved. Chung-erh fled to the Ti and Ta Wang went away from Pin,[35] wherefore both performed the functions of monarchs, bringing glory to their posterity. Surely it has grown very late. His Majesty must flee quickly."

Then they drew forward a carriage, set the imperial regalia inside, and trailed silken garments from beneath the inner curtain as though a court lady sat within. And helping the supreme highness to enter it, they went forth to the Yōmeimon Gate.

The warriors guarding the gate stopped the carriage, saying, "Who passes there?"

Fujifusa and Suefusa, who accompanied the carriage, answered them, "It is the Inner Princess, going to the Mansion of the Northern Hills[36] under cover of darkness."

And those warriors suffered the carriage to pass through, saying, "Why should it not be so?"

Perhaps because they had busied themselves with preparations, the Gen Middle Counselor Tomoyuki, the Great Counselor Kintoshi, and the Rokujō Lesser Marshal Tadaaki came behind the emperor, overtaking him at the Third Ward river bed. They left the carriage in that place, and the emperor sat down in a shabby covered litter.

There were no litter bearers (for it was a most sudden affair), but the litter was borne on the shoulders of Shigeyasu the Master of the Palace Table, Toyohara Kaneaki the Court Musician, and Hata no Hisatake the Escort. The nobles serving before and behind put off their high-crowned headgear and robes for folded caps and plain shirts and trousers, that they might appear to be menservants of a highborn lady going on a pilgrimage to the seven great monasteries of Nara.

As they passed the stone Jizō of Kozu, already the night lightened

---

[35] Chung-erh (697 B.C.–628 B.C.), a son of the Duke of Chin, fled to his mother's people, the Ti (a non-Chinese tribe in north China), to escape the enmity of his father's concubine. He later was able to return and make himself the ruler of the state. When barbarians attacked the principality of Pin, Ta Wang (traditional death date 1231 B.C.), the virtuous ancestor of the Chou rulers, moved to another place rather than subject his people to the hardships of war.

[36] A residence of her family, the Saionji.

Chapter 2

and the morning meal was brought forward. The emperor went in to the Southeast Cloister in the southern capital, a place where the monk reformer was not of two hearts, nor had any disloyalty in him; and that monk reformer sounded the hearts of his soldier-monks, speaking no word of the emperor's coming. Yet from fear of the monk reformer Genjitsu of Nishimuro there was none that would join himself to the imperial side; for Genjitsu was a most powerful abbot, a man bound to the Kantō by ties of blood.

So the emperor could not tarry in the southern capital, but on the morrow went forth to Mount Jubu at Watsuka (it being the twenty-sixth day). But because Mount Jubu was a place deep in the mountains and remote from settlements, ill-fitted for devising plans, the supreme highness resolved, "We shall go to a place that will be a strong fortress." And on the twenty-seventh day he went forth secretly to the rocky heights of Mount Kasagi, with a small number of soldier-monks from the southern capital.

Morokata Climbs the Mountain; the Battle of Karasaki Beach

On the night when the supreme highness went forth from the palace, Lord Morokata the Great Counselor attended upon him as far as the Third Ward river bed. There the emperor spoke a word to Morokata, saying:

"Do you ascend to the Mountain Gate in Our guise, that you may search the hearts of the monks and bring together warriors for a battle. Even such is the counsel of the Prince of the Great Pagoda."

Therefore Morokata put on the imperial dragon robes in front of the Hosshōji Temple and rode in the sovereign's litter to the West Pagoda Cloister of the Mountain Gate. With him were the Shijō Middle Counselor Takasuke, the Nijō Middle Marshal Tameakira, and Sadahira the Middle Marshal of the Left, all correct in high-crowned caps and robes[37] as though attending upon him, for the ceremony of the affair was most real.

---

[37] *Ikan*, a semi-ceremonial costume worn for visits to shrines and temples, weddings, and the like. It was less formal than full court dress (*sokutai*).

Taking the Sākyamuni Hall of the West Pagoda to be the imperial abiding place, they spread abroad the tidings of Morokata's coming, saying, "The supreme highness is come to entrust himself to the Mountain Gate." And thereupon all the warriors strove to be the first to hasten there: the men of Ōtsu, Matsumoto, Tozu, Hieitsuji, Ōgi, Kinugawa, and Wani, and likewise of Katata (we do not speak of Mount Hiei and Sakamoto), until their hosts enveloped the East and West Pagodas like clouds or mist.

At Rokuhara they knew nothing at all of these things. At daybreak the two eastern messengers went forth toward the palace, thinking to fetch the supreme highness to Rukuhara. But just at that time there came a messenger to Rokuhara from the Deacon Gōyo, called Jōrimbō, saying:

"During the hour of the tiger tonight, the supreme highness came here, placing his trust in the Mountain Gate, and the three thousand monks hastened to his side. They are resolved to attack Rokuhara tomorrow with men of war from Ōmi and Echizen. You must send a force quickly to the eastern base of Mount Hiei while this thing is of no great import. I will fall upon them from behind, so that the supreme highness will surely be captured."

Seized with amazement, the men of Rokuhara went to the palace to look. But they beheld only court ladies, gathered together in divers places weeping aloud, for the supreme highness was gone.

"Most assuredly has he fled to the Mountain Gate!" they said. "Let us attack the mountain before he is joined by men of war."

Thereupon five thousand riders went forth toward the base of Mount Seki and Sagarimatsu to strike from the front: the watchmen of the forty-eight places and the warriors of the five home provinces. And seven thousand riders went forth toward the Karasaki pine tree by way of Ōtsu and Matsumoto, to strike from the rear: the men of Sasaki Saburō Hōgan Tokinobu, Kaitō Sakon Shōgen, Nagai Munehira the governor of Tango, Chikugo-no-zenji Sadatomo, Hatano Kōzuke-no-zenji Nobumichi, and Hitachi-no-zenji Tokitomo, with men of Mino, Owari, Tamba and Tajima.

The two abbots, the Prince of the Great Pagoda and the Prince of the Myōhōin Cloister, had been awaiting a signal at Sakamoto. During the night, these brothers went up to the hill of the Eight

Regal Scions,[38] where they raised the imperial standard. And in answer to the call there came two disciples, the monk governor Yūzen of the Goshōin Cloister and the deacon Genson, called Myōkōbō. Moreover, by three hundreds and five hundreds riders galloped together from many places, so that in one night their strength became six thousand horsemen. Putting off his holy robes, the abbot of the Tendai faith took up strong mail and sharp weapons; and likewise the monks did the same. Strange indeed would it appear to the gods and buddhas, that this sacred ground was suddenly become a defending-place for men of war!

Now at Sakamoto a mighty clamor arose, of men saying, "Already the warriors of Rokuhara are beside the Tozu post station!" Impetuous monks hastened forth from the Enshūin Cloister on the south shore, and from the Shōgyōbō House of the central compound, bound for Karasaki beach to confront the enemy. But all went by foot; nor did their numbers exceed three hundred men.

When Kaitō beheld them, he said:

"The enemy are few indeed! We must chase them away before others come from behind. Follow me!"

He drew his three-foot sword, held his left arm above his head, galloped into the middle of the milling enemy, struck down three men, and stopped his horse at the water's edge to await the coming of other warriors.

Thereupon a monk kicked over the shield in front of him and sprang forward, whirling his short halberd like a water wheel; Kaijitsu of Harima. Kaitō received him with his left arm and struck at him with his right arm, thinking to cleave his helmet-bowl; but the glancing sword struck down lightly from Kaijitsu's shoulder-plate to the cross-stitching at the bottom of his armor. Again Kaitō struck mightily, yet his left foot broke through its stirrup, so that he was like to fall down from his horse. As he straightened his body, Kaijitsu thrust up his halberd, and twice and thrice drove its tip rapidly into his helmet. And Kaitō fell from off his horse headfirst, pierced cleanly through the glottis.

Swiftly Kaijitsu put down his foot on Kaitō's armor-braid, seized

---

[38] Adjacent to Mount Hiei on the north. The eight offspring of the Sun Goddess Amaterasu were said to have descended from heaven to its summit.

his side hair, and cut off his head, that he might fix it to his halberd. Rejoicing, he mocked at the enemy.

"We have slain a grand marshal of the military. An excellent beginning!"

Thereupon from among those that looked on, there came forth a boy of fourteen or fifteen years, clad in armor of pale green and widemouthed trousers pulled high at the side, with his hair rolled up after the manner of children. This boy pulled out a short gold-mounted sword and rushed against Kaijitsu, striking his helmet-bowl fiercely three or four times. Swiftly Kaijitsu turned to behold him, but when he saw the painted eyebrows and blackened teeth of a boy of fifteen years he resolved not to strike, since it would have been shameful for a monk to kill such a child. He danced around the boy harmlessly, striking at the air again and again, until it came to his mind to beat down the sword with his halberd and seize him in his arms. But just then men of Hiei-tsuji came over a path between the rice fields, and suddenly one among them shot an arrow through the child's breastplate from the side, so that he fell down dead.

Later men knew that the boy was Kaitō's eldest son, a child called Kōwakamaru, who had followed behind anxiously in the crowd of onlookers, not suffered by his father to go with him into battle. Seeing his father killed, he died on the same battlefield to leave a name behind him. Although Kōwaka was young, he sprang from a warrior house. How sad it was!

When Kaitō's retainers beheld these things they said:

"Shall any man of us return alive? We have suffered our two lords to perish before our eyes, and have allowed a head to be taken by the enemy."

Bridle to bridle, the thirty-six riders swept forward to give battle, each furious to die on his lord's body.

Kaijitsu laughed loudly, saying:

"You are odd fellows! Although you ought to be trying to take enemy heads, you seek to lay hands upon the heads of your own men. This is an auspicious sign, foretelling the self-destruction of the military! If you want it, here it is!"

And he threw Kaitō's head into the middle of the enemy.

Then Kaijitsu struck downward with his halberd grasped in both hands, sweeping away enemies in every direction until the sparks flew. The thirty-six horsemen, put to flight by him alone, were powerless to stay their horses' feet.

Standing in the rear, Sasaki Saburō Hōgan Tokinobu spoke an order, saying, "Do not allow our friends to be killed! Follow!" And clamorously three hundred riders galloped foward: men of Iba, Megata, Kimura, and Mabuchi. Kaijitsu was most like to be killed, had not four monks come from the left and right to give battle, who smote the enemy side by side: Keirimbō Akasanuki, Nakanobō Kosagami, Shōgyōbō Jōkai, and Konrembō Jikigen. And when Sanuki and Jikigen were struck down in the same place, fifty monks in the rear followed them into the fighting.

Now on the east at Karasaki lay the lake,[39] where broken and craggy ground extended to the water's edge; and on the west there were muddy rice fields, such as would not support a horse's feet; likewise sand flats stretched out widely around the narrow road. Men of war could not go around to an enemy's rear, nor might they encompass an enemy about. None might fight save those that were in the front line of battle, both the monks and the attackers; and the armies behind them were but spectators.

When it became known that a battle was set in array at Karasaki, three thousand disciples of the prince went forth toward Imamichi, passing by way of Shiroi; and seven thousand monks from the Main Cloister came down through Sannomiya Woods. Likewise men of Wani and Katata embarked in three hundred small boats to row toward Ōtsu, that they might cut off the enemy's rear. And then perhaps the warriors of Rokuhara thought in their hearts that they could not prevail; for they crossed in front of the Shiga Emma Hall and fell back to Imamichi.

Being well acquainted with the land, the monks gathered together in fitting places, wherefrom to let fly arrows in very great numbers. Nor might the warriors retreat easily, but being strangers to the land they galloped into ditches and over cliffs, and fell down

[39] Lake Biwa.

together with their horses. Eight of Kaitō's retainers, men who had drawn back to the rear ranks, perished at the bottoms of ravines. Thirteen of Hatano's retainers did the same, and the Mano lay monk and his son, and Hirai Kurō and one retainer. Also Sasaki Hōgan was surrounded by enemy hosts on the left and right, where he waited for another mount after losing his horse from an arrow, and the monks would have killed him, had not his retainers turned back to give battle, hungry for fame and careless of life. While these died in many places, their lord, escaping alive from a myriad deaths, retreated to the capital in full daylight.

Heretofore the realm had been at peace, with no talk of such a thing as war. But because of these marvelous happenings the spirits of men were alarmed and agitated, and everywhere it was spread abroad that soon heaven and earth would be overturned.

The Highnesses of the Jimyōin Go to Rokuhara

At the hour of the snake on the twenty-seventh day, the senior retired emperor[40] of the Jimyōin went forth from the Sixth Ward Mansion to the north compound of Rokuhara, and with him the heir apparent, fearing lest evil-hearted men lay hands upon them because of the troubled times. Courtiers clad in high-crowned caps and robes served before and behind their carriage: Lord Kanesue, the Imadegawa Former Great Subject of the Right; the Sanjō Great Counselor Michiaki; the Saionji Great Counselor Kimmune; the Hino Former Middle Counselor Sukena; the Bōjō Consultant Tsuneaki; and the Hino Consultant Sukeakira. But for the rest, the men of the escort wore ordinary tunics[41] with corselets underneath: the former emperor's military guards, the officials, and the lesser guards. How shocking it was, that within the capital all things were changed in an instant, and armies guarded the kingfisher flowers of the sovereign's banner!

---

[40] Go-Fushimi. The other retired emperor of the Jimyōin line was Hanazono.
[41] *Kariginu,* the everyday attire of the lesser nobility.

Medieval Japanese House

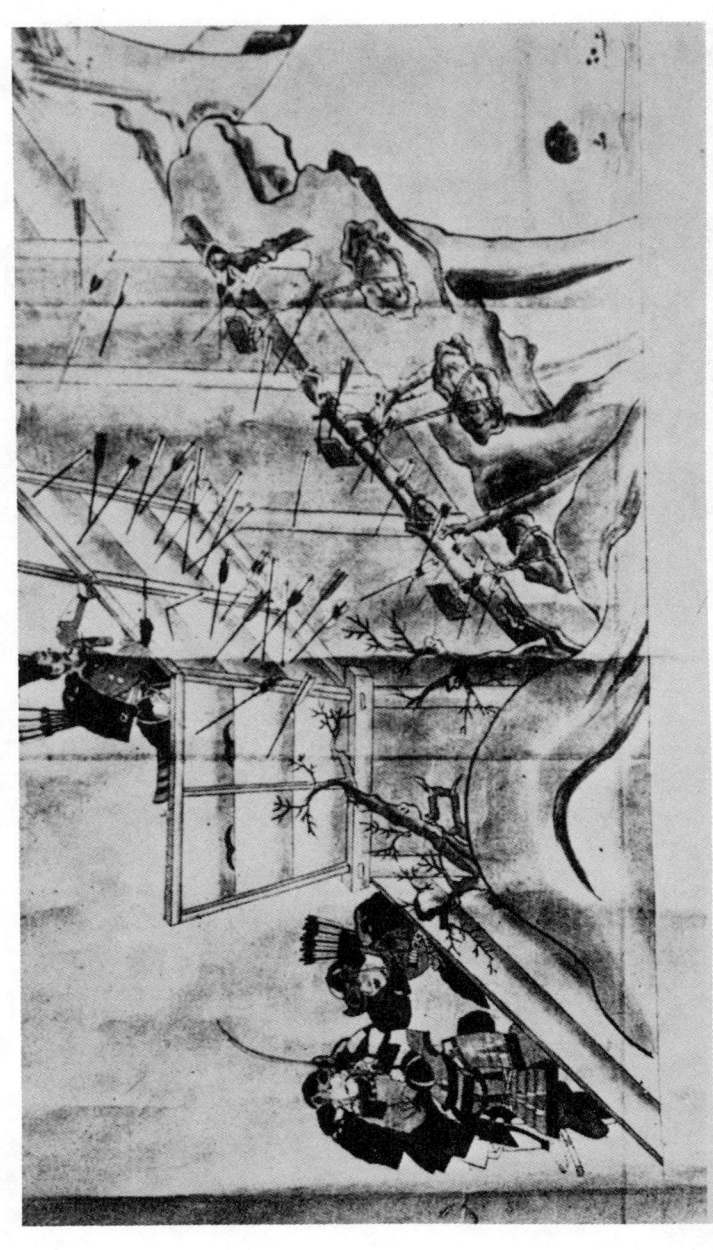

Medieval Uyesugi Castle Showing Tower

Chapter 2

The Coming of the Supreme Highness Is Found to Be a Deceit, Wherefore the Heart of the Mountain Gate Changes; Also, the Matter of Chi Hsin

After winning the battle of Karasaki, the monks of the Mountain Gate rejoiced greatly, saying, "An auspicious beginning!" They sent a message to the West Pagoda Cloister, saying:

"The designation of the West Pagoda as the imperial residence is a dishonor to the Main Cloister. When Go-Shirakawa-in relied upon the Mountain Gate long ago in Juei, he ascended to Yokawa first, but then quickly he removed to the Enyūbō in the South Valley of the East Pagoda. This is a previous example; this is an auspicious precedent. Let His Majesty be brought to the Main Cloister at once."

So they spoke, and bowing to reason the monks of the West Pagoda went to the emperor's abiding place to escort him to the Main Cloister. Yet just at that time a violent wind from off the mountain blew up the blinds, and they saw that it was not the supreme highness inside, but the Great Counselor Morokata, dressed in the imperial robes of the Son of Heaven.

"What goblins' work is this?" said the monks, and turned away; neither did any among them come again.

When the night was half spent, in secret the Great Counselor Morokata, the Shijō Middle Counselor Takasuke, and the Nijō Middle Marshal Tameakira fled toward Mount Kasagi from the Mountain Gate, fearing to trust to the monks. The deacon Gōyō Jōrimbō laid hands upon the steward of the Prince of the Great Pagoda, he who was called the Aguin Middle Counselor and Sign of the Law Chōshun, and sent him to Rokuhara (since from the beginning Gōyō's heart had inclined toward the military). Likewise, one of the chief of the prince's followers surrendered himself up to Rokuhara with all the men of his monastery, the monk governor Yūzen of the Goshōin Cloister, who doubtless believed that the imperial cause could not prevail, the monks having turned away their faces. And then by ones and twos the other monks fled from the hill of the Eight Regal Scions, until none remained but the teacher of discipline Kōrimbō Genson, Myōkōbō Kosagami, and Nakanobō Akurisshi.

Although the Prince of the Myōhōin and the Prince of the Great Pagoda had remained at the hill until that evening, in their hearts they thought:

"It is ill thus. Shall we not flee from here, that we may learn of His Majesty's fate?"

Late on the night of the twenty-ninth day they lighted watch fires at many places on the hill, as though a mighty host still waited there. And going forth in a small boat from the beach at Tozu with the three monks who had not run away, they fled first to Ishiyama.

It was not the counsel of wisdom that the two princes should flee to the same place; moreover the Prince of the Myōhōin could walk but ill, being weak of limb. Wherefore they tarried not, but parted at Ishiyama. The Prince of the Myōhōin took his way to Kasagi, but the Prince of the Great Pagoda fled toward the southern capital, seeking to go to the wilderness of Totsugawa.

So casting away their high estate, these two who had been the rulers of great monasteries wandered forth on unaccustomed endless journeys. Sore at heart, they broke the holy ties binding them to the Healing Monarch Yakushi,[42] and to the divine King of the Mountain,[43] distressfully thinking, "When shall these brothers meet again?" They parted tearfully, the one to the east and the one to the west, each gazing back upon the other until he was hidden. Sad indeed were their august hearts!

[*There follows a famous anecdote from Chinese history concerning the impersonation of a ruler by one of his subjects.*]

Now on this occasion the imperial design was not accomplished, since the supreme highness did not go to the Mountain Gate himself, and the monks turned away their faces quickly because of this. Yet carefully considered the plan was not lacking in wisdom. In ancient times, after the death of the First Emperor of Ch'in, Hsiang Yü of Ch'u and Kao Tsu of Han disputed the state for

---

[42] The buddha worshiped in the Central Hall of the Enryakuji.
[43] The god of the Hiyoshi Shrine on Mount Hiei.

Chapter 2

eight years, contesting together in more than seventy battles; and each time Hsiang Yü was victorious, while Kao Tsu suffered grievously. It came about that Kao Tsu defended Jung-yang Castle, which Hsiang Yü surrounded several hundredfold with men of war. With the passing of time, the warriors within the castle ate up the food that was there, and their bodies fainted from weakness. Kao Tsu could not fight; neither was there a means of escape for him.

Thereupon one of Kao Tsu's vassals, a warrior called Chi Hsin, spoke a word, saying:

"Hsiang Yü has surrounded our castle several hundredfold; likewise the food is eaten up and the army is weary. If the warriors are sent out to fight, assuredly Han will be captured by Ch'u. You must practice a deception upon the enemy, that in secret you may escape from the castle. I ask to be allowed to surrender to Ch'u, borrowing the name of the monarch of Han. When Ch'u loosens her encirclement to take me, then quickly the monarch of Han may go forth from the castle, and again raise a mighty host wherewith to crush Ch'u."

It was regrettable that Chi Hsin should surrender to Ch'u to be killed; yet for the sake of the state Kao Tsu could not hold his own life lightly. Though he grieved tearfully because of the parting, he accepted Chi Hsin's counsel.

Chi Hsin joyfully put on the robes of the monarch of Han, mounted up into the yellow-roofed imperial carriage, attached the plumes on the left thereof, and came forth from the east gate of the castle with a mighty shout, saying:

"Apologizing for his crimes, Kao Tsu surrenders to the great monarch of Ch'u!"

When the men of Ch'u heard Chi Hsin's shouting, they relaxed their four-sided encirclement to gather together in one place. But while their whole army was shouting, "Hurrah!" Kao Tsu fled out through the castle's west gate to Ch'eng-kao with thirty horsemen.

When the night lightened, the men of Ch'u saw that the surrendered monarch of Han was not Kao Tsu, but his vassal Chi Hsin. And Hsiang Yü stabbed Chi Hsin to death, greatly enraged.

Soon Kao Tsu led men of Ch'eng-kao against Hsiang Yü. When Hsiang Yü's armies were gone, they killed him at Wu-chiang, and for many years Kao Tsu governed the realm as the emperor of Han.

[*End of anecdote*]

Did the supreme highness recall this auspicious precedent? Did Morokata likewise think of Chi Hsin's loyalty? Chi Hsin practiced a deception to break an enemy encirclement, while Morokata sought to hold back enemy warriors. Likewise Yamato and Han differed in time. Yet truly were both of these wise plans, whereby subjects assumed their lords' guises, and perfect loyalty was transformed for a time.

3

The Dream of the Supreme Highness and the Matter of Kusunoki

IT WAS ON THE TWENTY-SEVENTH DAY of the eighth month of the first year of Genkō that the supreme highness went to Kasagi to take up his abode in the Main Hall.[1] For the first day or two after his coming, no man rendered allegiance to him there, since all feared the power of the military. But when it was known that the men of Rokuhara were beaten down in the fighting at the eastern base of Mount Hiei, the monks of Kasagi Temple hastened to assemble, and warriors of neighboring provinces galloped together from here and there. Yet there came no great lord who was a warrior of renown, leading one hundred or two hundred horsemen. And the heart of the supreme highness was made heavy thereby, so that he thought:

"Can these warriors alone protect Our abiding place?"

So he was thinking, when for a time sleep claimed his eyes. In a dream he beheld a place like to the courtyard of the Shishinden,[2] wherein stood a mighty evergreen tree with dense foliage, its branches stretching out luxuriantly toward the south. Beneath that tree sat the great lords and officials, each according to his rank; and there were thick mats piled high on a raised seat facing toward the south,[3] where no man sat.

In the dream the supreme highness thought, "For whom is this seat made ready?"

---

[1] The principal building of Kasagi Temple, situated on top of the mountain.
[2] One of the main ceremonial halls of the palace.
[3] The position of honor or authority (cf. the Chinese epithet "south-facer," used of the emperor).

As he stood there doubtfully, suddenly two children appeared, wearing their hair in rolls. They knelt in front of him and wept into their sleeves, saying:

"Nowhere in all the realm may you hide even briefly, yet beneath that tree there is a seat facing south. Sit there awhile. It was made ready for your sake."

He thought that those children rose up into the distant sky. And even then he awakened.

Now the supreme highness thought, "This was a dream conveying a heavenly announcement to Us." Considering the characters, he thought again:

"By writing the character for 'south' next to the character for 'tree,' 'camphor tree' is produced, which is to say *kusunoki*. When the two children called upon Us to sit down beneath the protection of that tree with Our face turned toward the south, it was a sign from the bodhisattvas Nikkō and Gakkō that We shall again exercise sovereign powers over the men of the realm."

Thus hopefully he interpreted the august dream.

When the night had lightened, he summoned the teacher of discipline Jōjubō, a monk of Kasagi Temple, and spoke to him, saying, "Is there perhaps a warrior called Kusunoki in these parts?"

Jōjubō answered him, saying:

"I have not heard that there is a person of such a surname hard by. In the province of Kawachi west of Mount Kongō, there is indeed one who has obtained a name as a wielder of bow and arrow, and he is called Kusunoki Tamon Hyōe Masashige. Men say he is a descendant of the Ide Great Subject of the Left, Lord Moroe of the Tachibana, a descendant in the fourth generation of the Emperor Bidatsu, whose family left the capital long ago to dwell among the common people. Likewise is it told that Masashige was born of a dream dreamt by his mother when in her youth she made a hundred-day retreat to Shigi Bishamon—wherefore he was named Tamon as a child." [4]

[4] Bishamon (Skt. Vaiśravana; also called Tamon in Japanese), one of the Four Heavenly Monarchs, is worshiped as a protector of the state, a war-god and a bringer of wealth. He is the principal deity enshrined at the Chōgosonshiji Temple on Mount Shigi in northern Kawachi (Nara Prefecture).

Chapter 3

So indeed he replied.

Now the supreme highness thought, "This is he of whom tonight's dream told Us."

"Call the warrior Kusunoki at once," he said.

And Lord Fujifusa made speed to summon Masashige, according to the imperial command.

When the imperial messenger came to Kusunoki's abiding place to speak concerning his commission, in his heart Masashige thought, "There can be no greater honor for a man of bow and arrow." Quickly he went forth in secret to Kasagi, not thinking about advantages or disadvantages.

The supreme highness spoke to Masashige through the mouth of Lord Fujifusa the Madenokōji Middle Counselor, saying:

"Thinking to rely upon you to subdue the eastern barbarians, We sent forth Our imperial messenger. We rejoice exceedingly that you have hastened to come here. What is your plan for swiftly winning a victory and pacifying the four seas, that the realm may be returned to Our hands? Speak freely all that is in your mind."

Respectfully Masashige said:

"Of late by their crimes the eastern barbarians have invited the censure of heaven. Wherefore then shall we not profit from their weakness to destroy them on heaven's behalf? Yet to control the realm we require not men of war alone, but clever devisings as well. Not by opposing strength against strength will we triumph, not though we assemble together the warriors of more than sixty provinces to contest against the men of Musashi and Sagami alone. But if we fight with a plan there will be nothing to fear, since the guileless eastern barbarians can do nothing beyond smashing what is sharp and destroying what is strong.[5]

"Since the way of warfare is as it is, let not the sovereign look at the outcome of a single battle. While he hears that Masashige alone still lives, let him believe that he will prevail at last!"

So he spoke firmly, and went home to Kawachi.

---

[5] He means that the eastern warriors are vulnerable because they are poor strategists, although they are so strong in battle that they can batter down enemy swords and destroy enemy positions.

The Battle of Kasagi; How Suyama and Komiyama Attacked by Night

When it was known in the capital that at Kasagi the supreme highness received the homage of loyal warriors from nearby provinces, the military were seized with trembling, lest with emboldened hearts the soldier-monks of the Mountain Gate come down against Rokuhara. They gave men of the province of Ōmi to Sasaki Hōgan Tokinobu, to go forth toward Ōtsu, and when it was said that this was not sufficient, they added the Kuge and Nagazawa families, residents of the province of Tamba, that camped with eight hundred riders at the post stations east and west of Ōtsu.

On the first day of the ninth month, the two Rokuhara examiners,[6] Kasuya Saburō Muneaki and Suda Jirō Saemon, went forth to the Byōdōin Cloister at Uji with five hundred riders to record the coming of the hosts. Men of war from many provinces galloped together continuously in daylight and darkness, not waiting to be urged, until their numbers became a hundred thousand riders. And they resolved to go against Kasagi at the hour of the snake on the second day of the ninth month.

May it not be that Takahashi Matashirō thought to win honor by acting before others? For on the first day of the ninth month he drew near to the foot of Kasagi Mountain with none but his three hundred kinsmen.

Although the loyal warriors inside the castle were not many, their spirit was valiant, and they hungered to do great deeds to save the realm. How could they fail to strike when they beheld Takahashi's miserable force? Their three thousand riders lay in wait beside the Kozu River, encompassed Takahashi's men about, and fell upon them fiercely. And forgetting the warlike ardor that had seized him in the beginning, Takahashi frantically whipped his horse in retreat, without looking back so much as once. Great numbers of his men were driven to their deaths in the whirling waters of the Kozu River, while those who escaped alive abandoned

---
[6] The second-ranking officials of the Rokuhara Samurai Office. They judged crimes, made tours of investigation and led the warriors stationed in Kyoto to battle.

their horses and arms, fleeing stripped to the capital in full daylight. An ignominious spectacle indeed! Someone must have thought it such a disgrace that he wrote a verse and put it up beside the bridge at the Byōdōin, saying, "Swift are the white waves of the Kozu River's many rapids—the High Bridge thrown across at once collapsed." [7]

Hearing of Takahashi's plan, a certain Kobayakawa had followed along behind him, thinking to win honor in his place if he retreated. Yet Kobayakawa's men, chased off at the same time, ran away as far as Uji without ever turning back. And a second bill was put up, saying, "Unable to stand, the High Bridge fell, bringing disgrace to the flowing water—O disgraced Small Swift Stream!" [8]

Now the two Rokuhara examiners thought:

"When it is known that the imperial forces were victorious in yesterday's battle, warriors will come hastily from many provinces to render allegiance to the sovereign, and it will be a troublesome thing. We must not delay."

Wherefore with the hosts at Uji divided into four armies for the four directions they went forth against Kasagi castle on the second day of the ninth month. To the south were sent seven thousand six hundred horsemen from the five home provinces, that circled around behind Mount Kōmyō to attack from the rear. To the east were sent twenty-five thousand horsemen from Iga, Ise, Owari, Mikawa, and Tōtōmi, all provinces of the Tōkaidō circuit, that headed toward Kongōsangoe by way of the Iga road. To the north were sent twelve thousand horsemen from the eight provinces of the San'indō circuit, that went from beside the Nashima post station, and circled around the foot of Mount Ichinobe to attack from the front. And to the west were sent thirty-two thousand horsemen from the eight provinces of the San'yōdō circuit, that went up the Kozu River and advanced in two armies by steep paths above the banks. Truly for two leagues on each side of Kasagi Mountain the more than seventy-five thousand attackers filled every foot of land.

When the sky lightened at the hour of the hare on the third day of the ninth month, the attackers drew together on all sides to shout

---

[7] A pun on Takahashi's name, which means "high bridge."
[8] Kobayakawa means "small swift stream."

out their battle cry. Like a hundred thousand thunderclaps was that sound, shaking heaven and earth! When they had shouted three times, they shot humming-bulb arrows to set the battle in array. Yet within the silent castle no man raised a battle shout, nor did any shoot an answering arrow.

White clouds buried the peak of the high mountain where Kasagi castle stood, and mossy crags dropped away below for a myriad fathoms. The twisting path leading upward was half a league long; likewise, rocks had been hewn away to make ditches, and boulders were piled up to serve as walls. Not easily might men ascend to such a castle, though it be not defended by a single warrior! But the men of Rokuhara thought:

"Within the castle all is silent, and no man can be seen. It must be that our enemies have fled."

The more than seventy-five thousand attackers from the four directions climbed over chasms and cliffs, clung to *kuzu* vines, and scaled rocks, until they came before the Hall of the Two Monarchs, close upon the outer castle gate. There they rested awhile, looking up into the castle. And then indeed they beheld the sovereign's brocade banner floating in the air, its sun and moon of gold and silver shining and sparkling in the bright sunlight. All the space beneath that banner was filled by more than three thousand armored warriors, standing like clouds or mist with joined sleeves and gleaming helmet-stars.[9] Moreover archers waited eagerly at the tops of towers and behind windows, where they moistened bowstrings with their mouths, untied packets of arrows and spread them out, and rubbed oil from their noses onto arrows from the middle of their quivers.[10] These were not men to be attacked hastily!

Now as the besiegers remained in their places with unquiet hearts, not venturing to advance nor yet able to fall back, a window board was removed from the tower above the gate, and a warrior named his name, saying:

"Honored by the trust of the master of the realm, Asuke Jirō Shigenori, a resident of the province of Mikawa, guards the outer gate of this castle. Am I wrong in thinking that these advancing

[9] Nailheads on the helmet-bowl.
[10] Possibly to make the arrow slide more easily against the bow and hand?

Chapter 3

banners are banners of men of Mino and Owari? I have been awaiting the coming of the lords of Rokuhara, since the master of the ten good acts[11] is staying in this castle. To welcome them I have made ready a few arrowheads, forged by smiths of Yamato. Please try one!"

He pulled a long arrow far back in his mighty bow strung by three men, steadied his aim a moment, and let go the singing arrow, that smote Arao Kurō, waiting across a valley two hundred and fifty yards distant, and drove hard and deep into his right side through the flap protecting his armor-cord. Though it was but a single arrow, most excellently was it aimed! Arao fell down headfirst from his horse, and died without sitting up.

Then Kurō's younger brother Yagorō stood in front of him, that his corpse might not be seen by the enemy. He came out from behind his shield [12] and spoke a word, saying:

"The strength of my lord Asuke's bow-arm is not as I have heard! Pray shoot here so that I may test the sinews of my armor with your arrow!"

So he mocked him, striking his bowstring-runner.[13]

"Judging from this person's manner of speaking," thought Asuke, "he must certainly be wearing a corselet or chain garment under his armor, that after seeing my first arrow he beats his chest, saying, 'Shoot here!' If I hit his armor, the shaft of the arrow will be smashed, the arrowhead will bend, and assuredly it will not go through. But if I hit the visor of his helmet, why should it not penetrate?"

He drew out a metal-headed arrow from his quiver and rubbed it with nose-oil, saying:

"If such is your desire, I will give you an arrow! Receive it if you can!"

He unfastened his armor, drew back the long arrow farther than before, until the bow recoiled strongly, and sent the arrow singing

---

[11] The emperor, so called because he was believed to have attained his high estate as a result of practicing the ten Buddhist virtues in a previous life.
[12] Rectangular wooden shields were frequently propped up on the ground in front of archers shooting on foot.
[13] A piece of leather worn over the chest to keep the bowstring from catching on the armor.

on its way. Nor did that arrow fail to hit its mark, but ripped through the visor of Arao Yagorō's helmet three inches above the edge, burying itself up to the shaft between his eyebrows. And so these brothers fell down dead on the same pillow without saying two words.

With this as the beginning of the battle, howling and shouting the attackers at the front and rear began to fight, and likewise the defenders inside the castle. Not even briefly did the battle cries cease, or the yells of the archers; but truly it seemed that great mountains would crumble and be carried off to the sea, and the axis of the earth would bend and sink down in an instant. And when evening came, in many ranks the attackers pressed forward behind their shields, as far as the castle gate.

Within the castle there was a monk called Honjōbō, a man of great strength, come as a messenger bearing prayer charms from the Hannyaji Temple in the southern capital. Honjōbō tied back the sleeves of his robe, easily picked up immense boulders, such as a hundred men might not move, and tossed them out like balls, twenty or thirty in succession. The shields of the attacking hosts were smashed to pieces, and every person touched by those rocks fell over backwards. On the east and west slopes an avalanche of men swept down, so that horses and riders were piled up manyfold, the one upon the other. Although the two valleys were exceedingly deep, dead men filled them up completely. Even after the battle was ended, the Kozu River was turned to blood, differing in no wise from the deep crimson color of water flowing beneath autumn leaves.

From this time on, no man sought to assail the castle, though the attackers were like clouds or mist. They merely surrounded the castle's four sides, attacking from a distance.

Now some time having passed in this manner, it came about that a fast messenger was sent to Rokuhara from the province of Kawachi on the eleventh day of that month, saying:

"The person called Kusunoki Hyōe Masashige has raised a standard in the imperial cause. Those of his neighbors who cherish unfulfilled desires have joined themselves to him, while the others have fled east and west to hide. Likewise Kusunoki has laid requisitions upon the commoners of the provinces, carrying away their food for his warriors to eat; and he has built a stronghold on Mount Akasaka above his home, where he shuts himself up with five hundred horsemen. Send men to subdue him at once, lest the affair become troublesome."

Thereupon a great clamor arose at Rokuhara of men saying, "What strange matter is this!"

Moreover on the evening of the thirteenth day there came another fast messenger, sent from the province of Bingo, who said:

"With his kinsmen the lay monk Sakurayama Shirō has raised a standard in the imperial cause, making the foremost shrine of the province[14] his stronghold. More than seven hundred rebels from nearby provinces have hastened to the side of this person, who thinks to cross into other provinces after conquering Bingo. Send men to chastise him quickly, lest the affair become troublesome. There must be no remissness."

So indeed it was reported.

In front of the capital, Kasagi castle stood firm against the hosts of the provinces attacking by day and by night, while to the rear the rebels Kusunoki and Sakurayama had risen in force, causing messengers to warn of danger daily. The Rokuhara personage of the north, he that was the governor of Suruga, was disquieted in his heart, thinking:

"Already traitors in the south and west are creating disturbances. Who can tell what will happen in the east and north?"

So he thought, and daily sent fast horses to Kamakura to ask for men of war from the eastern provinces.

Now sorely affrighted, the Sagami lay monk called upon as many as sixty-three men of consequence, both those who were his kinsmen and those who were not, that he might send a chastising army at once. And so it came about that 207,600 warriors went forth from Kamakura on the twentieth day of the ninth month, a most mighty host, whose foremost riders came to the provinces of Mino and Owari on the last day of the month, while yet the rearmost lay in the passes of Kōshi and Futamura.

Meanwhile according to the summons of Rokuhara two residents

[14] Kibitsu Shrine (Ashina-gun, Hiroshima-ken).

of the province of Bitchū had joined the attackers at Kasagi castle, where they camped across the river: Suyama Tōzō Yoshitaka and a certain Komiyama Jirō. When these heard that a great army from the east was come as far as the province of Ōmi, they gathered together their kinsmen and retainers to speak a word to them, saying:

"Tell us your minds. No man can say how many thousands or tens of thousands are fallen in these days of fighting, struck down by rocks or smitten by arrows from afar. Their bodies are not yet dried up, but already their names are forgotten, because they died without doing great deeds. Since no man is immortal, why should we not die fighting brilliantly, so that our fame may endure a thousand years, and rewards may bless the houses of our descendants? There are those who since the disturbances of the Heike have been renowned as mighty men of valor, yet truly their deeds were of no great merit. Kumagai and Hirayama took the lead at Ichi-no-tani because they relied upon the big force in their rear; likewise it was to save his son Genta that Kajiwara Heizō dashed forward twice. Sasaki Saburō's crossing at Fujito was the work of a guide, while only the speed of his horse Ikezuki enabled Sasaki Shirō Takatsuna to lead the way across the Uji River.[15] Even these are still talked about today, and their names are in the mouths of the realm's men. How much the more glorious if by our strength alone we bring down this castle, attacked vainly day after day by the assembled warriors of the land of Japan! Our fame will be unequaled for all time; our loyalty will stand above that of a myriad men. Come! Under cover of this night's rain and wind, let us secretly enter the castle precincts to amaze the men of the realm with a night attack!"

So they spoke, and their fifty kinsmen and retainers agreed, "By all means let it be so!"

Thereupon all of these drew holy pictures[16] to wear in prepara-

---

[15] The references are all to heroic acts performed by supporters of Yoritomo during the warfare between the Taira and the Minamoto at the end of the twelfth century.

[16] Mandalas representing the Pure Land paradise, into which they hoped to be born.

Chapter 3

tion for death, since they were resolved not to return alive. They took two lead ropes for horses, a hundred feet long, knotted them together at intervals of a foot, and tied a grapnel at the end, that by hanging the ropes from branches and boulders they might climb over the rocks.

On that night one could see nothing, however much one looked, for it was the last night of the lunar month. Moreover it was a night of furious rain and wind, when opposing armies would not go forth to clash in battle. With swords and daggers on their backs, the fifty men began to climb at the northern rampart of the castle, a rock wall fifteen hundred feet high, where even a bird could not fly easily. In divers ways they went up for seven hundred and fifty feet, until with perplexed hearts they beheld rocks like folding screens, rising in layers above them in a place of smooth green moss and ancient pines with drooping limbs.

Thereupon Suyama Tōzō ran up lightly over the rocks, hung the lead ropes onto the branch of a tree, and lowered them from above the rocks, so that the warriors passed over the difficult place easily by laying hold of them. And there was no other great precipice above.

Toiling sorely, they grasped *kuzu* roots in their hands and walked over moss on their toes, until with the passing of four hours they came to the edge of the wall. And when they had rested their bodies awhile, every man of them climbed over.

Then in stealth they spied upon the castle's interior by following a sentry making his rounds. They saw that a thousand warriors of Iga and Ise guarded the front gate on the west side of the mountain, five hundred men of Yamato and Kawachi guarded the eastern bastion in the rear, and seven hundred riders of Izumi and Kii watched in front of the Hall of the Two Monarchs on the south side. May it be that the defenders trusted to the steepness of the cliffs on the north side? No warriors watched there, but only two or three soldiers of low degree, who had lighted a campfire and gone to sleep on straw matting spread below a tower.

When Suyama and Komiyama had gone around the castle to see the enemy positions on the four sides, they turned their footsteps toward the Main Hall, thinking to search out the abiding place of the emperor. Hearing them, a man of a battle office[17] spoke a question, saying:

"It is strange indeed that many men pass thus stealthily in the night! Who are you?"

Quickly Suyama Yoshitsugu answered him, saying, "We are warriors of Yamato, guarding against attackers slipping in by night, for the wind and rain are violent, and there is much noise."

"To be sure," said the voice, and there was no other question.

Thereafter they ascended calmly to the Main Hall without seeking concealment, shouting aloud, "All positions be on the alert!"

When they beheld that hall, they saw that it was indeed the imperial abode, where candles burned in many places, and a bell rang faintly. There were three or four men in high-crowned caps and robes serving in the anteroom.

"Which of the warrior-guards are you?" these asked.

And the warriors lined up close together in the winding corridor, giving the names of such and such persons from thus and so provinces.

When Suyama and his men had beheld everything, even to the imperial abode, they made their hearts strong, bowed down in front of the god of the mountain, climbed to the peak above the Main Hall, lighted a fire in a deserted compound, and raised a battle cry all together.

"Aha!" said the attackers on the four sides. "Deserters within the castle have lighted a fire. Let us join our battle cries to theirs!"

Of the seventy thousand attackers before and behind, each shouted his own battle cry, their voices shaking heaven and earth with a sound that would shatter even the eight myriad leagues of Mount Sumeru.[18]

Now because Suyama's fifty warriors knew everything that was within the castle, they set fire to a battle-office here and raised a war cry there, raised a war cry there and set fire to a tower here, running around in every direction with a noise as of an army great enough to fill the interior of the castle.

---

[17] The headquarters of a chieftain.
[18] In Hinduism and Buddhism, the central mountain of the world.

"A mighty host has come up into the castle!" thought the emperor's warriors.

They cast off their armor, threw down their bows and arrows, and ran away, falling and tumbling over cliffs and into ditches.

When he beheld these things, Nishigori Hōgandai spoke a word, saying:

"What miserable behavior is this! We are men trusted by the master of the ten good acts, warriors worthy of meeting the Hōjō in battle. Shall we flee without a fight, saying, 'The enemy is mighty'? For what occasion must our lives be cherished?"

Again and again he ran toward the enemies facing him. After he had shot away all his arrows and broken his sword, then indeed he ripped open his belly, together with his son and thirteen retainers, and all fell down dead on the same pillow.

The Supreme Highness Flees from Kasagi

As spreading flames blew from the east and west and smoke descended upon the imperial abode, the supreme highness fled away aimlessly with naked feet, and the princes and great nobles did the same. For the first one hundred or two hundred yards, these others assisted the supreme highness, waiting upon him in front and behind. But at last they drew apart, since by reason of the fierce storm the path could not be seen, and enemy war cries sounded on every side. None but Fujifusa and Suefusa remained to take the imperial hands.

Even in this wise did the gracious Son of Heaven of the ten good acts deign to transform his august person into the figure of a rustic and wander forth without an object. How shocking it was! With all his heart he thought of going toward Akasaka castle in the night; yet he felt as though treading a dream-path, for he was not in the least accustomed to walking. Stepping once he rested; stepping twice he halted. By day he hid his body behind green hillocks close to the path, making sitting-cushions of the sparse blades of frozen grasses; by night he stumbled through the dewdrops on desolate moors, quite unable to dry his gauze sleeves.

Three days and nights having passed, in some way the supreme highness came to the foot of Mount Ariō, that lies in Taga district in the land of Yamashiro. Fujifusa and Suefusa were footsore and weary, since no food had passed their lips for three days; and the will to flee was dead within them, happen what might. Wherefore, pillowing their heads on the rocks of a secluded valley, they dreamt together in broken slumber, master with subject and brother with brother.

The supreme highness heard a wind sweeping the tops of the pine trees with a sound as of falling rain. And when he stood under a tree, the dew therefrom dripped down rapidly onto his sleeves. He recited: "Since leaving Kasagi Mountain, our journeying sedge hats have found no shelter in the realm." And restraining tears, Lord Fujifusa replied, "Alas! When one approaches trusted shelter, yet are one's sleeves drenched by dew beneath the pines."

Now there were two residents of the province of Yamashiro well acquainted with this region, the Misu lay monk and the Matsui archivist, who searched every mountain and peak until they found out the place where the emperor abode. And Misu drew near thereto.

The supreme highness spoke to Misu with imperial dignity, saying, "If you are men of prudence, accept the favor of the Son of Heaven, whereby you will prosper exceedingly."

Suddenly a new feeling came into the heart of the Misu lay monk.

"Ah," he thought, "would that I could hide this sovereign and raise a loyal force!"

But because it was impossible to know the mind of Matsui following after, he said nothing, fearful lest the matter become known and his devisings fail. How regrettable it was!

This lay monk put the supreme highness into a mean litter covered with straw matting, wherein he took him away to Uchiyama in the southern capital (not even a woven-bark litter was in readiness, it being a sudden affair). Indeed it was not different from the dreamlike past, when T'ang of Yin was shut up in Hsia prison, or when the monarch of Yüeh surrendered at K'uai-chi.[19]

---

[19] Allusions to famous events in Chinese history. T'ang is said to have suffered imprisonment at the hands of Chieh (d. 1763 B.C.?), the last Hsia ruler, before

Chapter 3

Of those who heard or saw, there was none whose sleeve was not drenched.

These were the persons taken alive in divers places at this time:

The First Prince, which is to say the Minister of Central Affairs and Prince of the Blood

The Second Prince, which is to say the Canonical Prince of the Blood Sonchō of the Myōhōin Cloister

The monk reformer Shunga of Mine

The monk reformer Shōjin of the Southeast Cloister

The Madenokōji Great Counselor Nobufusa

The Kazan'in Great Counselor Morokata

The Inspector and Great Counselor Kintoshi

The Minamoto Middle Counselor Tomoyuki

The Chamberlain and Middle Counselor Kin'akira

The Chief Police Commissioner and Left Gate Guards Assistant Saneyo

The Middle Counselor Fujifusa

The magistrate Suefusa

The Taira magistrate Narisuke

The Left Gate Guards Assistant Tameakira

The Middle Marshal of the Left Yukifusa

The Lesser Marshal of the Left Tadaaki

The Minamoto Lesser Marshal Yoshisada

The Shijō Lesser Marshal Takakane

The Sign of the Law Chōshun, the steward of the Myōhōin Cloister

And of the warriors of the imperial guards:

Saemon Ujinobu
Uhyōe Arikiyo
Tsushima Hyōe Shigesada
Taifu Shōgen Kaneaki
Sakon Muneaki
Hyōe-no-jō Noriaki

---

he founded the Shang (Yin) dynasty. Kou-chien, a king of Yüeh (acceded 496 B.C.), was forced to surrender at K'uai-chi Mountain after being disastrously defeated by a rival monarch. See Chapter Four for the full story of Kou-chien.

The university vice-president Nagaakira
Asuke Jirō Shigenori
The Palace Interior Aide Yoshiyuki
Ōkawara Genshichi Saemon-no-jō Arishige
And of the Nara monks:
> Shunzō
> Kyōmitsu
> Gyōkai
> Shigaragi Jibubō Enjitsu

Kondō Saburō Sahyōemon-no-jō Munemitsu
The lay monk Kunimura Saburō Jōhō
The lay monk Minamoto no Sahyōemon Jigan
The lay monk Oku Joen
The lay monk Rokurō Hyōe Jōen
And of the monks of the Enryakuji:
> Shōgyōbō Jōkai
> Shūzenbō Jōun
> Jōjitsubō Jisson

In all they were sixty-one persons, nor can one count the numbers of their retainers and kinsmen that were captured. Put into litters or mounted on post horses, they were fetched back to the capital in full daylight. Men and women who seemed to be connected with them stood lined up in the streets, weeping and lamenting unashamed before the eyes of others. How sad it was!

The Rokuhara personage of the north removed the supreme highness to the Byōdōin at Uji on the second day of the tenth month, guarding the road with more than three thousand horsemen. On that day also the two grand marshals of the host from the Kantō came straightway to Uji, not entering the capital. And these went before the dragon countenance to petition for the three imperial emblems,[20] that they might bear them to the new sovereign of the Jimyōin.

---

[20] The imperial regalia: the jewel, sword and mirror.

Chapter 3

Through Fujifusa, the supreme highness spoke a word to them, saying:

"When a new sovereign receives the throne from heaven, the former emperor himself must present the three imperial symbols, for thus has it been since ancient days. There have been rebellious subjects who have displayed their power in the four seas, and likewise there have been men who have held the realm in their hands for awhile, but never have We heard of one who willfully seized these three imperial symbols to deliver them up to a new sovereign. Moreover, the Sacred Mirror has assuredly burned to ashes, for We cast it away in the Main Hall of Kasagi. The Divine Jewel may again become the guardian of the land, since We hung it onto the branch of a tree while We wandered through the mountains. But as for the Treasured Sword, We Ourself shall fall upon it if the military profane Our person, heedless of the wrath of heaven, nor even briefly will We be separated from it."

So he spoke, and in silence the two eastern commissioners departed, with the men of Rokuhara.

On the following day these brought forth a litter, thinking to bear the sovereign to Rokuhara. But resolutely the supreme highness said to them, "If it be not with the ceremony of former days, We shall not go back."

Then they made ready the state litter with the golden phoenix on top, and prepared the imperial robes, for they could do no other. And when the emperor had remained for three days in the Byōdōin, then indeed did he go forth to Rokuhara.

Not as in former days was that imperial procession! Myriads of warriors encompassed the phoenix litter about, and the great nobles sat in shabby litters or rode on post horses. As they went toward the east in the Seventh Ward, ascended the Kamo River, and made haste toward Rokuhara, those who saw shed tears, and those who heard grieved in their hearts.

Was it not sad? Yesterday he sat on the imperial dais in the Shishinden, with the hundred officials dressed in their ceremonial robes; today he goes down into the rude dwelling of the eastern barbarians, with the stern gaze of a myriad men of war afflicting his spirit. Truly time passes and the world changes; happiness vanishes as sadness comes. Naught but a dream are the days of life.

There came to the emperor's mind divers memories of his cloud-topping palace, since the place where it stood was not far distant. When a shower of rain passed by, veiling the moonlight on the eaves, he wrote a verse, saying, "Though one but hears the sound of a shower on the eaves of an unfamiliar shingle roof, one's sleeves are drenched!"

When four or five days had passed, there came a lute to the supreme highness from the Inner Princess, with a poem saying, "Picture the tears I could not brush away, that struck the dust deep-piled on these four strings." And he answered, "Though veiled by tears the crescent[21] hide, We shall not forget the radiance of moon-lit nights together."

Now the examiners Takahashi Gyōbu Saemon and Kasuya Saburō Muneaki came to Rokuhara on the eighth day of that month, and delivered each of the captives into the hands of a powerful chieftain. The First Prince, which is to say the Central Affairs Minister and Prince of the Blood, they delivered up to Sasaki Hōgan Tokinobu; and the Second Prince, which is to say the Prince of the Blood of the Myōhōin, they delivered up to Nagai Sakon Takahiro; and the Minamoto Middle Counselor Tomoyuki to Chikugo-no-zenji Sadatomo; and the monk reformer of the Southeast Cloister to Hitachi-no-zenji Tokitomo. The Madeno-kōji Middle Counselor Fujifusa was detained at Rokuhara as though under house arrest, so that he might attend upon the supreme highness; and likewise the Rokujō Lesser Marshal Tadaaki.

On the ninth day the emperor gave up the three imperial symbols to the new sovereign of the Jimyōin.[22] The Horikawa Great Counselor Tomochika and the Hino Middle Counselor Sukena received them and sent them to the Chōkōdō Hall (which is to say the residence of the highnesses of the Jimyōin). The guards were the Nagai Rectifier and Archivist, the Mizutani Military Guard and

[21] Another name for the lute (biwa), derived from the shape of the aperture in front.
[22] Presumably because he was unable to keep up the pretense that two of them had been lost.

Archivist, the Tamba Popular Affairs Grandee, and Sasaki Oki no Hōgan Kiyotaka. And on the thirteenth day the new sovereign came to the palace from the Chōkōdō, that he might be placed upon the throne. The great nobles in his procession went forth in splendid raiment, while in helmets and armor the warriors of an escort guarded against untoward things.

Now it came about that the former sovereign's courtiers were distressed and fearful of every happening, both those that were guilty of offense and those that were not, each thinking in his heart, "What grievous fate will befall me?" But those who served the new emperor rejoiced, both the upright and the false, thinking, "Now is our prosperity begun!"

The maturing seed becomes the spreading tree; the falling flower forsakes the branch. Today's want is tomorrow's plenty; yesterday's honor is today's disgrace. Although this was not the beginning of the world of cares, it was in these times that dreams could not be distinguished from reality.

The Battle of Akasaka Castle

No man of the mighty host from the distant eastern lands was willing to enter the capital, so sorely were their spirits mortified because Kasagi castle had fallen before they were come to the province of Ōmi. All took their way instead toward Akasaka castle, where Kusunoki Hyōe Masashige was shut up, some crossing the mountains of Iga and Ise, others following the Uji and Daigo roads.

When these had passed beyond the Ishi River, they beheld the castle. Surely this was a stronghold of hasty devising! The ditch was not a proper ditch, and there was but a single wooden wall, plastered over with mud. Likewise in size the castle was not more than one hundred or two hundred yards around, with but twenty or thirty towers within, made ready in haste. Of those who saw it, not one but thought:

"Ah, what a pitiable spectacle the enemy presents! Even if we were to hold this castle in one hand and throw, we would be able to throw it! Let us hope that in some strange manner Kusunoki will endure for at least a day, that by taking booty and winning honor we may obtain future rewards."

Drawing near, the three hundred thousand riders got down from their horses, one after another, jumped into the ditch, stood below the towers, and competed to be the first to enter the castle.

Now by nature Masashige was a man who would "scheme in his tent to defeat an enemy a thousand leagues distant," one whose counsels were as subtle as though sprung from the brain of Ch'en-p'ing or Chang Liang.[23] Wherefore had he kept two hundred mighty archers within the castle, and had given three hundred riders to his brother Shichirō and Wada Gorō Masato outside in the mountains. Yet the attackers, all unwitting, rushed forward together to the banks of the ditch on the four sides, resolved to bring down the castle in a single assault.

Then from tower tops and windows the archers shot furiously with arrowheads aligned together, smiting more than a thousand men in an instant. And greatly amazed, the eastern warriors said:

"No, no! From the look of things at this castle, it will never fall in a day or two. Let us take time before going against it, that we may establish camps and battle-offices and form separate parties."

They drew back from the attack a little, took off their horses' saddles, cast aside their armor, and rested in their camps.

In the mountains Kusunoki Shichirō and Wada Gorō said, "The time is right." They made two parties of the three hundred horsemen, came out from the shelter of the trees on the eastern and western slopes with two fluttering banners, whereon were depicted the chrysanthemum and water crest of the Kusunoki house, and advanced quietly toward the enemy, urging their horses forward in the swirling mist.

The attackers hesitated doubtfully.

"Are they enemies or friends?" they thought.

Then suddenly from both sides the three hundred attacked,

---

[23] Two ministers of the Chinese emperor Han Kao Tsu. The quotation is a paraphrase of a speech by Kao Tsu recorded in the *Han shu*: ". . . in revolving plans in the tent and in making a victory certain at a distance of a thousand *li*, I am not as good as Tzu-fang [Chang Liang]." (Translation from H. H. Dubs, *History of the Former Han Dynasty* [Baltimore, American Council of Learned Societies, 1938—], I, 106.

shouting, in wedge-shaped formations. They smote the center of the three hundred thousand horsemen spread out like clouds or mist, broke into them in all directions, and cut them down on every side. And the attackers' hosts were powerless to form to give battle, so great was their bewilderment.

Next within the castle three gates opened all together, wherefrom two hundred horsemen galloped forth side by side to let fly a multitude of arrows from bows pulled back to the utmost limits. Although the attackers were a mighty host, they were confounded utterly by these few enemies, so that they clamored aloud. Some mounted tethered horses and beat them with their stirrups, seeking to advance; others fixed arrows to unstrung bows and tried vainly to shoot. Two or three men took up a single piece of armor and disputed it, pulling against each other. Though a lord was killed, his vassals knew nothing of it; though a father was killed, his sons aided him not, but like scattered spiderlings they retreated to the Ishi River. For half a league along their way there was no space where a foot might tread, by reason of their abandoned horses and arms. To be sure, great gains came suddenly to the common folk of Tōjō district! [24]

Perhaps the proud eastern warriors thought in their hearts that Kusunoki's strategy could not be despised, since blundering unexpectedly they had been defeated in the first battle. For though they went forth against Handa and Narahara,[25] they did not seek to attack the castle again quickly, but consulted together and made a resolution, saying:

"Let us remain awhile in this place, that led by men acquainted with the home provinces we may cut down trees on the mountains, burn houses, and guard thereby against warriors waiting in reserve to fall upon us. Then may we attack the castle with tranquil spirits."

But there were many among the men of Homma and Shibuya who had lost fathers and sons in the fighting. These roused themselves up, saying:

"What is the use of living? Though we go alone, let us gallop forth to die in battle!"

[24] The local inhabitants, who took possession of what was abandoned.
[25] Settlements near Akasaka.

And thereupon all the others took heart as well, and galloped forward eagerly.

Now Akasaka castle might not be attacked easily on the east, where terraced rice fields extended far up the mountainside. But on three sides the land was flat; likewise there was but a single ditch and wall. All the attackers were contemptuous, thinking, "No matter what demons may be inside, it cannot be much of an affair." When they drew near again, they went forward quickly into the ditch to the opposite bank, pulled away the obstacles and made ready to enter. Yet within the castle there was no sound.

Then the attackers thought in their hearts:

"As it was yesterday, so will it be today. After wounding many men with arrows to confuse us, they will send other warriors to fight in our midst."

They counted out a hundred thousand riders to go to the mountains in the rear, while the remaining two hundred thousand compassed the castle round about like thickly growing rice, hemp, bamboo, or reeds. Yet from within the castle not an arrow was released, nor was any man seen.

At last the attackers laid hold of the wall on the four sides to climb over it, filled with excitement. But thereupon men within the castle cut the ropes supporting that wall, all at the same time, for it was a double wall, built to let the outside fall down. More than a thousand of the attackers became as though crushed by a weight, so that only their eyes moved as the defenders threw down logs and boulders onto them. And in this day's fighting more than seven hundred of them were slain.

Unwilling to attack again because of the bitterness of the first two days of fighting, for four or five days the eastern hosts merely besieged the castle from camps hard by. Truly were they without pride, to watch thus idly from a nearby place! How mortifying it was that men of the future would make a mock of them, saying, "Although the enemy were no more than four or five hundred persons shut up in a flatland castle not five hundred yards around, the hosts of the eight eastern provinces would not attack them, but shamefully laid down a siege from a distance!"

Chapter 3

At last the attackers spoke among themselves, saying:

"Previously we attacked in the fierceness of our valor, not carrying shields or preparing weapons of assault, wherefore we suffered unforeseen injury. Let us go against them now with a different method."

All commanded the making of shields with toughened hide on their faces, such as might not be smashed through easily, and with these upheld they went against the castle once more, saying:

"There can be no difficulty about jumping across to the wall, since the banks are not high, nor is the ditch deep. Yet will not this wall also drop down upon us?"

They spoke with fearful hearts, reluctant to seize upon the wall lightly. All went down into the water of the ditch, laid hold upon the wall with grapnels, and pulled at it. But when the wall was about to fall, those within the castle took ladles with handles ten or twenty feet long, dipped up boiling water, and poured it onto them. The hot water passed through the holes in their helmet tops, ran down from the edges of their shoulder-guards, and burned their bodies so grievously that they fled panic-stricken, throwing down their shields and grapnels. How shameful it was! Although no man of them was slain, there were as many as two or three hundred persons who could not stand up from the burns on their hands and feet, or who lay down with sick bodies.

So it was that whenever the attackers advanced with new devisings, those within the castle defended against them with changed stratagems. Wherefore in consultation together the attackers said, "From this time on, let us starve them, for we can do no other." They forbore utterly to do battle, but only built towers in their camps, lined up obstacles, and laid down a siege.

Soon the warriors in the castle grew weary of spirit, since there was no diversion for them. Nor was their food sufficient, since Kusunoki had built the castle in haste. The battle having begun and the siege commenced, within twenty days the stores were eaten up; nor did food remain for more than four or five days.

Then Masashige spoke a word to his men, saying:

"In divers battles of late have we overreached the foe, whose slain are beyond counting, but these things are as nothing in the eyes of so mighty a host. Moreover, the castle's food is eaten up, and no other warriors will come to deliver us.

"Assuredly I will not cherish life in the hour of need, that from the beginning have been steadfast for His Majesty's sake, anticipating therein the warriors of the realm. But the true man of courage 'is cautious in the face of difficulties, and deliberates before acting.' [26] I will flee this castle for a time, causing the enemy to believe that I have taken my life, so that they may go away rejoicing. When they are gone I will come forward to fight; and if they return I will go deep into the mountains. When I have harassed the eastern hosts four or five times in this manner, will they not grow weary? This is a plan for destroying the enemy in safety. What are your views?"

All agreed, "It ought to be so."

Then quickly within the castle they dug a mighty hole seven feet deep, filling it with twenty or thirty bodies of the slain (who were fallen down dead into the ditch in great numbers), whereon they piled up charcoal and firewood. And they awaited a night of pouring rain and driving wind.

Perhaps because Masashige had found favor in the sight of heaven, suddenly a harsh wind came raising the sand, accompanied by a rain violent enough to pierce bamboo. The night was exceedingly dark, and all the enemy in their camps were sheltered behind curtains. This indeed was the awaited night!

Leaving a man in the castle to light a blaze when they were fled away safely five or six hundred yards, the defenders cast off their armor, assumed the guise of attackers, and fled away calmly by threes and fives, passing in front of enemy battle-offices and beside enemy sleeping places.

It came about that the eyes of an enemy fell upon Masashige, where he passed before the stables of Nagasaki. The man challenged him, saying, "What person passes before this battle-office in stealth, not announcing himself?"

In haste Masashige passed beyond that place, calling back, "I am a follower of the grand marshal who has taken the wrong road."

[26] From the *Analects*.

Chapter 3

"A suspicious fellow indeed!" thought the man. "Assuredly he is a stealer of horses! I shall shoot him down."

He ran up close and shot Masashige full in the body. But although the arrow looked to have driven deep at the height of the elbow-joint, it turned over and flew back again without touching the naked flesh.

Later, when that arrow's track was observed, men saw that it had struck an amulet wherein was preserved the *Kannon Sutra*, which Masashige had trusted and read for many years. Its arrowhead had stopped in the two-line poem, "Wholeheartedly praising the name." How strange it was!

When in this manner Masashige had escaped death from a certain-death arrowhead, he fled to a safe place more than half a league distant. And looking back he saw that the warrior had lighted fires in the castle's battle-offices, faithful to his covenant.

The hosts of the attackers were seized with amazement at the sight of the flames.

"Aha! The castle has fallen!" they shouted exultantly. "Let no man be spared! Let none escape!"

When the flames died away, they saw a mighty hole inside the castle, piled up with charcoal, wherein lay the burned bodies of many men. And then not a man of them but spoke words of praise, saying:

"How pitiful! Masashige has ended his life! Though he was an enemy, his was a glorious death, well befitting a warrior."

Sakurayama's Suicide

The lay monk Sakurayama Shirō was thinking that he would cross into Bitchū, or perhaps go forth to conquer Aki, since already he had taken half the province of Bingo. But when men came bearing tidings of the fall of Kasagi castle and Kusunoki's suicide, all the warriors of his following fled save twenty persons, kinsmen and retainers of many years' service.

In those days the Hōjō family were exceeding great, and their power extended over all the land. Wherefore Sakurayama Shirō thought in his heart:

"Not even a near kinsman can hide me, nor even less may I rely upon a stranger. Rather than fall into the hands of men who will expose my corpse. . . ."

Going forth to the foremost shrine of the province, he stabbed his dearly beloved son, who was in the eighth year of his life, and his faithful wife, in her twenty-seventh year. Then he lighted a fire on the altar, sliced open his belly, and suffered the flames to devour him. And his twenty-three kinsmen and retainers did the same.

Not unthinkingly did Sakurayama single out this altar from an abundance of places, whereon to kindle the flames that swallowed up his body. Sorrowing to see the decay of the shrine where he had bowed his head through many years, he had made a great vow to restore it; yet he had not the means for the performance of so sore a task, but only the resolve. It was solely to accomplish his vow that he had joined himself to the imperial plot.

Now perhaps the gods denied Sakurayama's right to be their servant, since the hour of his death approached while the vow remained unaccomplished. But so it was that he burned his body at that shrine, thinking with valorous heart:

"If we destroy this shrine by fire, the court and military can do no other than restore it. Though my body descend to the depths of hell, there will be nothing to regret if my vow is accomplished."

Good and evil alike are but different means of salvation, as we may learn from the vows of bodhisattvas come to earth to succor living beings. Assuredly Sakurayama believed deeply, "Through my crime in this life I shall meet the savior Maitreya in the life to come."

4

The Captives of Kasagi Are Put to Death or Sent into Exile; the Matter of Lord Fujifusa

NOW IT CAME TO THE SEASON when men busy themselves with the ending year, and for a time the Kantō turned aside from the matter of the Kasagi captives. But when in the new year the great nobles bowed themselves down in front of the throne, and the military took up the work of government again, then indeed to the capital there came two eastern commissioners, Kudō Jirō Saemon-no-jō and the lay monk of Shinano, Nikaidō Kōchin, who rendered judgments at Rokuhara according to the decisions of the Kantō, naming the names of men to be slain and laying down provinces of exile. According as their guilt was heavy or light, so they condemned the captives to exile or prison; the princely abbots of Mount Hiei and the southern capital, the great nobles, and even officers of the guards. But of Asuke Jirō Shigenori it was ordered, "Let his head be struck off at the Sixth Ward river bed."

Likewise the military laid hands upon the Madenokōji Great Counselor Lord Nobufusa, making him a prisoner for the offenses of his sons Fujifusa and Suefusa. Now in the hearing of Nobufusa, whose days were more than seventy years, men said that the emperor, the sacred master of a myriad chariots, would go forth in exile to a distant island. Likewise in his heart Nobufusa feared lest his sons be slain, and grieved that he too was become a prisoner.

"Alas!" he thought, "that I have lived so long merely to see and hear such distressing things as these!" And sadly he composed a verse, saying, "Why did I seek to make it longer—this life that brings only pain?"

Of the great nobles who had served the former emperor, the righteous even as the transgressors turned away from their duties to dwell in seclusion, or were bereft of their offices to taste the bitterness of want. Who knows whether it be illusion or reality, when men's fortunes alter in such wise? Truly times change and things pass away; grief follows upon joy, and joy upon grief. In a world of sorrow, what can happiness signify, or what can lamentation avail?

Lord Tomoyuki the Gen Middle Counselor was sent forth toward Kamakura in the keeping of the lay monk Sasaki Dōyo. Perhaps Tomoyuki knew that he would be struck down on the way, for at Ōsaka barrier he wrote, "Since I shall not come back, never again shall I journey past Ōsaka barrier." On crossing Seta Bridge he wrote, "Living but a short day in this world of dreams, I cross the Long Bridge of Seta."

Then truly at Kashiwabara in Ōmi an overseer came down upon them, pressing Sasaki Dōyo to fall upon this noble, since from the beginning it was ordained that he should perish on the way.

Dōyo went before His Lordship the Middle Counselor, saying:

"By some karma-tie from an earlier life, this lay monk was chosen before all others to be your guardian. As though devoid of mercy, I must say to you that your time is at hand; but indeed a person like myself is without power. Many days have I delayed, awaiting tidings of your pardon, but now urgently from the Kantō there has come a command to destroy you. Please console yourself by remembering that all things are the results of the deeds of previous lives."

So he spoke, pressing his sleeve to his face; and His Lordship the Middle Counselor likewise wiped away the tears that would not stay back, saying:

"Truly it is so. And truly I shall not forget what has happened of late, even in the next world.[1] As regards my death—it is said that the imperial lord of a myriad chariots must himself go away to a distant island, wherefore there can be no hope for lesser men. But indeed it would be impossible to repay you for such kindness as this, even were I to continue to live."

---

[1] He means that he will remember Sasaki's considerate behavior.

Chapter 4

So he spoke, and silently took up an inkstone and paper. When he had written a long letter, he said again to the lay monk:

"Please give it to a messenger to take to a certain lady."

As the day was ending they brought forth Tomoyuki's litter, put him inside, and bore him to a pine grove at the edge of the mountains south of the Tōkaidō Road. Then seated upright on an animal skin, Tomoyuki again took up the inkstone, and tranquilly composed a farewell verse in praise of the Buddhist Law.

> Forty-two years have I lived
> In the mortal sphere of nonaction.
> Heaven and earth disappear
> As now I bid farewell to life.

He wrote, "The nineteenth day of the sixth month," laid aside the brush, and sat erect with his hands folded together. And when Tago Rokurō Saemon-no-jō went around behind him, at once his noble head fell forward. It would be idle to call it pitiful!

With tears the lay monk made smoke of Tomoyuki's body and performed divers good works to pray for his enlightenment. In his heart he thought:

"How extremely regrettable it is! Morning and evening did this lord serve the former emperor zealously, even from the days when His Majesty was the princely vice-governor of the Dazaifu; day and night he labored faithfully, distinguishing himself beyond others. Wherefore by degrees his estate was raised, and the emperor loved him greatly. With what sorrow will His Majesty hear that Tomoyuki has perished in this manner!"

Now there was one Kogushi Gorō Hyōemon-no-jō, the guardian of the crossing of Ōhi-no-mikado and Abura-kōji.[2] This Kogushi seized the Tono Sign of the Law Ryōchū[3] on the twenty-first day of that month, and sent him to Rokuhara. And Nakatoki the governor of Echigo[4] spoke to Ryōchū through Saitō Jūrō Hyōe, saying:

"It is indeed strange and rash that one such as you devises against us, where even the master of all the realm could not prevail. Lawless beyond measure is a man who carries a map of Rokuhara to steal away the former emperor! Criminal beyond comparison is such a

---

[2] Two streets in the capital.
[3] A high-ranking Buddhist monk who was conspiring to rescue Go-Daigo.
[4] Hōjō Nakatoki, the Rokuhara chieftain of the north.

man! There is abundant testimony of your conspiracy. Describe your plotting fully, that we may report all to the Kantō."

The Sign of the Law answered him, saying:

" 'There is nothing under the vast heavens that is not the monarch's land, nor is there a person anywhere to the ends of the earth who is not of the monarch's folk.' Can there be anyone who does not grieve for the former emperor? Can anyone who is human rejoice in his distress? What is strange about planning to carry away the august person for His Majesty's sake? What is rash about consulting together to punish wickedness? Nor was I wrong to know of the emperor's desires from the start, or to go forth toward his abiding place at Kasagi. But just as I left the capital the castle's defenses fell, and the loyal warriors were defeated. Wherefore I talked to Lord Tomoyuki, received an imperial command from his hands, and sent it to the warriors of divers provinces. These are the things I have done."

So indeed he answered him.

Then at Rokuhara many opinions were spoken. The Shinano lay monk of the Nikaidō family came forward and said:

"Assuredly Ryōchū must die, for his guilt is beyond doubt. Yet would it not be well to ask about those that were in league with him, and likewise to send tidings of this matter to the Kantō?"

Nagai Uma-no-suke said:

"By all means let it be so. Such a serious thing as this ought indeed to be told to the Kantō."

And all agreed that it ought to be so. They delivered up the Sign of the Law to be imprisoned by Kaga-no-zenji, the guard of the Gojō-Kyōgoku crossing, and sent tidings thereof to the Kantō.

As for the Taira magistrate Narisuke, he was delivered up to the lay monk Kawagoe Enjū of Mikawa. Men said that he would go to Kamakura, but he perished on the way at Hayakawajiri in the province of Sagami. Likewise was it said that pardons had been granted the Chamberlain and Middle Counselor Lord Kin'akira and the chief of the police commissioners Lord Saneyo; yet watchfully the military held them in the hands of Hatano Kōzuke-no-suke Nobumichi and Sasaki Saburō Saemon-no-jō, without returning them to their homes.

Chapter 4

The Regulator and Great Counselor Lord Morokata was banished to the land of Shimōsa, where he was delivered into the hands of Chiba-no-suke. In no wise did Morokata grieve thereat, since long ago in his fifteenth year he had given himself over to Japanese and Chinese learning, indifferent to worldly honors. In his heart he thought:

"In the disturbances late in the years of T'ien-pao, Tu Shao-ling,[5] the poet of glorious T'ang, wrote of the bitterness of a strange place:

> The road passes beyond the Yen-yü River;
> My hair droops wearily.
> The sky drops down to the blue-green waves;
> A single fishing boat.

"Likewise a sage of poetry in Japan was sent away to the province of Oki, Ono no Takamura, who sang of his exile-heart to fisherfolk plying their lines, 'My boat rowed out over the vast sea, passing beyond many isles.' These did not lament the lamentable, for their minds understood the law of change; neither did they sorrow when sadness was present, for their hearts were acquainted with the inconstancy of fortune. Moreover indeed is it said, 'When the ruler is distressed the subject is shamed; when the ruler is shamed the subject dies.'[6] Even though my bones were to be pickled in brine or my body rent by carriages, there would be nothing to regret."

He did not mourn at all, but passed the days peacefully, amusing himself from time to time with composing verses. Earnestly he said that he longed to become a monk, since he had renounced the world of men entirely, and the Sagami lay monk agreed, saying, "There is no harm in it." Thus before his fortieth year he shaved off his raven hair to become a man of the holy order. But then suddenly he died of a disease in the early days of the Disturbance of Genkō—or so we have heard.

As for Suefusa, the secretary of the crown prince's household, he was exiled to the province of Hitachi, in the charge of the Naganuma governor of Suruga. The Middle Counselor Fujifusa was

---

[5] Tu Fu, who wandered through the provinces for many years after the rebellion of An Lu-shan in 755.
[6] From the *Shu ching* (*Book of History*).

exiled to the same province, where he was delivered into the hands of Oda Mimbu-no-tayū.

Although the sorrow of banishment was equally the sorrow of all, pitiful beyond others were the feelings of Lord Fujifusa! For in those days there was a lady in the Inner Princess's service, the fairest among women, called Lady Saemon-no-suke. On a certain occasion, the supreme highness journeyed forth to the Mansion of the Northern Hills (was it perhaps an autumn during the years of Genkyō?). There were dances to celebrate his coming, while below the hall musicians waved their sleeves and entertainers presented their songs, and the voices singing the quick songs were like gold and jade, clear and bright. Being commanded to play upon the lute, this Lady Saemon-no-suke played "The Waves of the Blue Sea." As a bush warbler in a flowering tree was the music of her playing, as a choked stream fretting against ice. Endlessly the strains obeyed the changing rhythm, now gay, now wrathful, now fresh, now weak. All together she struck the four strings with a sound of rending silk, and struck and struck again, until the clear voice of the melody was like a swallow soaring over a bridge, or a fish leaping in the water.[7]

When the Middle Counselor gazed upon this lady from a distance, secretly he began to love her with a passion which increased daily. But for three years he abode in silence, passing his nights in lamentation and his days in melancholy yearning, since there was no means whereby he might speak to her. Truly it was a very long time!

In the end did he not perhaps form a fleeting bond with her, unseen by the eyes of others? For as in a dream did those two exchange pillows on a certain night. Yet on the following night the supreme highness fled away in haste to Kasagi, and Fujifusa, putting away his high-crowned cap and robe for armor, made ready to accompany him.

In his heart Fujifusa thought:

"Who knows whether I shall ever see the lady again? How well

---

[7] Most of the description of the lady's playing is borrowed from Po Chü-i's famous "Song of the Lute" (*P'i-p'a hsing*).

Chapter 4

I remember her face on that night of dreams! If we could meet but once . . ."

So he thought, and went to the lady's dwelling place in the western wing. Those within said to him:

"Even now has Lady Saemon-no-suke gone forth to the Mansion of the Northern Hills, in answer to a summons from the Inner Princess."

The Middle Counselor cut off a lock of his hair and left it there with a poem, saying, "Since we have lived until a time when all is confused as tangled black hair, look upon this as a final memento."

When the lady returned she beheld the lock of hair and the verse. Reading she wept, and weeping she read, and sorely distressed she unrolled and rolled the paper a hundred and a thousand times, blotting out the writing with tears of passionate grief.

"Were I but to hear of his abiding place, assuredly would I wander forth to seek him," she said, "though it be to moors where tigers crouch, or to bays that whales approach."

Yet she could learn nothing of him; nor might she know whether they two would meet again in this world.

At last, unable to bear her affliction longer, she added a verse to the Middle Counselor's, saying, "Next to my body I place this precious message from my lord, a keepsake for the afterlife." And she threw herself into the depths of the Ōi River, with the lock of hair inside her sleeve. How pitiful it was! Even thus was the woman of T'ang, who sang, "For the sake of a day of my lord's favor, I destroy this body that would endure a hundred years." [8]

Now the Inspector and Great Counselor Lord Kintoshi was sent to the province of Kazusa, and the monk reformer Shōjun of the Southeast Cloister was sent to the province of Shimōsa. Men said that the monk reformer Shunga of Mine would go to the province of Tsushima; yet suddenly there was a change, and he was banished to the province of Nagato. And the Fourth Prince was banished to the province of Tajima, in the charge of Ōta Hōgan, the protector of the province.

[8] From a poem by Po Chü-i.

The Verse of the Seven-Year-Old Prince

The Ninth Imperial Prince remained in the capital in the care of Lord Nobuakira the Nakamikado Middle Counselor, since he was yet a child. Wise beyond ordinary men, this prince of seven years many times entreated Nobuakira sadly, saying:

"Why should I alone remain in the capital, when men say that the supreme highness must go away to the uninhabited land of Oki? Alas! That I too could be sent to a place close to the province where my lord will reside! Although we would not be together, at least I would receive tidings of him."

So he would speak, unable to hold back his tears. Again he said:

"My lord is shut up at Shirakawa, that I have heard of as a place close to the capital. Why cannot Nobuakira take me there?"

Restraining tears, Lord Nobuakira said to him:

"If it were but a place as close as the imperial palace, there would be no difficulty about my going with you. But Shirakawa is many hundreds of leagues distant, wherefore indeed the monk Nōin wrote, 'Though I left the capital in spring mists, autumn winds blow at Shirakawa barrier.' From this you may know that Shirakawa is a remote and impassable barrier."

Restraining his tears, the prince was silent for a time. But because he thought in his heart, "Nobuakira is unwilling to take me," soon he spoke a word:

"The Shirakawa barrier of the poem is in no wise akin to the Shirakawa River of the capital, but is a famous place of Ōshū. Wherefore, mindful of Nōin's verse, Tsumori no Kuninatsu has written of late: 'Since many days have passed, autumn winds indeed are blowing, even at the Shirakawa that reaches not to the barrier on the Eastern Road.' Moreover, when they were about to take away the dead cherry tree from the kickball field at the Saishōji Temple, Fujiwara no Ason Masatsune wrote, 'I did not know this was your final spring—O well-accustomed sight of Shirakawa's flowers!' These are both poems which prove that the places are different, though the names are the same. Very well! Henceforth I shall hold my thoughts in my heart without speech."

Chapter 4
101

So he spoke in resentment against Nobuakira.

Thereafter the prince left off entreating, nor did he speak of yearning after his father.

Now it came about that this prince was standing dispirited at Nobuakira's middle gate, when faintly from afar he heard a temple's evening bell. And he composed, "Passing the days in constant grief, how I long for my lord at the sound of the sunset bell!"

Because "the heart finds words," this was a poem such as a master might write. With compassionate thoughts, monks and laymen and men and women of the capital copied it onto paper handkerchiefs and fans, nor was there a person who did not interest himself in it, saying, "This is the poem of the seven-year-old prince."

The Matter of the First Prince and the Prince of the Myōhōin

The First Prince, the Central Affairs Minister Prince of the Blood, was sent away to Tosa-no-hata on the eighth day of the third month, with Sasaki Hōgan Tokinobu guarding him on the way. This prince had looked up to the sky and fallen down to the earth, praying, "Let me be slain and buried in the moss 'on Lung-men's moor,' [9] if only I may remain close to the capital." But then to his ears came the converse of warriors of his guard, who said, "The former sovereign[10] was sent away into exile yesterday." And he lost faith in prayer, mourning deeply. As a multitude of warriors drew near to the middle gate with his litter, he recited, weeping, "My streaming tears no weir restrains—O whither fares this drifting life?"

On the same day the Second Rank Prince of the Blood of the Myōhōin was banished to the province of Sanuki, with Nagai Takahiro guarding him on the way. This prince's heart was heavy within him, since it was noised abroad that yesterday the supreme highness had gone away into exile, and the First Prince today. Even as the grief of the two princes was the same, so the roads

---

[9] A reference to a poem by Po Chü-i which speaks of a burial at Lung-men.
[10] Go-Daigo.

that they followed were not different, yet each went forth alone. Sad indeed was the august heart of the prince of the Myōhōin!

In the beginning the princes went down separately from the capital, but on the evening of the eleventh day they arrived at Hyōgo, both the First Prince and the Prince of the Blood of the Myōhōin. The Prince of the Myōhōin sent a word to the First Prince, that would go down thence by boat to Tosa-no-hata, saying, "After seeking the same hostels until this time, how sad it is to hear of trackless waves!" And the First Prince replied, "Though from tomorrow I wander over trackless waves, let your heart go back and forth to be my guide."

Since it was to Shikoku that both of these princes were banished, they prayed in their hearts, "At least let us be in the same province, that bits of news to comfort our anguish may be brought by the tale-bearing wind."

Yet it was not to be. In a fragile boat the First Prince rowed out over the unsteady sea to Tosa-no-hata, where men built him a room beside the house of Arii Saburō Saemon-no-jō. Mountains rose up on the south of Hata, and the sea lay low on the north. Damp on his door the piny dew roused him to bitter tears, while on the beach the noisy waves stole from his eyes the path of dreams, that alone might lead to home. For a thousand days from the day of his coming, thrice daily he lighted ritual fires to pray for the former emperor's return to the capital—or did he perchance think to attain deliverance thereby?

Taking a different course, the Prince of the Myōhōin traveled by land to Fukiage in Kojima district in the province of Bizen, whence by ship he went forth to Takuma in Sanuki. This too was a place close to the shore, where poisonous fogs encompassed his august person about, and tainted sea vapors were an affliction upon him. Evening sounds of fishers' songs and oaten flutes, autumnal views of moonlit seas and cloud-bound hills—these and all else that touched his ears and eyes grieved his spirit and drew forth his tears.

Now at Kamakura it was ordained that the former emperor should be exiled to the land of Oki, according to the precedent of Shōkyū. Yet perhaps even the men of the Kantō feared to deal scornfully with an emperor, for they conspired together, saying,

"Let us place the eldest princely scion of Go-Fushimi-in upon the throne, that he may issue a decree to exile the former sovereign."

Likewise they said:

"This emperor must not hope to sit upon the throne again. He must enter into holy orders before he goes forth into exile."

And they came bearing clove-dyed garments of brown.

Yet the former sovereign said, "Not soon shall We lay aside worldly things." Nor would he put off the imperial dragon robes, but bathed himself daily in the morning, purified his transient dwelling, and worshiped the Grand Shrine of Ise at a place modeled after the altar in the Seiryōden.[11] Though there are not two suns in the heavens, there were two princes in the land; and the Hōjō were sore perplexed thereat. Truly it was because of a certain belief that the former emperor acted in this wise.

Chün Ming-chi Visits the Palace

In a former day, around the spring of the first year of Genkyō, there came to Japan from the land of Yüan a wise meditation teacher called Chün Ming-chi.[12] Although no Son of Heaven had ever before deigned to receive a foreign monk in audience, the emperor commanded this meditation teacher to enter the palace to speak of the Buddhist Law. For His Majesty was pleased to look with favor upon the Zen teachings, and sought knowledge of them in many places.

The great ministers and courtiers arranged their official robes; and carefully the controllers and scholars made ready to stand in attendance, that our court might not be shamed through lack of ceremony.

When the hour had grown late and tapers had been set up, the meditation teacher entered the palace. The supreme highness came into the Shishinden, where he advanced to the Jade Seat. The meditation teacher bowed low three times, burned a pinch of

---

[11] A building in the great palace enclosure; the emperor's usual place of residence.

[12] The author courteously refers to Chün Ming-chi by a title (meditation teacher) which has not yet been bestowed upon him.

incense, and wished the emperor eternal life. And thereupon the supreme highness spoke a word to this monk, saying:

"Now that the Harmonious Reverence has successfully crossed over mountains and seas, how will he cross over from this world to Nirvana?"

And the meditation teacher answered him:

"I shall cross over by means of the essential teachings of the Buddhist Law."

Again the emperor asked, saying:

"How is it that you have come here in this manner?"

And Chün Ming-chi answered:

"As all the stars of heaven bow to the north, so among mankind no water fails to pay court to the east."

When the talk of the Law was ended, the meditation teacher bowed and withdrew.

On the following day an imperial commissioner Lord Saneyo, the Chief of the Police Commissioners, came to confer the title of meditation teacher upon Chün Ming-chi. The meditation teacher said to Saneyo, "I have seen in your master's face that the dragon soaring on high will fall; yet assuredly will he sit upon the throne a second time."

Now indeed was the dragon fallen, since this ruler was seized by his military subjects. But by reason of the physiognomizing of the meditation teacher, the supreme highness believed trustingly that he would ascend the imperial throne again. Because of this, he insisted that he would not soon take holy orders.

The Grief of the Inner Princess

After it was made known that the former sovereign would be sent away to the province of Oki on the seventh day of the third month, the Inner Princess went forth to the imperial abiding place at Rokuhara in the darkness of night. When she drew near to the middle gate, the supreme highness came out to her, and she rolled up the blinds of her carriage. The emperor's heart was filled with thoughts of the time to come, when leaving the Inner Princess in the capital he would wander forth to listen to the waves at travel hostels and gaze at the moon on distant beaches. Likewise, when she imagined the supreme highness far off in a strange land, the Inner Princess was as one wandering without hope in an endless night. Had they sought for the sake of remembrance to say all that was in their minds, yet would unspoken words have remained at dawn, though the night had been a thousand autumn nights in one. Wherefore they uttered no words (since not by speech might the sadness of their hearts be made known), but bitterly wept until the sinking of the pitiless pale moon. Then, the dawn being near, the Inner Princess went back, saying tearfully, "My only thought —O cruel life, when will you end?" And grieving sorely she returned to the palace. How miserable was her heart, that feared never to meet him again!

The Former Sovereign Goes into Exile

On the seventh day of the third month, five hundred horsemen guarded the streets, commanded by Chiba-no-suke Sadatane, Oyama Gorō Saemon, and Sasaki Sado no Hōgan, the lay monk Dōyo. And they took the former sovereign away toward the land of Oki.

In company with His Majesty there went forth none but the Ichijō Chief Archivist Yukifusa and the Rokujō Lesser Marshal Tadaaki, and the Lady Sammi to minister to his needs. For the rest he was encompassed about by armored warriors carrying bows and arrows, who took the carriage creaking westward through the Seventh Ward and down Higashi-no-tōin, while the people of the capital stood lined up in byways: the high and the low and the men and the women, fearlessly filling the streets with their voices, saying:

"How astonishing it is, that like a subject the rightful lord of all the realm is sent away into exile! No longer will fortune look kindly upon the military!"

So like infants wailing for their mothers they cried and lamented. All who heard were grieved, and the very warriors of the guard wept into their armor-sleeves.

When the former emperor had passed beyond the post station of Sakurai, he came to Hachiman Shrine. He commanded them to put down his litter while he prayed to return again to the capital, thinking with deep faith, "Assuredly will this god cast protective eyes upon the Son of Heaven, though he be in a far-off place, for most miraculously has the great bodhisattva Hachiman sworn to bless the generations of emperors with peace and safety."

When he had crossed the Minato River, he beheld the capital of Fukuhara,[13] and thought with comforted heart:

"Taira no Kiyomori the Great Subject of the Grand Preceptorate held the four seas in the palm of his hand and moved the city of Heian to this low and damp place, yet soon he was destroyed. Heaven's punishment fell upon the man who arrogantly sought to set aside those above him."

Gazing ahead to Inano Moor, he passed beside the Bay of Suma, and thought again:

"When long ago Genji the grand marshal brought shame to the Lady of the Misty Moonlit Night, it was at this bay that he suffered in exile through the autumns of three years. How natural it was that he lamented those autumns away from home, when 'it seemed that the waves were coming all the way up to him, and his pillow grew wet with sudden tears'!"[14]

When he went forth from Akashi Bay in the morning mist, dimly the coast of Awaji fell away, and high the incoming waves rolled up, as he journeyed toward the windswept pine of Takasago-no-onoe. Passing beyond Sugisaka, he came into the province of Mimasaka (for truly he crossed over many mountains and rivers). Likewise he passed beyond Sara Mountain in the district of Kume.

Far distant among the clouds he beheld a snowy mountain peak, though indeed it was not the season of snow. He summoned a warrior of the guard, asking that he might know the name of that mountain.

"It is the Grand Mountain of Hōki," the man said.

Whereupon the emperor stopped the august litter for awhile, and with reverent heart recited holy words.

Quickly he set forth in the mornings, when "cock crows greeted

---

[13] Established by Taira no Kiyomori during his brief hegemony. It was soon abandoned.

[14] From the *Tale of Genji*.

Chapter 4

the moon, setting behind a thatched roof," and "horses' feet trampled the frost on wooden bridges." [15] Many were the days of his journeying, until on the thirteenth day of his going forth from the capital he came to the harbor of Mio in the land of Izumo. There a boat was made ready, and he waited for a fair wind to cross over the sea.

The Matter of Bingo no Saburō Takanori; the Fighting between Wu and Yüeh

In those days in the province of Bizen, there lived a person called Kojima Bingo no Saburō Takanori. When the supreme highness went to Kasagi, this Takanori thought to rally warriors for his sake. Yet before the thing was accomplished, he heard of Kasagi's fall and Kusunoki's suicide, and losing heart fell idle. When men said that the supreme highness would be sent away to the province of Oki, Takanori gathered together the loyal men of his family, saying:

"It is said, 'The resolute man and the man of virtue do not prize life at the expense of virtue; rather will they destroy their bodies to achieve virtue.' [16] So in days of old when the northern barbarians slew Duke I of Wei, his minister Hung Yen could not bear to look, but cut open his own belly and put Duke I's liver inside, perishing to requite his master's favors.[17] 'He who sees what is right and fails to act is lacking in manhood.' [18] Come! Let us go to a place where the emperor will pass by, that we may take him away, raise a mighty host, and leave names to posterity, though our corpses lie exposed on the battlefield."

And all his loyal kinsmen agreed.

Now these thought, "Let us await our opportunity at a steep place on the road." They lay down and hid themselves on the peak of Funasaka Mountain, on the border between Bizen and the land of Harima, waiting eagerly. But because the emperor's coming was exceedingly slow, they sent forth a man running to look upon the procession. And the man saw that the warriors of the guard did not

---
[15] Allusions to a poem by Wen T'ing-yün.
[16] From the *Analects*.
[17] The barbarians devoured all of Duke I except his liver.
[18] From the *Analects*.

follow the San'yōdō Road, but took the sovereign along the San'indō Road from Imashuku in Harima. Wherefore Takanori's preparations were set at naught.

Again Takanori said:

"If it be thus, let us wait at Sugisaka in the land of Mimasaka, where there are excellent deep mountains."

Going forth obliquely from Three Stones Mountain, they crossed the clouds of trackless hills to Sugisaka. But the people of Sugisaka said, "Already the supreme highness has entered Innoshō." And thereupon the kinsmen scattered, for they could do no other.

"In some way I should like to convey a thought to the august ears," said Takanori in his heart.

He put on coarse garments and stealthily drew near to the former sovereign to await an opportunity; yet in no wise might he meet him. And therefore he whittled away the bark from a great cherry tree in the courtyard of the emperor's lodging place, whereon he wrote a stanza of Chinese poetry in bold characters:

> Heaven will not destroy Kou-chien;
> A Fan Li is not lacking today.

Now although the warriors of the guard beheld this verse in the morning, they knew not the meaning of it.

"What is this, and who has written it?" they said.

When tidings thereof were borne to the august ears, quickly the supreme highness recognized the meaning, and a smile of pleasure appeared on his dragon countenance. But the warriors were without suspicion, since they did not know the meaning.

[*The author next relates a famous episode from Chinese history in order to explain Takanori's allusion.*]

Now let us speak of this poem's inner meaning.

Long ago in a different land there were two countries called Wu and Yüeh. The princes of those countries would not govern virtuously, but strove to rule over others by the strength of their arms. Wu sought to attack and seize Yüeh, and likewise Yüeh sought to destroy and annex Wu, and it was thus for many years. Ever did Wu and Yüeh strive together, winning and losing by turns, and

Chapter 4

their enmity descended from father to son, since it is shameful to live under the same heaven as the enemy of one's father.

When the days of Chou[19] were far gone, the prince of the country of Wu was called Fu-ch'ai King of Wu, and the prince of the country of Yüeh was called Kou-chien King of Yüeh. It came about that the king of Yüeh summoned his minister Fan Li and spoke a word to him, saying:

"Wu is the enemy of my ancestors. If without attacking Wu I pass the years in doing vain things, the men of the realm will make a mock of me; likewise I will shame the dead bodies of my ancestors beneath the moss of the grave. It is in my mind to gather together the country's warriors, cross over into the land of Wu, and destroy Fu-ch'ai King of Wu, that my ancestors may be avenged. Do you remain in this country for awhile to guard the national altars."

So he spoke, but Fan Li answered him with words of admonition, saying:

"I myself believe that it will in no wise be possible for Yüeh to destroy Wu now. If we count the warriors of the two countries, Wu possesses two hundred thousand horsemen, while Yüeh possesses but one hundred thousand. Truly one cannot contend against the large with the small. This is the first reason why we cannot destroy Wu. Likewise the season is inauspicious for chastisement, it being the beginning of spring. Spring and summer are seasons of yang, when loyalty is rewarded, but autumn and winter are seasons of yin, when evildoers are punished. This is the second reason why we cannot destroy Wu. Likewise that country is strong to which wise men render allegiance, and I have heard that there is a person called Wu Tzu-hsü among the subjects of Fu-ch'ai King of Wu, one who with deep wisdom wins the hearts of others, and with farsighted prudence admonishes the ruler. While he remains in the country of Wu, it will be impossible to destroy Wu. This is the third reason. The unicorn bears flesh on its horn and does not present a fierce aspect; the concealed dragon hibernates during the three months of winter to await the heavens of the winter solstice. If my lord would make Wu and Yüeh as one, if he would conquer

---

[19] The Chou dynasty (*ca.* 1027 B.C.–256 B.C.).

the Middle Kingdom and sit facing south upon the imperial throne, then he must hide his warriors awhile from men's sight, concealing his arms until the coming of an auspicious time."

The king of Yüeh was angered exceedingly thereat.

"It is said in the *Collected Ritual* that one may not remain under the same heaven with the enemy of one's father," he said. "Now that I have attained the years of a man, shall I not be humbled before others if I share the light of the sun and moon with Wu, instead of destroying her? Nor is there reason in your three impossibilities, that you speak to stop me when I would assemble warriors in this cause. Although it is true that Yüeh cannot stand against Wu if one wages war by counting soldiers, the outcome of a battle by no means depends upon numbers, but upon the fortunes of the occasion and the strategy of the generals. Wherefore many times have Wu and Yüeh exchanged victory and defeat in their struggles, as is well known to you. Why do you admonish me now, saying, 'With Yüeh's small strength it is impossible to fight a great enemy like Wu'? Your first objection shows that you are deficient in military strategy. Moreover if the outcome of a battle were to be determined by the season, who could fail to win, since all men know the seasons? Although you say that there must be no punishments in spring and summer, since they are seasons of yang, yet it was in the spring that King T'ang of Yin chastised Chieh, and it was in the spring that King Wu of Chou destroyed Chou.[20] Therefore it is said, 'An auspicious season is less to be desired than an advantageous location; and an advantageous location is less to be desired than accord among men.' Yet you admonish me, saying, 'It is not the season for inflicting punishment.' This, your second objection, is caused by lack of wisdom. Moreover, if I may not destroy Wu while Wu Tzu-hsü remains in the land, I cannot strike down the enemy of my ancestors, nor avenge the wrongs of those who have passed to the nether world. If I wait aimlessly for Wu Tzu-hsü's death, who can tell which of the two of us will die first? 'There is a fate that determines life and death.' The young may perish before the old. Shall I withhold my hand, not heeeding this truth? This, your third objection, is a mark of stupidity.

[20] The first Chou is a dynasty; the second is a ruler of another dynasty.

Chapter 4

"If I wait until another time to gather together warriors, assuredly will tidings thereof reach the country of Wu, and the king of Wu will come against me because of my delay. It will be useless to repent on that day. It is said, 'He who is beforehand controls others; he who is behindhand is controlled by others.' The matter is decided. I shall not stop even briefly." [21]

And early in the second month of the eleventh year of his reign, Kou-chien personally led his hundred thousand horsemen against the land of Wu.

Now hearing of this, Fu-ch'ai King of Wu said, "An enemy must not be despised merely because his numbers are few." He made speed to lead his two hundred thousand horsemen to a place called Fu-chiao-hsien, on the border between Wu and Yüeh, where he camped with K'uai-chi Mountain behind him and a mighty river in front. That he might destroy the enemy utterly, he revealed but thirty thousand of his horsemen, hiding the others deep in the mountains behind his camp; one hundred and seventy thousand riders.

Soon the king of Yüeh came to Fu-chiao-hsien. When he saw that the men of Wu were but twenty or thirty thousand riders waiting here and there, he despised them, thinking, "A strangely small force!" And he commanded his hundred thousand warriors to cross the river, all of them at once.

The warriors of Yüeh urged their horses into the water, lined them up close together, and crossed. The day was bitter cold, since it was early in the second month, and there was ice in the river. The hands of the warriors froze, so that they could not bend their bows; the horses stumbled in the snow, and could not easily go forward or backward. Yet the king of Yüeh advanced with attack-drums beating and warriors galloping forward neck by neck, each striving to be first.

From the beginning the warriors of Wu had thought to destroy the men of Yüeh by drawing them into a difficult position and surrounding them. Wherefore without fighting they retreated toward K'uai-chi Mountain from their camp at Fu-chiao-hsien, while for

---

[21] The arguments in these two paragraphs are reinforced with quotations from *Mencius*, the *Analects*, and the *Shih chi*.

thirty leagues the warriors of Yüeh pursued them, making their four lines into one and not looking to the right or left. Each for himself, they chased after them until their horses were without breath.

But at dusk the warriors of Wu came out of the mountains on every side, two hundred thousand riders, that according to their desire had drawn the enemy into a difficult place. They encompassed Kou-chien King of Yüeh round about, and attacked furiously.

The warriors and horses of Yüeh were weary, since they had galloped a long distance in that morning's fighting; moreover their numbers were inferior. And because of these things they drew together in one place when the great host of Wu surrounded them. If they advanced against the enemy in front, there were warriors waiting on steep cliffs with arrowheads ready; if they fell back seeking to break through behind, the enemy were many and they were weary. Assuredly they must taste defeat, who could neither advance nor retreat.

In destroying the strong and smashing the sharp, Kou-chien King of Yüeh surpassed the strength of Hsiang Yü and exceeded the bravery of Fan K'uai.[22] His men swept into the middle of the great host, crossing and circling to beat it down and drive it away. They came together in one place and scattered in three places; they forced back the enemy in four directions and smote them on eight sides; they changed from moment to moment, fighting a hundred times. Yet in the end the king of Yüeh was defeated, and more than seventy thousand of his riders were killed. Kou-chien went up onto K'uai-chi Mountain, unable to stand against the enemy. And when the warriors of Yüeh were numbered, but thirty thousand horsemen remained, whereof half were wounded and all had used up their arrows and broken their spear tips.

In the beginning the lords of neighboring countries had watched the fighting, not joining themselves to Wu nor yet to Yüeh, until they might behold which of the two would win a victory. But now in great numbers they galloped to the side of the king of Wu, and the warriors of Wu, strengthened mightily, became three hun-

---

[22] Famous heroes of Chinese history. Hsiang Yü was the adversary whom Kao Tsu had to overcome in order to found the Han dynasty. Fan K'uai was one of Kao Tsu's ministers. See note 2, Chapter Seven.

Chapter 4

dred thousand horsemen, who encompassed the four sides of K'uai-chi Mountain like thickly growing rice, hemp, bamboo, or reeds.

The king of Yüeh entered his tent and gathered together his warriors, saying:

"Through no remissness in battle have I encountered ill fortune and suffered encirclement. It is heaven that has destroyed me. On the morrow I shall break through the enemy siege in company with all of you, gallop down into the king of Wu's camp, and perish. In the life to come I shall seek my revenge!"

So he spoke, and piled up the sacred regalia of Yüeh to burn them. The king's beloved eldest son, a child of seven years known as Shih-yü, had followed him to that camp. The king called Shih-yü to him, saying:

"It would be pitiful if you were treated harshly by the enemy after my death, for you are very young. Likewise life would be insupportable to me if I were captured by the enemy and lived on after your death. I think it is best to send you before me, tranquilly resign myself, and perish in tomorrow's battle, that the love between parent and child, preserved beneath the moss of the grave, may continue in the life hereafter."

He wiped away his tears with his left sleeve, and with his right hand held out a sword, begging his son to kill himself.

But a minister called Ta-fu Chung, the king of Yüeh's General of the Left, came forward, saying:

"To remain alive and await one's fate is tedious and difficult; to hold death lightly and obey principle is direct and easy. Let my lord desist awhile from burning the sacred regalia of Yüeh, and from killing his eldest son. Although I am not clever, I believe that I can deceive the king of Wu, save my lord's life, and return home to raise another great army to wipe out this disgrace. In former days I was a friend of T'ai-tsai P'i, the supreme commander of Wu surrounding this mountain; and through long acquaintance I have come to know his heart. Truly he is a man of blind daring; yet his heart overflows with greed, and he gives no thought to evils to come. Likewise I have heard him speak of the actions of Fu-ch'ai King of Wu, wherefore I know that the king's wisdom is shallow and his planning is lacking in intelligence. Moreover, he is addicted to carnal delights and deficient in virtue. Both lord and minister will be easy to deceive.

"Assuredly it is because my lord would not heed the admonitions of Fan Li, that now Yüeh fights without success and is surrounded by Wu. I ask my lord to save the lives of the myriads of his defeated warriors by accepting my humble planning."

So he admonished him. And the king of Yüeh bowed before his reasoning, saying:

"Although it is said that the leader of a defeated army does not again devise strategy, henceforth I shall trust to Ta-fu Chung."

And he forbore to burn the sacred regalia, nor caused his eldest son to kill himself.

According to his master's command, Ta-fu Chung took off his helmet, furled his standard, and galloped down from K'uai-chi Mountain, calling out, "Having exhausted his strength, the king of Yüeh surrenders before the camp-gate of Wu." And the three hundred thousand warriors of Wu all raised a victory shout, crying, "Hurrah!"

Then Ta-fu Chung entered the camp of Wu, saying, "The insignificant minister Chung, an attendant of the great king's rear-vassal Kou-chien of Yüeh, respectfully acts as the under-servant of the supreme commander of Wu." He moved forward on his knees, touched his head to the ground, and laid down his body in front of T'ai-tsai P'i's abiding place.

T'ai-tsai P'i seated himself on a couch and granted an audience to Ta-fu Chung, ordering his curtain to be rolled up. Ta-fu Chung would not look at him directly, but hung his head tearfully, saying:

"The luck of my unworthy master Kou-chien is ended, his strength is exhausted, and he is surrounded by the warriors of Wu. Through the tongue of the insignificant minister Chung he asks that the king of Yüeh may forever render homage as the least of the subjects of Wu. I beg that you will forgive yesterday's trespasses and spare the king today. If the general will save Kou-chien from death, the country of Yüeh will be offered up to the king of Wu to be his land, and the sacred regalia of Yüeh will be presented to the general. Likewise the beautiful Hsi Shih will be given to the king for a handmaiden, to serve his pleasure throughout the day.

Chapter 4

If unsatisfied you demand the punishment of Kou-chien, then assuredly will I burn the sacred regalia of Yüeh, unite the hearts of my warriors, and come down against the camp of the king of Wu to perish.

"Because my friendship with the general has always been stronger than glue or lacquer, therefore I ask this favor of a lifetime. I beg the general to go in haste to the king of Wu to speak of these things, that while I live I may learn the fate of my petition."

So with passion he spoke, and again with lamenting, exhausting all the words in his mouth. And T'ai-tsai P'i looked kindly upon him, saying, "The affair will not be difficult. I shall surely prevail upon my lord to lessen the punishment of the king of Yüeh."

At once T'ai-tsai P'i went in to the king of Wu, where, drawing near, he spoke of these things. But the king was sorely vexed, saying:

"Not today alone have Wu and Yüeh called together warriors to dispute lands; yet now Kou-chien has lost his luck and become our prisoner. Is this not a gift to me from heaven? You are no loyal minister, if, knowing this, you would spare Kou-chien's life!"

T'ai-tsai P'i said again:

"Though I am as nothing, yet for a time has it been granted to me to bear the name of general. Going forth into battle against the warriors of Yüeh, I have destroyed a mighty host by my planning on the day of battle, and heedless of life have won a victory. Yet all these are but the labors of an honest heart, that for my lord's sake seeks to bring peace to the realm, unwilling to relax its loyalty even for a day, or to fail to put forth its uttermost exertions.

"Although one may say, 'The king of Yüeh has lost the battle and his strength is exhausted,' the warriors remaining to him are thirty thousand men, all mighty men of war and excellent riders. The warriors of Wu are many, but having won yesterday's battle they will be thinking of preserving their lives to enjoy rewards. The warriors of Yüeh are few, but their hearts are united; moreover, they know that they cannot escape. It is said that cornered rats bite cats, and fighting sparrows are not afraid of men. If Wu and Yüeh fight again, Wu will certainly be close to danger. If my lord spares the life of the king of Yüeh, giving him a little land to make him a vassal of Wu, then not only will my lord join together the two states of Wu and Yüeh, but likewise none among the states of Ch'i, Ch'u, Ch'in, and Chao will fail to render allegiance to him. This is the way to make the foundation deep and the base strong."

So he spoke, exhausting reason, whereupon with avaricious heart the king of Wu said to him, "If it be so, quickly raise the siege of K'uai-chi Mountain, and let Kou-chien be spared."

And T'ai-tsai P'i returned to speak of these things to Ta-fu Chung.

Rejoicing exceedingly, Ta-fu Chung galloped back to K'uai-chi Mountain to bear tidings thereof to the king of Yüeh. Color returned to the warriors' faces; and every man of them rejoiced, saying, "That we have escaped certain death is due solely to the resourceful mind of Ta-fu Chung."

Then the king of Yüeh raised a flag to surrender, and the king of Wu stopped the siege of K'uai-chi. The warriors of Wu returned to Wu, the warriors of Yüeh returned to Yüeh, and Kou-chien sent home his eldest son Shih-yü with Ta-fu Chung.

Kou-chien himself mounted up into an unpainted chariot of white wood drawn by a white horse.[23] With the seal-cord of Yüeh hung around his neck, he proclaimed himself the rear-vassal of Wu and surrendered at the enemy camp.

May it not be that there was fear in the heart of the king of Wu? For he refused to show his face to Kou-chien, saying, "'The man of honor does not draw near to a condemned person.'"[24] He gave Kou-chien over into the keeping of prison officers, with whom he journeyed toward the Ku-su castle of Wu, galloping from one post station to another in a single day. Of those who saw him, there was none whose sleeve was not wet with tears.

When Kou-chien came to Ku-su castle, they bound him with manacles and leg irons in a dirt prison. Though the nights grew light and the days grew dark, he beheld not the radiance of the sun

---

[23] White was a sign of mourning, or, as here, an admission of guilt.
[24] Lest he become prone to look upon capital punishment lightly. A quotation from the Kung-yang commentary to the *Spring and Autumn Annals*.

Chapter 4

or moon, but abode in darkness, ignorant of the passing of the seasons. Deep indeed was the dew on his tear-soaked floor!

Sojourning in the country of Yüeh, Fan Li heard of these things, and his wrath against Wu entered unbearably into the marrow of his bones. Distressfully he thought:

"Ah! In some way I must preserve the life of the king of Yüeh until the day of his return to our country, that together we may devise a means of wiping out the disgrace of K'uai-chi Mountain."

Disguising his person and altering his appearance, he put fish into a basket and went forth toward the land of Wu in the guise of a fishmonger. When he came before Ku-su castle, he asked concerning the abiding place of Kou-chien, and there was one who told him of it fully.

Then joyfully Fan Li went to his master's prison. Although the place was guarded very strictly, he threw a fish inside with a letter in its belly. And because it was a strange thing, Kou-chien opened the fish's belly and discovered the message:

> Hsi-po[25] was imprisoned at Yu-li
> And Chung-erh[26] fled to the Ti;
> Yet both of them became princes.
> Do not submit to the enemy by dying.

So indeed it was written.

Beholding the vigor of the brush and the style of the words, Kou-chien knew that it was from the hand of Fan Li. His heart was touched by Fan Li's spirit, and hope moved within his breast.

"In this world of sorrows Fan Li lives on, busying himself for my sake," he thought.

He began to cherish his life, of which he had complained, "It is misery to exist even for a day or a moment."

Now it came to pass that suddenly Fu-ch'ai King of Wu was afflicted by the disease called bladder stone, wherefore his body and mind were everlastingly tormented and distracted. Although shamans prayed for him, both the male and the female, there was no manifestation; although doctors treated him, he was not cured.

---

[25] A Chinese political figure of the Era of Warring States (403–221 B.C.). He later became a powerful ruler.
[26] See note 35, Chapter Two.

When his fleeting life was nearly gone, from a foreign land there came a physician of renown, saying:

"Although the august affliction is most severe, it is not beyond the healer's art. Without difficulty could I cure it, if some person would but taste a bladder stone to tell me whether it be salty, bitter, acid, pungent, or sweet."

Thereupon it was asked, "Let some person take this bladder stone into his mouth, that he may make known its taste." Yet the great ministers of state on the left and right looked at one another, none willing to taste it.

When tidings of these things came to Kou-chien, he said weeping:

"It is due entirely to the benevolent favor of the great king that I was not struck down after the encirclement of K'uai-chi, but have remained alive to await his pardon. When shall I discharge my obligation, if it be not now?"

In secret he obtained a bladder stone, put it into his mouth, and told the doctor of its taste. And the doctor applied a treatment that cured the king of Wu instantly.

Greatly pleased, the king of Wu thought, "Kou-chien is a kind man who has saved me from death. How can I refrain from thanking him?"

"Let the king of Yüeh go free from his prison," he commanded. "Let him receive again the country of Yüeh, and return to his own land."

Thereupon the king's minister, Wu Tzu-hsü, admonished him, saying:

"It is said that those who refuse heaven's gifts incur heaven's censure. It will be like setting a tiger free to roam over a thousand-league plain, if instead of taking the territory of Yüeh you send Kou-chien home. Disaster is close at hand!"

But the king of Wu, unwilling to listen, sent Kou-chien back to his own country.

When the king of Yüeh turned his carriage shafts toward the country of Yüeh, a vast multitude of frogs came leaping before the carriage. Kou-chien got down and bowed to them, saying, "From

Chapter 4

this auspicious omen I learn that brave warriors will come to my side, whereby the object of my desire will be accomplished."

So Kou-chien returned to the country of Yüeh, to his palace of former days, that in three years had become a desolate wilderness, where owls hooted from the branches of pine and cinnamon trees, foxes hid in thickets of orchids and chrysanthemums, and fallen leaves filled quiet unswept courtyards. And when it was known that the king had escaped death and come back, Fan Li came to the palace with Shih-yü.

Now the consort of the king of Yüeh was a beautiful woman called Hsi Shih. Because she was fair beyond others and beautiful beyond comparison, the king cherished her tenderly, never leaving her side even briefly. While the king was in the hands of Wu, this lady lived in hiding to escape calamity, but on hearing of his return she came back again to the rear palace.[27] Plain indeed were the marks of her three years of bitter grief! Strange indeed were her neglected hair and thin body, more touching than a pear blossom opening in the spring rain!

Quickly from here and there the great nobles and dignitaries assembled, with the hundred civil and military officials. Chariots galloped through the dust of the capital streets, the ornaments on caps and girdles tinkled in the moonlight at the Cinnabar Courtyard,[28] and again the palace apartments were as a blooming garden.

Just at that time there came a messenger from the country of Wu. Fearfully the king of Yüeh questioned him through Fan Li, saying, "Why are you come here?" And the messenger said:

"Throughout the breadth and compass of the realm has my master the king of Wu sought a fair woman, for he is a passionate man enamored of beauty, yet nowhere has he seen the equal of Hsi Shih's face. Now there was a promise made when the king of Yüeh emerged from the siege of K'uai-chi Mountain, that at once Hsi Shih would be sent to enter the rear palace of Wu. I am come to make her ready to be the queen of Wu."

---

[27] The women's quarters.
[28] A courtyard with red lacquered paving stones; by extension, the palace precincts in general.

Hearing him, the king of Yüeh said:

"By no means was it to preserve the state or my own person that I surrendered at the camp of Fu-ch'ai King of Wu, or saved my life by shamelessly tasting the bladder stone. It was solely for the sake of Hsi Shih that I did those things. I care nothing for ruling a great country if, parted from her during this life, I can but look forward to seeing her after death. I shall never send Hsi Shih to another country, even though I become Wu's captive again by violating the treaty between Wu and Yüeh."

With flowing tears Fan Li spoke to the king, saying:

"Truly it is grievous to me to consider the great sorrow my lord must feel. Yet by refusing to give up Hsi Shih he will violate the covenant between Wu and Yüeh, whereupon assuredly the king of Wu will send an army against him. Then not only will the country of Yüeh be annexed to Wu, but Hsi Shih will be taken away by force, and the national altars will be overthrown.

"Now the king of Wu is a lascivious man, one who lusts thirstily after pleasures of the flesh. If His Shih enters the rear palace of Wu, beyond doubt he will forget the government of the state, so excessive will be his enjoyment of her. When his country grows weak and his people become rebellious, it will be within my lord's power to win a victory swiftly by invading Wu with armed men. In this way his seed will flourish throughout the ages, and his conjugal vows will endure forever."

So with tears he spoke, and again with admonitions, exhausting reason, until submissively the king of Yüeh commanded Hsi Shih to be sent away to the country of Wu.

Hsi Shih went forth from the palace she had not thought to leave for a time as short as a small deer's horns, parting from her beloved husband, the king of Yüeh, and sadly leaving the young Shih-yü, with no words in her mouth. Never on that unaccustomed journey did her tears of sorrow cease to flow, nor ever were her two sleeves dried.

Likewise the king of Yüeh, cast down by a great grief, thought in his heart that they would not meet again. As he gazed afar toward the skies of her dwelling place, his tears were like the rain that falls from clouds drifting slowly over the mountains at dusk. Retiring alone to an empty couch, he lay propped up on the pillow, longing to meet her even in a dream. Yet they could not be united, though the image of her face was clear before him. How natural it was that he should grieve despairingly!

Now Hsi Shih was the most beautiful woman of the realm, one who in her fair raiment would ravish a lord's eyes with a hundred delights, though she smiled but once, for the flowers of the earth were as nothing before her. When she but gazed in silence, by a thousand graceful poses she would melt a man's heart, causing the moon to pale suddenly as though hidden behind a cloud. And therefore she seduced the heart of the king of Wu from the day when first she entered the palace to serve at his side. By night the king turned away his face from the government of the realm, and nightlong gave himself to carnal joys; by day he heeded not the peril of the state, but thought only of drinking and banqueting throughout the day. That he might divert himself while feasting with Hsi Shih, he built the cloud-piercing Golden Chamber, where from his pillow he looked down upon mountains and rivers for three hundred leagues in every direction. Were there a spring day without flowers, he would command men to bury musk bags to scent the courtiers' shoes on the carriage-roads; were there a summer night without a moon, he would command men to gather fireflies, that even as lamps they might illumine the royal villa. Day after day without pause his wantonness continued, bringing decline above and ruin below, yet slavishly the fawning ministers refrained from admonition. And in all things the king of Wu was as though in an intoxicated oblivion.

Beholding these things, Wu Tzu-hsü spoke words of reproof, saying:

"Does not my lord know that King Chou of Yin brought disorders upon the realm through being bewitched by Chieh Fei, and King Yü of Chou destroyed his state through love of Pao Szu? [29] Yet my lord's infatuation with Hsi Shih exceeds these precedents. The ruin of the state is not far distant. I implore my lord to put away Hsi Shih."

---

[29] Two well-known episodes in early Chinese history. For the story of Pao Szu, see note 8, Chapter Ten.

So with words of admonition he braved the royal countenance; yet the king of Wu heeded him not.

Now it came about that the king of Wu, having summoned his courtiers to a banquet for Hsi Shih, was drinking to drunkenness among the flowers of the South Apartment when with dignified mien Wu Tzu-hsü made his appearance. As Wu Tzu-hsü prepared to ascend the jade stairway strewn with jewels and inlaid with gold, he raised his skirts high, as though to cross water. When they asked him about it (since it was very strange), he said:

"Not distant is the time when this Ku-su Tower will become a place of thick grasses and heavy dews, destroyed by the king of Yüeh. If I live to visit the ruins of this my dwelling place, surely the dew from my sleeves will be thick and deep. It is in anticipation of a future autumn[30] that I train myself to lift my skirts."

So indeed he spoke.

Perhaps Wu Tzu-hsü thought in his heart:

"Although a loyal minister offers reproofs, the king will not heed them. Rather than admonish excessively, I will try to turn peril aside by killing myself."

For on a certain occasion he entered bearing his Blue Snake Sword, newly come from the whetstone. And he drew it out and leaned on it in the presence of the king, saying:

"To expel evil and drive away enemies have I sharpened this sword, yet when I enquire closely into the source of the nation's decline, all proceeds from Hsi Shih. There can be no greater enemy than she. I beg of you to cut off Hsi Shih's head in order to avert the danger to the national altars."

So he spoke, grinding his teeth where he stood.

The king of Wu, mightily enraged, thought to kill Wu Tzu-hsü, since a master of men does not scruple to be unrighteous when honest counsels offend his ears. Yet Wu Tzu-hsü uttered no lamentations, but said:

"It is the duty of a subject to strive, remonstrate, and die for principle. I rejoice in the midst of regret that I am to die by the hand of the great king instead of by the hand of a warrior of Yüeh. But that my lord kills me through anger against my loyal admoni-

---

[30] The season of melancholy.

Chapter 4

tions—this indeed is a sign that heaven has forsaken him. Not three years will pass before my lord is conquered and killed by the king of Yüeh.

"When my head is struck off, I ask to have my two eyes plucked out and hung up on the East Gate of Wu. Before those eyes wither, they will smile with pleasure to see my lord going toward his execution, defeated by Kou-chien."

So he spoke, and the king's anger waxed stronger, so that he indeed put Wu Tzu-hsü to death, plucked out his eyes, and hung them up on the flag-spear at the East Gate of Wu.

Thereafter no minister offered admonitions, though the king's deeds were exceedingly wicked. The assembled officials held their peace; the myriad people spoke with their eyes alone.

Hearing of these things, Fan Li rejoiced, saying, "The hour is come." And he led two hundred thousand horsemen against the country of Wu.

Just at that time Fu-ch'ai King of Wu had gone forth toward the country of Chin, since men had come saying that Chin would rise against Wu, wherefore there were no warriors left behind to defend Wu. Fan Li took back Hsi Shih, sent her home to the palace of the king of Yüeh, and burned down the Ku-su Tower. Likewise the two countries of Ch'i and Ch'u made an agreement with the king of Yüeh, whereby they sent three hundred thousand horsemen to strengthen Fan Li's arms.

Hearing of these things, the king of Wu left off fighting with the country of Chin and went back to contend against Yüeh. Yet in front of him the waiting warriors of Yüeh, Ch'i and Ch'u were like clouds or mist, while in the rear a powerful enemy came after him, the state of Chin pressing its victory. In no wise might he flee, when these strong enemies encompassed him before and behind.

For three days and nights the king of Wu fought fiercely, but unceasingly Fan Li smote him with fresh warriors, until but a hundred of the thirty thousand men of Wu remained unslain.

When the king of Wu had personally fought against the enemy thirty-two times, he broke through the encirclement in the night, and with sixty-seven horsemen climbed up to Ku-su Mountain, whence he sent a messenger to the king of Yüeh, saying:

"When the great king suffered affliction at K'uai-chi Mountain, his minister Fu-ch'ai stretched forth his hand to help him. I ask that from this time on I may live beneath the jade foot of the great king as a rear-vassal of Yüeh. If my lord has not forgotten the obligation of K'uai-chi, let him spare his minister's life today."

So with humble words and proper decorum he begged to surrender.

Hearing his words, the king of Yüeh was moved to pity, thinking in his heart, "Even as I suffered in a bygone time, so another grieves today." Nor could he endure to kill the king of Wu, but resolved to let him live.

But hearing these things, Fan Li went before the king and spoke all that was in his heart freely, saying:

" 'When one hews an ax handle, the model is not far away.' [31] Although heaven delivered Yüeh into the hands of Wu at K'uai-chi, the king of Wu would not accept that gift, wherefore quickly he encountered calamity. Now that heaven delivers Wu to Yüeh, Yüeh likewise will encounter calamity if the gift is not accepted. For twenty-one years my lord and I have striven mightily to overcome Wu. Would it not be regrettable to cast away the fruit of our labors in a single morning? The loyal minister does not follow when his lord's actions are unrighteous."

Fan Li personally beat the attack-drums even before the king of Wu's messenger went back. He gathered together his warriors, captured the king of Wu alive, and brought him before the camp of Yüeh.

Then passing through the East Gate of Wu with his hands bound behind him, the king of Wu beheld the two eyes that he had put up on the flag-spear, when he had struck down the loyal minister Wu Tzu-hsü because of his admonitions. Nor after three years were those eyes withered, but the pupils were opened wide, and it was as though they laughed to see him. Perhaps the king of Wu felt shame before them, for he drew his sleeve in front of his face and passed with lowered head. Of the myriads of warriors who watched, not one but shed tears.

[31] One models it after the ax in one's hand. An allusion to a poem in the *Book of Odes*.

Chapter 4

Then the king of Wu was given over into the hands of jailers, who cut off his head at the foot of K'uai-chi Mountain. Wherefore since ancient times have men had the saying, "to wipe out K'uai-chi shame."

Thereafter the king of Yüeh took the land of Wu for his own. Likewise he subdued Chin, Ch'u, Ch'i, and Ch'in, and became the head of the league of military rulers.[32] He sought to reward Fan Li's merit by making him the lord of a myriad households, but Fan Li refused, saying:

"He who has a great name cannot endure for long. It is following the way of heaven to retire after achieving success and winning fame."

Thereafter Fan Li changed his name to T'ao Chu-kung and shut himself away from the world in a place called Five Lakes. Fishing, he sheltered on reedy banks, where he kept off the snow with half a straw coat; reciting poems, he floated below scarlet maple leaves, carrying autumn in his solitary boat. He watched the moon moving across the vast heavens behind the red evening dust, and watching became a white-headed old man.

[End of episode]

Truly all these things were in Takanori's mind when, drawing a comparison, he wrote a thousand thoughts in a single verse, and secretly made them known to the supreme highness.

When the former sovereign had sojourned for some ten days at Mio harbor in Izumo, his boatmen cast off their lines to depart in a fair wind, and he rowed away toward the distant clouds, encompassed about on every side by three hundred war boats.

Now where the broad sea lay peaceful, there in the northwest the sun sank below the waves; where the cloud-veiled mountains rose far away, there in the southeast the moon climbed up in the sky. Among the willows of an island shore a single lamp flickered, as of a fishing boat returning home. By night the sovereign's boat was moored in the vapors of reedy shores; by day its sail was spread in the breeze from Matsue. Many days he journeyed over the wave

---

[32] Formed in 681 B.C. for mutual protection during the warfare between petty feudal states which followed the decline of the Chou dynasty. It lasted for more than two hundred years.

paths, until at last the boat came to the land of Oki, even on the twenty-sixth day of his going forth from the capital. And he took up his abode in a house of unpeeled logs at a place called Kofu-no-shima, made ready by Sasaki Oki no Hōgan Sadakiyo.

Of personal attendants to serve His Majesty, there were but the Rokujō Lesser Marshal Tadaaki and the Chief Archivist and Grandee Yukifusa; and of ladies in waiting there was but Lady Sammi. No more did the supreme highness behold the stately apartments and splendid chambers of a former day. His eyes met rafters of bamboo, with knots clustering together thick as manifold sorrows, and hedges of pine-brush clinging together close as falling tears. Where the voice of the palace watchman had cried the dawn, the shouts of warrior guards pressed hard upon his pillow, not suffering him to slumber even briefly in the imperial bed-chamber. But though no morning audiences awaited the opening of the Lespedeza Room,[33] never did he neglect his dawn prayers or fail to worship the pole star, not though he had dreamed in the night of Wu-shan's clouds and rain.[34]

What sort of year was this year, when blameless officials shed tears of sorrow beneath the moon of exile, and the first person under heaven changed his estate to grieve amid the winds of a strange land! Never since the beginning of heaven and earth had such extraordinary things been heard of! Was there any man for whose sake the sun and moon could shine, hanging in the heavens unashamed of their brightness? These were things that would bring sadness even to insentient plants and trees, or make flowers forget to open.

[33] A chamber in the Seiryōden.
[34] A Chinese euphemism for love-making.

5

The Enthronement of the Highness of the Jimyōin

THE FIRST PRINCELY SON of Go-Fushimi-in ascended the imperial throne in the nineteenth year of his life, on the twenty-second day of the third month of the second year of Genkō. (His mother was the daughter of Kimpira the Chikurin'in Great Subject of the Left, she who was later called Kōgimon'in.) After purifying himself at the Kamo River on the twenty-eighth day of the tenth month, this emperor offered up new rice to the gods on the thirteenth day of the eleventh month.[1] The regent was Lord Fuyunori, the Takatsukasa Great Subject of the Left, and the chief of the police commissioners was Lord Sukena, the Hino Middle Counselor. Whatsoever the men of his following desired, instantly was it granted them, so that their gateways were as market places and their halls as gardens.

Son'in was named to be head of the Tendai faith, he who was called the Kajii Canonical Prince of the Blood of Second Rank. Likewise he was named to be abbot of the Enryakuji and Nashimoto,[2] where with solemnity he celebrated the hall-worshiping rites[3] before the assembled multitudes of his monks. Hōshu, the Omuro Canonical Prince of the Blood of Second Rank, was named to be abbot of the Ninnaji, where he gave his heart to spreading the teachings of the Eastern Temple, and to offering up prayers for the sake

---

[1] Two rituals traditionally performed by a new emperor.
[2] A popular name for the Kajii Ennyuin Cloister in Yamashiro, a branch of the Enryakuji.
[3] A ceremony held when the new head of a large temple entered it officially for the first time.

of the throne, that it might be established forevermore. These were both sons of Go-Fushimi-in and brothers of the new emperor.

Lord Nobufusa Serves Two Masters

For many years the Madenokōji Great Counselor Nobufusa had served the former sovereign as a favored minister. Moreover, Nobufusa's sons Fujifusa and Suefusa had been taken up at Kasagi and sent away into exile, wherefore in no wise did it seem that this lord might be guiltless. But because Nobufusa was a man of excellent talents, the men of the Kantō forgave him his transgressions, making an exception for his sake, and praying the new emperor to bring him into the court. And the emperor sent Lord Sukeakira the Hino Middle Counselor to summon him.

Lord Nobufusa spoke to the imperial messenger, saying:

"Though unworthy, through many years of labor I obtained favor in His Majesty's sight, advancing in office and emoluments. Yet I have defiled the name of counselor of state. For it is said: 'The right conduct in serving a master is to brave his august countenance when one finds him at fault, and to admonish and strive with him according to the Way. If one admonishes three times unheeded, one must sacrifice oneself and retire. To be possessed of the loyalty that corrects faults and not to be a favor-currying subordinate: this is the duty of the honest minister. To see something that requires admonition and not to admonish: this is called holding an empty position; to see that one ought to retire and not to retire: this is called attachment to favor. Those who are attached to favor and those who hold empty positions are a state's treacherous men.' [4] So it is said. Now for unrighteous deeds is His Majesty put to shame by his military subjects; yet I uttered no word of admonition. Though I knew nothing of his planning, how will the men of the realm say that I am not at fault?

"Moreover, for whose sake shall I seek prosperity, since my two eldest sons are sentenced to banishment, and I myself am a man of more than seventy years? Nor can my heart fail to feel shame for

---

[4] A quotation from a well-known commentary on the *Classic of Filial Piety* (*Hsiao ching*).

past mistakes. Far better would it be to starve like Po-i at Shouyang[5] than to serve two masters, bearing shame in my bosom when I am thin and old."

When he spoke thus with flowing tears, Lord Sukeakira was silent for a time, powerless to hold back tears of sympathy. Yet soon Sukeakira said to Nobufusa:

"It is said, 'By no means does the loyal minister choose his ruler. He perceives that by serving he can govern the state well; that is all.' Therefore Po-li Hsi served Duke Mu of Ch'in, maintaining his rule for many years; and Kuan I-wu assisted Duke Huan of Ch'i, nine times causing the lords to swear allegiance. Men say that Duke Huan spoke no word of the crime of shooting his buckle, while all looked upon the shame of being sold for hides as something that could not be helped.[6]

"Now since the military look thus kindly upon you, may there not be an order that will fetch home your two sons from their exile? Indeed what did it avail that Po-i and Shu-ch'i starved? Because Hsü Yu and Ch'ao Fu fled, they were of no use.[7] Which is the way of merit: to hide away and cover the name of one's family in darkness, or to keep alive the memory of one's ancestors by serving the

---

[5] According to Chinese tradition, Po-i and his brother Shu-ch'i starved to death in the mountains of Shansi in the twelfth century B.C., rather than render allegiance to a new dynasty.

[6] Po-li Hsi, an official in the service of the Duke of Yü in the seventh century B.C., fled from Yü after its destruction by Chin and was later captured by Ch'u. Duke Mu of Ch'in, aware of his exceptional abilities, ransomed him from Ch'u, offering only five rams' skins in order to conceal his true value. At first Po-li refused to serve a new master, but he finally agreed to become a minister of state, and served with great distinction. Kuan I-wu was a minister of Ch'i under Duke Li. When Duke Li died, Kuan and Shao Hu, another minister, fled to Lu with Li's son Ch'iu to escape the tyranny of the new lord, Ch'iu's uncle. Later, upon the death of the uncle, Ch'iu's brother Huan, who had also fled, succeeded in returning to Ch'i in advance of Ch'iu, made himself duke, and forced the Duke of Lu to execute Ch'iu. Kuan ultimately returned to Ch'i, became Huan's prime minister, and raised Huan to the position of head of the league of military rulers (see note 32, Chapter Four). The "crime of shooting his buckle" occurred during a battle between supporters of the two brothers, when an arrow shot by Kuan hit the clasp of Huan's girdle.

[7] Hsü Yu, a recluse during the reign of the mythical Chinese Emperor Yao, is supposed to have washed his ears to cleanse them of defilement after having been offered an official appointment by Yao. Ch'ao Fu shared his sentiments so completely that he refused to permit his calves to drink from the stream in which Hsü Yu had washed his ears.

emperor? To consort with birds and animals as though they were no different than ourselves is something Confucius will not accept."

When Lord Sukeakira reproved him thus, exhausting his logic, Lord Nobufusa looked submissively upon him. On the back of the imperial message he wrote down some lines of Ts'ao Tzu-chien of Wei: "He who ends his life for a mistake remembers not the words of the sage, 'Correct the morning's faults by night'; he who lives in disgrace heeds not the poet's dart, 'Has he no shame, that lingers on?' " Yet, saying, "You are quite right," in the end he agreed that he would come to serve.

The Extinction of the New Perpetual Lamp of the Central Hall

Around that time there were many extraordinary and marvelous happenings in the capital and the countryside. At the Mountain Gate a pair of turtledoves came flying into the image chamber of the Central Hall, beat their wings in the oil cup of the new perpetual lamp, and quickly put out the flame. Then losing their way in the darkness of the hall, those doves came to rest on the Buddha-altar. And from a heavy beam a weasel, of a color as though vermilion had been poured over his body, came running out, bit them to death, and disappeared.

Now this perpetual lamp was a lamp that the former sovereign[8] himself put up when he visited the Mountain Gate. Even as Kammu Tenno put up the lamp in ancient days, so with his own hands His Majesty made ready a bundle of a hundred and twenty wicks, poured oil in the silver oil cup, and turned the wick. It was not fitting that this lamp should ever be extinguished, since he put it there to be a prayer for the everlasting life of the imperial line, thinking in his heart of the bright light of the Buddhist Law illumining the darkness of the multitudes in the six existences.[9] How strange it was that turtledoves came flying to extinguish it! It was also strange that those birds were killed by a weasel.

[8] Go-Daigo.
[9] The worlds of hells, hungry ghosts, animals, malevolent nature spirits, human existence, and divine existence.

The Sagami Lay Monk Amuses Himself with Field Music; the Matter of the Dog Fights

Around that time in the capital, men made much of the dance called field music,[10] and high or low there was none that did not seek after it eagerly. Hearing of this the Sagami lay monk called down the New Troupe and the Original Troupe to Kamakura, where he amused himself with them day and night and morning and evening, with no other thought in his mind. Zealously he gave over a dancer to each of his great captains, that they might embellish their costumes, so that it was said, "This is Lord Such and Such's dancer," and "That is Lord Thus and So's dancer"; and the lords bestowed gold and silver and precious stones upon them, and fine garments of damask and brocade. When those dancers danced at a feast, the Sagami lay monk and all his kinsmen and captains took off their robes and trousers and tossed them out, none willing to be outdone.[11] Most like to a mountain were the garments that they piled up together, nor can any man say how many thousands and tens of thousands they spent.

Now drinking on a certain night, the Sagami lay monk grew merry with wine, so that he rose up and danced. (His dancing was not to entertain the young men, nor yet to inspire *farceurs* with clever words, but was only the vain dancing of a drunken old lay monk of more than forty years.) Suddenly from nowhere there came more than ten field music dancers of the New and Original Troupes, who lined up in the room dancing and singing with surpassing skill. And soon these changed their song, chanting, "How we long to see the unnatural star of the Tennōji Temple!"

There was a lady in waiting who looked through a crack in the sliding door, irresistibly diverted by the sound of those voices. And

---

[10] The dance form known as field music (*dengaku*) appears to have arisen in the Heian period (794–1185), probably as a planting ritual performed in the fields, and to have moved gradually to the precincts of Shinto shrines. By this time, it had become a theatrical entertainment for city dwellers and members of the upper classes, performed chiefly by men known as field music teachers of the Law (*dengaku hōshi*) because they shaved their heads like monks. It was the direct antecedent of the Nō drama.

[11] This was done to applaud and reward the performers.

she saw that of those who had seemed to be dancers of the New and Original Troupes, not one was a human being, but all were specters of divers kinds and shapes who had changed themselves into men. Some among them had curved beaks like kites, while the bodies of others were winged and bore the semblance of wandering monks.

Sorely affrighted, the lady sent a man running to the castle lay monk,[12] who made haste to go toward that room, sword in hand. But when the lay monk's footsteps advanced violently through the middle gate, the phantoms vanished as though wiped out. And all the while the Sagami lay monk slept drunkenly, knowing nothing of it.

When the castle lay monk called for lamps to be lit that he might look upon the room, he beheld a multitude of bird and animal tracks on the soiled floor mats, as though goblins had assuredly assembled there. He stood with eyes glaring, yet nothing dared to obstruct his sight. And when a little time had passed, the Sagami lay monk awoke and rose as one dazed, knowing nothing at all.

Afterward these things were made known to Nakanori the Lesser Assistant of the Ministry of Justice, a Confucian scholar of the Southern House of the Fujiwara.

"It is said that an evil star descends to bring calamity when the realm is soon to be disturbed," said Nakanori. "It is most strange that those spirits sang of an unnatural star at the Tennōji, the oldest of the sacred places of Buddhism, where Shōtoku Taishi himself laid down the *Forecast of the Future of Japan*.[13] Will not disorders come upon the land from that temple, and a deadly destruction strike down the state? Ah! How desirable it is for the emperor to cultivate virtue and the military to walk in ways of righteousness, that these strange portents may become as nothing!"

So he spoke, and in the end the world became as he predicted. Marvelous indeed was the great learning by means of which Nakanori prophesied evil visitations of the future!

The heart of the Sagami lay monk was not affrighted because of these apparitions, but more and more his fancy inclined toward

---

[12] Takatoki's maternal grandfather, Adachi Tokiaki.
[13] A book of prophecy said to have been deposited in the Tennōji by this famous regent-prince (574–622), who was the temple's founder.

curious things. It came to pass on a certain occasion, that dogs gathered together in his courtyard to fight; and this lay monk's enjoyment of their battle penetrated to the very marrow of his bones, so that he sent out orders to the provinces, commanding dogs to be paid in for taxes, or asking for gifts of dogs from powerful families of high rank and people of elevated status. Each of the provincial protectors and governors raised up ten or twenty beasts to take to Kamakura; likewise, the Hōjō kinsmen and great vassals of divers places did the same. The expense thereof was exceeding great, since they fed them with fishes and birds and tethered their necks with chains overlaid in gold and silver. On days when those dogs were traveling in their litters, hurrying wayfarers dismounted from their horses to kneel before them, and villagers working in the fields were seized to carry them on their shoulders. Truly they were highly esteemed! Kamakura was filled up with strange animals surfeited with meat and dressed in brocades, as many as four or five thousand.

Twelve days of every month were named to be days of dog-fighting, when the Hōjō kinsmen and great lords sat in the halls and courtyards to watch, with the hereditary retainers and other vassals. Two armies of dogs would be set free, of one hundred or two hundred each, who wildly chased after one another, sprang together, and rolled over and over, making the heavens echo and the earth tremble with the sound of their fighting. Frivolous persons thought, "How amusing they are! It is exactly as though the outcome of a battle were being decided." But wise men lamented, "How disgusting! It is as though they fought over corpses in a field."

Although the combatants were dogs and not men, yet when one thinks of comparisons, assuredly these were omens of human warfare and death. How shameless was such behavior!

How Tokimasa Shut Himself Up at Enoshima to Pray

Now the realm having fallen beneath the sway of military houses in the days of the latter end of the Buddhist Law, the dominion thereof passed more than once between Minamoto and Taira. Those that were raised up perished in a single generation, or were struck down before the ending of a lifetime, for it is the way of heaven to diminish what is full. Yet for nine generations the family of the Sagami lay monk protected the realm. And this was the reason thereof:

Long ago when the government at Kamakura began, Hōjō Shirō Tokimasa shut himself up at Enoshima to pray for his descendants, that they might be blessed forever. Suddenly on the night of the twenty-first day there appeared before him a fair and stately lady, dressed in a robe lined in willow green over a red skirt, who spoke to Tokimasa, saying:

"In an earlier life you were a monk of Hakone Shrine, who achieved rebirth on this earth by meritoriously copying out sixty-six copies of the *Lotus Sutra* to present to sacred places in the sixty-six provinces. Long will your descendants rule over Japan, and mighty will their prospering be, yet if they be not righteous they will not endure for more than seven generations. If you are doubtful of these my words, look upon the sacred places in the provinces where the sutras were laid down."

So she spoke, and turned away without waiting for an answer.

All at once that same stately lady became a great snake two hundred feet long, which entered into the sea. And when Tokimasa gazed upon the place where the snake had passed, he saw three large fallen scales, that he took up to be a crest for his banner, rejoicing in the granting of his petition. This is the present three-scale crest of the Hōjō family.

Because of this revelation from Benzaiten,[14] Tokimasa sent forth men to the sacred places of the provinces, that they might look upon the places where the *Lotus Sutras* had been presented. And they saw that the lay name Tokimasa had been changed into a monk's name; for on the dedicatory cylinders was written, "The Great Teacher of the Law Jisei." [15] How strange it was!

Thus was it owing to the divine favor of Enoshima Benzaiten, and to the effect of a past good cause, that still the Sagami lay monk ruled the realm after more than seven generations. But as regards the strange doings of Takatoki, may it not be that the time was

---

[14] The patron goddess of Enoshima Island.
[15] Jisei is the Sino-Japanese reading for the characters used in the Japanese name Tokimasa. It was usual for monks to assume Sino-Japanese names.

Chapter 5

come for the Hōjō to be cut off? For already the seventh generation was past, and the ninth generation was reached.

The Prince of the Great Pagoda Flees to Kumano

The Prince of the Great Pagoda had hid himself for a time at the Hannyaji Temple in the southern capital, thinking to hear tidings of Kasagi castle. When men came saying that Kasagi was fallen and the supreme highness was made a prisoner, the prince's peril was even as that of one treading on a tiger's tail, since nowhere in the wide realm was there a place wherein his august person might be concealed. Yet mindful of past travail he thought, "Even so, I shall tarry here awhile." Despite the brightness of the sun and moon, his heart had been as the heart of one lost in a long night, when he hid his body by day in the grasses of moors, rivaling with his tears the dew on the dew-couched quails' beds, or wandered by night through the lanes of isolated hamlets, fearful of barking village dogs.

But then in some way the presence of this prince was made known to the Eye of the Law Kōsen, an official of the Ichijōin Cloister, who came against the Hannyaji in the grey dawn with five hundred horsemen.

The prince could not escape by fighting a defensive fight, since just at that time there was no man ministering to his needs, nor could he steal away in the guise of another, since the warriors were entering every part of the monastery.

"Behold, I shall take my life!" he thought, and laid bare his body to the waist.

Again he thought:

"Nothing can be easier than to rip open my belly when hope is vanished utterly. Shall I not seek to hide my body and escape alive?"

In the Buddha Hall he saw three great Chinese boxes with legs, containers of the *Daihannya Sutra*, left out where a monk had begun to read. The lids of two of them were still closed, but more than half the sacred writings were taken out of the other one, that stood open. The prince laid himself down inside that open box, pulled the sacred writings on top of him, and silently recited incantations to hide his person from the eyes of men. He had an icy dagger against his belly, thinking, "If they seek me out, then quickly will I drive it in!" How little can one imagine the feelings in his august heart as he waited for an enemy to say, "He is here!"

Soon warriors entered the Buddha Hall in disorder, seeking the prince from the altar to the ceiling. Not finding him, they said: "There is something suspicious over there. Let us open those *Daihannya* boxes."

Vainly they opened the two boxes that were closed, took out the sacred writings, and turned the boxes over. And then all of them went away from the interior of the monastery, scorning to look into the box that was open, while the prince lay as one journeying in a dream, his life most strangely preserved.

Now the prince thought, "May not the warriors return to enquire more diligently?"

He made speed to change over, and lay down in a box that they had searched before.

Without fail the warriors came back again into the Buddha Hall, saying, "It had been meet to look into the open box." And they moved all the sutras to look at it. Then one among them laughed loudly, punning:

"Although we examined these *Daihannya* boxes most zealously, it was not the Prince of the Great Pagoda that we found, but Hsüan-tsang the Tripitaka of Great T'ang!" [16]

And all the warriors went away beyond the gate laughing.

Reverence filled the prince's heart, and grateful tears wet his sleeve.

"That I have been saved is due solely to the divine assistance of Marishiten," he thought, "and to the protection of the Sixteen Excellent Gods." [17]

Since it was thus, the prince could not hide near the southern

---

[16] Tripitaka is a term used to refer either to the three divisions of the Buddhist canon or to monks versed in the sacred writings, notably to Hsüan-tsang (602–664), famous for his travels in India and his scholarly translations of Buddhist texts. The pun involves the homophones ōtō (Great Pagoda) and ōtō (Great T'ang).

[17] Marishiten (Skt. Marīci), a goddess of Indian origin, protects those who recite incantations to render themselves invisible. The Sixteen Excellent Gods protect those who have faith in the *Daihannya Sutra* (*Prajñāpāramitā*).

Chapter 5

capital, but went forth from the Hannyaji to flee toward Kumano. Those who went together with him were nine men: Kōrimbō Genson, the teacher of discipline Akamatsu Sokuyū, Kidera Sagami, Okamoto Mikawabō, Musashibō, Murakami Hikoshirō, Kataoka Hachirō, Yata Hikoshichi, and Hiraga Saburō. The prince and all those others strapped panniers onto their backs over persimmon-colored robes, covered every man his head with a close-fitting cloth cap down to his eyebrows, and assumed the guise of provincial wandering monks bound on a pilgrimage to Kumano, with the eldest among them as their leaders.

Since this prince had grown to manhood within the Dragon Pavilion and Phoenix Gate,[18] never had his foot stepped outside of splendid vehicles and perfumed carriages. Those who attended upon him were troubled, thinking, "How may he travel on his feet during a long journey?" Yet he wore the unaccustomed coarse socks, leggings, and straw sandals, and as though unwearied presented offerings at shrines and performed holy works at temples where they lodged. Pilgrims who passed him on the way saw nothing to question, nor holy men rich in austerities.

Journeying onward [19] the prince gazed out over Yura harbor, where in the distance a boat drifted with severed oar-rope, and a plover cried over boundless waves, many-layered as stalks of coastal beach-cotton. Endlessly the mountains of Kii ran on, and shore-waves beat on the pines of Fujishiro. Only from afar might he look upon Waka and Fukiage; yet surely was he protected by the god of Tamatsushima, shining jewellike in the moonlight. Ever must a traveler's heart be chastened, as he makes his way by long beaches and winding inlets; but melancholy indeed on this journey were "the dripping trees of a lonesome village, and the evening bell of a remote temple," [20] when at dusk this prince came to Kirime-no-ōji.

That evening the prince spread his sleeping robe on the dew of a thicket-shrine. All through the night he offered up a prayer, saying: "Devoutly I lay my head at the feet of the three buddha-mani-

---

[18] Chinese names for the imperial palace.
[19] This paragraph is a brief *michiyuki*, containing a succession of involved literary allusions and plays on words.
[20] From a verse by the T'ang poet Lu Lun.

festations[21] of the shrines of Kumano, and of the ten myriad beneficent spirits who guard Kumano as protectors of the Buddhist Law, and of the eight myriad guardian gods of warriors. May the moon of the tempered radiance of the buddha-manifestations brightly illumine the darkness of the common dwelling of the classes of beings.[22] May rebellious subjects be destroyed in an instant, and the court be resplendent once more. I have heard that two of the gods of Kumano are manifestations of Izanagi and Izanami,[23] of whom our emperor is most assuredly the seed. Yet suddenly the morning sun is hidden by drifting clouds, and darkness covers the earth. How grievous a thing is this! As nothing is the protection of the gods! If the gods are true gods, surely the emperor will be an emperor!"

So indeed he spoke, throwing his body onto the ground and praying with all his heart. For within himself he thought that the gods would in no wise refuse an answer to devotions of perfect sincerity.

Tired by his nightlong worship, the prince bent his knees to make a pillow. As he slept, a boy with hair bound up in rolls came to him in a dream, saying:

"At the three shrines of Kumano, men's hearts are still out of harmony, so that it will be difficult for righteousness to prevail. Go from hence toward Totsugawa to await the coming of an auspicious time. I am sent by the two gods as a guide to show the way."

The prince awakened out of his sleep when he had dreamt this dream, thinking hopefully, "It is a revelation from the gods."

He made an offering of thanksgiving before dawn, and went forth quickly into the mountains toward Totsugawa.

Because there was no human habitation on that road of more than thirty leagues, the prince lay wakeful among the clouds of lofty peaks and spread his sleeve on mats of moss. He slaked his thirst from water trickling through the rocks, and trembling trod

---

[21] I.e., the Shinto gods of the shrines, who were regarded as manifestations of buddhas.

[22] When buddhas assume the form of gods, their nature is partially obscured; hence the use of the phrase "tempered radiance." "The common dwelling of the classes of beings" is the earth.

[23] Divine progenitors of the Japanese ruling line and creators of the Japanese islands; alternative forms of buddhas.

on moldering bridges. "No rain fell on the mountain road, yet ever with tree-shaded air were his garments damp." [24] Cliffs as sheer as though chiseled by a sword rose above him for tens of thousands of feet; deep waters lay myriads of feet below, blue as though dyed with indigo.

When for many days the prince had passed through these steep and perilous places, his august body was wearied, his sweat ran down like water, and blood from his torn feet stained his straw sandals. Likewise, those who journeyed together with him were starved and weary, since their bodies were not made of iron or stone. But although they could no longer walk steadily, they pushed at his back and pulled him by his two hands, until on the thirteenth day they indeed came to Totsugawa.

While the prince waited in a certain crossroads temple, these others went into a man's house, saying, "We are wandering monks, lost on a pilgrimage to Kumano." The people of the house, moved with compassion, brought out boiled millet and horse-chestnut gruel wherewith to stay their hunger; and they took these things to the prince as well. So in this way they passed two or three days.

At last Kōrimbō Genson went forth to a certain house, of which he thought, "Assuredly is this the dwelling place of a person of consequence," for it was not well that they should tarry thus. He stopped a serving-boy coming out and asked concerning his master's name, whereupon the boy said:

"This is the home of the honorable Tono Hyōe, a nephew of His Lordship the lay monk Takehara Hachirō."

"Indeed, I have heard that Tono Hyōe is a person skilled with bow and arrow," thought Genson. "If we could but call upon him in some way!"

He went inside the gate to look and listen. And thereupon he heard a voice, as of one who lay within stricken of a disease, saying:

"Ah! That a holy wandering monk would appear to offer up a prayer!"

And Genson thought, "Truly an excellent thing!"

Then loudly Genson called out:

---

[24] An allusion to a poem by Wang Wei (699–759).

"We are wandering monks, buffeted for seven days by the threefold falls[25] and sequestered a thousand days in Nachi. We are bound on a pilgrimage to the thirty-three places,[26] but having lost our way we have emerged at this village. Please grant us a night's lodging and a day's respite from hunger."

A wretched-looking maidservant came out to him from within.

"I believe that this is surely the doing of a benevolent buddha or god," she said. "The lady of the master of this place is afflicted by an evil spirit. Will you not pray for her?"

Genson answered her, saying:

"Since I am a monk of low degree, my prayers would be of no avail. But our leader resting his feet in the crossroads temple is a person whose efficacy in such matters is of the first rank. When I speak to him of this thing, assuredly will he agree to help her."

Hearing Genson's words, the lady of the house rejoiced greatly, saying, "If such is the case, please bring in that august monk who is your leader," and her joy was exceedingly great.

When Genson had made speed to return with these tidings, the prince and all his followers went to the house. The prince entered in to the sick person to pray that her affliction might pass away, recited the *Thousand-Arm Darani*[27] loudly two or three times, and clicked the beads of his rosary. The sick person babbled divers things foolishly, drew in her arms and legs as though bound by the rope of the Bright Monarch,[28] and struggled perspiring. Then indeed the evil spirit fled away, whereupon she was healed instantly.

The master her husband rejoiced greatly, saying:

"Since I have no stored-up things, I cannot give you any special presents, but please bring yourselves to stay here at least ten days to rest your feet. I think that most wandering monks are restless men who will steal away secretly, so I ask most respectfully to receive these as a pledge."

[25] The Nachi Falls in Kii.

[26] Thirty-three holy places dedicated to Kannon, corresponding to the thirty-three forms in which the bodhisattva is represented in Buddhist art. Of numerous "thirty-three places," the oldest and most famous were the Thirty-three Places of the Western Provinces, the first of which was in Kii.

[27] An incantation of esoteric Buddhism celebrating the efficacy of Thousand-Armed Kannon.

[28] Fudō. See note 20, Chapter Two.

Chapter 5

So he spoke, and gathering together all their panniers laid them inside. Although the faces of the prince's companions showed nothing, inwardly they were delighted beyond measure.

One evening when the prince had tarried for more than ten days in this manner, the master Hyōe-no-jō came to the guest hall, caused a fire to be lit, and spoke of divers matters.

"Surely all of you have heard of it," he said, "yet I wonder if it is true that the Prince of the Great Pagoda has fled away from the capital to journey toward Kumano. I do not believe he can hide there, since the abbot of the three shrines cleaves steadfastly to the military, the monk governor Jōhen. Ah, that he would come hither to this village! Narrow though its confines may be, on all sides there are mountains so steep that for ten or twenty leagues not even a bird can cross. Moreover the people's hearts are honest, and in taking up bow and arrow the men are preeminent in the world. So we are told the offspring of the eldest son of the Heike hid here, he who was called Koremori, and by relying on our ancestors lived safely in the world of the Genji."

So he spoke, and the prince showed in his face that he was well pleased. The prince asked:

"If the Prince of the Great Pagoda trusted to this place and entered here, would you put forth your hand to help him?"

"Is it necessary for me to speak?" said Tono Hyōe. "Although I am a man of no importance, if I alone say, 'It is such and such an affair,' there will be none to oppose me among the men of Shishigase, Kaburazaka, Yuasa, Azegawa, Obara, Imose, Nakatsugawa, and the eighteen districts of Yoshino."

Then the prince signed swiftly with his eyes to Kidera Sagami, who came up beside Hyōe, saying:

"What is there to hide now? That august monk who is our leader is indeed the Prince of the Great Pagoda."

Doubtfully Hyōe gazed at all their faces, until Kataoka Hachirō and Yata Hikoshichi took off their caps and laid them aside, saying, "How hot it is!" And thereupon Hyōe beheld traces of shaved places on their heads, since they were not true wandering monks.[29]

---

[29] Wandering monks (*yamabushi*) wore their hair uncut, whereas laymen shaved a half-moon-shaped area under their caps.

"Indeed you are not wandering monks," he said. "It is well that I spoke of this thing. Alas, how disgraceful! You must certainly have considered our former behavior discourteous."

Seized with amazement, he touched his head to the floor, and with folded arms went down from the mats to prostrate his body.

Tono Hyōe hastened to build a dwelling place of unpeeled logs wherein to guard the prince, established barriers in the mountains on all sides, cut off and blocked the roads, and kept a strait watch. Likewise he sought aid of his uncle, the lay monk Takehara Hachirō, saying to him that he feared lest these devisings be not sufficient to protect the prince. And quickly yielding to Tono's persuasions the lay monk brought the prince into his own house.

Then for half a year the prince sojourned in that place, his heart set at ease by these loyal deeds. Assuming the semblance of a layman lest men's eyes find him out in days to come, he summoned to his bedchamber the daughter of the lay monk Takehara Hachirō, whom he favored beyond all others. More and more the loyalty of the lay monk increased; more and more the men of neighboring villages rendered allegiance to the prince and spoke ill of the military.

Although these things came to the ears of the Kumano abbot Jōhen, by no means might he approach Totsugawa; not with a host of ten myriads of horsemen. Wherefore he put up signs at crossroads, that by arousing the cupidity of the country people he might draw the prince away to another place. The signs said:

AN ORDER FROM THE KANTŌ

The manor of Kuruma in Ise will be given in reward to the man who kills the Prince of the Great Pagoda, regardless of whether he holds an official position or is a person of consequence. And within three days Jōhen will present six thousand *kan* of money to him.[30]

Likewise five hundred *kan* will be given to the man who kills a personal attendant or retainer of the prince, and three hundred *kan* will be given to any man who comes forth to surrender, the money in each case to be settled and paid without fail within the day.

---

[30] A substantial sum. One *kan* was equal to a thousand *mon*, or farthings.

Chapter 5

At the end the words of a written pledge were inscribed. Truly it was a most severe order!

Now the promises were designed to make the pledge firm, and the rewards were to steal men's hearts. When the rapacious bailiffs of the eight estates[31] beheld these signs, then quickly their hearts changed, their manners altered, and strange deeds were heard of.

"Since it is thus," said the prince, "in the end it will not be well to remain in this place. It will be best to go from hence toward Yoshino."

But earnestly the Takehara lay monk pressed him to abide there, saying, "What can happen?" And loath to wound him the prince passed the days and months in fear and trembling.

At last the prince heard that the very sons of the Takehara lay monk conspired to kill him, heedless of their father's orders. And thereupon he went forth toward Kōya from Totsugawa in stealth.

The prince's road was a road that passed through Obara, Imose, and Nakatsugawa, all dangerous enemy places. Straightway he went to the bailiff of Imose, thinking, "By all means must I seek to win the heart of the enemy." Yet the bailiff would not take him into his house, but left him in the Buddha Hall hard by, saying by means of a messenger:

"From the military there has come an order to Jōhen the abbot of the three shrines, commanding him to speak to the Kantō of any man who joins himself to a plot. I shall be blamed on a day to come if I suffer the prince to pass freely over this road, nor will there be aught wherewith to excuse my deed. Yet to detain a prince is an awesome thing. Will His Highness not give over into my hands one or two men of renown among his attendants, such as I may deliver to the military? Or let me receive the banner which bears his august crest, so that I may say to the military, 'Here is testimony of the battle I fought.' If the prince will not accept either one of these two things, then I must shoot an arrow against him."

So he spoke, nor did it seem that he would yield at all.

The prince did not answer him, for he thought that both of these things were impossible. But the teacher of discipline Akamatsu Sokuyū came forward, saying:

[31] The eight manors in the Kumano district.

"It is the duty of a warrior to sacrifice his life in the hour of danger, even as Chi Hsin surrendered to the enemy to deceive them, and Wei Pao remained to guard the castle.[32] Did not these two leave names in the world by substituting their lives for the life of their lord? There can be no difficulty about my coming out in the prince's stead, if only the bailiff will suffer him to pass."

Hearing him, Hiraga Saburō said:

"Although it is not proper for one who sits in the lowest seat to offer counsel, in this grievous time I believe that our lord would sooner lose a thigh, elbow, ear, or eye than give up a single one of his followers. Since it is quite impossible to dispute the words of the Imose bailiff, why should we not choose the easy way by giving him the banner? On the battlefield there is no great shame in abandoning horses and armor, or in letting swords fall to be taken by the enemy. Please by all means deliver up the banner to him, that it may be as he desires."

In his heart the prince thought, "Quite right!" He delivered up to the Imose bailiff the august banner of brocade, whereon the sun and moon were worked in gold and silver, and passed far beyond that place.

Within a while thereafter came Murakami Hikoshirō Yoshiteru, hastening to overtake the prince from far behind. By chance Murakami met with the Imose bailiff on the way, and beheld the banner carried by one of the Imose servants, which was indeed the august banner of the prince. With mistrustful heart Murakami questioned that bailiff, and the bailiff spoke to him of what had passed.

"What is this?" said Murakami. "Ought such a thing to be done by a common fellow like yourself, that falls in with a prince on the road, where he goes to chastise the enemies of the throne; he who is the seed of the Son of Heaven, the gracious ruler of the four seas?"

He took away the banner, laid hands on the servant who bore it, and flung him fifteen yards away (though truly the servant was a

---

[32] The story of Chi Hsin appears in Chapter Two. Wei Pao, another of Kao Tsu's warriors, was surrounded and killed by a Ch'u force while defending Jung-yang castle.

large man). The Imose bailiff said no word, since doubtless his heart was affrighted by Murakami's marvelous strength. And soon with the banner over his shoulder, Murakami overtook the prince.

When Yoshiteru knelt in the august presence to tell his story, the prince smiled with a joyful smile. Graciously he said:

"Sokuyū's loyalty is faithful to the precepts of Meng Shih-she.[33] Hiraga's wisdom is equal to the planning of the minister Ch'en,[34] and Yoshiteru's manliness surpasses the vigor of Pei-kung Yu.[35] With these three superior persons, why should I not bring order to the realm?"

That night the prince laid his pillow in a woodsman's hut where a thin row of live oak trees grew round about, and in the morning he went forth again, thinking to go toward Obara. He spoke to a mountain dweller carrying firewood, one whom he met on the way, questioning him concerning the state of the road ahead. And perhaps even that ignorant woodcutter recognized the prince, for he put down his firewood and knelt on the ground, saying:

"On the road from this place to Obara, there dwells a person who cleaves steadfastly to the side of the military, His Lordship the bailiff of Tamaki. However strong your force, I do not believe you can pass in front of that person without obtaining his consent. Although I speak with awe, please by all means send ahead one or two men as messengers, that they may hear his thoughts."

Attending closely, the prince said:

[33] From *Mencius*: "Mang Shih-she had this way of nourishing his valour:—He said, 'I look upon not conquering and conquering in the same way. To measure the enemy and then advance; to calculate the chances of victory and then engage:—this is to stand in awe of the opposing force. How can I make certain of conquering? I can only rise superior to all fear.'" (Translation from James Legge, *The Chinese Classics* [1939], II, 186-87.)

[34] Ch'en P'ing (d. 178 B.C.), a minister of Han Kao Tsu, was famous as the author of a series of clever political stratagems, the Six Wonderful Plans.

[35] From *Mencius*: "Pih-kung Yu had this way of nourishing his valour:—He did not flinch from any strokes at his body. He did not turn his eyes aside from any thrusts at them. He considered that the slightest push from any one was the same as if he were beaten before the crowds in the market-place, and that what he would not receive from a common man in his loose large garments of hair, neither should he receive from a prince of ten thousand chariots. He viewed stabbing a prince of ten thousand chariots just as stabbing a fellow dressed in cloth of hair. He feared not any of all the princes. A bad word addressed to him he always returned." (Translation from Legge, II, 186.)

"Well is it said, 'There is value even in the words of grass- and wood-gatherers!' [36] There is reason in this woodcutter's speech."

He sent two men to the bailiff of Tamaki, Kataoka Hachirō and Yata Hikoshichi, that they might speak to him, saying:

"The prince will pass this way. Let those who are guarding the road open the gates and remove the obstructions."

The bailiff of Tamaki came out to receive these messengers, but when he had heard their words he went inside, not returning an answer. Instantly there was a great tumult, where he caused his retainers and servants to arm themselves and saddle their horses.

The two messengers turned away quickly.

"No, no!" they said. "It is quite impossible! We must return with all speed to bear tidings to the prince."

Now fifty or sixty of the retainers of Tamaki came chasing after the two, swords in hand. Kataoka and Yata stopped, leaped out from the shelter of two or three young pines, and slashed the knees of the foremost warrior's horse, so that it reared up and cast the man to the ground. And when they had cut off that warrior's head with their second blows, they stood waiting, straightening their bent weapons.

Of those coming up from behind none dared to draw near, but all shot arrows from afar, seeking to make Kataoka and Yata cower down in that place. And two of their arrows struck Kataoka.

Kataoka Hachirō thought in his heart that he would die. He spoke insistently many times, saying:

"Indeed, my lord! My lord Yata! I shall perish here, for I am wounded unto death. Do you hasten to bear tidings to the prince, that he may flee at once."

Although Yata had thought to die in the same place, he could not but turn his back on his dying comrade, since truly it would have been disloyal not to bear tidings to the prince. How sad it is to imagine the feelings in his heart! After he had fled a long distance, he looked around and saw that Kataoka Hachirō had surely perished, for there was one bearing a head on the tip of his sword.

---

[36] An allusion to the *Book of Odes:* "The ancients had a saying:—'Consult the grass and firewood-gatherers.'" (Translation from Legge, VI, 501.)

Chapter 5

When Yata ran back in haste with these tidings, the prince said, "We have come to the end on a road from which there is no escape. Now that our luck is finished, it is useless to lament."

Nor did any of those with him show agitation.

"Since things are as they are, we cannot remain here," they thought. "Let us go as far as we may."

And the thirty warriors high and low passed over the mountain road with the prince at their head, asking the way many times.

When these made to cross the pass of Nakatsugawa, they beheld five or six hundred men on a mountain-top ahead, who looked to be the men of Tamaki. All of them wore helmets and carried shields, and they raised a battle shout with archers on the left and right.

With a grave smile the prince smiled to behold them. He spoke a word to his companions, saying:

"After shooting defensive arrows while our stores endure, let us tranquilly take our lives, that our names may survive for a myriad generations. But take care not to rip open your bellies before me. You must strip the skin from my face after I have killed myself, cut off my ears and nose so that none may know me, and throw away my head. If my head is hung up to be exposed at a prison gate, those in the realm who think to support our cause will lose heart, and the defiant spirit of the military will increase. Even as the dead K'ung-ming made the living Chung-ta run,[37] so a good general makes his power linger in the realm after he is dead. Now that we can in no wise escape, let all take care not to be laughed at by the enemy for cowardice."

So he spoke, and the warriors said, "How can we be cowardly?" Placing themselves in front of the prince, they went down the hillside halfway, where the enemy host was charging up. Yet since they were but thirty-two men, they could not engage and fight an enemy of more than five hundred, even though each rider of them could be called a warrior in a thousand.

The attackers climbed upward, covering their heads with shields

---

[37] The Chinese general Chu-ko Liang (K'ung-ming) was the hero of many campaigns in the third century B.C. An opposing general, Ssu-ma I (Chung-ta), was so reluctant to meet him in battle that he retreated before an army led by one of Chu-ko's subordinates, unaware that Chu-ko himself had died of sickness shortly before.

aligned like a hen's feathers, the left in front of the right. The defending warriors drew their forged weapons, and both sides went forward to fight.

But now from a mountain-top to the north there galloped six or seven hundred horsemen, their three red banners tossing in the pine gale, who split into three parts as they gradually drew near, and raised a battle cry against the Tamaki bailiff. In a mighty voice the warrior advancing in the lead cried out:

"We are residents of the province of Kii, known to men as Rokurō and Shichirō of the Nonagase family, come to meet the Prince of the Great Pagoda with a force of more than three thousand horsemen. Who is it that confronts this gracious prince with bows pulled back and shields lined up? Are we wrong in thinking it is His Lordship the bailiff of Tamaki? Where in all the realm will you find a resting place—you who stand against a prince soon to be blessed by fortune, choosing to obey the traitorous orders of a military family about to be destroyed? Heaven's punishment is not far off. We shall subdue this traitor in a single battle. Let none remain! Let none escape!"

So he attacked, shouting and roaring. And perhaps the five hundred horsemen of Tamaki thought that it was impossible to resist him, for they threw away their shields, rolled up their banners, and fled away instantly in every direction.

The Nonagase brothers took off their helmets, put their bows under their arms, and stood respectfully in the distance.

Then the prince called these close to question them, saying:

"Because I could not labor fruitfully in His Majesty's cause in the mountains, I went forth to gather together warriors in Yamato and Kawachi. But by reason of the late behavior of the Tamaki bailiff, my warriors believed that they could in no wise escape alive. Truly is heaven still to be trusted, that now we meet with this unexpected assistance! How was it that you knew of these things, and galloped to this battlefield to subdue the great numbers of the traitor?"

Respectfully the Nonagase said:

"Around noon yesterday there was a youth of thirteen or fourteen years, one who called himself Oimatsu, spreading a rumor. 'The

Prince of the Great Pagoda will leave Totsugawa tomorrow to go to Obara,' he said, 'yet I believe that he will certainly encounter trouble on the way. Let men of goodwill go quickly to meet him.' So we came, believing that he was a messenger from the prince."

When the prince had meditated on this matter, he thought that it was not an ordinary thing. And when he beheld his amulet bag, which for many years had not left his body, its mouth was slightly open. Looking inside with astonished heart, he saw that sweat was pouring from all parts of the body of the gilded copper god of the Oimatsu chapel of Kitano Shrine, and dirt was clinging to its feet. How strange it was!

"Assuredly does it please the gods to bring me good fortune," he thought. "What doubt can there be about subduing the traitors?"

Afterward the prince went to Makino castle, built by Makino Kōzukebō Shōken. Yet because he thought that the castle was not a good place (since it was exceedingly narrow), with persuasive words he won the hearts of the warrior-monks of Yoshino,[38] made a stronghold of the Aizen Treasure Pagoda,[39] and shut himself up with three thousand horsemen behind the rock-piercing Yoshino River. Or so indeed we have heard.

[38] The monks of Kimpusan Temple at Mount Kimpu in Yamato Province (Nara Prefecture), near the Yoshino River.
[39] A pagoda at Kimpusan Temple.

6

The Dream of Lady Mimbukyō

AS AN ARROW IN FLIGHT is the passing of time, even as waters running down to the sea. After happiness there is sorrow, and after sorrow happiness. Even as a tree's blushing glory and yellowed shedding, so the one follows after the other. Verily who can say if the things of this world be dreams or reality?

Not for the first time in those days were sleeves moistened with the dew of tears, since ever by rejoicing as by affliction are the hearts of men stirred. Yet when Kasagi castle was brought down in the ninth month and the former emperor was sent away to the land of Oki, the officials and courtiers shut themselves up sadly in divers places, and the three thousand court ladies[1] wept and mourned inconsolably.

Although such things are but the way of this world of sorrows, pitiful indeed was Lady Mimbukyō of third rank, the beloved of the former sovereign and the honored mother of the Prince of the Great Pagoda, she who among the imperial handmaidens and consorts was as a garden flower among pale and scentless wild plants. In the imperial palace where all was altered, there was no longer an appointed place wherein she might dwell, and her unquiet heart was as the heart of a fisher adrift in his boat on a stormy sea. When men told how the emperor wept with fast-falling tears among the never-returning waves of the western sea, vainly her thoughts turned

[1] A bit of hyperbole based on Po Chü-i's "Song of Everlasting Sorrow" (*Ch'ang-hen ko*), which speaks of the three thousand ladies in the palace of the T'ang emperor Hsüan Tsung.

upon the far-riding moon of dawn, shining on him as well. And though there came tidings of the Prince of the Great Pagoda, how he wandered to an uncertain lodging place through the clouds of trackless southern mountains, yet she could send no word to him (for might she entrust a letter to a wild goose winging through the spring dusk?). While bitterly she grieved for the one and for the other, her blue-silk hair grew thin, and she marveled, "Old age has come very suddenly"; her red-jade skin faded, and she thought, "Would that my life could end today!"

Sorely stricken, this lady thought to make a retreat for seven days in the cloister of a monk of Kitano Shrine, who for many years had served her with prayers, sutra-readings, and rituals of purification. The monk built her a narrow chamber hard by the Worship Hall, such as might be the retreat of an ordinary court lady of low degree, saying to himself, "Although it will be ill if the military hear of it, I cannot harden my heart against her, since the burden of my obligations is heavy and her present grief is most extreme."

Alas! In a former day brocade curtains would have concealed Lady Mimbukyō's elegant robes and gauze windows veiled her fair countenance, while on the left and right a brilliant multitude of attendants cared for her tenderly. Yet now there was none to visit her, though the capital was very near, for it was a secret retreat and a sudden thing. Only the wind awakened her from dreaming, passing through the pines that grew up in a single night, or the fragrance of the plum, blown from a tree faithful to its master, recalled an ancient spring. Thinking in her heart of the emperor's affliction —how it was even as the affliction of one who dwelt afar in wearisome Tsukushi, and in the last years of Shōtai became a mighty god—[2] she left off her holy chanting to write with flowing tears, "Be merciful, O god, if you have not forgot the ancient journey to wearisome Tsukushi!"

That night Lady Mimbukyō dreamed a dream, dozing briefly. She beheld a careworn old man of more than eighty years beside

[2] Sugawara no Michizane (845–903), a minister of state who fell afoul of the Fujiwara and died in exile in Kyushu (Tsukushi). He is worshiped as the god Temman Tenjin at Kitano, where through his divine power he caused a thousand pine trees to grow up overnight in 955. See Chapter Twelve for the story of the faithful plum tree.

her pillow, correctly attired in high-crowned cap and robe, with a spray of plum blossoms in his left hand and a staff, carved at the top in the semblance of a dove, in his right hand.

In her dream the lady asked:

"In this place of flourishing mugwort outside the capital, I had believed that the possibility of a visitor was as slight as the distance between the knots of the dwarf bamboo's tiny plants. How strange this is! Who wanders from his way to stop here?"

The old man looked upon her with compassionate eyes. In silence he put down the blossoms before her, turned and departed. And gazing perplexed, Lady Mimbukyō beheld a poem on a strip of paper attached to the branch: "With the passing of time the moon's light will shine forth. Why should one regret that for awhile it is obscured by clouds?"

Thereupon she awakened from the dream.

When Lady Mimbukyō considered the meaning of the poem, she thought fervently, "This was an auspicious vision, wherefrom I know that the emperor will return at last to dwell above the clouds."

Because a greatly benevolent and greatly compassionate buddha has assumed the guise of the god called Temman Tenjin, his holy shrine is a place which brings good fortune in this life and the next even to one entering it but a single time. To one who but speaks the sacred name every desire will be granted. Wherefore when this lady prayed wholeheartedly for seven days and nights, with encarmined tears furrowing her face a thousand and ten thousand times, most assuredly her devotion was made known to that god, who answered her at once with a divine revelation.

"Though it is said that the world has reached the age of decline," she thought trustfully, "still are the gods and buddhas cognizant of faith and sincerity."

Kusunoki Goes to the Tennōji; the Matter of Suda, Takahashi, and Utsunomiya

Sakon-no-shōgen Tokimasa and Nakatoki the governor of Echigo went up from the Kantō on the fifth day of the third month of the second year of Genkō, that the two Rokuharas might be committed to their hands. Men said that they came because Tokiwa Norisada the governor of Suruga had firmly laid down his duties, since for three or four years he had managed the affairs of the two places by himself.

Now in the first year of Genkō the military were deceived by Kusunoki Hyōe Masashige, when fleeing away he feigned to have died in the fire at Akasaka castle. They sent forth Yuasa Magoro to be the steward of the place, he who was called the lay monk Jōbutsu, thinking with easy hearts, "There is nothing more to fear in the province of Kawachi." Yet suddenly Kusunoki rode furiously against Yuasa's castle with five hundred horsemen, on the third day of the fourth month of the second year.

May it not be that little food was laid up in the castle? For it came to Kusunoki's ears that five or six hundred commoners would approach by night bearing stores from Yuasa's lands at Asegawa in the province of Kii. And thereupon he sent forth warriors to an advantageous place on the road, who took away all of those stores and put arms into the straw bags in their stead. Kusunoki loaded some of the bags onto horses, and gave others to commoners to carry. And he named two or three hundred warriors to put on the semblance of guards, in order that they might enter into the castle. Then his force gave battle against these their comrades, chasing them back as though to scatter them, so that the Yuasa lay monk thought, "The warriors bringing our stores are fighting against Kusunoki's men." And unwittingly the lay monk emerged from the castle to lead the enemy warriors in.

When Kusunoki's men were come inside the castle according to their plan, they drew forth weapons from the bags, gathered together in one place, and raised a battle shout, while at the same time the warriors outside broke down the gates and climbed over the walls. And the Yuasa lay monk, now pressed irresistibly by enemies within and without, quickly stretched out his neck in surrender.

After Kusunoki had taken that lay monk's warriors for himself, with seven hundred horsemen he subdued the two provinces of Izumi and Kawachi, and his army waxed exceeding strong. On the seventeenth day of the fifth month, he went forth toward Sumiyoshi and the Tennōji Temple, encamping southward from Watanabe Bridge.

Now a great clamor arose in the capital, where many fast messengers from Izumi and Kawachi reported that Kusunoki thought to advance against the city. Warriors galloped away to the east and west, and noble and base alike were sorely agitated. Like clouds or mist the hosts of the home provinces and neighboring places galloped together to wait at Rokuhara, thinking, "Kusunoki will attack now!" Yet it was not so.

Then these said:

"What we have heard is not true. Assuredly Kusunoki's is but a small force. Let us go forth to smite it!"

The lords of Rokuhara made Suda and Takahashi their two battle commissioners, commanding them to go against the Tennōji with five thousand horsemen: the watchmen of the forty-eight places, the warriors in the capital, and the forces of the home provinces and nearby places. And these went forth from the city on the twentieth day of that month to make their camps at Amagasaki, Kanzaki, and Hashiramoto, where they lighted watch fires to await the coming of the dawn.

Upon hearing of these things, Kusunoki divided his two thousand horsemen into three parties, whereof the chief were hidden in the neighborhood of Sumiyoshi and the Tennōji, while three hundred remained south of Watanabe Bridge, to burn great watch fires in two or three places over against the enemy. This was to draw the enemy warriors across the bridge, that Kusunoki's men might win a victory by chasing them back into the deep water.

At dawn on the twenty-first day of the fifth month, the five thousand warriors of Rokuhara gathered together in one place. Gazing toward Watanabe Bridge, they saw that the enemies across the river were but two or three hundred horsemen. Moreover, they were but poor warriors riding thin horses bridled with straw rope.

"Indeed, the quality of the men of Izumi and Kawachi is as we believed," thought Suda and Takahashi. "There is not a single worthy foe among them! Let us capture all these fellows, cut off their heads at the Sixth Ward river bed, and enjoy the gratitude of the lords of Rokuhara!"

Chapter 6

Quickly Suda and Takahashi forded the river in a straight line below the bridge, not waiting for others. And beholding them, their five thousand horsemen urged their horses, each striving to be first, some riding over the bridge cautiously, and some crossing at shallow places to dash up onto the opposite bank.

The army of Kusunoki went back toward the Tennōji, not fighting a battle, but only shooting a few scattered arrows from afar. Jostling and shoving, the victorious men of Rokuhara pursued them as far as the commoners' houses northward from the temple, nor did men or horses rest for an instant.

When Kusunoki had wearied the enemy's men and horses according to plan, he divided his two thousand horsemen into three parties, whereof one came out attacking from eastward of the temple, and received the enemy on its left, one attacked with a wedge attack from the stone torii at the west gate, and one attacked from beneath the Sumiyoshi pines, spreading itself out like chicken wings to encompass the enemy warriors round about.

Although the army of Rokuhara was such a mighty host as Kusunoki's men might not be thought to stand against, yet was it like to be surrounded by his lesser force, so sorely disordered were its groupings. Suda and Takahashi uttered words of command, saying:

"The enemy have deceived us by concealing a large force in the rear. This is an ill place, where horses cannot keep their footing. Let us draw out the enemy to a wide place, calculate the degree of their strength, and attack again and again until the battle is won."

Then the five thousand horsemen went back toward Watanabe Bridge, lest the enemy cut off their rear. And shouting a victory shout, Kusunoki's warriors chased after them from three sides.

Suda and Takahashi turned back their horses' feet when they drew near to the bridge, commanding:

"By no means is the enemy a large force. Unless we turn back here, we will suffer the ill of a large river behind us. Turn back, warriors!"

Yet the mighty host would not turn back, for their hearts yearned to run away. As they galloped together onto the perilous bridge, each striving to be first, countless numbers of men and horses were pushed off to drown in the water. Some perished when they rushed across heedless of the water's depth; others died when they galloped their horses off from the bank, so that they fell over. No man sought to turn back to give battle, but all thought only of abandoning their horses and arms and running away. And so the small remnants of the five thousand warriors crept back toward the capital.

On the next day a notice board appeared at the Sixth Ward river bed, with a verse saying, "Perhaps because of the swiftness of Watanabe's waters, the High Bridge fell; the Corner Field washed away!" [3] And these scoffing words were put into poems to be told to others with laughter, as is the way of the capital's slanderous tongues. Sorely dishonored, Suda and Takahashi for a time would not go forth to discharge their duties, but abode in their dwelling places feigning illness.

With unquiet hearts, the chiefs of the two Rokuharas thought to advance against Kusunoki again, wherefore they summoned Utsunomiya Jibu-no-tayū, a warrior sent up from the Kantō in those days to strengthen the capital.

"Since ancient times it has been the way of warfare for luck to determine victory and defeat," they said to him. "Yet our defeat in the fighting to the south was due entirely to the ill-made strategy of our captains and the cowardly hearts of our warriors. Truly in no wise may we stop the jeers of the men of the realm! Now as regards your coming to the capital after the coming of Nakatoki, assuredly was it designed that you would confront and subdue all such outlaws as might rise against us. Since things are as they are, we cannot fight a good fight by gathering together the warriors of the defeated army, though we send them forth time upon time. We pray you to face Kusunoki and subdue him, for it is a most grave matter of state."

So they spoke, nor did Utsunomiya seek to refuse.

"There is some doubt about going out with a small force after a mighty host has been defeated," he said. "But since the day of my departure from the Kantō I have been resolved not to cherish life in an affair of such moment. I shall advance alone to put the battle in array. By no means is it possible to know the outcome now, wherefore if I fail let others be sent forward."

[3] Puns on the names of the two generals, Takahashi and Suda.

Chapter 6

So he spoke resolutely, and took his leave. And straightway he went forth from Rokuhara toward the Tennōji, it being the hour of the horse on the nineteenth day of the seventh month. Nor did he return to his lodging place at all, for he could not cherish life, when alone he received the military's order to stand against a mighty enemy.

As far as the Eastern Temple, of lord and retainers alike there were but fourteen or fifteen riders in Utsunomiya's party. But at Yotsuzaka and Tsukurimichi these became more than five hundred, by reason that followers came galloping to join themselves to him from many places within the capital. As they rode forward, they spoiled passers-by of their horses, even such as were of powerful families; likewise, they took away commoners to labor for them, so that travelers traveled by roundabout ways and village folk closed their doors. That night they encamped at Hashiramoto to await the dawn, no man of them believing that even one would return alive, so firm was their resolution.

Upon hearing of these things, Wada Magosaburō of Kawachi spoke a word to Kusunoki, saying:

"Pricked to wrath by their recent defeat, the military have sent Utsunomiya against us from the capital, who camps tonight at Hashiramoto. Yet I have heard that his army numbers but six or seven hundred horsemen. Now previously when Suda and Takahashi confronted us with more than five thousand horsemen, we indeed scattered them with our small force! Moreover we are a superior force on this occasion, one which has won a victory, while the enemy is a defeated army of inferior size. Though Utsunomiya may be an outstanding warrior, how can he prevail? Let us rather attack him tonight, that we may scatter his warriors and drive them back."

After considering Wada's words awhile, Kusunoki said:

"By no means does the outcome of a battle depend upon numbers, but upon the united hearts of those who fight. Wherefore is it said, 'When you see a great enemy, practice deceit; when you confront a small enemy, be afraid.' Not one of Utsunomiya's followers thinks to return alive, since with none but this small force he confronts us, men who have defeated and driven back a mighty host. There is no better warrior than Utsunomiya east of the barrier;[4] likewise, the Ki and Kiyowara have ever held life more cheaply than dust when they have gone forth to give battle.[5] It is certain that more than half our warriors will be struck down, even though they may have no thought of retreat, for the enemy's seven hundred will fight with united hearts.

"The fate of the realm does not depend upon this day alone. Who will fight in battles to come if our small loyal army is smitten in its first encounter? It is said that a good general wins without fighting. On the morrow I shall draw back from this camp, allowing the enemy to feel pride in their hearts, but after four or five days I shall light watch fires on the peaks in all directions, as though about to attack them. Then quickly Utsunomiya's warriors will lose heart, such being the way of men from east of the barrier, and not one but will say, 'No, no! It is no good staying here forever. Come! Let us withdraw while the honor is ours.' Thus do I apply the saying, 'It is the occasion which determines advance and retreat.'

"Now assuredly the enemy will draw near soon, since dawn is at hand. Let us go forth at once."

So Kusunoki departed from the Tennōji with Wada and Yuasa.

As the night lightened, Utsunomiya advanced against the temple with his seven hundred horsemen. He burned the commoners' houses at Kōzu and raised a battle shout, but, not being there, the enemy did not come out to meet him.

"Assuredly Kusunoki seeks to deceive us," he said to his men. "The footing is ill for horses in this place, and the road is narrow. Do not allow your center to be ripped by a charging enemy or suffer your rear to be cut off."

Thereupon, with horses' feet aligned, the Ki and Kiyowara galloped in from the east and west entrances of the temple. Twice and thrice they charged; yet they beheld no enemy, but only lingering smoke from abandoned watch fires in the dawning day.

Then Utsunomiya got down from off his horse in front of the

---

[4] The barrier at Lake Hakone, regarded as a dividing line between the east and the west.
[5] The Ki and Kiyowara families traditionally accompanied the Utsunomiya into battle.

Main Hall to offer up a prayer to Shōtoku Taishi, thinking in his heart that he had won a victory without fighting. Reverently he rejoiced, saying, "Not through strength of arms did this thing come to pass, but through the protection of the gods and buddhas."

Utsunomiya made haste to send off a fast messenger to the capital, saying, "The enemies at the Tennōji were driven away instantly." And all men praised him, from the chiefs of the two Rokuharas down to the lowest warriors in the service of hereditary retainers and other vassals, saying, "Truly it was an extraordinary deed that Utsunomiya did."

Although it was an honor to Utsunomiya to have chased away the enemy from the Tennōji without difficulty, he could not advance against Kusunoki at once, his numbers being too small, nor could he turn back willingly, since he had not fought a true battle. But when four or five days had passed, Wada and Kusunoki assembled five or six hundred outlaws of Izumi and Kawachi, together with two or three hundred mighty men of valor, and caused them to light watch fires in the neighborhood of the temple. And then the warriors of Utsunomiya raised a clamor, saying, "Aha! The enemy has come out!"

As the darkness deepened, the fires at "Akishino's foothill village" [6] and Mount Ikoma burned thicker than stars on a cloudless night. Beacons flared strangely at Shigitsu-no-ura where salt grass grows, and at Sumiyoshi and Naniwa village, like fishing boats burning up the waves. In all the land of Yamato, Kawachi, and Kii, there was no mountain or bay of note where Kusunoki's men failed to light a watch fire, as though theirs was an army of untold myriads of horsemen. For two or three nights they did in this wise, drawing together little by little until they filled up every space in every direction, and changed the darkness of night into noon.

On beholding these fires, Utsunomiya resolved, "I shall stand against the enemy if they come upon me, that the outcome may be decided in a single battle." He kept himself in readiness, never taking off the saddle from his horse's back or removing the overgirdle of his armor; yet after all there was no battle. And thereupon

---

[6] A phrase from a poem in the *Shinkokinshū* anthology (1206).

Utsunomiya lost courage before the enemy encirclement, and thought with dismay, "Alas! That I could but retreat!"

Likewise there were men of the Ki and Kiyowara who said:

"What will happen if our small force fights against this mighty enemy? Let us return to the capital, considering it a cause for pride that without difficulty we chased the enemy from this place before."

And so they all agreed to retreat. Utsunomiya went back to the capital from the Tennōji deep in the night of the twenty-seventh day of the seventh month, and early in the morning of the next day Kusunoki came in to take his place.

Truly would both Utsunomiya and Kusunoki have perished, had those two met in battle, even as with the fighting of paired tigers or dragons. May it not be that each of them knew this thing in his heart? For Kusunoki drew back to lay plans far away, while Utsunomiya retreated honorably after a single encounter. There was none who did not praise them, saying, "All was done in this wise because both are fine generals, skilled in planning and mindful of days to come."

Now although Kusunoki's power waxed strong after he came out at the Tennōji, he forbore to spoil the commoners' dwellings, or to behave himself toward his warriors with other than the strictest propriety. Wherefore his host grew exceedingly great, since hearing of these things the warriors of nearby provinces galloped eagerly to join themselves to him, and likewise leaders of men from far-off places. Assuredly did it appear that not even from the capital itself might an attacking army be sent against him easily!

Masashige Beholds the FORECAST of the Tennōji

On the third day of the eighth month of the second year of Genkō, Kusunoki Hyōe Masashige went to Sumiyoshi Shrine with an offering of three sacred horses. On the next day he went to the Tennōji to present a horse with a silver-plated saddle, a sword with a silver-trimmed scabbard, and a suit of armor, all thank offerings for an abbreviated reading of the *Daihannya Sutra*.

Chapter 6

When the reading was done, an aged monk of the temple came bearing a list whereon were inscribed the names of the chapters that had been read. Kusunoki called this monk into his presence, saying:

"Assuredly must it appear presumptuous for such a humble person as myself to seek to set His Majesty on the throne again; yet it is not fitting that I should think of danger to my body and spirit when an imperial command has been issued. I have won some small advantage in two battles, wherefore the warriors of many provinces have galloped to join themselves to me, not waiting to be invited. Surely this is because heaven has made the times auspicious, and gods and buddhas have watched with protective eyes.

"Although I know not if it be true, men say that Shōtoku Taishi in his day wrote down a book called the *Forecast of the Future of Japan*, treating of the future of the imperial throne; and it is said that he laid it to rest in this temple. If there be no harm in looking, I should like to see only the scroll which speaks of our own time."

So he spoke, and the ancient monk answered him, saying:

"When Shōtoku Taishi subdued the traitor Moriya, he built this temple to propagate the Buddhist Law.[7] Thereafter he wrote a book in thirty scrolls, speaking of matters from the age of the gods to the august reign of Jitō Tennō,[8] and the book was called the *Chronicle of Antiquity*. That book was handed down from one to another of the Urabe no Sukune, men of a house learned in ancient tradition. Likewise the prince left a secret writing of one scroll, which from the time of Jitō Tennō tells of the deeds of emperors to come, and of war and peace in the realm. Not easily may men's eyes behold it; yet to you alone will I reveal it in stealth."

Turning the silver key of a secret treasury, he drew out a scroll rolled up on a roller of gold; and Masashige gazed joyfully thereon, beholding a curious discourse, which said:

---

[7] Shōtoku Taishi and Mononobe no Moriya (d. 587) were on opposite sides in a struggle between two court factions in the middle of the sixth century. At the time of the battle in which Moriya was finally crushed, the prince vowed to build the Tennōji (Shitennōji) if his side won.

[8] Reigned 689–697. There is an obvious inconsistency here, since Shōtoku Taishi died in 622.

In the reign of the ninety-fifth mortal emperor, violence shall rise up in the land; distress shall afflict the sovereign. In those days fish shall come out of the east to swallow the four seas. Three hundred and seventy days after the sun shall have sunk in the western heavens, birds shall come out of the west to devour the eastern fish; and thereafter for three years the state shall be one. Again a man like a monkey shall spoil the realm; yet after thirty years' time the evil shall pass away, and it shall be as before.

When Masashige had considered these words well (since they were most strange), he said trustingly, "Soon there will be a great change in the realm. Even such is the import of that which is written here." For he thought:

"Since Go-Daigo Tennō is the ninety-fifth of mortal emperors, therefore it was of our time that Shōtoku Taishi wrote, 'Violence shall rise up in the land; distress shall afflict the sovereign.' As for the fish that come out of the east to swallow up the four seas, assuredly these are the followers of the traitorous Sagami lay monk. Likewise the western birds which eat the eastern fish are men who will destroy the Kantō. By the sun sinking in the western heavens is meant the former sovereign's removal to the province of Oki. And 'three hundred and seventy days' means that in the spring of next year the emperor will come back from Oki to sit upon the throne once more."

He gave a gold-mounted sword to the ancient monk, bidding him return the book to the secret treasury.

Now when these things are considered in a later day, in no wise mistaken were Masashige's words. Truly that was a book written down by a living buddha, mindful of things to come, a marvelous prophecy, faithfully revealing the happenings of future generations.

The Prince of the Great Pagoda Issues a Command to the Lay Monk Akamatsu Enshin

Around that time in the province of Harima, there was a matchless man of valor called the lay monk Akamatsu Jirō Enshin, an offspring of the line of Suefusa of junior third rank, who was a descendant in the sixth generation of the Prince of the Blood Guhei, the seventh son of Murakami Tennō. Enshin was a man of large ideas, such as would not willingly give place to others. In his heart he thought, "Indeed I should like to continue what has been stopped and revive what has been abandoned, that I might make my name known and display a loyalty surpassing others."

Just at that time it chanced that Enshin's son came to him, bearing a princely command from the Prince of the Great Pagoda. This was the teacher of discipline Sokuyū, a companion of the prince for the past two or three years, who had passed through the trials of Yoshino and Totsugawa. The command said:

"Make speed to gather together loyal warriors, that you may lead an army to destroy the enemies of the court. Success will be rewarded in accordance with your desires."

Added thereto were seventeen articles of written details, graciously decreed, that did honor to Enshin's family and answered his desires. And Enshin rejoiced greatly thereat.

Then Enshin built a castle at Mount Kokenawa in Sayo-no-shō in the land of Harima, whence he sent out a call for followers. He extended his power to neighboring places, and the warriors of Harima galloped to join themselves to him, quickly becoming more than a thousand horsemen. (Even so did a man of the people rise up at Ta-che against the weakness of faltering Ch'in: Ch'en Sheng of Ch'u.)[9] And he hastened to establish barriers at Sugisaka and Yama-no-sato, whereby he blocked the San'yōdō and San'indō Roads to the western provinces, so that their armies might not go to the capital.

A Host from the Kantō Goes Up to the Capital

Now to the Kantō came fast messengers from Rokuhara with tidings of rebels rising up daily in the home provinces and western lands. And sorely distressed the Sagami lay monk assembled his kinsmen, summoned the great captains of the eight eastern prov-

[9] The collapse of the Ch'in dynasty (221–207 B.C.) started with Ch'en Sheng's revolt.

inces, and sent forth an attacking army. More than 307,500 horsemen departed from Kamakura on the twentieth day of the ninth month, a mighty host, whereof the foremost riders came to the capital on the eighth day of the tenth month, while yet the rearmost lay at Ashigara Hakone. Moreover, Kōno Kurō came up to the lower capital [10] from Amagasaki, with men of Shikoku riding in three hundred great ships, and the Kōtō lay monk, Ōuchi-no-suke, and Aki no Kumagai came up from Hyōgo to the west capital,[11] with men of Suō and Nagato riding in two hundred warships. More than seven thousand men of the Kai and Shinano Genji came to Higashiyama by way of the Chūsandō Road, and the Ema governor of Echizen and Aikawa Ukyō-no-suke came to the upper capital [12] by way of East Sakamoto, with thirty thousand horsemen from the seven provinces of the Hokurikudō Road. In this wise did all the hosts of all the provinces and circuits gallop to the capital, each striving to be first, so that the houses of the city and Shirakawa were filled to overflowing. There was no place where warriors were not encamped: not Daigo, Ogurusu, Hino, Kanjuji, Saga, Ninnaji, Uzumasa, Nishiyama, Kitayama, Kamo, Kitano, Kōdō, Kawasaki, Kiyomizu, the space below the Rokkakudō gate, or even the interiors of bell towers. With wondering hearts men said, "Although Japan is a small country, yet its men are as numerous as this!"

On the last day of the first month of the third year of Genkō, the lords of Rokuhara divided the hosts of the provinces into three parties, eight hundred thousand horsemen in all, to go forth against the castles at Yoshino, Akasaka, and Mount Kongō. Toward Yoshino there advanced three armies, following upper, lower, and middle roads: twenty-seven thousand riders, with Nikaidō Dōun the lay monk of Dewa as their grand marshal. Toward Akasaka there advanced eighty thousand horsemen, that first encamped at the Tennōji and Sumiyoshi, with Aso no Danjō Shōhitsu as their grand marshal. Toward Mount Kongō there advanced two hundred thousand horsemen from the Nara road, and the grand marshal of this army attacking from the rear was Mutsu Uma-no-suke.

[10] The section of the capital which lay south of what is now Sanjō Avenue.
[11] The western section of the capital.
[12] The area north of Sanjō Avenue.

Chapter 6

Also there was one Nagasaki Akushirō Saemon-no-jō, a warrior grand marshal [13] sent to attack from the front, who set forth one day later than the others, as it were that men might observe the quality of his army. Truly the splendor of his procession was amazing to behold! Foremost behind the standard-bearer appeared eight hundred warriors armored all alike, mounted on strong fat horses decked out with thick tassels. Two hundred and fifty yards behind them rode the grand marshal, Nagasaki himself, clad in purple armor of a hue that deepened toward the skirt, with a dappled underdress and short widemouthed trousers of heavy silk. Eight golden dragons surmounted the silver-starred five-flap helmet pushed back on his head; likewise his iron greaves were plated with silver, and his two swords fitted with gold. His mount Ichinoheguro was the finest horse of the eastern land. Sixteen hands high he stood, decked out with thick tassels of bright yellow and a saddle adorned with a small boat on a beach at ebb tide, traced in thin gold leaf on gold lacquer. Nagasaki's thirty-six arrows were white, with large black center markings and silver notches, and he grasped a rattan-wound bow in the middle. Narrow indeed was the street where Ichinoheguro stepped forward! In two lines before and behind marched five hundred soldiers of middle grade, wearing corselets and bow-arm gauntlets. And a hundred thousand horsemen rode five or six hundred yards behind, each armored according to his liking, with helmets gleaming and sleeves aligned, filling the road like tacks in a shoe for five or six leagues. Well might heaven and earth shake before their resolute will, and mountains and rivers tremble!

Likewise were other vassals sent against those castles in parties of two and three thousand horsemen, one after the other, by day and by night, until the thirteenth day. There was none who did not think in his heart, "Never was such a mighty host sent forth by T'ang, India, Great Yüan, or the southern barbarians, to say nothing of our own land!"

---

[13] A retainer, as distinguished from a chieftain with retainers of his own.

The Battle of Akasaka; How Hitomi and Homma Went Before Others

Aso no Danjō Shōhitsu spoke an order, he who was the grand marshal of the advance against Akasaka castle, saying:

"We shall encamp for two days at the Tennōji to await our rearmost forces, even until the hour of the horse on the second day of the second month. Not until then shall we shoot arrows to set the battle in array. If any man goes against the enemy in advance, the appointed hour not being come, assuredly he shall be punished."

Now there was a resident of the province of Musashi called the lay monk Hitomi Shirō On'a, and On'a spoke persuasive words to one Homma Kurō Sukesada, saying:

"We shall certainly bring down the enemy castle, since our warriors are as clouds or mist. But truly it is the way of heaven to diminish the full. How may the men of the Kantō escape this law, when for more than seven generations they have governed the realm with full authority? Moreover, destruction must surely be the portion of subjects who wickedly banish their emperor.

"Although I am a person of no consequence, the Hōjō have looked kindly upon me for more than seventy years. It would be an affliction to my old age and a hindrance in my dying hour, should I endure until their fall, needlessly prolonging this life, which will no longer bear fruitful memories. I think that I shall anticipate tomorrow's battle, die ahead of others, and leave a name for the men of a later day."

In his heart Homma Kurō thought, "Quite right!" Yet he said:

"How foolishly you speak! In a battle where the attack is such as this, there is little glory in going ahead of others to perish needlessly. I myself shall behave like an ordinary person."

So he spoke, and thereupon Hitomi went away toward the Main Hall angrily. But Homma sent a man to spy secretly on Hitomi, since it was strange that he went to that place. The man saw that Hitomi drew out an inkstone, wrote upon the stone torii, and returned to his lodging place. And Homma Kurō thought in his heart, "If it be thus, Hitomi will surely go out ahead of us tomorrow."

Chapter 6

Without remissness Homma rode forth before the night was done, took his way alone toward Tōjō, and awaited the dawn at the Ishi River. Soon, to the south, he beheld a bay horse advancing toward Akasaka castle through the morning mist, carrying a warrior clad in armor threaded with blue Chinese damask, with a white mantle hanging down from his helmet in back. And riding forward he saw that the warrior was the lay monk Hitomi Shirō.

When Hitomi saw Homma he laughed, saying, "If I am to believe your words of yesterday, I ought not to be forestalled by a person who is young enough to be my grandson!" He urged his horse forward eagerly.

Homma followed after him, saying:

"Why should we struggle to be first now? Let us expose our corpses in a single place and journey together to the nether regions."

Hitomi answered, "Need it be said?"

So these went on their way talking together, the one in front and the one behind, until they drew near to Akasaka castle. Then they galloped to the edge of the ditch with their horses' noses aligned, rose up in their stirrups, leaning on their bows, and shouted their names in loud voices.

"We are the lay monk Hitomi Shirō On'a, aged seventy-two, a resident of the province of Musashi, and Homma Kurō Sukesada, aged thirty-six, a resident of the province of Sagami, who since leaving Kamakura have been resolved to perish in battle ahead of our comrades! Let those who are self-confident come forth to observe the degree of our skill!"

So they shouted loudly, glaring at the castle. But those within said:

"To be sure! Such is the way of eastern warriors! They are but men envious of Kumagai and Hirayama, who began to fight ahead of others at Ichi-no-tani.[14] No warriors follow them, nor do they bear the semblance of great chieftains. It is of no avail to throw away one's life by leaping forward to meet reckless outlaws. Let us simply wait."

So all remained silent and made no answer.

---

[14] A famous battle in the twelfth-century struggle between the Minamoto and the Taira. Kumagai and Hirayama were two of Yoritomo's captains.

Then in anger Hitomi spoke to them again, saying:

"Although we have duly made our names known after journeying toward this place since early morning, no arrow has been shot from within the castle. Are your hearts afraid, or do you seek to shame us? Enough! We shall show you our quality!"

He jumped down from his horse, ran nimbly over a narrow bridge across the ditch, and together with Homma followed along the side of a buttress, seeking to cut down the castle gate.

Thereupon a clamor arose within the castle. Arrows flew like falling rain from openings in walls and the tops of towers, lodging in the armor of those two until they resembled straws in a raincoat. But Homma and Hitomi would not give back so much as a foot, since from the beginning they were resolved to die. They fought while their lives endured, and fell down together on the same spot.

Now there was a holy man who followed Homma to that place, and for his sake recited the name of Amida Buddha ten times at the last.[15] This monk begged Homma's head to take back to the Tennōji, where he spoke of all that had passed to Homma's son, Gennai Hyōe Suketada.

When Suketada beheld his father's head, tears choked his throat. He threw his armor over his shoulder and saddled a horse as though to go forth alone (since doubtless he was resolved to take his revenge).

In alarm the holy man pulled at the sleeve of Suketada's armor, saying:

"What would you do? Assuredly would your father have taken you as well, had it been merely to win fame that he went forth before others. His purpose was to offer his life to His Lordship of Sagami, that the reward thereof might bring prosperity to his descendants. If heedlessly you rush against the enemy to die with him, who will succeed you? Who will enjoy the reward? It is said that descendants display filial piety toward their ancestors by prospering abundantly. It is natural for you to wish to die with him, since your heart is thus afflicted, but please stop awhile."

So he restrained him strongly, until Suketada took off the armor that he had put on, holding back his tears.

---

[15] So that Homma could be reborn in the Pure Land, Amida's paradise.

Chapter 6

Then the holy man rejoiced, thinking, "He has bowed before my persuasions." He wrapped up Homma's head in his sleeve and went away to bury it in a field hard by.

But when there was none to stay him, Suketada set forth. First he went before Shōtoku Taishi to worship, and weeping prayed with all his heart.

"I do not pray for prosperity in this life," he said, "since today is my last day. Yet if the mighty vow of great compassion[16] be not false, let me be buried beneath the moss of the battlefield where my father died, and let me be born together with him on the same lotus calyx in the Pure Land."

So he spoke, and went forth weeping.

When Suketada passed beside the stone torii, he beheld the poem written by the lay monk Hitomi Shirō, he who had fallen with Suketada's father. He bit the smallest finger of his right hand and wrote a verse with his blood, thinking, "Assuredly is this a thing that will be preserved in the tales of generations to come." And then indeed he took his way toward Akasaka castle.

When Suketada had come to a place hard by the castle, he got down from his horse and beat upon the gate with his bow pressed to his side, shouting, "I would speak a word to those within."

Soon two warriors stretched out their heads from the window of a tower, asking, "What man are you?"

Suketada answered them, saying:

"I am a person called Gennai Hyōe Suketada, the eldest son of that Homma Kurō Sukesada who died when he approached your castle in the morning. It is the way of men's fathers to be led into false paths through pity of their beloved sons. My father perished alone, not letting me know of it, because he grieved to have me die together with him. Yet I am sure that he will lose his way on the road of the middle existence,[17] and therefore I have come here alone to die like him, that I may fulfill my filial duty even after death. Please tell this to the castle's grand marshal and open the

---

[16] This probably refers to the vow to save mankind made by the bodhisattva Kannon, of whom Shōtoku Taishi was believed to have been an incarnation.

[17] The period between a person's death and his rebirth.

gate. I wish to attain my desire by ending my life on the spot where my father fell."

So he spoke courteously, with tears choking his throat.

At once the fifty warriors at the outer rampart opened the gate and pulled away the obstacles, their hearts moved to pity by his high resolution and noble devotion to duty. Suketada got up onto his horse, galloped into the castle, and fought with flying sparks of fire against them, until at last he put his sword in his mouth and fell down on his face, even on the spot where his father had died.

How regrettable it was! The father Sukesada was an unmatched wielder of bow and arrow, a person of whom the state had need. Likewise the son Suketada was a hero of unequaled loyalty and filial piety, an honor to his family. And although Hitomi was old, he looked upon life as a man of principle, living and dying as was fitting to the times. There was none but grieved to hear that these three had perished at the same time, neither of those who knew them nor of those who knew them not.

Now the grand marshal galloped forth from the Tennōji toward Akasaka castle, since it was known to all that certain warriors had perished before the castle in advance of others. As he passed in front of Shōtoku Taishi he got down from his horse, whereupon he beheld a verse, written on the left pillar of the stone torii: "Though withered and flowerless the ancient cherry tree, beneath the moss its name will not be hidden." [18] Next to it there was indeed written, "Hitomi Shirō On'a, aged seventy-two, a resident of the province of Musashi, is heading toward Akasaka castle on the second day of the second month of the second year of Shōgyō,[19] that he may die in battle to requite the benefactions of the Hōjō family." Likewise on the right pillar there was written, "Wait a bit! I shall guide you on the Six Roads,[20] lest in the darkness of parental love you lose the way." And it was written, "Gennai Hyōe Suketada, aged seventeen,

---

[18] Hitomi compares himself to the tree.

[19] The era name adopted by the new emperor. It was not recognized by the adherents of Go-Daigo, who continued to use the name Genkō.

[20] Hades; the place where six roads lead to the six worlds into which the dead are reborn. See note 9, Chapter Five.

Chapter 6

the eldest son of Homma Kurō Sukesada and a resident of the province of Sagami, will die on his father's body on the second day of the second month of the second year of Shōgyō."

Most admirably do the virtues of loyalty and filial piety shine forth in these two poems! Though the bones of the three molder under piles of yellow earth, their fame is loftier than the ninefold heavens above the clouds. Even today no man but sheds tears of sympathy at the sight of their poems, still remaining on the pillars of stone.

Soon Aso no Danjō Shōhitsu advanced against Akasaka with his host of eighty thousand horsemen, encompassing the castle's four sides like clouds or mist for three thousand yards. And their battle shout shook the mountains and made the earth to tremble, as it were to rend the heavens in an instant.

Tall cliffs like folding screens fell away below this castle on three sides, while on the south side, that alone was near to flat land, there was a wide and deep ditch with a wall on its bank bearing a line of towers. Not easily might such a castle be attacked, however great the strength or agile the feats! But the mighty host left back their shields disdainfully, ran down into the ditch within range of the enemy arrows, and sought to climb the steep bank.

Thereupon with careful aim skilled bowmen shot as they willed from within the castle. And it was thus on all the days that followed, and on every day five or six hundred men were killed or wounded.

Thinking nothing of those that were killed, the attackers did not cease to send in new warriors until the thirteenth day, yet in no wise did it appear that the castle was weakened. At last a person called Yoshikawa Hachirō, a resident of the province of Harima, came before the grand marshal, saying:

"Not easily can this castle be brought down through force alone. Nor will its stores soon fail, for assuredly Kusunoki has laid up food in abundance, since for the past one or two years he has held Izumi and Kawachi in the palm of his hand.

"Now truly it appears that there is no place whence water can be obtained for the castle, since on three sides there are deep gorges, and on the fourth side flat land; moreover, the mountains are far distant. Yet they extinguish our fire arrows with water jets. Assuredly they have brought a stream from the southern mountains by a pipe under the ground, since they possess water in this abundance, although no rain has fallen of late. Will not my lord gather together laborers to dig where the mountains draw near to the flat land?"

So he spoke, and the grand marshal thought, "Truly!"

When the assembled laborers had dug straight through the sloping ground hard by the castle, they uncovered a trough twenty feet below the ground, with stone walls, and cypress tiles on top, bringing water from a place more than a thousand yards distant. And the attackers stopped the water.

Thereupon there was such a dearth of water in the castle that the warriors could not support the thirsting of their mouths. For four or five days they waited for rain to fall, licking the morning dew from green things and pressing their bodies to ground moistened by the night air; yet no rain fell. Meanwhile the attackers took their advantage, and shot fire arrows in great abundance, that burned down two towers in front.

When the warriors inside the castle had not drunk water for twelve days, their limbs grew faint, and there was no means whereby they might defend themselves. They opened the gate to go forth together, saying, "Since we must perish, let us go out before our strength is decayed utterly, that we may die as is fitting, exchanging sword thrusts with an enemy." But the commandant of the castle, the lay monk Hirano Shōgen, ran down from his high tower to hold their sleeves, saying:

"Refrain awhile from rash action. You cannot stand against worthy enemies when you are thus wearied and athirst, and truly it would be a grievous and shameful thing to become captives of nameless soldiers of low degree. Now the castles at Yoshino and Mount Kongō are still holding fast, nor are the disturbances quieted in the western provinces. I believe that those who come out as prisoners here will not be cut down, lest they become a warning to

Chapter 6

others who might surrender. Since we can do no other, let us surrender ourselves and remain alive to await the coming of an auspicious time."

So he spoke, and all of them agreed that it ought to be so, giving up the idea of dying in battle on that day.

During the fighting on the next day, Hirano climbed up to his high tower and spoke a word to the enemy, saying:

"There is that which I would say to the grand marshal. Stop the fighting awhile to hear it."

The grand marshal sent Shibuya Jūrō to ask concerning this matter, and Hirano went out through the gate to meet him. Hirano spoke to Shibuya, saying:

"When Kusunoki subdued the lands of Izumi and Kawachi, and his power waxed strong therein, with reluctant heart I joined myself to your enemy, desiring to escape affliction thereby. I thought to go up to the capital to speak of this thing, but just at that time your mighty host came forward to attack me, wherefore I let fly an arrow, as is the way of warriors. If this transgression be forgiven, I will stretch out my neck to surrender, but if it be not forgiven, then I must shoot an arrow and expose my corpse on the battlefield. Let the grand marshal be informed of all these my words."

The grand marshal rejoiced greatly thereat. He replied to Hirano that the lords of Rokuhara would not only suffer him to retain his lands, but would give rewards to meritorious warriors among his men. And he indeed stopped the fighting.

Then the two hundred and eighty-two warriors in the castle came forth to surrender, for they knew not but that they would perish on the morrow, nor could they support their thirst for water. But when Nagasaki Kurō Saemon-no-jō received them, he spoiled them of their armor and swords, saying that such was the rule for prisoners, and sent them away toward the capital with their lower arms tied against their upper arms. Then to be sure they repented vainly, saying, "We ought to have died in battle!"

When the prisoners were come to the capital, the men of Rokuhara guarded them straitly.

"Since this fighting is but newly begun," they said, "let us make these a sacrifice to the gods of war and a warning to men." And they brought them to the Sixth Ward river bed, struck down every man of them, and hung up their heads.

On hearing of this, the warriors entrenched at Yoshino and Mount Kongō ground their teeth like lions, nor did any man think of coming out to surrender.

7

The Battle of Yoshino Castle

ON THE SIXTEENTH DAY of the first month of the third year of Genkō, with sixty thousand riders the lay monk Nikaidō Dōun of Dewa drew near to Yoshino castle, wherein the Prince of the Great Pagoda entrenched himself. When the host of the attackers looked up toward the castle from the wide pools of the Natsumi River, they beheld banners of white, red, and brocade streaming in the breeze on the mountain-top, most like to clouds or flowers, while at the foot of the mountain five or six thousand warriors waited with glittering helmet-stars and linked armor sleeves, vesting the ground with the semblance of damask or embroidery. Moreover, the peak was a high peak gained by a narrow way, a place of steep heights and slippery moss. Though the host of the attackers be many myriads of horsemen, not easily might they bring down such a castle!

Now these two armies exchanged arrows at the hour of the hare on the eighteenth day, and strove together mightily in battle, sending forward fresh men many times. By reason of knowing the ground, the prince's men ran out from blocked-up places, scattered apart over impassable places, fought together, fought separately, and shot their arrows terribly. Likewise the besiegers, fearless warriors from east of the barrier, looked not to the death of parent or child, counted as nothing the fall of lord or retainer, and pressed forward again and again over the corpses of the slain. During seven days and seven nights they fought, never stopping to rest their bodies. Of those within the castle three hundred were slain, and of the attackers eight hundred; nor can any man say how many thousands or tens of thousands were brought to the point of death through being stricken with arrows or rocks. But although green things were dyed with blood and dead bodies lay across the paths, it seemed that the castle was in no wise weakened. The hearts of the attackers grew troubled, and they were sorely perplexed.

Among the attackers there was a man well acquainted with the mountain, the Yoshino abbot Iwagikumaro. Gathering together his men, Iwagikumaro spoke a word to them, saying:

"I have heard that already the grand marshal of Tōjō, His Lordship Kanazawa Uma-no-suke, has brought down Akasaka castle and taken his way toward Mount Kongō. How mortifying it is! Being acquainted with the land, we are entrusted with an attack point at this mountain; yet vainly have we passed several days here, and the castle still stands. We shall never capture such a stronghold from the front, but shall merely lose men.

"Now I believe there will be few defending warriors on Mount Kimpu behind the castle, since the enemy will place their trust in the steep cliffs. I shall choose a hundred and fifty foot-soldiers, men acquainted with the mountain, to steal inside the castle in the darkness and raise a battle shout when the light of dawn appears on the Aizen Pagoda. While the castle's warriors are bewildered by the shouting, the forces in front will attack them from three sides; whereupon assuredly we shall bring down the castle and capture the prince alive."

So he commanded them, and chose a hundred and fifty soldiers to go around to Mount Kimpu at dusk on that day.

When the hundred and fifty had climbed up over the rocks, they beheld no defending warriors at all, but only banners bound to treetops in divers places. They stole inside the castle as it pleased them, laid their bows and arrows under trees or behind rocks, and made pillows of their helmets to await the dawn.

When the hour of the signal drew near, the fifty thousand horsemen in front pressed upward from three directions, whereupon five hundred monks of Yoshino came down to the places of attack to give battle against them. But while attackers and defenders fought with flying sparks of fire, driving one another up and down the mountain without regard for life, the attackers in the rear, the one hundred and fifty warriors who had come around by Mount Kimpu, descended from the Aizen Pagoda, lighted fires in many places, and raised a battle shout. Powerless to stand against the enemies in front and behind, the monks of Yoshino perished each after his own fashion, cutting open their bellies and running into the blazing fires to die, or laying hold upon enemies and fighting them with their swords until attacker and attacked were dead. Truly the ditch in front became as level ground, filled up with the bodies of the slain!

Suddenly the enemy in the rear pressed forward from Katte-no-myōjin Shrine to the Vajrasattva Hall, the abiding place of the Prince of the Great Pagoda. And thinking that he could not escape, the prince tranquilly clothed his body in a new suit of scarlet-braided armor over an underdress of red brocade, tied the cords of his dragon-head helmet, girded on a short sword, and burst into the middle of the enemy host with twenty mighty men of valor round about him. Although the attackers' numbers were great, they were defeated by this small force, that drove them back in every direction and raised the dust like black smoke as they cut them with their swords, until like leaves scattering in the wind they ran away to the gorges on the four sides.

When the enemy had fled, the prince gathered together his warriors in the courtyard of the Vajrasattva Hall, where he caused his outer curtain to be pulled up, that they might drink together for the last time. Seven arrows were lodged in his armor, and blood spurted from his upper arm and cheek like a waterfall. Yet he did not pull at the arrows or wipe away the blood, but tipped the large saucer three times, seated on an animal skin.

Kidera Sagami danced in front of the prince with an enemy head fixed to the point of his four-foot sword, singing:

> As the flashing of lightning was the lowering of halberds and swords;

As the falling of spring rain was the scattering of crags and boulders.
Yet they drew not near to the person of Indra,
But thereby was Asura brought down!¹

Truly he was most like to the valiant Fan K'uai, who opened the curtains to glare at the Hsiang prince from the courtyard when the lords of Han and Ch'u met at Hung-men, and Hsiang Po and Hsiang Chuang of Ch'u danced the sword dance.²

Now as the fighting in front raged furiously, the battle cries of enemies and friends mingled together. Into the prince's presence came Murakami Hikoshirō Yoshiteru, looking to have striven against many a foe, with sixteen arrows drooping in his armor like lingering winter grasses bowing before the wind on a withered moor. Murakami spoke to the prince, saying:

"For these several hours have I fought at the second gate in front, since regrettably the enemy has broken through the outer gate. I come here now because I have heard the sound of drinking in the prince's abiding place. I do not believe that we can prevail at this castle, since the enemy's strength is beyond resistance, and the hearts of our warriors are dispirited. His Highness must seek to break through in one direction before the enemy's strength spreads to other places. Yet if no warrior remains behind to fight, the enemy will perceive that he has escaped, and there will be no end to their pursuing after him. I ask His Highness most respectfully to give me his underdress of brocade, and likewise his armor, that by assuming his guise I may deceive the enemy and substitute my life for his."

So he spoke, but the prince answered him, saying:

"How can such a thing be? If we are to die, let it be in the same place."

---

¹ Kidera sings this song (of unknown provenance) to compare the prince's battle against the eastern warriors with the famous struggle in which the Hindu god Indra defeated the hosts of the demon Asura.

² When the two great rivals, Han Kao Tsu and Hsiang Yü of Ch'u, were meeting together at Hung-men, Hsiang Chuang drew his sword and began a dance which seemed likely to end in the murder of Kao Tsu. (Hsiang Po, who was also dancing, was protecting Kao Tsu by the motions of his body.) Hearing of what was happening, Fan K'uai of Han hurried to the scene and confronted Hsiang Yü angrily. The crisis passed when Hsiang Yü gave Fan wine to drink in admiration of his courage.

Chapter 7

Then with rough words Yoshiteru spoke again, saying:

"Strange indeed! Did Kao Tsu of Han turn away his face when Chi Hsin begged to assume his guise to deceive the eyes of Ch'u at the encirclement of Jung-yang? How regrettable it is that His Highness thinks to subdue the realm with such a weak spirit as this! Let him take off his armor quickly!"

And he untied the overgirdle of the prince's armor.

Then perhaps the prince thought in his heart that it ought to be so, for he took off and exchanged his armor and underdress, saying, "If I live, I shall offer prayers on your behalf. If both of us are smitten by the enemy, we shall follow the same path to the nether regions." And weeping he fled away southward from before Katteno-myōjin Shrine.

Yoshiteru mounted up to the high tower at the second gate, where he watched until the prince had fled far away. When the time was right, he cut off the board from a window in the tower to show his person, naming his name with a mighty shout.

"I am the Prince of the Blood Son'un of first rank, minister of military affairs and second son of Go-Daigo Tenno, the ninety-fifth mikado since Jimmu Tenno, the august scion of Amaterasu Ōmikami. Beaten down by rebels, I destroy myself to avenge my grievances in the afterlife. Mark me well, that you may know how to rip open your bellies when fortune fails the military!"

Stripping away his armor, he cast it down from the tower. Next he took off the narrow-sleeved coat of his underdress, fashioned of a woven double thickness of raw and glossed silk; and clad only in brocade trousers, he pierced his fair white skin with a dagger. He cut in a straight line from left to right, flung out his bowels onto the board of the tower, thrust his sword into his mouth, and fell forward onto his face.

When the attackers before and behind saw this, every man thought in his heart, "Aha! The Prince of the Great Pagoda has killed himself! I must take his head before the others!" But while they broke the four-sided encirclement to gather in one place, the prince fled away toward the Tennokawa River.

Just at this time, five hundred followers of the Yoshino abbot came around from the south, men well acquainted with the land for many years, who made a circle and sought by superior numbers to cut off the prince's road. But together with the prince there rode one Hyōe Kurando Yoshitaka, a son of Murakami Hikoshirō Yoshiteru. When this Yoshitaka had beheld his father Yoshiteru preparing to take his life on the tower in the prince's place, he had galloped there to die with him. Yet strongly his father admonished him, saying, "Although such is the proper thing as between parent and child, live on awhile, that you may remain with the prince to the end." Wherefore Yoshitaka fled with the prince, prolonging his brief life.

Now Yoshitaka alone stood forth against the enemy, thinking: "The prince's peril is most extreme. He cannot escape unless I die here."

He cut the knees of the pursuing enemy's horses, so that they dropped down, and smote the sides of their necks, so that the riders fell off; and for an hour he held back the five hundred horsemen on the narrow winding path. But although Yoshitaka's loyalty was like a rock, his body was not made of metal. Arrows wounded his flesh in more than ten places, shot by enemies surrounding him. And doubtless he thought, "Though I die, it shall not be at an enemy's hands." For he ran into a thicket of small bamboo, ripped open his belly, and perished. But while father and son of the Murakami were dying in battle to hold back the enemy, the prince escaped from the tiger's jaws and fled away toward Mount Kōya.[3]

Now Dōun the lay monk of Dewa, deceived when Murakami cut his belly in the prince's stead, took Murakami's head to the capital to be inspected by the lords of Rokuhara. But these said, "It is the head of another." Nor did they hang it up at the prison gate, but merely buried it beneath the moss in the place of the dead.

Then Dōun's heart was troubled within him that, although he had fought loyally until the fall of the castle of Yoshino, he had allowed the Prince of the Great Pagoda to escape. Soon he advanced against Mount Kōya, and camping at the Great Pagoda sought to find out the abiding place of the prince; but all the monks of the

---

[3] A mountain in the province of Kii; one of the headquarters of the Shingon sect. Its principal monastery, the Kongōbuji, was founded in 816 by Kōbō Daishi (Kūkai).

Chapter 7

monastery concealed him. Wherefore, when Dōun had passed five or six days vainly in this manner, he went forth toward Chihaya castle.

The Battle of Chihaya Castle

When the armies from Akasaka and Yoshino had galloped to join themselves to the eight hundred thousand attackers of Chihaya castle, then like a show place or wrestling ring the castle was encompassed about by a million riders, who filled every foot and inch of ground for two or three leagues on all sides. Thicker than plumes of pampas grass on an autumnal moor were their banners, fluttering and streaming in the breeze; as morning dew on withered herbs were their weapons, glittering and gleaming in the sunlight. The mountain trembled at the advance of the mighty host; the axis of the earth was shattered in an instant by their battle shout. Valiant indeed was the heart of Kusunoki, who feared not the great enemy, but defended his castle with fewer than a thousand men, depending on nobody and expecting nothing!

Now there were deep chasms eastward and westward of this castle, so that a man might not climb up, while northward and southward it stood over against Mount Kongō in a region of high and steep peaks. Yet the attackers looked upon it scornfully, for it was a small castle, barely seven hundred feet high and not a league around. At first for one or two days they forbore to build positions against it, nor prepared their attack, but with upheld shields climbed together as far as the gate, each striving to be first. Undismayed, the warriors within the castle threw down mighty rocks from the tower tops to smash the enemy's shields to pieces; and while the attackers were afflicted thereby, the defenders shot them terribly with arrows, so that they fell down from the slopes on the four sides, one on top of the other. In one day the killed and wounded were five or six thousand men; wherefore, when the battle commissioner Nagasaki Shirō Saemon-no-jō inquired concerning them, twelve scribes recorded their names day and night for three days without laying aside their brushes.

Thereupon it was commanded, "Henceforth any man will be

punished who seeks to do battle without the permission of the grand marshal." And the hosts gave over fighting for awhile, to make themselves positions.

Now Kanazawa Uma-no-suke, the grand marshal from Akasaka, spoke a word to the grand marshals Daibutsu and Ōshū, saying:

"By no means was it the valor of our warriors which brought down Akasaka castle. Divining the state of things within the castle, we stopped the water, whereupon quickly the enemy bowed before us. I do not think there can be water on the summit of such a trifling hill as this, nor is there a conduit to bring it from another mountain, yet it seems that there is an abundance of it inside the castle. Assuredly in some way they draw it nightly from the stream flowing at the bottom of the cliff to the east. So, please by all means speak a word to one or two of your captains, such as will prevent the drawing of this water!"

So he spoke, and the two grand marshals agreed that it ought to be so. They made the Nagoya governor of Echizen the grand marshal of three thousand horsemen, who encamped hard by the water, pulled obstacles onto the paths that men would follow from the castle, and awaited the coming of the enemy.

By nature Kusunoki was a person valorous in spirit and subtle in devisings. Considering the supply of water when first he built this castle, he found on the mountain the springs called the Secret Waters of the Five Places, where wandering monks drank secretly when they crossed the peaks, places that in one night gave up two hundred gallons of water. Never had those springs run dry, however severe the drought, so that assuredly they would always moisten men's mouths. Also Kusunoki made two or three hundred troughs from great trees, that he filled with water, thinking, "During a battle the spring water will not be enough, since we must both extinguish fire arrows and quench the thirst which will parch our throats." Moreover he attached joined gutters to the eaves of the battle-offices constructed in several hundred places, so that every raindrop falling from the eaves might be brought into the troughs; and he laid red earth on the bottoms of the troughs, resolved to lose no water. For again he thought, "With this water I shall endure even if no rain falls for fifty or sixty days. But how can rain fail to fall?" This was no ordinary intelligence!

Therefore no man went forth from the castle to draw water. Yet nightly the warriors guarding the stream waited eagerly, thinking, "Now! Now!" But to be sure this was only in the beginning, for gradually their hearts grew negligent, their spirits flagged, and they gave over their watchfulness, saying, "Assuredly they will not draw this water."

Then Kusunoki chose three hundred mighty men of valor to go forth from the castle in the darkness of night. And advancing out of a concealing mist before the eastern clouds were lightened fully, these struck down more than twenty of the men beside the water, nor could the Nagoya governor of Echizen stand against the fury of their attack, but fell back toward his former camp. Though the myriads of the attackers' hosts clamored to join themselves to Nagoya, no man of them could gallop to his side, by reason of the hills and valleys barring their way, wherefore Kusunoki's men retired tranquilly to the castle with Nagoya's abandoned banners and curtains.

The next day the defenders hung out a banner on the castle's front gate, one which bore a crest of three umbrellas, and likewise a curtain with the same crest. They laughed aloud, saying:

"Both of these have we received from His Lordship of the Nagoya family, yet since they bear his crest they are of no use to others. We would like to have his men come in to take them!"

Thereupon there was no warrior of the realm who did not say with all the others, "Ah! His Lordship of the Nagoya has been dishonored!"

The men of the Nagoya were greatly angered.

"Let every man of our force perish at the castle gate," they commanded.

Their five thousand warriors, resolved to die, rode again and again over the bodies of the slain without regard for rocks and arrows, pulled away obstacles, broke them into pieces, and came to the base of the far side of the ditch. But although their hearts were valiant, they could not climb up that high and steep side. They stood vainly glaring at the castle, helpless to do aught but swallow their anger.

Just at that time the warriors within the castle let fall ten great trees laid down flat above the ditch in readiness, by which four or five hundred attackers were smitten, who fell over dead like chessmen. And while the remainder clamored discomfited, seeking to escape the falling trees, the castle warriors shot at them according to their will from towers on all sides, until but few of the five thousand remained. So that day's fighting was ended.

Although the resolution of Nagoya's warriors had been most fierce, they had done no glorious deeds, but had been grievously smitten by the enemy. Wherefore men gossiped endlessly, saying, "Ah! Loss has been added to shame!"

Perhaps the attackers thought in their hearts that Kusunoki might not be despised, since his manner of fighting was not as that of others. For no man of them sought to press forward boldly to attack as in the beginning. Nagasaki Shirō Saemon-no-jō commanded the host, saying:

"In attacking this castle we but cause men to perish vainly. Let us besiege it until its stores of food are used up."

Now when the fighting was stopped, the warriors' spirits were wearied beyond endurance by lack of occupation. They brought down linked verse teachers of the Hana-no-moto school from the capital and began a linked verse of ten thousand stanzas,[4] whereof the opening stanza on the first day was composed by Nagasaki Kurō Saemon-no-jō: "Forestalling the rest, show your triumphant colors, O wild cherry!" Kudō Uemon-no-jō added a supporting stanza: "The tempest indeed will prove the blossoms' foe."

To be sure, the words of both these stanzas were skillfully allusive; likewise the form was superior. But was it not inauspicious to call their own side blossoms and compare the enemy to a tempest? So indeed it was later understood.

Perhaps because no other diversion was available to the hosts who had left off fighting according to the grand marshal's order, they spent the days at playing checkers or backgammon, and passed the

---

[4] The composition of such verses was a popular pastime. Each two- or three-line stanza was composed by someone other than the author of the preceding stanza.

nights with tea judging and poetry contests. And these things were a torment to the warriors inside the castle, who lacked all amusement.

Soon Masashige said, "If it be thus, we shall practice a deceit upon the attackers to open their eyes."

With rubbish he made twenty or thirty figures of a man's stature, clad them in helmets and armor, armed them with weapons, and set them up behind folding shields at the foot of the castle in the night. In the rear he stationed five hundred mighty men of valor, to raise a great battle shout when the dawn mists began to brighten.

"Aha! They have come out of the castle," said the besiegers, at the sound of the shouting. "Assuredly has fortune deserted them, that in desperation they emerge in this way!"

So they spoke, each striving to be the first to attack.

When the warriors from the castle had shot a few arrows, all went up to the castle before the great host approached, but the false men remained in the shelter of the trees. And the attackers gathered together to smite the false men, thinking that they were warriors.

After the enemy had been drawn close according to his plans, Masashige let fall forty or fifty mighty boulders all at once, killing more than three hundred of the men assembled in one place, and sorely wounding more than five hundred. And the fighting being ended, the attackers saw that the warriors of iron facing them were not men, but only straw figures. There was no glory for those who had been killed by the enemy's rocks and arrows while attacking these! And how cowardly were those who had trembled before such figures, not daring to advance! No man failed to mock at them, both at those that had died and at those that had held back.

Thereafter the besiegers left off fighting utterly, nor did the hosts of the provinces do any deeds of merit, but only looked up at the castle vainly. An unknown person posted a parody of an ancient verse in front of a grand marshal's camp, saying, "Must one merely gaze at it from afar—the *kusunoki* tree on Kazuragi's Takama Peak?" [5]

---

[5] The original, a lover's lament in the *Shinkokinshū*, has "white clouds" instead of *"kusunoki* tree," but is otherwise identical. Takama is an old name for Mount Kongō, the site of Chihaya castle. Kazuragi is the mountain from which the peak rises.

Then to their camps the grand marshals summoned women of pleasure from Eguchi and Kanzaki to amuse them in divers manners, for they wearied of watching the castle without fighting. It happened that two grand marshals of the Nagoya family were encamped together hard by the attack point, the lay monk of Tōtōmi and his nephew Hyōgo-no-suke. On a certain day each of these killed the other with his sword, where they played at backgammon in front of some courtesans (for perhaps they fell into a trifling dispute over the spots on the dice). Whereupon without cause their retainers began to stab one another, until quickly more than two hundred men were struck down.

Beholding these things from inside the castle, the defenders mocked at the attackers, saying, "See how these destroy themselves, punished by heaven for setting their faces against the master of the ten good acts!" Truly this was no ordinary occurrence, but a strange and curious thing, such as might have been the work of evil spirits.

On the fourth day of the third month there came a messenger bearing orders from the Kantō, saying, "You must not pass the days vainly without fighting." And thereupon the greatest of the grand marshals consulted together and made a plan, saying, "Let us lay down a bridge over the deep chasm between our camp and the enemy's castle, that we may enter the castle." They summoned five hundred carpenters from the capital; gathered together timbers six, seven, ten, and eleven inches thick; and made a bridge five yards wide and more than sixty-five yards long. When the bridge was made, they tied on two or three thousand great ropes and wound them up with a pulley, so that the bridge fell on top of the castle's cliff. How skillfully it was done! Even such must have been the cloud-ladder of Lu Pan! [6]

Now five or six thousand warriors went out onto the bridge to advance against the castle, men of bold and hasty heart, each striving to be first. Truly it seemed that the castle must be brought down! But Kusunoki's men threw lighted torches onto the bridge, piling them up like stacks of firewood (for doubtless they had made them

---

[6] An artisan of the Chinese principality of Lu. He built a similar bridge to help the ruler of Ch'u attack an enemy castle during the Era of Warring States (403–221 B.C.).

ready beforehand), and with a pump pumped out oil like a flowing waterfall. As the beams of the bridge took fire, the canyon wind fanned and spread the flames. The rash warriors who had thought to cross the bridge were scorched by the great flames when they advanced, yet behind them pressed the mighty host, heedless of trouble ahead. Nor might they leap away toward the sides, for their hearts were affrighted by the deep chasm and towering cliffs. They clamored and jostled, not knowing what to do, until the beams burned through and the bridge fell down abruptly to the bottom of the chasm. And then all together these thousands of warriors fell down in a heap into the fierce fire, where every man of them burned to death. Even so must be the torment of sinners in the eight great Buddhist hells, transfixed on sword trees and sword mountains, or burned by fierce fires and molten iron baths!

There were more than seven thousand outlaws hidden in mountains and valleys: men of Yoshino, Totsugawa, Uda, and Uchino-kōri, assembled together by command of the Prince of the Great Pagoda. When these had blocked off the roads traversed by the besiegers of Chihaya, the stores of the warriors of the provinces were used up quickly, and men and horses grew weak from hunger. Wherefore, suffering sorely, the attackers turned back toward their homes in groups of one or two hundred riders. The outlaws waited to kill them in many advantageous places, being well acquainted with the land, so that no man can say how many of them perished during every day and night. If one chanced to escape alive, he lost his horse, his armor, and all his garments. Daily in every direction men fled hiding their nakedness with tattered straw coats, or revealing their shame with plant leaves wound around their loins. Never was there such a disgraceful thing! Truly in this generation were lost all the precious heirlooms of the warriors of the land of Japan, the armor and swords and daggers.

Now in a vain dispute two men of the Nagoya had perished, the lay monk of Tōtōmi and Hyōgo-no-suke. Likewise was it so of the other armies, that when a father was killed, the son cut off his hair to become a monk, disappearing from the camp; and when a lord was wounded, his vassals ministered to him and took him away home. Though it was said that there were eight hundred thousand horsemen in the beginning, those who remained were but a hundred thousand.

Nitta Yoshisada Receives an Imperial Mandate

There was a resident of the province of Kōzuke called Nitta Kotarō Yoshisada, a scion of the Minamoto descended in the seventeenth generation from Hachiman Tarō Yoshiie,[7] who went forth against Mount Kongō from the rear, obedient to the demand of the Kantō. Truly in those days the house of Taira ruled the realm, and the four seas bowed before its strength! But may not Yoshisada have held certain thoughts in his mind? It came about that he summoned his steward, the lay monk Funada Yoshimasa, saying:

"In ancient times the house of Minamoto served the court by quieting the disturbances of rebellious Heishi; and even so the Taira family struck down those Genji who transgressed against their masters. Yet through my unworthiness the Minamoto have exchanged prosperity for decay, and for many years our family has lacked power in the realm. Is it not regrettable? Although I have not failed to think of restoring the prosperity of our house, I have remained silent through fear of the Kantō's strength. But now from the deeds of the Sagami lay monk one may know that his destruction is not far off. If I were to receive an imperial mandate, I would go home and gather together warriors to comfort the heart of the former sovereign. Is there no means of receiving a command from the Prince of the Great Pagoda?"

Readily the Funada lay monk assented to his words, saying respectfully, "The Prince of the Great Pagoda hides himself in the mountains hard by. I shall devise a means of obtaining a command quickly." And he went back to his abiding place.

On the morrow Funada sent forth thirty of his retainers in the guise of outlaws, to climb up to Kazuragi Mountain in the night. Then in the concealing mists before dawn he fought against these

---

[7] Minamoto no Yoshiie (1041–1108) was one of the most renowned of the Genji warriors. He fought so valiantly as a youth that he was called Hachiman Tarō (the Eldest Son of Hachiman [the god of war]).

his men, leading a force as though fleeing, and for an hour chasing them and driving them back, until the outlaws of Uda and Uchino-kōri came down from their mountains to render aid, saying, "Truly they are friendly outlaws." But when these drew near, they were encompassed about by Funada's force, and eleven of them were captured.

Funada untied the bonds of the captives and spoke to them secretly, saying:

"It is by no means to kill you that I have deceived and captured you in this manner. His Lordship of the Nitta seeks to return home to his province to raise the august standard, but he cannot act without a command from the Prince of the Great Pagoda. I have captured you to learn the prince's abiding place. If your lives are precious, let a guide lead my messenger to him."

Rejoicing greatly, the outlaws said:

"If such is your desire, it will be a very easy thing. Pray grant one of us a brief leave, that he may return with a command from the prince."

And one of them went forth toward the prince's camp, while the ten remained in that place.

When Funada had waited eagerly for a day, the outlaw came bearing the command. It was not a princely command after all, but a mandate from the sovereign himself, saying:

> I proclaim the words of the emperor received by me:
> Diffusing virtue, the enlightened sovereign governs the myriad lands; quelling disorders, the loyal warrior pacifies the four seas. Of recent years the Teacher of the Law Takatoki and his followers have despised the decrees of the court, wilfully wielded a treasonable power, and done many evil deeds. Yet assuredly the day of heaven's punishment is come. Deep indeed is Our gratitude, since now you seek to gather together men of war to end Our years of distress, nor will your reward be inconsequential. Quickly devise a plan to chastise the Kantō, that peace may return to the realm.
> The decree of His Imperial Majesty,
> Given on the eleventh day of the second month of the third year of Genkō,
> By the Lesser Marshal of the Left,
> To His Lordship Nitta Kotarō.

Yoshisada rejoiced beyond measure at these words honoring his house. And the next day he hastened toward his home province, feigning illness.

Now to Rokuhara there came men saying:
"For this reason and that, the foremost of the fighting forces are returning to their provinces. Likewise the roads are cut off, whereon stores of food must be carried. And therefore the besiegers of Chihaya castle have lost heart greatly."

Thereupon Utsunomiya was sent to join the attackers with more than a thousand riders of the Ki and Kiyowara, fresh men whose spirits were still undaunted. At once these climbed as far as the edge of the castle's ditch, where they attacked for more than ten days, never retreating by day or by night. And they weakened the castle's defenses by destroying the ditch-side obstacles. Yet not even the men of the Ki and Kiyowara could soar through the heavens, since they could not borrow the body of King Deer Foot;[8] nor might they split the mountain in twain, lacking the strength of the Lord of Lung-po.[9]

Next the attackers entrusted the fighting to the foremost warriors alone, while those in the rear sought to undermine the mountain with spades and mattocks. And when three days and nights had passed, the front tower was brought down by their digging.

"It had been well to stop fighting and dig in the beginning," all said regretfully.

But although they dug eagerly, not easily might they undermine a great mountain more than a league around!

The Rising of Akamatsu

Now to the ears of the lay monk Akamatsu Jirō Enshin came tidings of the strength of Kusunoki's castle, and of the capital's weakness. He went forth from Kokenawa castle in the province of Ha-

---

[8] King Kalmasada-pada, the subject of a legend which appears in the *Ninnōkyō* and other Buddhist sutras. The offspring of an Indian king and a lioness, he had wings on his body and deer hooves in place of feet.
[9] Lung-po was a mythical land of giants; the Lord of Lung-po was presumably its ruler.

rima, blocked the San'indō and San'yōdō Roads, and encamped between Yama-no-sato and Nashi-ga-hara. And when armies from Bizen, Bitchū, Bingo, Aki, and Suō gathered together at the Mitsuishi post station and chased away his warriors from Yama-no-sato (for they sought to pass by, that they might go to the capital according to the orders of Rokuhara), Enshin's son, the Akamatsu governor of Chikuzen, came down against them from Mount Funasaka, capturing more than twenty of their chieftains.

Enshin did not raise his hand against these captives, but dealt with them kindly. And thereupon, with grateful heart, Itō Yamato no Jirō[10] turned away abruptly from the military to join himself to the imperial cause. In the beginning Itō made a fortress on Mitsuishi Mountain above his dwelling place, and afterward he took possession of Bear Mountain, where he gathered warriors together. In a battle he defeated the protector of Bizen, Kaji no Genjirō Saemon, so that this protector fled away toward Kojima. Thereafter the roads to the western lands were cut off, and there was great disorder in the central provinces.

Soon Akamatsu brought down the castle of Takada Hyōgo-nosuke, since all was secure behind him, where Itō guarded against forces coming up from the west. Nor did this lay monk rest his feet even briefly thereafter, but attacked toward the San'yōdō Road. Warriors on his way galloped to join themselves to him, until quickly his followers became seven thousand horsemen, and it was in his mind to destroy Rokuhara with this army. But first he built a castle at a mountain temple called Maya, northward of Hyōgo, to be a refuge to men and horses in time of need. Maya was but twenty leagues removed from the enemy at Rokuhara.

Doi and Tokunō Raise Their Banners

The lords of Rokuhara consulted together, saying, "Let us send an army from Shikoku against Maya castle," for the mighty Utsunomiya was gone to Chihaya castle, and the armies of the western provinces were cut off by Itō. Yet on the fourth day of the second

---

[10] One of the warriors captured by Akamatsu.

month, a fast messenger was dispatched from the province of Iyo,[11] saying:

"Raising their banners on the side of the court, Doi Jirō and Tokunō Yasaburō advanced toward Tosa with warriors of this province, whereupon on the twelfth day of last month the military governor of Nagato, Kōzuke-no-suke Tokinao, came here with more than three hundred ships of war, and fought against them at Hoshiga-oka. The men of Nagato and Suō were defeated, nor can any say how many of them were killed or wounded. Moreover, no man has seen Tokinao or his son. All the warriors of Shikoku have joined themselves to Doi and Tokunō, that with more than six thousand riders prepare boats at Utatsu and Imahari harbors, seeking to attack the capital. Pray take care."

So indeed it was reported.

The Former Sovereign Goes to Funanoe

Now truly were the military's hearts as hearts of men treading on thin ice, and the Kantō's peril was as that of one looking into an abyss. For still the fighting in the home provinces continued, and daily Shikoku and the western provinces grew more disturbed. Orders were sent to Oki no Hōgan, saying:

"The present disturbances in the realm have all arisen in the heart of the former sovereign. Take heed that you guard him well, lest traitors steal in to carry him away."

And Hōgan called together the Hōjō vassals and stewards of nearby provinces, established strict day watches and night patrols, locked the palace gates, and guarded the former emperor zealously.

It came about that the last third of the intercalary second month was the watch of Sasaki Fujina no Hōgan Yoshitsuna, the guard of the middle gate. In his heart Yoshitsuna thought, "Ah, would that I could carry away this sovereign and raise a revolt!" Yet his mind was troubled, for there was no way of telling his thought to the emperor.

On a certain night the emperor sent wine to Yoshitsuna by a

[11] On Shikoku.

court lady. And receiving it, Yoshitsuna took his opportunity to speak secretly through that lady, saying:

"Perhaps His Majesty has not yet been informed of it, but Kusunoki Hyōe Masashige has built a castle at Mount Kongō, where he shuts himself up. A host of more than a million horsemen from the eastern provinces began an attack against Kusunoki early in the second month, yet the castle is so strong that already the attackers make as if to withdraw. Moreover, Itō Yamato no Jirō has built a castle at a place called Mitsuishi in Bizen, blocking the San'yōdō Road. And in Harima the lay monk Akamatsu Enshin has advanced as far as the province of Settsu with a mandate from the Prince of the Great Pagoda, and is encamped at a place called Maya, northward of Hyōgo, where with more than two thousand horsemen he threatens the capital, captures land, and makes his power felt in the neighboring provinces. In Shikoku Doi Jirō and Tokunō Yasaburō of the Kōno family have raised their banners in the imperial cause, defeating the military governor of Nagato, Kōzuke-no-suke Tokinao, who has fled to an unknown place, and all the warriors of Shikoku have joined themselves to them. Some say that they have made ready large vessels to come here to fetch His Majesty, while others say that they will first attack the capital.

"Now truly I believe that the hour of His Majesty's deliverance is at hand. Let him go out in secret while I guard the gate, set forth in a boat from Chiburi harbor, fare with the wind to a bay in Izumo or Hōki, and entrust himself to a suitable warrior. Though I speak with awe, I shall feign to go forward to attack him; yet quickly will I join myself to him."

Hearing these words from the court lady, the supreme highness thought, "Perhaps he speaks deceitfully." And he presented that court lady to Yoshitsuna, that he might know his mind.

Thereupon Yoshitsuna showed more and more that his heart was loyal, for he thought that he was honored beyond his station, and likewise he cherished the lady with deep devotion.

At last the former emperor commanded Yoshitsuna, saying, "If it is so, go before Us to the province of Izumo, win over a family of good will, and come to fetch Us." And thereupon Yoshitsuna crossed to Izumo, where he talked persuasively to En'ya Hōgan. Yet

En'ya shut up Yoshitsuna, nor suffered him to return to the province of Oki.

For a time the supreme highness awaited Yoshitsuna. But when his coming was long delayed, he thought, "We shall go forth alone, trusting to fortune." In the darkness of a certain night he got into Lady Sammi's litter, causing it to be said, "The lady must depart from the palace, by reason that the time of her lying-in draws near." [12] And in secret he went forth from the palace, with none but the Rokujō Lesser Marshal to accompany him, Tadaaki no Ason.

Soon the emperor put away the litter lest men's hearts be excited to wonder (nor were there bearers to bear it). And then the gracious Son of Heaven of the ten good acts stained his august feet with the dust where straw sandals trod, and personally walked over the muddy ground. How shocking it was!

With uncertain steps the supreme highness wandered over the paths of a vast moor, lost in the moon-awaiting dark (for it was the twenty-third day of the third month).

"Surely We have come a very great distance," he thought. Yet faintly to his ears there came the sound of water falling in the mountains behind.

Again he thought fearfully, "May not men come pursuing Us?" and "Let Us go forward, be it but a single step." Yet as in a dream he stood in one place. When might he have learned the manner of walking?

With unquiet heart, Tadaaki pulled at the former sovereign's hands and pushed at his hips, striving earnestly to come to the harbor before dawn, until his body and spirit grew weary, and he wandered lost with the emperor through the dews of the moor paths. But when the night was far spent, their ears heard the sound of a temple bell, lonesome in the lonesome moonlight, coming as from a village near at hand. And making it a guide, they drew near to that place.

Tadaaki no Ason knocked at the gate of a certain house, asking, "What is the way to Chiburi harbor?"

A man of common appearance came out to them from within. Beholding the supreme highness, he said:

---

[12] The birth of a child within the palace would defile it.

Chapter 7

"Although it is not four miles from here to Chiburi harbor, I am sure that you will lose the way where the road divides to the north and south. I will go with you to be your guide."

So he spoke, since doubtless there was sympathy in his heart, though he was but an ignorant countryman. And quickly he brought them to the harbor, bearing the supreme highness lightly on his back.

As the drum made known the beginning of the fifth watch,[13] this man who had become their guide ran around the harbor busily. With soft words he spoke to the master of a merchant vessel making ready to row back to the province of Hōki, put the supreme highness into his cabin, and making his farewells remained behind. Surely this was no ordinary mortal! When the emperor ruled the realm again, he asked for him through all of the province, that he might reward him, but in the end there was none who said, "I am he."

The dawn being come, the boatmen loosed their ropes, raised their sail in the fair wind, and rowed away from the harbor. The master of the vessel bowed respectfully in front of the cabin (for doubtless he thought that the supreme highness was not an ordinary man).

"To furnish a boat at such a time is the greatest honor of our lives," he said. "We shall steer our vessel toward any place that you command us to approach."

So he spoke, with a face as that of an honest man.

Thereupon Tadaaki no Ason called this master close, thinking that it would be ill to practice a deception upon him.

"Now that you have guessed this much, what is there to hide?" he said to him. "He who is within the cabin is truly the lord of the land of Japan, the gracious emperor of the ten good acts. No doubt you have heard that he has been shut up since last year in the dwelling place of Oki no Hōgan, but I have stolen him away from there. Please take your boat quickly to a good harbor in Izumo or Hōki. I will surely make you a warrior, and the master of an estate, if fortune looks kindly upon His Majesty."

Then the master's face became as that of one glad at heart. Swiftly

[13] 4:00 A.M. to 6:00 A.M.

he sent his boat forward, steering skillfully this way and that, with his sail slanted in the wind.

When they had traversed the surface of the sea for twenty or thirty leagues, they saw ten vessels hurrying toward Izumo and Hōki, their sails spread in the fair wind. They were not craft of Tsukushi, nor yet merchant vessels, but boats wherewith Oki no Hōgan Kiyotaka pursued the supreme highness.

Beholding them, the master of the boat said, "Please hide yourselves here, since we cannot stand against them."

He put the supreme highness and Tadaaki no Ason in the bottom of the boat beneath piled bales of dried fish, such as are called *aimono*, and the sailors stood on top of them pushing their oars.

Within a while after, a pursuing vessel drew near to the august boat, and men entered its cabin, searching vainly in divers places. They spoke to the master of the boat, saying:

"Well, he is not on this boat. Has a suspicious-looking boat passed you?"

The master answered them, saying:

"There were two men riding in a boat that set forth from Chiburi harbor at the hour of the rat last night. They bore the guise of nobles from the capital, the one wearing a ceremonial cap, and the other an informal standing cap. That boat is perhaps five or six leagues ahead of us now."

"There can be no doubt about it," they said. "Let us go forward quickly in our boats."

And they put up their sails, corrected their direction, and drew away rapidly.

Then with tranquil hearts those in the emperor's boat thought, "It is well." But looking back over the wave paths again, they beheld more than a hundred pursuing vessels, that but a league distant came toward them like flying birds. The master took up his oar below the spread sail and pushed, shouting loudly, as though to travel ten thousand leagues in an instant, yet the boat would not move forward, for the wind had ceased its blowing and the current ran against them. And the sailors raised a great clamor, saying, "What shall we do?"

Thereupon the supreme highness came out from the bottom of

the boat, took a bit of Buddha-bone from his amulet, and set it afloat on the waves in a piece of paper. May it not be that the dragon god accepted it? At once the wind shifted on the surface of the sea, so that the emperor's boat was sent eastward and the pursuing vessels were blown back toward the west. Thus indeed did the supreme highness escape as from a tiger's jaws!

Soon the boat came to Nawa harbor in the province of Hōki. Tadaaki no Ason went forth alone to inquire of men, saying, "In this place, who has become known as a wielder of bow and arrow?" And one passing by stopped and said:

"In this place there is a person called Nawa Matatarō Nagatoshi. He is not the most famous of warriors, but his house is wealthy, his kinsmen are many, and he is a man broad of mind."

So he spoke, and Tadaaki no Ason asked him many things carefully. Then quickly Tadaaki sent a messenger to Nagatoshi, saying:

"The supreme highness has escaped to this harbor from the dwelling place of Oki no Hōgan. It is in his heart that he will call upon you, because men have spoken to him of your bravery. Say quickly whether or not you will be relied upon."

Just at that time Nawa Matatarō had called together his kinsmen to drink wine at a banquet. Hearing the messenger's words, he could not say yes or no, for his heart was troubled within him. But his younger brother came forward, Kotarō Saemon-no-jō Nagashige, saying:

"From ancient times until the present, the desire of men has been for honor and advancement. Is it not the greatest honor of our lives, that the gracious emperor of the ten good acts places his trust in us? Will it not bring us glory among generations to come, even though we perish on the battlefield? You must resolve to help him at once."

So he spoke, and all agreed that it ought to be so, Matatarō and the twenty and more kinsmen with him in that place.

Nagashige spoke again, saying:

"If it is thus, we must make ready quickly to give battle, for assuredly pursuers will follow the supreme highness to attack him. I will go to fetch him to Funanoe Mountain at once, and do you likewise take your way to Funanoe."

He ran forth, settling his armor on his body. And five of his kinsmen threw on their corselets, tightened their laces, and went together with him to fetch the supreme highness.

There was no litter wherein the supreme highness might ride, so sudden was the affair. But Nagashige wound fresh straw matting around his armor, put the supreme highness onto his back, and took him into Funanoe like a flying bird. Meanwhile, Nagatoshi sent men around to the houses of that place, proclaiming:

"Even now has Lord Nagatoshi resolved to transport stores of food to Funanoe. He will present five hundred coppers to every person who carries up a load of grain from his storehouse."

Five or six thousand laborers came from the ten directions to carry away the grain, none willing to be outdone, wherefore in a single day they carried more than twenty-four thousand bushels. And Nagatoshi gave away all his family treasures to the commoners and farmers, burnt his house, and galloped to Funanoe to guard the emperor with a hundred and fifty horsemen.

Now there was one Nawa Shichirō, a kinsman of Nagatoshi, who was a person subtle in military devisings. This Shichirō made banners of five hundred pieces of white linen, aged them with smoke from pine needles that he burned, and painted them with the crests of all the warriors of neighboring places. And he put them under trees and on the tops of peaks, so that they blew in the gale from the peaks in great numbers, fluttering in the camps as though a mighty host filled up all the mountain.

The Battle of Funanoe

On the twenty-ninth day, Oki no Hōgan and Sasaki Danjō Saemon-no-jō came against Nawa from the north and south with a force of more than three thousand horsemen.

Funanoe was a mountain that towered up toward Grand Mountain on the north, and on the other three sides rose high above the land around it, a lofty peak, compassed about by white clouds far down toward its base. But no ditch had yet been dug at the castle, nor had any wall been erected, for it was a very sudden matter. The defenders had merely cut down a few great trees to serve as obstacles, and broken off roof tiles from houses to use as barricades.

When the three thousand attackers were come halfway up the mountain, they looked into the castle. Thickly growing pines and oaks hid the numbers of the defenders in a dense shade; yet there were four or five hundred banners to be seen, fluttering in the clouds and shining in the sun. They feared to advance, thinking, "Indeed, all the warriors of neighboring places have galloped here. We cannot attack them with our force alone."

For their part, the warriors inside the castle lay hidden in the shadows so that the enemy might not know their numbers, now and again sending out a bowman to shoot a distant arrow. And so they passed the time.

Meanwhile, Sasaki Danjō Saemon-no-jō, the leader of the attackers on one side, had encamped far back at the base of the mountain, when suddenly an arrow flying from an unknown place pierced his right eye, so that he fell down dead. And thereupon his five hundred followers changed color, unwilling to give battle. Moreover, Sado-no-zenji, who had advanced toward the rear of the castle with more than eight hundred horsemen, rolled up his banner, took off his helmet, and surrendered. But Oki no Hōgan, who knew nothing of these things, thought, "Assuredly the forces in the rear are drawing close now," and fought against the outer gate without stopping, sending in fresh warriors one after another.

As the sun made ready to hide itself behind the western mountains, suddenly the sky darkened, the wind blew, a great rain fell, and thunder rumbled as though to destroy the mountain. Trembling with fear, the attackers crowded together under this tree and that, whereupon Tarō Saemon-no-jō Nagashige and Kojirō Nagataka, Nawa Matatarō Nagatoshi's younger brothers, sent forth archers on the right and left, who shot them mercilessly. And when the enemy shields wavered, they drew their swords and sprang forward, shouting, "Hurrah! They are ours!" And they drove back the thousand attackers at the front, so that they fell down to the bottoms of the gorges. No man can tell how many of them perished, pierced by the swords and daggers of their comrades.

Oki no Hōgan alone entered alive into a small boat to go back to his province. Yet the men of that place guarded the inlets and bays against him, by reason that their hearts had changed abruptly. He drifted with the waves and winds to Tsuruga in Echizen, but very soon he cut open his belly in a wayside temple at Bamba in the land of Ōmi (it being the time when Rokuhara was brought down).

Although the age was an age of decline, did not heaven's justice still prevail? It was strange indeed that Oki no Hōgan was himself destroyed utterly in thirty days, and his head hung up on a warrior's banner-halberd,[14] he who had thus grievously distressed the former sovereign!

Now when men knew that the supreme highness had come back from the province of Oki to sojourn at Funanoe, warriors from all the provinces galloped to join themselves to him, the one after the other. Nor could Funanoe Mountain contain the mighty host, but for two or three leagues in every direction from its base there was no empty place, not even beneath a tree or bush.

[14] A halberd with a small crested banner attached at the top.

8

The Battle of Maya, and the Battles of Sakabe and Segawa

Now there came many fast messengers to Rokuhara from Izumo and Hōki, saying, "The former sovereign has come to Funanoe, whither all the warriors of neighboring provinces gallop to join themselves to him; for Oki no Hōgan has been defeated in battle." And with colorless faces those who heard thought in their hearts, "The hour of calamity is come."

"Still, we cannot permit the enemy to stay in a place near the capital," said the lords of Rokuhara. "We must first attack Maya castle in the province of Settsu, that we may subdue Akamatsu."

Then to the forces of Sasaki Hōgan Tokinobu and Hitachi-nozenji Tokitomo they added the watchmen of the forty-eight places, as well as three hundred Miidera monks and warriors of the capital, to go forth against Maya castle, more than five thousand riders, that departed from the city on the fifth day of the intercalary second month. And these advanced from Motomezuka and Yahata Woods at the southern base of Maya castle, at the hour of the hare on the eleventh day.

When he beheld the enemy, the Akamatsu lay monk thought to draw them to a perilous place. He sent down one or two hundred foot archers toward the bottom of the mountain, who merely shot a few distant arrows before retreating again toward the castle. And the five thousand jubilant attackers climbed after these up the steep south hillside, jostling and shoving, neither men nor horses stopping for an instant to breathe.

There was a steep and narrow path on this mountain, called the Seven Bends. As the attackers hesitated there, not able to climb up easily, the teacher of discipline Akamatsu Sokuyū and Akuma Kurō Saemon-no-jō Mitsuyasu descended to a place where the mountain bulged out southward, whence they shot quickly many times without grudging their arrows. The attackers wavered, each seeking shelter behind the other, whereupon two sons of the Akamatsu lay monk advanced against them from the second of Maya's eminences, Norisuke the governor of Shinano and Sadanori the governor of Chikuzen, with Sayo, Kōzuki, Kodera, and five hundred men of the Hayami band, who came down like the crumbling of a great mountain with sword points aligned.

Although the captains of the attackers commanded, "Let those in the rear withdraw first," their warriors would not listen, since each thought to go back before the other. Yet they could neither retreat nor fight a defensive fight, by reason that muddy rice fields lay hard against the path, where horses sank down beyond their knees; likewise the narrow way was encompassed about by thick brambles. Soon for three leagues men and horses lay dead in heaps, from the foot of the castle to the west bank of the Muko River, nor could travelers make their way past them. Although it was said that seven thousand horsemen rode forth in this army from Rokuhara, not a thousand returned. Great indeed was the dismay in the capital and Rokuhara!

Nevertheless there were those who said:

"Still, this enemy has arisen from a nearby place, nor have we heard that many warriors have joined themselves to him. Even if he gains one or two victories, what will it amount to?"

When the enemy was thought of in this way, no advantage had been lost by retreating.

Now again men came, saying that even the stewards and housemen of the Hōjō family were gone over to the enemy in the province of Bizen.

"We must send attackers against Maya castle before its strength increases," said the lords of Rokuhara, and they dispatched another

Chapter 8

army of ten thousand horsemen on the twenty-eighth day of the month.

Upon hearing of this, the Akamatsu lay monk said, "To win a victory in fighting, nothing can be better than coming out suddenly, oppressing the spirit of a great enemy, quickly changing to new devisings, and being beforehand in acting." He led his three thousand horsemen out of Maya castle to camps at Sakabe.

On the tenth day of the third month, one came to Akamatsu, saying, "The army of Rokuhara is come to Segawa." Yet Akamatsu's heart was at ease, for he thought, "Doubtless the battle will not be set in array until tomorrow." And there being a passing shower, this lay monk entered a small hut to dry his armor and wait for the ending of the rain. But while he abode therein, suddenly Awa no Ogasawara advanced against him with more than three thousand riders, come onto the land from boats at Amagasaki.

Although the warriors with Akamatsu were scarcely more than fifty men, they galloped into the middle of the mighty host to fight against them, not looking to the right or left. Yet how might they prevail against the enemy's great numbers? Forty-seven of them were struck down, and only five warriors remained with Akamatsu. But these six cast off the tokens whereby men might know them, and rode around among the enemy. Perhaps the enemy could not distinguish them, or perhaps heaven helped them in their need, for every man of them escaped from the tiger's jaws, and galloped safely into the middle of their own force, the three thousand horsemen waiting west of Koyano post station.

Thereafter the men of Rokuhara thought, "Though the enemy are few, they cannot be held lightly, since from yesterday's fighting we know that they are valiant and skilled in warfare."

They hung back at Segawa post station, unable to advance. Nor did Akamatsu attack, but only sought to bring together his defeated warriors, waiting for men who were lagging behind. And the two sides camped apart, not deciding the outcome.

At last, on the eleventh day, Akamatsu led his three thousand horsemen toward the enemy camp, thinking, "If our warriors grow weary of fighting, assuredly will their spirit bow before the enemy." Yet as these approached, they beheld two or three hundred family banners, fluttering in the breeze from the treetops eastward and westward of Segawa station, as though the enemy were indeed a great host of twenty or thirty thousand riders.

At the sight of these banners, seven of Akamatsu's warriors thought, "Not even one or two can we match against a hundred, if our force meets them in battle. Nonetheless, we must fall on this field, since there is no way of gaining a victory without fighting."

They moved up toward the southern mountains from the shelter of some bamboo: Sadanori the governor of Chikuzen, Sayo Hyōgo-no-suke Noriie, Uno Kuniyori the governor of Noto, Nakayama Gorō Saemon-no-jō Mitsuyoshi, Akuma Kurō Saemon-no-jō Mitsuyasu, and two retainers. Beholding them, the enemy moved the edges of their shields as though to attack; yet after all they but watched hesitantly while the seven flew down from off their horses to the shelter of a thick clump of bamboo, wherefrom they shot arrows furiously. By no means might the enemy escape those arrows, crowded together as close as tacks in a shoe for more than thirty-five hundred yards northward and southward of Segawa station, but sorely stricken twenty-five of the closest men fell down headlong from off their horses. And the enemy warriors shielded themselves behind the foremost of their numbers, fearful lest their horses be wounded.

Then seven hundred of Akamatsu's riders struck their quivers and raised a victory shout, saying, "Aha! The enemy wavers!" They attacked with bridles aligned: the young men in the service of Hirano Ise-no-zenji, and the warriors of Sayo, Kōzuki, Tanaka, Kodera, Yagi and Kinugasa.

When the foremost men of Rokuhara fell back, the rearmost failed to come forward in their stead, for it is ever thus when a mighty force wavers. Although the leaders commanded, "Withdraw in good order! The road is narrow!" heedlessly did sons desert their fathers and retainers forget their lords, and all fled thinking only of themselves. So they made their way back toward the capital, but more than half of their host were slain.

Akamatsu cut off the heads of three hundred wounded men and prisoners at Shuku-ga-wara, hung them up, and was making ready to go back again to Maya castle, when his son, the teacher of discipline Sokuyū, came forward and spoke a word, saying:

"The best way to gain the advantage in warfare is to press one's victory by pursuing those who flee. Having heard the names of the attackers, I am sure that all the armies of the capital were facing us. Those armies are weary, since they have fought a losing battle for four or five days, and neither men nor horses will be of any use in a fight. If we attack again before the spirit of cowardice awakens in us, why should we not destroy Rokuhara in a single battle? Was this not set forth in T'ai-kung's military teachings? Was it not kept secret in his innermost heart by Tzu-fang?" [1]

So he spoke, and all agreed that it ought to be so.

That night they left Shuku-ga-wara without delay, pursuing the fleeing enemy in the direction of the capital and burning houses on their way to make a light.

The Battle of the Twelfth Day of the Third Month

At Rokuhara no man dreamt of such things as these, for all believed with tranquil minds that soon the mighty host sent forth against Maya castle would defeat the enemy. Yet as they eagerly awaited tidings thereof, suddenly it was rumored, "The attackers flee in defeat toward the capital." And though the truth was not known, men's hearts were filled with wonder and doubting.

At the hour of the monkey on the twelfth day of the third month, the men of the capital beheld fires, lighted at more than thirty places over against Yodo, Akai, Yamazaki, and Nishi-no-oka. To those that asked it was said, "The armies of the western provinces have drawn near from three directions." And a great clamor arose in the capital.

Then in alarm the two lords of Rokuhara rang the bell of the Jizō Hall to assemble the warriors of the capital, but the chief part of the armies had run away and hidden themselves in divers places, chased back from Maya castle. Of others there were four or five hundred magistrates and civil officials—fat, puffed-out men raised

---

[1] T'ai-kung was a general of the Chou dynasty. For Tzu-fang, see note 10, Chapter Two.

up onto their horses by others—but these were absurd warriors, not fit to fight a battle.

Thereupon the Rokuhara Personage of the North, Nakatoki the governor of Echigo, spoke a word, saying:

"In no wise would it be proper strategy to meet the enemy in the capital. We must gallop outside the city to fight a defensive battle."

He entrusted the twenty thousand warriors in the capital to the two examiners, Suda and Takahashi, and sent them forth toward Imazaike, Tsukurimichi, West Suzaku, and West Hachijō to fight with the Katsura River in front of them, for it was a time when snows were melted by the south wind, and the waters overflowed their banks.

Meanwhile, the lay monk Akamatsu Enshin divided his three thousand riders into two parts, to advance from Koganawate and West Shichijō. When his warriors attacking at the front came to the west bank of the Katsura River, across the waters they beheld the army of Rokuhara, waiting with the banners of many families fluttering in the wind from Toba Akiyama, and like clouds or mist filling all the land from the west gate of the Seinan Imperial Villa to Tsukurimichi, Yotsuzuka, the east and west of Rashōmon Gate, and the entrance to West Shichijō. Truly it was a mighty host!

Now not a man of the defenders crossed the river, since it was commanded them, "Fight a defensive fight behind the Katsura River." Likewise, the attackers were loath to advance quickly, thinking, "This is a force mighty beyond expectation." Wherefore these two armies passed their time in shooting arrows, with the river between them.

In the beginning the teacher of discipline Sokuyū got down from his horse, untied a bundle of arrows, and shot furiously from behind a single-plank shield. Yet in his heart he said, "Not by shooting arrows will this battle be decided." He put his discarded armor over his shoulders, tied the strings of his helmet, tightened his horse's girth, and rode down from the bank alone, pulling at the reins to cross the river.

Beholding Sokuyū from afar, his father the lay monk rode up in front of him to restrain him, saying:

"It is true that Sasaki Saburō rode across at Fujito in ancient times, and Ashikaga Matatarō forded the Uji River.² Yet this river is a great river, swollen with water from snows melting above, nor can one see its deep and shallow places. Moreover, you will surely perish if you gallop into that mighty host alone, even should your horse's strength carry you across. The fate of the realm does not depend upon this one battle. Have you no desire to preserve your life, that His Majesty may sit upon the throne again?"

So he spoke over and over, restraining him strongly. But Sokuyū pulled up his horse, put back his drawn sword, and spoke a word, saying:

"Were our numbers such as might stand against the enemy, then without devisings of mine might we entrust our fate to the battle's outcome. Yet we are but three thousand riders, while the enemy is a hundred times greater. In no wise can we win this battle if we do not fight quickly, before the enemy knows the smallness of our size. It is said in T'ai-kung's writings touching on the military arts, 'To win a battle one must observe the enemy in secret, quickly take an advantage, and attack strongly when he is unprepared.' Is this not a means of destroying the mighty enemy with our few warriors?"

And spurred by the whip, his swift horse swam out, leaving a wake in the swollen current.

Next five riders made haste to enter the river: Akuma Kurō Saemon-no-jō, Itō Taifu, Kawarabayashi Jirō, Kidera Sagami, and Uno Kuniyori the governor of Noto. Uno and Itō rode across the current in a straight line, so strong were their mounts. Kidera Sagami was separated from his horse in the backward curling water, wherefore those who watched saw only the top of his helmet. But whether he swam through the water or walked on the bottom, he came to the opposite side before the others, and stood on a sand bar, shaking off the water from his armor.

Of the twenty thousand warriors of Rokuhara, east or west there was no man or horse but shrank back fearfully, not daring to attack those five (for assuredly they thought that they were not ordinary men). The edges of their shields fell into disorder, and they wavered uncertainly.

² Famous exploits during the struggle between the Minamoto and the Taira.

Again two men of Akamatsu's army led the way into the river, Norisuke the governor of Shinano and Sadanori the governor of Chikuzen, saying, "Do not let them strike down those who have gone ahead! Follow!"

Then all at once three thousand warriors of Sayo and Kōzuki plunged in, damming up the current with their horses until it flowed back over the banks in every direction, making the former pools and shallows into dry land. And the three thousand climbed up onto the opposite bank valiantly, resolved to hold their lives as nothing in the battle.

May it be that the warriors of Rokuhara despaired of success? They cast away their shields and drew back their banners without fighting, some retreating north on Tsukurimichi road toward the Eastern Temple, and others fleeing up the Takeda river bed toward Hōshōji Ōji. For twenty-five or thirty-five hundred yards along their way, their castoff armor covered the ground and lay buried in the dust from horses' feet.

Meanwhile, fires were lighted at more than fifty places in the neighborhood of Ōmiya, Inokuma, Horikawa, and Abura-no-kōji, as though already the army attacking from West Shichijō had entered the capital (which is to say, the warriors of Kodera and Kinugasa, and of Saemon-no-suke the son of the Takakura Lesser Marshal). Likewise it seemed that men were fighting in the Seventh, Eighth, and Ninth Wards, where sweating horses galloped east and west, while battle shouts shook heaven and earth. It was quite as though the three calamities had come upon the city all at once: fire, water and wind, or as though the world were to be consumed utterly in the flames of the kalpa-fire.[3]

Since this battle in the capital was fought at night, war cries were heard here and there, but none could tell the numbers of the forces or the plan of the fighting, nor did the warriors know whither to go to put the battle in array. The defenders of the capital but galloped together at the Sixth Ward river bed, where they waited with amazed hearts.

[3] In Hindu mythology, the fire which burns when a universe is being destroyed; the fire of the kalpa (eon) of destruction.

Chapter 8

The Highness of the Jimyōin Goes to Rokuhara

Now the Hino Middle Counselor Sukena and the Hino Great Controller of the Left Sukeakira came to the imperial palace together in the same carriage. The four gates of the palace had been left open carelessly, with no warriors guarding them. And though the supreme highness had come out to the South Pavilion, asking, "Who is on duty?" it seemed that all the officers of the guards headquarters had gone elsewhere, and likewise the officials of the Orchid Dais and Golden Horse.[4] There were but two persons to attend upon His Majesty, a lady in waiting and a young page.

Sukena and Sukeakira went in to the august presence, saying:

"To our surprise, rebels have come attacking the capital, so ineffective has been the fighting of the court's armies. It may be that these traitors will mistakenly enter the imperial palace to make a disturbance. His Majesty must go at once to Rokuhara, sending the three sacred treasures on ahead."

Then quickly the supreme highness rose up, entered the imperial litter, and went forth toward Rokuhara from the Second Ward river bed. More than twenty great nobles came after him on the way to go with him: the Horikawa Great Counselor, the Sanjō Minamoto Great Counselor, the Washinoo Middle Counselor, the Bōjō magistrate, and others. Likewise, hearing of this, the retired emperor went forth toward Rokuhara, and the priestly retired emperor did the same, and the crown prince and the empress, and even the Kajii Prince of the Blood of second rank. The great nobles in their trains mingled with the armies, and the voices of those who cleared their way were heard constantly. In amazement, the men of Rokuhara hastened to open the northern compound, to make it into palaces for the supreme highness and the retired emperors, and there was a great clamor.

Soon the two lords of Rokuhara awaited the enemy at the Seventh Ward river bed. Yet Akamatsu's warriors did not advance,

[4] Chinese names for controllers and personal attendants.

but only ran about in divers places, lighting fires and uttering battle shouts. (Doubtless even such hearts as theirs were dismayed to see the mighty enemy.)

"Indeed! We perceive that the enemy's numbers are few," said the lords of Rokuhara. "Let us force them back!"

They gave three thousand riders to Suda and Takahashi, to go toward the end of Hachijō Avenue, and to Kōno Kurō Saemon-no-jō and Suyama Jirō they gave two thousand riders, to go toward the Hall of the Lotus King.

Now Suyama spoke to Kōno, saying:

"If we fight these contemptible attackers by mingling with them, we shall but obstruct ourselves so that we cannot attack or retreat quickly. Let us rather leave behind the warriors we have received from the Rokuhara lords, commanding them to utter battle shouts at the Eighth Ward river bed, and let us fall upon the enemy with our own men from eastward of the Hall of the Lotus King, rip into them from every direction, and shoot on their left and right as at a dog-shoot." [5]

So he spoke, and Kōno agreed that it ought to be so.

They sent the two thousand vassal warriors to the front of Shio-no-kōji Seminary, divided themselves into Kōno's force of three hundred riders and Suyama's force of one hundred and fifty riders, and went around eastward of the Hall of the Lotus King.

When the time of the signal was come, the force at the Eighth Ward river bed raised a battle cry, and the enemy turned their horses' heads to the west to fight against them. But thereupon, with a sudden shouting, the four hundred riders of Suyama and Kōno galloped into the middle of the greater force from the undreamt-of rear. They ripped into them from every side, not attacking in one place, but attacking by chasing, separating when they came together, and coming together when they separated, and in this manner they smote them seven or eight times.

Wearied by their long journey, Akamatsu's foot-soldiers fell in great numbers before these warriors riding swift horses, until at last

---

[5] Shooting at dogs was a popular form of target practice for mounted archers. The simile suggests itself to Suyama because the enemy warriors are on foot. (They were probably soldier-monks who had joined forces with Akamatsu.)

Chapter 8

they abandoned their wounded and ran away across the road in disorder.

Heedless of the enemy's flight, Suyama and Kōno rode westward across the Seventh Ward river bed to Shichijō Ōmiya, thinking, "Who can say what is happening in the fighting at West Shichijō?"

In the direction of Suzaku they beheld two hundred enemy riders, men of Takakura Saemon-no-suke, Kodera, and Kinugasa, galloping after the three thousand warriors of Suda and Takahashi, who were powerless to stop their horses' feet.

"Our side will be defeated!" said Kōno. "Let us attack!"

But Suyama restrained him, saying:

"Wait awhile! If we add our strength before the battle is decided on this field, Suda and Takahashi will claim the honor for themselves, so evil are their tongues. Look on for awhile. Though the enemy may gain an advantage, it cannot be a serious thing."

So they stood in that place, while the lesser numbers of Kodera and Kinugasa chased the greater numbers of Suda and Takahashi, who tried vainly to turn back as they fled up Suzaku toward Uchino and retreated eastward on Shichijō. (To be sure, there were those among them who lost their horses and unwillingly turned back to perish at the enemy's hands.)

At length Suyama said:

"It is foolish to watch until our side is enfeebled utterly. Let us join the battle now."

And Kōno agreed that it ought to be so. Their two forces came together in one, galloped into the middle of the greater army, and fought against them fiercely. With the classical four-sided attack they smashed the firm; with matchless valor they met the unexpected. And they defeated the attackers on this field as well, driving them away with Terado on the west.

It chanced that Sadanori the governor of Chikuzen chased after the fleeing enemy when first Akamatsu's army crossed the Katsura River; likewise his brother, the teacher of discipline Sokuyū, did the same. Not knowing that no friendly warriors followed after them, these went up Takeda toward Hōshōji Ōji to the Sixth Ward river bed with but four retainers, resolved to attack the dwelling place of the Hōjō at Rokuhara. Yet it seemed that Akamatsu's warriors had been defeated and driven back quickly, they who had advanced from the Eastern Temple, for these six beheld none but enemies on all sides.

Now the six cast away the tokens whereby men might distinguish them[6] and drew together in one place, thinking, "We shall mingle with the enemy until friendly warriors arrive." But Suda and Takahashi rode around shouting:

"Most assuredly have men of Akamatsu's army mingled with our warriors. Since they are enemies who have crossed a river, their horses and armor cannot fail to be wet. Let that be a sign to you to grapple with them."

Thereupon Sadanori and Sokuyū thought, "By no means will it be well to seek to mingle with the enemy." The six riders aligned their bridles, shouted a mighty shout, galloped into the middle of the two thousand enemy horsemen, and fought against them, announcing their names in this place and intermingling in that place.

Raising a great clamor on all sides, the enemy fought among themselves for several hours, without understanding how few were the attackers. Yet at last all of the four retainers perished in divers places, since the great host could not be deceived forever. The governor of Chikuzen was separated from his brother, and Sokuyū alone fled westward on Rokujō and down Ōmiya.

Eight retainers of the Igu governor of Owari pursued Sokuyū, saying:

"Though an enemy, you are indeed an extraordinary man! Tell us your name."

Tranquilly Sokuyū spurred his horse.

"Since I am a person of no consequence," he said, "you would not know me even if I were to tell you my name. You must simply take my head to show to people."

When the enemy drew near, he turned back and fought against them; when they fell back, he allowed his horse to walk; and so for more than two thousand yards he fled calmly, taking the eight enemy horsemen with him.

As Sokuyū emerged in front of the West Hachijō Temple to go to the south, he beheld three hundred of Sadanori's retainers cool-

---

[6] Badges attached to the helmet or sleeve for purposes of identification.

ing their horses' feet in a shallow place in the stream in front of Rashōmon Gate, where they waited with banners high to gather together the warriors of the defeated army. He galloped in among them, beating his saddle flaps with his stirrups. And the eight enemy pursuers turned back their horses' noses, saying, "We have allowed a desirable foe to escape! How annoying it is!"

Within a while after, more than a thousand of the warriors of Akamatsu galloped together again from many places, they who had been scattered at the Seventh Ward river bed and West Suzaku. Akamatsu brought these men forward from the streets on the east and west to raise a battle shout in the neighborhood of the Seventh Ward. But with the Rokujō Cloister at their backs, seven thousand riders from Rokuhara chased them and drove them away. And then for four hours the one attacked the other, so that no man might tell when the battle would be decided.

At last the warriors of Kōno and Suyama came down to that place by way of Ōmiya, more than five hundred horsemen, who went around behind to encompass the enemy's rear, beat down the hindmost attackers, and killed them in great numbers. And Akamatsu's force, sorely reduced thereby, turned back toward Yamazaki.

Pressing their victory, Kōno and Suyama chased after the enemy as far as Tsukurimichi. But when they saw that Akamatsu would retire, they turned back in front of the Toba Mansion, saying:

"Let this be the end of the battle. There is no need to pursue them so far."

Now the prisoners that Kōno and Suyama captured alive were more than twenty men. And when they galloped back toward Rokuhara, smeared with blood, they bore seventy-three heads affixed to the points of their swords.

The supreme highness caused his screens to be rolled up that he might behold them. Likewise, the two lords of Rokuhara, seated on animal skins, examined the heads, and spoke to Kōno and Suyama, saying:

"Though your actions are ever thus, yet assuredly there would have been no victory in this night's battle, had you not personally joined in the fighting, counting your lives as nothing."

So they spoke, and praised them again and again.

That night by an extraordinary imperial decree Kōno Kurō was made the governor of Tsushima, and presented with a sword, and Suyama Jirō was made the governor of Bitchū, and presented with a horse from the imperial stables. The warriors who saw and heard these things said enviously, "Ah! What an honor for the bow and arrow!" And their names resounded throughout the land.

On the day after they had been chased away in the fighting, Suda and Takahashi galloped through the capital gathering up the heads of wounded and dead men from ditches here and there, and hung them up in rows at the Sixth Ward river bed, eight hundred and seventy-three of them. Yet not so many of the enemy had been struck down. Some among them were merely heads brought forth by Rokuhara warriors who had not joined in the fighting, but sought to gain honor for themselves: heads of commoners from the capital and other places, labeled with divers names. Among them were five heads labeled, "The lay monk Akamatsu Enshin," which were all hung up in the same way, since all of them were heads of unknown men. Seeing them, the urchins of the capital laughed, saying, "The people who have borrowed heads are going to return them with interest," and "The Akamatsu lay monk is dividing his person. Is this a sign that the enemy cannot be exhausted?"

The Sacred Rituals in the Palaces of the Emperor and the Retired Emperor; the Battle of Yamazaki

In those days the four seas were greatly disturbed, and the fires of war darkened the sky. There was no season wherein the emperor's[7] heart was not oppressed with cares of state, nor was there a time when his military ministers might rest their banners. And therefore a command was handed down to divers shrines and temples, to perform great rituals and offer up secret prayers. For it was said, "When shall peace return to the realm, if the rebels be not destroyed by the virtue of the Buddhist Law?"

The Kajii Prince, he who was brother to the emperor and abbot of the Mountain Gate, established an altar in the palace whereon to perform the Buddha-eye rites, while in the palace of the retired

---
[7] Kōgon, the new emperor who had replaced Go-Daigo.

emperor the monk reformer Jiyū of Uratsuji performed the Yakushi rites. Likewise the military presented estates to the Enryakuji, the Kōfukuji, and the Onjōji, that they might enjoy divine protection by winning the hearts of the monks. They gave them many kinds of holy treasures as well, and called upon them to recite prayers. Yet though these offered up prayers, the gods did not accept their unrighteousness; though they talked persuasively, men were not blinded with avarice. For the court governed without justice, and by many evil deeds the military invited ill fortune. Wherefore daily from the provinces came men bearing tidings of trouble, nor was there any end of their coming.

Now Akamatsu had fled away toward Yamazaki, vanquished in battle on the twelfth day of the third month. Doubtless would he have found no resting place, had the men of Rokuhara but chased after him quickly with an attacking army. Yet because these were remiss, thinking, "What more is there to fear?" the warriors of the defeated army galloped together from this place and that, until rapidly they became a mighty host.

Then Akamatsu singled out the Naka-no-in Middle Marshal Sadahira, and proclaimed him as the imperial prince of the Shōgoin Cloister.[8] And from camps at Yamazaki and Yahata he blocked the river mouth and cut off the road to the western provinces, so that there was no more trading within the capital, and all the warriors therein suffered for lack of stores.

On hearing of these things, the two lords of Rokuhara sent forth an order, saying:

"Akamatsu alone afflicts the capital, causing our warriors to suffer grievously. Truly it will be a shame to the military in generations to come, that with cowardly hearts we have trembled before rumors and allowed these enemies to remain within our borders, though from the battle of the twelfth day it is clear that their army is not large. Let the warriors of the court[9] go forth now against the enemy,

---

[8] A son of Go-Daigo who had become a monk. Akamatsu pretended that Sadahira was the prince in order to gain prestige and encourage other warriors to join the imperial cause.

[9] In order to establish the legitimacy of its cause, each side referred to itself as the army of the court and to the enemy as rebels. The court meant here is that of the new emperor.

destroy the camps at Yahata and Yamazaki, chase the rebels into the river, and take their heads to be exposed at the Sixth Ward river bed."

So indeed they commanded. The watchmen of the forty-eight places came together at the Fifth Ward river bed, with the five thousand riders dwelling in the capital, and they went forth toward Yamazaki at the hour of the hare on the fifteenth day of the third month.

In the beginning this army was divided into two parties, but at the Eighth Ward they became one, since it was said, "At Koganawate the road is narrow and the rice fields are deep, so that horses cannot go forward and backward easily." They crossed the Katsura River, passed southward of Kōshima, and drew near to the enemy from in front of Mozume and Ōharano.

Hearing of their coming, Akamatsu divided his three thousand riders into three parties. One, made up of five hundred foot-archers, he sent around to Oshio Mountain; one, made up of a thousand outlaws with a few warriors mounted on swift horses, he left beside the Kitsune River; and one, made up of eight hundred riders skilled in the use of forged weapons, he hid in the pine trees behind Mukai-no-myōjin Shrine.

Unwittingly the men of Rokuhara advanced farther than was meet, not thinking that this enemy would come out so far to meet them. They burnt the houses at Terado, and the foremost among them made to pass before Mukai-no-myōjin Shrine. But thereupon Akamatsu's foot-archers came down with their single-plank shields from Yoshimine Peak and Iwakura Mountain, shooting furiously. The attacking warriors sought to gallop against these to scatter them, yet in no wise could they climb the steep mountains. Nor might they draw them out to the plain to destroy them, for, understanding their minds, the men of Akamatsu would not attack.

Then the men of Rokuhara said:

"Enough, warriors! What is the use of exhausting our bodies by fighting against a band of inconsequential outlaws? Let us give this up and go on toward Yamazaki."

As they rode southward past Nishioka, suddenly with fifty horsemen Bōjō Saemon-no-jō galloped forth to smite the center of their mighty host from the small pine grove of Mukai-no-myōjin Shrine. The warriors of Rokuhara despised the lesser enemy, compassed them about, and strove to kill every man. But thereupon the warriors of Tanaka, Kodera, Yagi, and Kanzawa galloped out from divers places in groups of one or two hundred, advancing in wedges like the scales of a fish, or seeking to envelop the enemy like the wings of a chicken. Moreover, at the sight of these things the five hundred riders at the Kitsune River came traversing field paths and crossing roads to cut off the rear of the Rokuhara army. And then perhaps the warriors from the capital thought that they could not prevail, for they retreated, whipping their horses mightily.

The warriors of the capital were not grievously injured, since the fighting had endured but briefly, yet through falling into ditches and muddy fields their horses and armor were covered over with filth. When they passed through the city in full daylight, no beholder but laughed, saying, "Ah! If only Suyama and Kōno had been sent, they would not have been defeated so shabbily!" So because of this defeat the fame of Suyama and Kōno increased, although they had not gone forth against the enemy, but had stayed behind in the capital.

The Soldier-Monks of the Enryakuji Invade the Capital

Now there were those who came to the Prince of the Great Pagoda, saying, "A battle has begun in the capital, wherein the imperial armies are like to suffer defeat." And thereupon the prince sent forth a messenger to speak persuasive words to the soldier-monks of the Mountain Gate. All the monks of the mountain assembled in the courtyard of the Great Lecture Hall on the twenty-sixth day of the third month, and consulted together, saying:

"Our mountain is a sanctuary that shelters and protects the generations of emperors, and a holy ground, wherein buddhas have manifested themselves as the deities of the Seven Shrines. Now when the great teacher Dengyō first established this monastery, before the window of abstraction and contemplation we gazed upon the moon of permanent reality, which is the only illumination; but suddenly after the abbacy of the monk reformer Jie, we girded on the autumn frost of forged weapons over our garments of forbearance, that we might conquer interfering demons therewith. And thenceforth through the power of the Buddhist Law we expelled the evil that appeared in the realm, and through the strength of our god drove back treachery that disordered the state.

"Although the four seas are disturbed today, and the imperial heart is not at ease, yet from many portents is it known to wise men and fools alike that soon heaven will punish the wickedness of the military. It is said, 'There must be no remissness in serving the monarch.'[10] Although we who are monks have shaken off the dust of the world, how can we fail to render faithful service to the state? We must turn away quickly from the impropriety whereby we followed after the military. With loyal hearts we must help the court in its time of peril."

So indeed it was said, and the three thousand all agreed, "Entirely so, entirely so." Going back again to their cloisters and valleys, they gave themselves over to plans for chastising the military.

It being made known that the monks of the Mountain Gate would go against Rokuhara on the twenty-eighth day, the men of their subsidiary shrines and temples came forth to join them, and likewise warriors from nearby provinces galloped together like clouds or mist. When the arrivals were recorded in front of Ōmiya Shrine on the twenty-seventh day, they were more than 106,000 horsemen.

Now it was ever the way of the soldier-monks of the Mountain Gate that there was no limit to the hastiness of their hearts.

"The men of Rokuhara will flee without resistance when they but hear of the coming of this army against the capital," they thought contemptuously.

Nor did they send tidings to the friendly forces at Yahata and Yamazaki, or consult together with them, but proclaimed abroad, "The army will assemble at the Hosshōji Temple at the hour of the hare on the twenty-eighth day." And without putting on their armor or eating, they came down from Imamichi and Nishizaka.[11]

On hearing of these things, the two lords of Rokuhara said:

---

[10] From the *Book of Odes*.

[11] Apparently they caught up their armor hastily, intending to put it on later, since they are represented below as wearing heavy armor.

"Although the mountain monks are many, not a man of them will be riding a horse. We shall send mounted archers to await them at the Third Ward river bed, that they may gallop around them, get on their left and right sides, and shoot as though at a dog-shoot. However valorous the monks may be, they will quickly become weary from fighting on foot with heavy armor on their shoulders. This is the way to crush the many with the few and destroy the strong with the weak."

And they divided their seven thousand riders into seven parties, that waited in positions eastward and westward on the Third Ward river bed.

Not dreaming that it was thus, each one of the monks resolved to be the first to enter the capital, take possession of desirable lodgings, and lay hands upon valuable things. And carrying twenty or thirty lodging signs[12] apiece, they went forth toward the Hosshōji.

At Imamichi and Nishizaka stood that force, at Furutōge and Yase, at Yabusata, Sagarimatsu, and Sekisanguchi. When the foremost ranks were come to the Hall of Eternal Reality of the Hosshōji, still did the rearmost fill up Mount Hiei and Sakamoto to overflowing. As the striking of lightning was the morning sun flashing on their armor; as dragons and snakes were their banners moving in the wind from the mountain. It was natural indeed that these should look down confidently upon Rokuhara, thinking, "Assuredly with this army it will be an easy matter!" For their numbers were more than ten times the numbers of the military.

Now as the foremost of the monks were waiting briefly for the rearmost at the Hosshōji, with loud war cries the seven thousand riders of Rokuhara came against them from three directions. And startled by their shouting the monks clamored, "Armor! Swords! Halberds!"

The monks went out before the west gate of the temple, a mere thousand men, unsheathing their weapons and battling against the enemies drawing near. But these pulled back their horses and retreated nimbly when the monks attacked, and galloped around to the rear when the monks stood in their places, as it was planned

---

[12] These were to proclaim occupancy and warn off others who might try to take possession of the same place.

from the beginning. In this wise they galloped and harassed them six or seven times, until at length the bodies of the monks grew weary, by reason that they fought on foot wearing heavy armor. And seizing their advantage, the warriors put forward archers to shoot them mercilessly.

Then the monks sought to find shelter within the temple (for perhaps they thought that they could not prevail against those arrows in a flat place). Yet an enemy warrior called Saji Magoro, a resident of the province of Tamba, brought his horse up sideways in front of the west gate and easily slashed the bellies of three enemies with his five-foot sword, such a long sword as had never before been seen. Then this warrior struck the sword against the door of the gate, straightening it where it had bent a little, and turned his horse's head to the west to await the enemy.

It may be that the mountain monks were affrighted by the strength of Saji Magoro, or perhaps they thought that there were enemies within the temple as well. For they turned their feet northward from the west gate without entering the temple, divided themselves into two parties that went in front of the Hall of Eternal Reality and in back of Kaguraoka, and thought only of retreating to Mount Hiei.

Now there were two warlike monks, famous among the Three Pagodas, who lived together at the Zenchibō Cloister in the South Valley of the East Pagoda, and their names were Gōkan and Gōsen. As these were being carried along unwillingly toward North Shirakawa by the great size of their army, Gōkan called out to Gōsen to stop him, saying:

"There are times when one wins and times when one loses, since such is the way of warfare. Nor is there any shame in something which depends upon the luck of the moment. Yet because today's battle was such as might allow the realm to mock at the Mountain Gate, let us go back together to meet the enemy and die, that by sacrificing the lives of two men we may wipe out the disgrace of the Three Pagodas."

So he spoke, and Gōsen said:

"Is it needful to speak? I would like nothing better."

Chapter 8

Stopping their feet before the north gate of the Hosshōji, these two named their names in a mighty shout, saying:

"Well may you know that we are the bravest men of the Three Pagodas, since we turn back alone from the great host drawing us along. Doubtless you have heard our names! We are known to the entire mountain as Gōkan and Gōsen, residents of the Zenchibō Cloister in the South Valley of the East Pagoda. Draw near, self-confident warriors! Use your forged weapons to provide a spectacle for the men of your army!"

So they spoke, whirling their great four-foot halberds like water wheels. Again and again they leaped and attacked with flying sparks of fire. Many were the warriors whose horses' legs were cut when they sought to smite these two; many were they who fell to the ground and perished with smashed helmets!

For an hour the two fought there, although no monk came to join himself to them. But when they were wounded in more than ten places by enemy arrows shot like falling rain, they made a compact, saying:

"We have no chance now. Let us journey together to the nether regions."

They stripped off their armor to bare their upper bodies, cut their bellies crosswise, and lay down on the same pillow. Of all the warriors who saw them, not one but said regretfully, "Ah! They were the stoutest fellows in Japan!"

After the foremost monks had returned defeated, the great force in the rear went back to the Mountain Gate from the road, not so much as looking upon the battlefield. Only the conduct of Gōkan and Gōsen did honor to the Mountain Gate.

The Battle of the Third Day of the Fourth Month, and the Valor of Mega Magosaburō

The military were ever victorious after Akamatsu fell back defeated on the twelfth day of the third month, and the enemies that they slew were five or six thousand men. Yet the four seas remained unquiet. Moreover, the monks of the Mountain Gate turned away their faces from the Hōjō, and men said that they lit beacon fires on the Great Peak,[13] assembling forces at Sakamoto to go against Rokuhara a second time. But then the military sought to win the hearts of the monks by presenting thirteen large estates to the Mountain Gate, while to each of the principal soldier-monks they gave one or two pieces of desirable land, saying, "These are for prayers." And thereupon the counsels of the Mountain Gate were riven in twain, and many monks became friendly toward the military.

Now the imperial armies at Yahata and Yamazaki were diminished by more than half, and were become fewer than ten thousand riders, since many had been killed and wounded in the fighting at the capital. But again Akamatsu divided his seven thousand horsemen into two parties, that he sent toward the capital at the hour of the hare on the third day of the fourth month, thinking, "There is nothing to fear from the warriors of the Hōjō, nor yet from the state of the city."

In the one party were men of Itō, Matsuda, and Hayami, the band of Tonda Hōgan, and outlaws from Maki and Kuzuha: three thousand riders, led by the Tono Sign of the Law Ryōchū and Naka-no-in Sadahira, that lighted fires at Fushimi and Kobata and advanced from Toba and Takeda. In the other party were warriors of the lay monk Akamatsu Enshin, and of Uno, Kashiwabara, Sayo, Majima, Tokuhira, Kinugasa, and the Kanke band: thirty-five hundred riders, that lighted fires at Kōshima and Katsura-no-sato and advanced from West Shichijō.

The hearts of the Rokuhara warriors were valiant within them, since they had won victories in many battles, and likewise their numbers were more than thirty thousand riders. They were in no wise affrighted when they heard tidings of the enemy attack, but gathered together calmly at the Sixth Ward river bed to divide themselves into parties.

Three thousand horsemen were given to Sasaki Hōgan Tokinobu, Hitachi-no-zenji Tokitomo, and Nagai Nui Hidemasa, that they might go forth toward Tadasugawara. (For it was thought, "Though

[13] Another name for Mount Hiei.

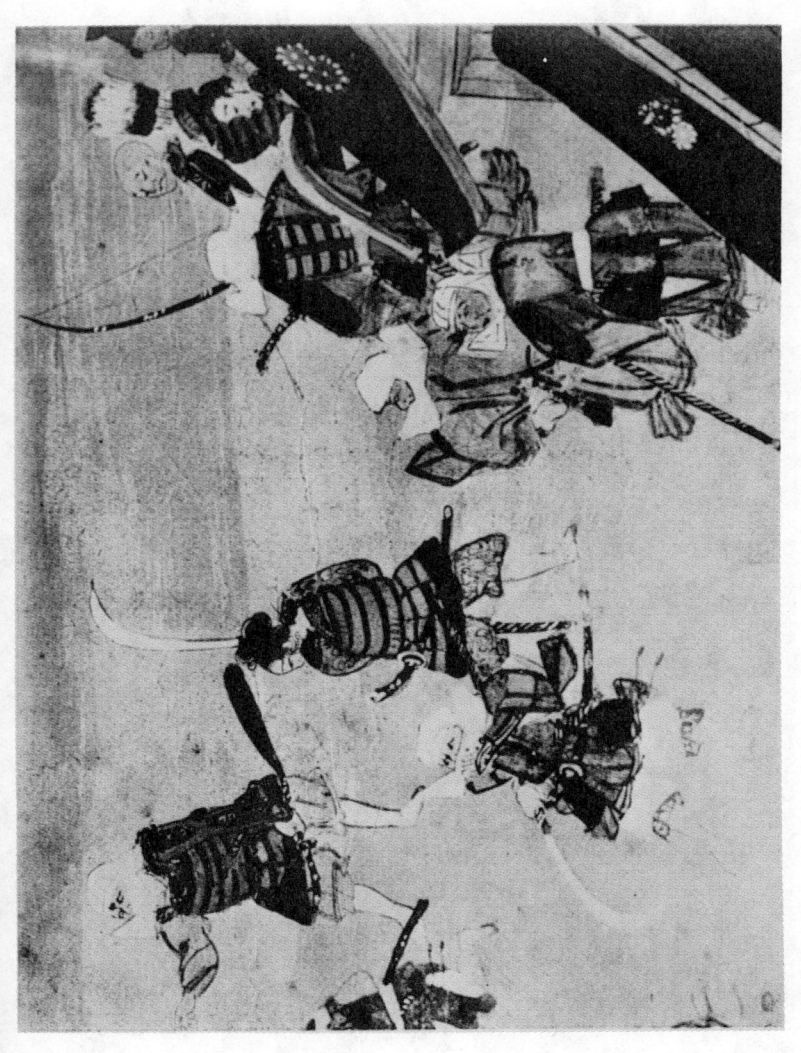

Soldier-Monks

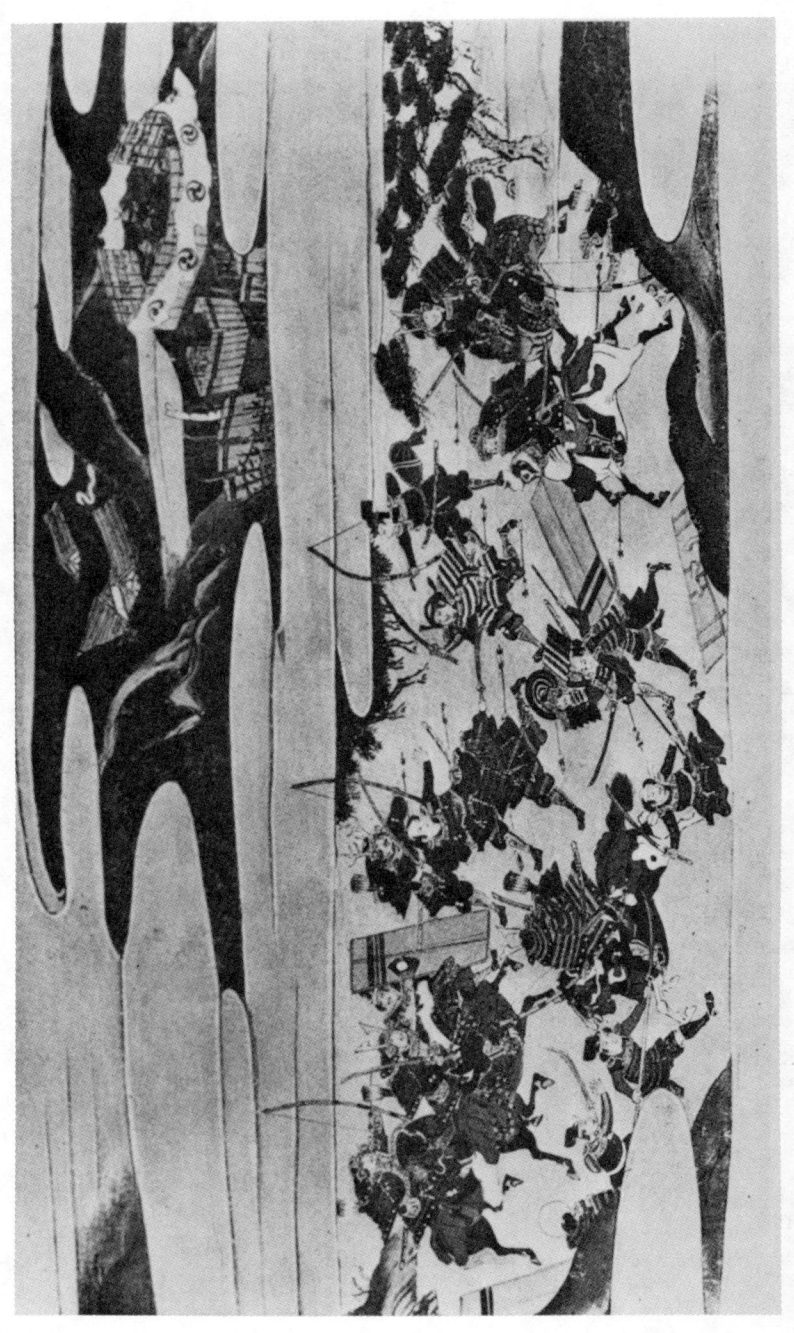

Chapter 8

the monks of the Mountain Gate now incline their hearts toward the military, who can say what wickedness they may devise? There must be no remissness.") And with five thousand riders the lords of Rokuhara sent forth Kōno and Suyama toward Hosshōji Ōji, saying, "It will be well to go there, since we won a victory in that direction in the fighting on the twelfth day of last month." They added six thousand warriors to the men of Togashi, and the Hayashi family, and Shimazu, and Kobayakawa's two forces, and sent them toward the Eighth Ward and the Eastern Temple. And to the end of West Shichijō they sent the Kōtō governor of Kaga, Kaji Genta Saemon-no-jō, Suda, Takahashi, Kasuya, Tsuchiya, and Ogasawara, with seven thousand riders. A thousand riders were kept at Rokuhara to take the places of others in the fighting.

All at once at the hour of the snake the battle began in three directions. Sending forth fresh warriors again and again, the two sides strove together. Among the attackers, warriors mounted on horses were few but foot-archers were many, wherefore these blocked up the streets, shooting arrows furiously together. Within the army of Rokuhara, foot-soldiers were few and mounted warriors were many, wherefore these galloped backward and forward, seeking to encompass the enemy about. Yet neither side could beat down or surround the other, for both were acquainted with Sun-tzu's thousand-charge strategy, and likewise with Wu-tzu's eight-position tactics.[14] They strove together mightily, neither winning nor losing.

When in this wise they had fought until the setting of the sun, Kōno and Suyama joined their three hundred riders together and galloped forward with their bridles in a row. And the attackers from Kohata, beaten down utterly, drew back toward the Uji road.

Next Suyama and Kōno rode across Takeda beach past the north gate of the Toba Mansion to Tsukurimichi, heedless of the fleeing enemy, that they might encompass the attackers before the Eastern Temple. And perhaps those attackers thought that they could not stand against them (though they filled the eighteen blocks of Tsukurimichi), for they crossed westward of Rashōmon Gate and drew back toward Terado.

[14] Sun-tzu and Wu-tzu were ancient Chinese military strategists.

Thereupon chagrin burned in the hearts of Kobayakawa and Shimazu Aki-no-zenji, who had met the attackers at the Eastern Temple, and had chased them and fought against them.

"It is a defeat for us that the enemies we faced were driven away by Kōno and Suyama," they thought. "Let us fight a glorious fight against the enemies attacking in the direction of West Shichijō." And they went up West Hachijō to West Suzaku.

Now the Akamatsu lay monk had made a stand in that place with three thousand mighty men of valor, and it did not seem that he would be defeated easily. Yet Shimazu and Kobayakawa set their battle in array from the side, whereupon the weary warriors of Rokuhara gained strength again to attack from three directions. And Akamatsu's force, wavering suddenly, fell back separately to three places.

Then there came four warriors from out of Akamatsu's army, advancing without hesitation to fight the thousands of the enemy. Truly their resolution surpassed the fury of Fan K'uai or Hsiang Yü![15] As they drew near, the men of Rokuhara saw that they were seven feet tall, with divided beards and upslanting eyes. They were clad in armor on top of chain mail, with metal thigh guards and knee armor. Dragon-head helmets were pushed back on their heads, five-foot swords hung at their waists, and lightly in their hands they held octagonal iron clubs eight feet long, whereof two feet were rounded that they might grasp them.

Beholding these four men, the thousands in the Rokuhara host fell back in three directions, not waiting to fight against them. The four invited the enemy, and named their names with a mighty shout, saying:

"We are residents of the province of Bitchū, known as the lay monk Hayami Matajirō, his son Magosaburō, Tanaka Tōkurō Morikane, and his brother Yakurō Moriyasu. Proclaimed to be outlaws in the far-off days of our youth, we have passed our lives enjoyably as mountain bandits. Now we have joined ourselves to the side of the gracious master of a myriad chariots, since by good fortune the realm has become disordered. Our hearts are ashamed because our side was vanquished in a previous battle, and failed to fight a good

---

[15] Chinese heroes. See note 2, Chapter Seven.

Chapter 8

fight. We shall refuse to give back today, even though our side draws away defeated, nor shall we fear the enemy's strength. It is in our minds to enter the presence of the lords of Rokuhara by breaking through the middle of the enemy!"

So freely they spoke all that was in their hearts, drawing up their bodies fiercely like the Two Deva Kings.[16]

Hearing them, Shimazu Aki-no-zenji spoke a word to his sons and retainers, saying:

"Behold the peerless strong men of the western provinces, even those of whom men speak in these days! Not by numbers alone will they be slain! Do you others go elsewhere for awhile to give battle against the remaining enemy. My two sons and I will draw near to them, to afflict them for a time by advancing and retreating, and then why should we not be able to kill them? However strong they may be, they cannot fail to be struck by arrows. However fast they may run, assuredly they cannot overtake a horse. If we do not make use today of our many years of dog-shooting and hat-shooting, when shall we do it? Come, come! Let us fight a glorious battle for men to see!"

Thereupon these three riders went forth alone to meet the four enemies.

Tanaka Tōkurō mocked at them, saying:

"Though we do not know your names, courageous indeed is your resolution! If it is all the same to you, we will capture you alive so that you may fight on our side!"

He walked toward them calmly, shaking his iron club. And calmly Shimazu and his sons rode their horses forward.

When the distance was meet, Aki-no-zenji pulled back his bow, strung by three men, and with a singing sound the arrow flew away, a shaft measuring twelve hands and the breadth of three fingers. Nor did that arrow fail to find its mark, but pierced Tanaka's right cheek to the cross-stitched bottom flap of his helmet, where it buried half its length. Notwithstanding his great strength, Tanaka's eyes grew dim, nor could he advance further, for he was grievously wounded in a vital place. But his brother Yakurō ran up to him, drew out the arrow, and threw it aside, saying:

---

[16] Fierce deities whose statues guard the gates of Buddhist temples.

"The men of Rokuhara are the emperor's enemies. You are my brother's enemies. None shall be spared!"

He took up his brother's club to whirl against them. And leaping for joy, Hayami and his son followed after, ready to draw their five-foot swords. Yet the hearts of the Shimazu were tranquil, since they were wise in the ways of horsemanship, and excelled in shooting arrows rapidly. When Tanaka and the others advanced against them, they shot strongly, whipping their horses and turning around in their saddles; when the enemy circled to the right, they crossed on the left, shooting at them strongly. So these strove together all alone, the one chasing and passing the other, the famous wielders of forged weapons from the west and the peerless horsemen of the north. Truly it was a sight such as former generations dreamed not of!

When the Shimazu had used up their stores of arrows, they made ready to fight with forged weapons. But then perhaps Kobayakawa thought that they could not prevail, for his two hundred horsemen attacked shouting, they who had waited north of the Jizō Hall of Suzaku. And the warriors behind Tanaka and the others drew back quickly.

Each of the two Tanaka brothers was stricken with twenty to thirty arrows, driven into the cracks of his armor and the inner parts of his helmet, and it was even thus with the Hayami lay monk and his son. Wherefore the four leaned on their upturned swords and perished standing on their feet. Of those who saw or heard of these things, there was none that ceased to feel regret.

Meanwhile three hundred horsemen of the Kanke family came into the capital as far as Shijō Inokuma, residents of the province of Mimasaka, who fought fiercely against the thousand warriors of Takeda Hyōgo-no-suke, Kasuya and Takahashi. When the Kanke beheld Akamatsu's warriors retreating behind them, perhaps it was a shame to them to show their backs to the enemy, or perhaps from the beginning they were resolved not to draw away. For three brothers of the Arimoto Kanke galloped beside the enemies drawing near, Shirō Sukehiro, Gorō Sukemitsu, and Matasaburō Sukeyoshi, and grappled with them until they fell down to the ground. Takeda Shichirō held down Sukehiro and cut off his head. (Sukehiro's kneecap had been smitten during the morning's fighting, and it may be that his strength had weakened.) Sukemitsu took the head of Takeda Jirō, and Sukeyoshi and a retainer of the Takeda stabbed each other mortally. Thereupon Sukemitsu and Takeda Shichirō thought in their hearts:

"Since they were two brothers, and likewise ourselves, we cannot live on alone. Let us strive together to seek a decision."

They cast aside the heads that they bore, grappled together, and cut at one another with their swords.

Thereupon four men turned back their horses all at once, Fukumitsu Hikojirō Sukenaga, Uetsuki Hikogorō Shigesuke, Harada Hikosaburō Sukehide, and Takatori Hikojirō Tanesuke. They grappled mightily with the enemy, brought them down to the ground, and cut them with their swords, until twenty-seven persons were smitten in that place. And in that fighting the warriors of Akamatsu were beaten down.

Likewise, in Akamatsu's army there was one Mega Magosaburō Nagamune of the province of Harima, the seed of Satsuma Ujinaga, a man whose strength exceeded the strength of others, and whose body was excellent beyond comparing. Since his twelfth spring this Magosaburō had sported joyfully with wrestling. There was no man able to stand against him, though he used but a single hand, not in any of the more than sixty provinces of Japan. Moreover, Magosaburō's seventeen kinsmen who followed after him were all superior to ordinary persons, since it is the way of mankind for like to come together with like.

These eighteen men went forward alone as far as Rokujō-no-bōmon Ōmiya. But three thousand warriors of Rokuhara, who were returning victorious from the Eastern Temple and Takeda, compassed them about and smote the seventeen mortally, so that Magosaburō alone remained.

"Though mine is a worthless life," said Magosaburō, "not yet is His Majesty's great work completed. I shall live on alone to render aid in a time to come."

And he drew back toward West Suzaku.

Now fifty riders of the Igu governor of Suruga pursued after Magosaburō. Among them was a young warrior of about twenty years, who galloped near to grapple with Mega Magosaburō where he fled, and laid hands on the sleeve of his armor. Magosaburō thought nothing of it, but unbent his long arm, grasped that warrior's armor-braid, and rode holding him in the air for three hundred and fifty yards.

May it not be that that warrior was a person of consequence? The fifty riders chased after him, saying, "Do not allow him to be killed!"

But Magosaburō glared at them, saying:

"The enemy depends upon the enemy! [17] Do not make the mistake of coming up to me because I am a single rider. If you want this fellow, I will let you have him. Here he is!"

Moving the armored warrior from his left hand to his right hand, he tossed him away with a shout. The warrior flew over the heads of six horsemen riding behind and struck into the mud of a paddy field so deeply that no part of him could be seen. And beholding this, the fifty hastily turned back their horses.

In divers places were eight hundred of Akamatsu's kinsmen slain, warriors whom he trusted above others in this day's fighting. And with fainting spirits and wearied bodies his men drew back again toward Yahata and Yamazaki.

The Supreme Highness Performs the Rites of the Golden Wheel; Lord Chigusa Fights in the Capital

Now to Funanoe there came men bearing tidings of how the imperial armies were smitten again and again in the fighting at the capital, and the warriors at Yahata and Yamazaki were become few in number. The supreme highness was afflicted thereat, thinking, "How will it be with the realm?" He raised up an altar in the imperial dwelling place at Funanoe to perform the rites of the golden wheel,[18] the Son of Heaven himself. And on the night of the seventh day the three radiant sons of heaven appeared in a cloud of glory above that altar.[19]

---

[17] I.e., one enemy may be stronger than another.

[18] A calamity-averting rite in which the Gold Wheel Monarch was the object of worship. See note 25, Chapter One.

[19] Three bodhisattvas, the divine sons of the sun, the moon, and the bright stars.

Chapter 8

Then fervently the emperor believed that his prayer would be granted soon.

"If it be thus," he said, "we shall send forth a grand marshal at once, that he may join himself to the Akamatsu lay monk in the advance on Rokuhara."

He gave an appointment to the Rokujō Lesser Marshal, Tadaaki no Ason, making him a chief archivist and middle marshal, and sent him toward the capital as the grand marshal of the warriors of the San'yōdō and San'indō Roads.

Although it is said that Tadaaki's warriors were but a thousand riders before he took his way from the province of Hōki, the hosts came galloping to join themselves to him, until quickly their numbers became more than 207,000 horsemen. Moreover, Ōta Saburō Saemon-no-jō the protector of Tajima lifted up the young sixth prince,[20] he whom the military had sent away to Tajima as a prisoner at the beginning of the Disturbance of Genkō. And gathering together warriors from nearby provinces, Ōta went forth to Shinomura in Tamba to meet Tadaaki the Middle Marshal, who joyfully raised the august standard of brocade, greeted the prince as superior grand marshal, and in the prince's name sent forth commands for the assembling of warriors.

On the second day of the fourth month, the prince departed from Shinomura to make his camp at the Mine-no-dō Temple in the hills westward of the capital. Nor might all the two hundred thousand horsemen of his host be contained in the Tani-no-dō Temple, Hamuro, Kinugasa, Mangoku-ōji, Matsunoo, or Katsura-no-sato, but the half thereof slept in the fields.

The Tono Sign of the Law Ryōchū was encamped at Yahata, and the lay monk Akamatsu Enshin was at Yamazaki, but six thousand yards removed from the camp of Lord Chigusa.[21] Assuredly was it meet that all should concert together to go against the capital, yet the Chigusa Middle Marshal appointed his day in secret. (Perhaps he relied upon the great numbers of his host, or perhaps he sought to win honor alone.) And he indeed advanced toward Rokuhara at the hour of the hare on the eighth day of the fourth month.

---

[20] One of Go-Daigo's many sons.
[21] Tadaaki.

There were those who were affrighted thereby, saying:

"Strange indeed! On this day which is the birthday of the Buddha, it is the way of wise men and fools alike to purify their hearts in the baptismal waters,[22] and to expel evil and cultivate virtue with flowers, burning incense, and the recitation of sacred texts. Why should anyone follow the way of demons and fiends by beginning a battle on a holy day? Truly there are many other days."

But the warriors of Tadaaki's host took up pieces of white silk, cut them into lengths of one foot, wrote the character "wind" thereon, and fastened them to the sleeves of their armor, saying, "Well may it be that friend will strike down friend if there be no tokens to distinguish them, since our warriors will mingle with the enemy, and Minamoto and Taira will be in company together." Doubtless the words of Confucius were in their minds, who said, "Those in high position are as wind, and those below are as grass. Assuredly must the grass bow before the wind."[23]

Meanwhile the men of Rokuhara made ready to receive the enemy on the west by building mud-covered walls on the outer edge of Ōmiya from the Third Ward to the Ninth Ward. They erected towers on the tops of these, whereto archers were dispatched, and in every street they placed a thousand or two thousand riders, to advance in wedges like the scales of a fish or encompass the enemy like the wings of a chicken.

When they enquired concerning the grand marshal of the attackers, there were those that said:

"He is the sixth young princely son of the former sovereign. The general serving below him is the Chigusa Middle Marshal, Tadaaki no Ason."

Thereupon the men of Rokuhara said:

"Indeed, it is needless to worry about the outcome of the battle. Though Tadaaki be a Minamoto, 'the mandarin orange south of the river becomes a quince when it is moved north of the river.'"[24]

[22] The Buddha's image was ceremoniously bathed on his birthday.
[23] From the *Analects*.
[24] Minamoto was a surname granted to numerous sons and grandsons of early emperors when they became commoners. Some of the families thus founded moved to the provinces and became warriors, while others remained in the capital as courtiers. Since Tadaaki belonged in the second category, there was no particu-

Chapter 8

When followers of the way of bow and horse strive in battle against versifying courtiers, the warriors cannot fail to win."

And valiantly their seven thousand riders made their way toward the outer edge of Ōmiya, awaiting the coming of the enemy with eager hearts.

Meanwhile, Tadaaki no Ason divided his host before the Office of Shrines, whence he sent a thousand attackers into every street from Ōtoneri to Shichijō.

Now the men of Rokuhara had built fortresses and put archers in front of them, and in the rear they had established mounted warriors, to gallop out and chase back the enemy when they wavered. Likewise the imperial armies had placed fresh men two and three deep, wherefore when the first line drew away, a second line came forward in their stead, and when the second line were beaten down, a third line came forward in their stead. The dust of their attacking obscured the heavens, nor did any man or horse rest his weariness. Because both of these armies prized virtue and disdained life—because they esteemed honor and welcomed death—no man of them drew back to escape an enemy, although many advanced to aid a friend. Most assuredly did it seem that the outcome would not be decided quickly!

Suddenly fires burned up in divers places, lighted by men of the Tajima and Tamba forces[25] sent into the city secretly, and great billows of smoke rose up like a screen (since just at that time the wind blew violently). And the foremost men of Rokuhara drew back into the city beyond Ōmiya.

Then the lords of Rokuhara called upon the warriors held in readiness to aid the weak, sending them forth with five thousand riders toward the Ichijō and Nijō approaches to the city: Sasaki Hōgan Tokinobu, Suda, Takahashi, Nambu, Shimoyama, Kōno, Suyama, and Kobayakawa. And in combat against these new forces the protector of Tajima Ōta Saburō Saemon-no-jō was struck down.

On the side of the attackers, Ogino Hikoroku and Adachi Saburō

---

lar reason to fear his military prowess. The saying quoted, which means that men are molded by their environment, appears in the Chinese philosophical text *Huai-nan-tzu* and elsewhere.

[25] Partisans of Go-Daigo.

of Tamba advanced as far as Shijō Abura-no-kōji with five hundred riders, but seven hundred defenders fought against them, followers of Yakushi Hachirō, Nakayoshi Jūrō, and Tankodama from the province of Bizen, until Ogino and Adachi gave back, thinking that the attackers at Nijō were defeated. Likewise, with seven hundred horsemen Kanaji Saburō attacked as far as Shichijō Higashi-no-tōin; yet he was so grievously wounded that he could not withdraw, and the Koezuka family of Harima captured him alive by surrounding him with three hundred riders. Eighty soldier-monks from Miike in Tamba advanced as far as Gojō Nishi-no-tōin, fighting without knowledge of the withdrawal of their allies, but Shō Saburō and Makabe Shirō of Bitchū surrounded them with three hundred riders and killed every man.

So on every side the attackers were smitten and beaten down, until they drew away beside the Katsura River. Only at Ichijō did they hold fast, where Nawa Kojirō and Kojima Bingo no Saburō led their warriors, galloping and fighting furiously.

The defenders at Ichijō were Suyama and Kōno, and the attackers were Nawa and Kojima. Kojima and Kōno were kinsmen, and Nawa and Suyama had been comrades together. Yet perhaps their hearts were shamed by words that had been spoken, or perhaps they thought of troubles to come. For they fought with great shouts, not holding life dear, but saying, "Though we perish here, we will not dishonor ourselves by fleeing!"

Soon there came one to the Middle Marshal Tadaaki, where he drew back at Uchino, saying, "At Ichijō our warriors stand and fight." Wherefore Tadaaki went before the Office of Shrines again, and sent a messenger to call back Kojima and Nawa.

Kojima and Nawa made their farewells to Suyama and Kōno, saying, "This day has already drawn to a close. We shall meet another time." And the two armies drew apart, the one to the east and the one to the west.

Lord Chigusa took his way back to his camp at the Mine-no-dō, for the sun declined in the heavens, and the army was scattered in many places. When he made an accounting of the wounded and slain, they were more than seven thousand men, and among the

Chapter 8

dead were several hundred trustworthy chieftains: Ōta, the Kanaji family, and others.

Then Lord Chigusa summoned Kojima Bingo no Saburō Takanori. (For perhaps he thought that Takanori might become a warrior marshal.) He spoke a word to Takanori, saying:

"Our defeated warriors are powerless to give battle. It is in my mind that we do ill to encamp thus hard against the capital. Rather would I draw back a little, gather together a new host from nearby provinces, and attack the city once more. What is your opinion?"

So he spoke; yet Kojima Saburō would not agree.

"By no means is defeat a shameful thing," he said. "The outcome of a battle rests with the fortune of the moment. A general can be blamed only when he draws back wrongly, or fails to attack when attacking is meet. With but a thousand riders the Akamatsu lay monk has gone against the capital three times, and drawn away unable to prevail; yet he has never given up his camps at Yahata and Yamazaki. As regards my lord's warriors, even if the greater half of them were to be struck down, they would still be more numerous than the men of Rokuhara. Moreover, there are deep mountains behind this camp, and a great river runs before it, so that it is an excellent fortress in time of attack. It is not proper to think, 'Ah! I should like to withdraw from this position.'

"I shall make a camp at the end of the Shichijō bridge, lest the enemy come against us by night, trading upon the weariness of our warriors. Do you send forth four or five hundred trustworthy warriors to guard the Umezu and Hōren crossings."

Thereupon, with three hundred riders Kojima Saburō Takanori encamped westward from the Shichijō bridge. Likewise, for a time Lord Chigusa abode at the Mine-no-dō, shamed by Kojima's words. Yet when the night was half spent, then indeed did this lord set the prince upon a horse and flee toward Yahata from in front of Hamuro. (For perhaps his heart was stricken with fear by the words, "It may be that the enemy will attack in the night.")

Although Bingo no Saburō knew nothing of this, in the late watches of the night he beheld the fires that had glittered like stars at the Mine-no-dō, how one by one their numbers lessened, and in many places they died away. He climbed up toward the temple from Hamuro-ōji to observe the state of things, asking in his heart, "Alas! Has the grand marshal run away?" And when he came before the Jōjūji Temple, he fell in with Ogino Hikoroku Tomotaka.

"The grand marshal fled in the night at the hour of the rat, wherefore we too were obliged to come down from the mountain," said Ogino. "We are going toward Tamba. Come along! We will take you with us."

Greatly angered, Bingo no Saburō said:

"It was indeed a grievous error to make a grand marshal of such a cowardly man as this! I must behold the state of things at once, lest it be a distress in times to come. Pass by swiftly! I will climb to the temple to seek the prince, but afterward I will come behind you."

Leaving his men at the foot of the mountain, he pushed upward alone through the fleeing hosts. When he came to the Main Hall, the abiding place of the grand marshal, he beheld the imperial banner of brocade, where it was left behind, and even the grand marshal's underdress, for with sorely affrighted heart had Tadaaki run away.

Wrathfully Bingo no Saburō said to himself, "Would that this grand marshal would perish by falling into a ditch, or plunge over a precipice!" And he stood for a time on the veranda of the hall, gnashing his teeth.

Soon Bingo no Saburō rolled up the brocade banner for a servant to carry, thinking, "My men will be waiting anxiously." He ran down quickly in front of the Jōjūji, spurred his horse forward at the head of his followers, and came up with Ogino Hikoroku beside Oiwake post station. Ogino took with him three thousand warriors fleeing toward Tamba, Tango, Izumo, and Hōki, who were gathered together at Shinomura and Hieda, and routing the outlaws along his way he shut himself up in Kōsenji castle in the province of Tamba.

The Fire at the Tani-no-dō Temple

Now to the capital came men saying that the Chigusa Middle Marshal was fled from his camp in the western hills; wherefore on the ninth day of the fourth month the warriors of Rokuhara entered the Tani-no-dō in disorder, and the Mine-no-dō, and the Jōjūji, and Matsunoo, and Mangoku-ōji, and Hamuro and Kinugasa. They destroyed the Buddhist pavilions and god halls, took possession of the monks' cloisters and commoners' dwellings, and carried away all the precious things. And when they had done, they burnt the houses. In an instant more than three hundred sacred buildings turned to ashes at the Jōjūji and the Saifukuji, and at Hamuro, Kinugasa, and the Nison'in Cloister. Five thousand commoners' houses were destroyed as well, since just at that time a wind blew furiously. Buddhist images turned to smoke in an instant, and holy objects of the way of the gods, and sacred writings of many kinds.

Now the Tani-no-dō was a sacred place established by His Holiness Enrō, a son of the eldest son of Yoshichika the governor of Tsushima, the eldest son of Lord Hachiman.[26] In the far-off days of his youth this holy man separated himself from his family of many generations of warriors to dwell humbly in a lonesome cell. Practicing the three studies, which are abstinence, decision, and wisdom, he attained the merit of cleansing the six sense organs.[27] Before the window where he chanted the words of the *Lotus Sutra*, the bright divinities of Matsunoo[28] sat in a row with inclined ears; within the door where he performed the mysteries of the True Word, a child guardian of the Law[29] waited upon him with folded arms.

Because this temple was a place founded by such a wise and virtuous man, its sacramental waters had flowed purely during the stars and frosts of more than five hundred years; even to the present

[26] Minamoto no Yoshiie. See note 7, Chapter Seven.
[27] The eyes, ears, nose, tongue, body, and spirit.
[28] Shinto gods worshiped at Matsunoo Shrine.
[29] A messenger from the beneficent deities who protect the Buddhist faith.

era of degeneration had the radiance of the lamp of the law shone brightly. Therein were treasured more than seven thousand scrolls of sutras and commentaries, transmitters of the teachings of the Buddha, stored in a library eighteen feet long on the four sides. The towers of forty-nine cloisters stood above the rare trees and curious rocks of its pond, most like to the inner close of the Tuṣita heaven.[30] On twelve balustrades pearls and costly stones were offered up to heaven; on a pagoda of five stories gold and silver beckoned to the moon. Surely the splendor of the seven treasures of the Pure Land [31] is even thus!

Likewise, the Jōjūji was a place whence the disciplinary teachings were spread abroad, a place for the labors of the Ritsu faith. When the blessed Śākyamuni entered Nirvana, a demon called Nimble Spirit secretly drew near beneath the paired trees before the golden coffin was closed, to break off one of the Buddha's holy teeth. Sorely amazed, the four classes of disciples sought to detain him; yet with a leap of two million leagues he fled away in an instant to the Heaven of the Four Kings halfway up Mount Sumeru. But fleet-footed Skanda chased that demon and recovered the tooth, which in a later day was given to the monk Tao-hsüan of the land of Han. Thereafter it was handed down from one to another, until crossing to Japan it came to rest in this temple in the reign of Saga Tenno.

Now all the people spoke words of censure, saying:

"Extraordinary indeed! Still does the body of the Buddha pass everywhere throughout the world, though more than twenty-three hundred years have elapsed since the Great Sacred One entered Nirvana, the Revered of the World. A shameless thing was the destruction of this auspicious and praiseworthy temple, a sign signifying the ruin of the Hōjō family."

How strange it was that the men of Rokuhara were struck down at Bamba within a very short time after, and all the Hōjō perished at Kamakura! Truly there was none but believed, "Of such things is it said, 'In a family where wickedness accumulates, there will surely be abundant misfortunes.' "

[30] Maitreya's heaven.
[31] Gold, silver, lapis lazuli, crystal, agate, rubies, and cornelian.

9

Lord Ashikaga Goes Up to the Capital

Now FAST MESSENGERS FROM ROKUHARA were sent galloping to the Kantō, one after the other, saying, "The former sovereign abides at Funanoe, whence he sends forth armies to attack the capital," and "Already the matter is grave."

Greatly amazed, the Sagami lay monk said, "If it is thus, yet another mighty host shall we send up, that the half thereof may guard the capital, and the great chieftains may go forward against Funanoe." And making the Nagoya governor of Owari his grand marshal, he summoned twenty powerful vassals.

Among these vassals called to go up to the capital was Ashikaga Jibu-no-tayū Takauji, who had been afflicted of a disease, so that his body was yet infirm. But notwithstanding they summoned him again and again. Lord Ashikaga was angered in his heart because of this thing, thinking:

"Not for the space of three months have I mourned my father's death, nor yet are my grievous tears dried. Moreover a disease smites my body, such as will not let me rest from suffering. How distasteful it is, that still they summon me to a war of chastisement!

"It is said that the great are brought down with the passing of time, and the lowly are exalted. Yet Takatoki is but a descendant of Hōjō Shirō Tokimasa, whose clan long ago came down among the commoners, while I am of the generations of the house of Genji, which left the imperial family not long since. Surely it is meet that Takatoki should be my vassal, instead of contemptuously handing down orders such as these! If he requires this thing of me another time, I shall take all my kinsmen toward the capital, and shall join myself to the cause of the former sovereign, that by attacking and destroying Rokuhara I may decide the fate of my family."

So he thought, while no man knew aught thereof. Not dreaming of such a thing, the Sagami lay monk twice in one day sent a messenger, Kudō Saemon-no-jō, to urge Takauji, saying, "Why is it that you delay to go to the capital?"

Lord Ashikaga in no wise turned away his face from Kudō, but answered him, saying, "I shall go up very soon," for in his heart he was resolved to rebel. And joining night to day, he made ready to depart.

Now there came men to Kamakura saying, "Not only will Lord Ashikaga lead his kinsmen and retainers toward the capital, but also he will take his women, with the infant lords his sons"; wherefore with unquiet heart the lay monk Nagasaki Enki went hastily to the Sagami lay monk.

"Can it be true that Lord Ashikaga takes his wife and young lords to the capital?" he said. "This is a most suspicious thing. At such a time as the present, we must watch even those bound to your family by close ties.[1] Moreover, Lord Ashikaga is a noble of the Genji, who may perhaps nourish a plan in his breast, for many years have elapsed since the Minamoto became without influence in the realm.

"In another country the military rulers assembled their great vassals in times of disorder, killed sacrificial victims, sipped blood, and covenanted together not to be false.[2] Even such a thing is the written pledge of our day. Likewise there have been men who have given up their sons as hostages, that none might look upon them with doubtful eyes or call them treacherous. Was not Shimizu-no-kanja, the son of Lord Kiso,[3] sent to the grand marshal Yoritomo? Since there are these precedents, I believe that you must by all means detain the son and wife of Lord Ashikaga in Kamakura, and you must prevail upon him to write a pledge."

[1] Takauji's wife was a Hōjō.
[2] In China during the Chou dynasty.
[3] Yoritomo's cousin and rival, Minamoto no Yoshinaka (1154–1184).

Chapter 9

Perhaps the Sagami lay monk thought that it ought to be so. For quickly he sent a messenger to Lord Ashikaga, saying:

"Since the eastern provinces are tranquil, it will be well to leave your young sons to abide in Kamakura, so that your heart can be at ease concerning them. Likewise I venture to ask you to leave a written pledge, such as will dispel the doubts of certain persons—though indeed there can be no lack of trust between you and me, since our two houses are as closely united as a fish and water, and moreover you are akin to Akahashi Sōshū[4] by marriage. I think this will be proper, both as regards what is public and as regards what is private."

Because of these words, the anger in Lord Ashikaga's heart waxed fierce, yet he held his wrath, nor showed it in his countenance, but sent back the messenger, saying, "I shall reply later."

Then Lord Ashikaga summoned his younger brother, Lord Hyōbu-no-tayū, to ask for an opinion, saying, "What ought to be done in this matter?"

When Lord Hyōbu-no-tayū had considered awhile, he said:

"By no means is it for your own profit that you plan this great thing. Your purpose is to punish wickedness in heaven's stead, and to beat down unrighteousness for His Majesty's sake. Moreover, there is a saying, 'The gods do not recognize pledges.' Though you set down the words of a pledge deceitfully, will not the buddhas and gods protect your loyal resolve? Do not vex your heart, that you leave your sons and wife to dwell in Kamakura, for it is a small matter alongside a great one. Let a few retainers abide with the young lords to carry them away and hide them in time of peril, and do not fear for your lady while Lord Akahashi lives. It is indeed said, 'In great undertakings one does not consider trivial things.'[5] There can be no delay in such a matter as this. By all means agree to the words of the Sagami lay monk, so that he may eye you no longer, and go up to the capital to begin your devisings."

So he spoke and, bowing before his logic, Lord Ashikaga left his son Master Senjuō in Kamakura, together with his wife, the younger sister of Akahashi Sōshū. Moreover, he delivered a written pledge to the Sagami lay monk.

[4] A Hōjō; the brother of Takauji's wife.
[5] From the *Shih chi*.

The lay monk doubted Takauji no more, but rejoicing greatly called him into his presence and praised him many times.

"There is a white banner used by the generations of your ancestors," he said, "a rare treasure, handed down to the heads of the family from the time of Lord Hachiman. At length the Nun of the Second Rank received it, the widow of Lord Yoritomo,[6] so that it came to rest in this house. Truly it is a rare treasure; yet it is of no use to another family. I shall bring it forward as a farewell present on this occasion. Let it be held aloft while you beat down the rebels!"

He put the banner into a bag of brocade, and himself presented it to Takauji. He gave him ten horses of his own breeding, saddled with silver-mounted saddles, saying, "Use one of them when you have need of a fresh horse"; and likewise he gave him ten suits of armor with silver trimmings, and a sword trimmed with gold.

Lord Ashikaga and his brother went forth from Kamakura on the twenty-seventh day of the third month of the third year of Genkō. With them rode thirty-two of their kinsmen: Kira, Uesugi, Nikki, Hosokawa, Imagawa, Arakawa, and the others, and forty-three allies of high estate, altogether more than three thousand horsemen. And Takauji, appointed to be the grand marshal of the host attacking the rebels from the front, came to the capital on the sixteenth day of the fourth month, three days before Nagoya Takaie the governor of Owari.[7]

The Attack on Yamazaki and the Battle of Koganawate

Because the two lords of Rokuhara had won many battles, they thought contemptuously, "Why should we fear the enemies from the western provinces?" Yet suddenly a valiant and trusted chieftain became an enemy, Yūki Kurō Saemon-no-jō, who joined himself to the armies at Yamazaki. Likewise, by fives and tens the hosts of the provinces returned home, weary of transporting stores, or allied themselves with the enemy, seeking to follow the trend of the times.

[6] Hōjō Masako. She became a nun after Yoritomo's death.
[7] The other commanding general appointed by Takatoki.

Chapter 9

The court's armies increased manyfold, notwithstanding their defeats, but daily the warriors of the Hōjō grew fewer, notwithstanding their victories. And many in the capital were fearful of things to come.

When like clouds or mist the two armies of Ashikaga and Nagoya advanced into the city, men's hearts changed quickly, color returned to pale faces, and all were of good cheer, saying, "What can happen now?" But on the next day after Lord Ashikaga's arrival in the capital, in secret he sent forth a messenger to Funanoe in Hōki, to speak of joining himself to the side of the court. And joyfully the emperor commanded him to gather together imperial armies from the provinces to strike down the enemies of the court.

The lords of Rokuhara knew nothing of these designs of Lord Ashikaga, nor did the Nagoya governor of Owari. Daily they met with him to speak privately of going forth against Yahata and Yamazaki, not concealing anything that was in their minds. How imprudent they were!

> The road of Ta-hsing often breaks carts,
> Yet by comparison with men's hearts it is a level road.
> The water of Wu-hsia often upsets boats,
> Yet by comparison with men's hearts it is a peaceful stream.
> Far from ordinary is the love of evil in men's hearts! [8]

So indeed it is said. Yet for many generations the house of Ashikaga had found favor in the sight of the Hōjō and received kindnesses from their hands, so that there was none in the realm to match its prospering. Likewise Takauji had taken to wife a kinswoman of Akahashi the former governor of Sagami, who had borne him many young lords. Not without reason did the Sagami lay monk believe in him, thinking, "By no means will this man be faithless!"

Now it was decided at Rokuhara, "We shall set a battle in array at Yahata and Yamazaki on the twenty-seventh day of the fourth month." The grand marshal of the army advancing from the front was the Nagoya governor of Owari, who went forth with seven thousand six hundred riders from Toba Tsukurimichi, and the

---

[8] From a poem by Po Chü-i.

grand marshal of the army attacking from the rear was Ashikaga Jibu-no-tayū Takauji, with five thousand riders from Nishi-ga-oka.

Hearing of their coming, the imperial armies at Yahata and Yamazaki said, "If it be thus, we will lie in wait to meet the enemy at advantageous places, that by confounding them we may win a victory." Tadaaki no Ason crossed Ōwatari Bridge with five thousand horsemen and waited at Akai beach. Yūki Kurō Saemon-no-jō Chikamitsu went forth toward the Kitsune River with three hundred men. And with three thousand men, the lay monk Akamatsu Enshin encamped at Yodo, Furukawa, and Koganawate road; three places, north and south.

The hearts of Akamatsu's warriors were ardent to crush the mighty enemy, and their spirit was a spirit to overturn heaven and earth; yet it did not seem that they might prevail against this host of a myriad riders, come up freshly to the capital from the eastern provinces. Neither did they look trustfully to Lord Ashikaga (though men had brought tidings of his secret words) but, fearful lest he deal treacherously with them, they sent the Bōmon Lesser Marshal Tadamasa toward Iwakura with five or six hundred outlaws of Terado and Nishi-ga-oka.

Meanwhile, in the capital men said, "Before the night lightened, Lord Ashikaga went forth from the city, he who is the grand marshal of the army attacking from behind." And the Nagoya governor of Owari, the grand marshal of the army in front, was disquieted by these tidings, thinking, "I have let him go ahead of me!" He rode into the deep mud of Koganawate, where no horse's feet could stand, and made speed to go forward.

This governor of Owari, a fiery young warrior, had planned from the beginning, "In the coming battle I will amaze men's eyes and ears, that my name may be great in the land." Splendid to behold was his mount when he set forth on that day, and likewise his armor, and even the badge whereby men might know him! All his body was covered closely with purple-threaded armor garnished abundantly with metal, worn over garments of crimson flowered damask; and the silver-studded five-flap helmet pushed back on his head [9] bore a sun and moon carved on its wings in open-work of

---

[9] It was a sign of bravery to push one's helmet back so that it did not protect the head.

Chapter 9

gold and silver. Sheathed in a scabbard of gold hung his gold-handled sword Onimaru, a treasure of the generations of his house, together with another sword more than three feet long, while high on his back he carried a quiver of thirty-six arrows feathered with black-striped feathers. His horse was a stout and muscular golden bay, saddled with a lacquered saddle whereon three parasols were inlaid in precious metal, and he was fitted out with vermilion lines and long thick tassels. Truly this was a warrior marvelous to behold, shining in the light of the morning sun!

Because it was the way of this warrior to ride in advance of his army, he galloped boldly forward alone, whereupon there was no enemy but thought, "Assuredly is this the grand marshal of the army approaching from the front today!" By his horse and armor they knew him, and by his manner of going forth to give battle. They turned away their eyes from the common warriors with him, drew away in this place and attacked in that place, and thought only of smiting this one man. Yet no arrow drove through Nagoya's stout armor, nor did he fail to cut down the foes who approached, since he was a man skilled in the wielding of forged weapons. And the myriads of the imperial armies shrank before his might, wavering as if to run away.

Now there was a kinsman of Akamatsu called Sayo Saemon Saburō Noriie, one who let fly arrows rapidly from a strong bow, and was versed in the fighting ways of outlaws and the secrets of Cho Hsüan-kung.[10] Stripping off his armor, Noriie took his way between rice fields and through thickets in the guise of a foot-archer, crawled near the grand marshal behind a high path, and waited to shoot an arrow.

Meanwhile the governor of Owari drove back the enemy on three sides, wiped the blood from Onimaru with his badge, and stood fanning himself, not dreaming of such a thing. But when Noriie had drawn closer and closer with his bow aimed, at last he pulled back the string to release the singing arrow. Nor did that arrow stray from its mark, but struck the governor of Owari in the middle of the forehead, just at the edge of his helmet. It smashed his brains, shattered his bones, and came forth whitely at the tip of his neck-

---

[10] Apparently a Chinese military writer. Nothing is known of him.

bone. And the mighty general's limbs fainted, so that he fell down from off his horse headfirst.

Noriie beat upon his quiver, shouting aloud:

"With but a single arrow have I struck and killed the Nagoya governor of Owari, a grand marshal of the attackers! Follow me!"

Then from three directions the wavering imperial armies rode shouting mightily against the seven thousand followers of the governor of Owari, who fell back in confusion. Some among these came again to die in battle, thinking, "Where shall we turn, now that our grand marshal is smitten?" while others galloped their horses into deep paddy fields, where they took their own lives. And the bodies of the slain filled the road from the Kitsune River to the houses of Toba, more than six thousand yards distant.

Lord Ashikaga Crosses Beyond Ōe Mountain

In this manner did the attackers in front set the battle in array at the hour of the dragon on that morning. The dust from their horses' feet rose up on the east and west, and heaven and earth were seized with trembling by the sound of their battle cries, yet Lord Ashikaga, the grand marshal of the attackers in the rear, feasted with wine on the left bank of the Katsura River.

When several hours had passed, there came men saying, "The attackers are defeated in the fighting in the front, and their grand marshal is slain."

"If it be thus," said Lord Ashikaga, "let us cross beyond the mountains."

And all his warriors mounted their horses to hasten westward toward Shinomura on the Tamba road, far away from Yamazaki.

Now in the division of forces two men had been joined to the attackers of the rear, Nakagiri Jūrō of the province of Bizen and Nuka Shirō of the province of Settsu. At the foot of Ōe Mountain, Nakagiri Jūrō rode up above the road and called out to Nuka Shirō, saying:

"Is it not strange? Although a battle raged furiously in front from the hour of the dragon on, the attackers of the rear took their ease on the grass, feasting with wine for many hours. And when at last men came saying that Lord Nagoya was struck down, Lord Ashikaga spurred his horse toward the Tamba road. Assuredly he devises a wicked thing! If it be thus, how far shall we follow him? Let us turn back here to bear tidings to the lords of Rokuhara."

So he spoke, and Nuka Shirō answered him, saying:

"Well said! Though I also marveled at these things in my heart, I thought, 'Perhaps he has devised a stratagem of some kind.' But it is indeed impossible to be at ease, now that we have turned aside from today's battle. Lord Ashikaga has become our enemy! Yet I think that I will shoot an arrow before I turn back. It would be cowardly simply to go away."

He drew forth an arrow from the middle of his quiver, arranged it along the string, and made ready to gallop furiously in front of Lord Ashikaga's warriors. But Nakagiri restrained him, saying:

"Are your wits disordered? Do you seek to die a dog's death, that you would attack the mighty host with our twenty or thirty riders? It is better to do nothing than to become known to men by a foolish act. If we turn back safely, preserving our lives for battles to come, we will always be remembered as men who understood the meaning of loyalty."

So he spoke, and perhaps Nuka thought that it ought to be so, for he indeed turned back his horse at Ōe Mountain to return to Rokuhara with Nakagiri.

When these two galloped up and spoke of what had passed, the lords of Rokuhara were as men who feel rain dripping through the branches of a trusted tree. The Nagoya governor of Owari, their shield and halberd, was dead, and Lord Ashikaga was become an enemy, of whom they had thought in close friendship, "The heart of this man will never be false. He is as our very bones and flesh." Nor was there any warrior but was cast down and ill at ease, thinking, "Assuredly will others do the same, that have thus far remained loyal."

Lord Ashikaga Comes to Shinomura, Whereupon the Men of the Provinces Gallop to Join Him

Soon Lord Ashikaga made his camp at Shinomura, whereto he summoned the armies of nearby provinces. First of all a resident of the province of Tamba came galloping to join him with two hundred and fifty men, a person called Kuge Yasaburō Tokishige, whose banner and badges bore the legend, "First." Marveling thereat, Lord Ashikaga summoned Kō Uemon-no-jō Moronao, asking, "Is it the family crest, or is it because they are the first to come here that the men of Kuge have written 'First' on their badges?" And respectfully Moronao answered him, saying:

"It is a crest with a history. When the grand marshal Yoritomo raised his banner at Doi no Sugiyama, Tokishige's ancestor Kuge Jirō Shigemitsu, a resident of the province of Musashi, was the first to gallop to join him. The heart of His Lordship the grand marshal was moved thereby. 'If the realm comes within my grasp, you shall be the first to receive a reward,' he said, and himself wrote the word 'First' to present to him, wherefore soon it became that family's crest."

Then Lord Ashikaga rejoiced greatly, saying, "Truly it suits well with their family's tradition that they are the first to come."

Now there were those that had been encamped at the Kōsenji Temple: men of Adachi, Ogino, Kojima, Wada, Inden, Honjō, and Hirajō. These crossed over from Tamba into Wakasa to attack the capital from the Hokurikudō Road, saying, "Let us not be ruled by another." But no other family failed to gallop to Lord Ashikaga's camp, not Kuge, Nagasawa, Shiuchi, Yamanouchi, Ashida, Yoda, Sakai, Hagano, Oyama, or Hahakabe, nor even the men of neighboring provinces. Rapidly the armies gathered together at Shinomura, until their numbers were more than thirty-two thousand horsemen.

Hearing of these things, the men of Rokuhara said:

"Our fate will be decided in the battle to come. If we are beaten down, we shall take the supreme highness and the former emperors

Chapter 9

to the Kantō, establish a capital at Kamakura, and raise another mighty host to destroy the traitors."

So they spoke, and made palaces for the supreme highness and the retired emperors in the northern mansion of Rokuhara. And the Kajii Prince of the Blood of second rank came to Rokuhara also. (To be sure, there could be no fear for his person, whatever calamities might befall, since he was the Tendai abbot. But perhaps he wished to be near his brother, the emperor, and to pray for the eternal preservation of the throne.) The emperor's mother came, and the empress, the imperial nun, the wife of the regent, the great nobles, the courtiers of the three houses of the Fujiwara clan, the civil and military officials, the monks of the prince's following, the guards of the ex-emperors and noble families, and even page boys and ladies in waiting. When all of these had crowded together eagerly, the city was left desolate; even as the leaves of a storm-tossed tree were the people scattered. But Shirakawa[11] flourished like the brief blooming of a flower.

Now it is said, "The Son of Heaven makes the four seas his house";[12] moreover, Rokuhara was very near to the capital. There was no need for the emperor to grieve because he sojourned in a traveling-palace "on the Wei River eastward from the city." [13] But he lamented sorely, blaming himself alone that in his reign the realm was unquiet and the offices of state were soiled with the dust of a place outside the city. "It is solely because We have offended against heaven," he said. Nor did he ever enter his night apartments until the fifth watch,[14] but summoned venerable and wise courtiers to ask them concerning the ancient days of Yao, Shun, T'ang, and Wu.[15] He did not listen to foolish talk having to do with marvels, violence, disturbances, or supernatural things.[16]

Although the sixteenth day of the month of the hare was the second day of the monkey in that month, men did not celebrate the

[11] Shirakawa and Rokuhara were both east of the capital.
[12] I.e., the emperor is at home anywhere in the land.
[13] The Kamo River is meant. The Wei River flowed beside the Chinese capital of Loyang.
[14] 4:00 A.M.
[15] Model Chinese rulers.
[16] These are things that Confucius refused to discuss.

Hiyoshi festival,[17] but left the gods of the land desolate, and suffered the fine fish, meet to be an august offering, to sport aimlessly in the lake waters. Likewise, although the seventeenth day was the second day of the cock, they did not celebrate the Kamo festival,[18] but in the First Ward the people were few, and no carriages strove together for place. The silver face was covered with dust; the pearls of the clouds left off their shining.[19] It is indeed said, "Festivals are not increased in years of abundance nor decreased in years of famine";[20] yet now for the first time men forbore to celebrate the festivals of these two shrines, that had never been passed over since the days of their founding. These were fearful things, for none might know the thoughts of the gods.

Now the imperial armies resolved to go forth against the capital on the seventh day of the fifth month. In the night the foremost warriors drew near to the city from Shinomura, Yahata, and Yamazaki. They burned watch fires at Umezu and Katsura-no-sato on the west and at Takeda and Fushimi on the south, and stopped up the San'yōdō and San'indō Roads. Likewise, in the capital men said, "The armies from the Kōsenji Temple are drawing near from the Kurama Road and Takao, those that have come by the Wakasa Road." The Tōsandō Road alone was open; yet the hearts of the Mountain Gate were rebellious as before, and Seta too was like to be closed up. As birds in a cage were the warriors of Rokuhara, as fish in a net. Although their faces were valiant, their hearts fainted within them, for there was no way whereby they might escape.

It is said, "When there were three men in a household, the far-ranging army of Yünnan took one of them." [21] But not only one of three had the lords of Rokuhara sent forth to attack the single small castle of Chihaya, but every man from every province. And now within their own gate screens calamity beckoned while still that castle stood; for suddenly on the west the banners of righteousness pressed against Ch'ang-an.[22] They could not fight a defensive fight,

---

[17] The festival of the Hiyoshi (Hie) Shrine on Mount Hiei.
[18] The festival of the Kamo Shrine, a major social event in the capital.
[19] The moon and the stars.
[20] From the *Li chi*.
[21] From a poem by Po Chü-i.
[22] An ancient Chinese capital. Kyoto is meant.

so few were their numbers, nor might they receive aid of others, the roads being cut off. The lords of Rokuhara repented vainly, and all the others with them, saying, "Alas! Had we but known that these things would come to pass, not thus would we have thinned away the capital's armies!"

Now from the beginning the men of Rokuhara said:

"In no wise may we prevail if we fight on flat land alone, for the enemy is become a mighty host striking from many directions at the same time. We must make ready a strong place wherein to rest our horses now and again, and to save our warriors from danger. When the enemy approaches, we must fight by galloping out again and again."

So they spoke, and dug a deep ditch beside the Kamo River, fifteen or twenty acres in size, whereto they conducted the waters of the river. (Truly it was most like to K'un-ming Lake,[23] swallowing the sinking sun of spring in its still depths.) On the other three sides of the dwelling place at Rokuhara they built high turfed walls of mud, lined with towers and protected by many rows of obstacles. (Surely even thus was the strength of Shou-hsiang castle in Yen-chou!)[24] Yet were the builders of this cunningly contrived fortress deficient in wisdom. For those men fell down who relied on the steepness of Chien-ko Peak, because the root was not deep or the foundation firm; and those men fled who trusted to the depth of Tung-t'ing Lake, because the people were not cherished, nor was the state governed justly.[25]

Moreover, it was meet that the defenders should "cast away their food and sink their boats,"[26] since by this battle the destiny of the divided realm would be determined. Yet from this day forth they hesitated, resolved to shut themselves up in a small fortress of no consequence. How deplorable was their strategy!

[23] A large body of water in southern China (described in the *Han shu*).
[24] A fortress built by the Chinese in 104 B.C. as a protection against the Hsiung-nu nomads.
[25] Allusions to Chinese history and philosophy, intended to show that strength cannot prevail where virtue is lacking.
[26] Burn their bridges behind them. An allusion to an incident in Chinese history recorded in the *Shih chi*.

Takauji Offers Up a Petition at Shinomura Hachiman Shrine

At the hour of the tiger on the seventh day of the fifth month, Ashikaga Jibu-no-tayū Takauji led forth more than twenty-five thousand horsemen from Shinomura post station. As he rode quietly through the night, he beheld an ancient shrine southward of the station, standing in the shadow of old willows and straggling pagoda trees. Dimly he discerned the fluttering sleeves of a priest where a sacred fire burned low, and faintly heard the sound of a bell.

"Though I do not know what shrine this may be," thought Lord Ashikaga, "it is meet that I should worship here before going into battle."

He got down from his horse, stripped off his helmet, and knelt before the shrine. Fervently he prayed, "Let all be well with the battle today, and vouchsafe the might of thy protection, that the enemies of the court may be beaten down."

Just at that time there was a shamaness there, come to return thanks for a divine favor. Lord Ashikaga spoke to her, asking:

"What god is worshiped at this shrine?"

And she answered him, saying, "Since the enshrinement of Hachiman here in the middle ages, it has been called the New Hachiman Shrine of Shinomura."

Lord Ashikaga said:

"That is none other than the wonder-working god reverenced by my family! Most assuredly will he heed my prayers! I should like to offer up a written petition, as would be suitable."

Thereupon, Hikida Myōgen took out writing materials from his armor-fastening, made ready a brush and wrote:

"Respectfully I offer up this my prayer:

"Wondrous are the works of the Great Bodhisattva Hachiman, the guardian of the tombs of my ancestors, who will vouchsafe to raise the house of Minamoto once again. High in the heavens of the Pure Land hangs the moon of his enlightened true being; brightly the glory of his harmonious god-manifestation covers the seven thousand deities. As regards the forming of affinities, he guards and instructs; yet he does not accept the worship of the unrighteous. As regards the dispensing of benevolence, he helps living beings; yet he abides with the upright alone. Great is his virtue, that causes all the world to believe on him!

"Now since the years of Shōkyū, capriciously the four seas have been ruled by men who were the ministers of the generations of my ancestors, the eastern descendants of the house of Taira. Wickedly for nine generations have these walked in the ways of violence. They have sent away the emperor to the waves of the western seas; they have afflicted the abbot of Tendai, so that he abides in the clouds of the southern mountains. Surely their iniquity passes the knowledge of man! Is it not a subject's duty to give up his life against these who are the court's bitter enemies? Will not the justice of heaven strike down these who are the foremost foes of the gods?

"Beholding the accumulation of their iniquities, I thought nothing of my own distress, but made myself as thin fish flesh lying below a sharp knife on the chopping block. When loyal warriors gathered together to make their camps in the west and in the south, the supreme marshal camped at Dove Peak and I camped at Shinomura. So the two of us have dwelt within the shadow of Hachiman's shrine fence, and together we go forth beneath his protection. Consorting together as a box with its lid, how can we fail to smite the enemy?

"To the divine promise I raise up my eyes, which blesses the generations of emperors with peace and protection. Nor shall my courage waver sooner than sweat shall start forth from the body of a stone horse. My trust is in the destiny of the house of Minamoto, wherein the generations of my ancestors have placed their faith, wherefore I await even such a prodigy as the gnawing of the golden rats.[27] Let the god join my righteous battle! Brilliantly let him show forth his wondrous power! When the virtuous wind strikes the grass, then for a thousand leagues around will the enemy be brought down. When the divine radiance replaces the sword, then in a

---

[27] A horde of golden rats with iron teeth is said to have rescued a beleaguered Chinese army by attacking its enemies, consuming their weapons and biting their soldiers to death.

single battle will the victory be won. The true heart is sincere; the divine vision is without error.

"Reverently presented by Minamoto no Ason Takauji on the seventh day of the fifth month of the third year of Genkō."

When Hikida read this prayer in a loud voice, faith lifted up the hearts of all who heard him, and every warrior placed his trust in the god.

"As precious gems are the sentences of this prayer; clear and profound are its words and arguments. Assuredly it will find favor in the sight of the god," they thought.

After Lord Ashikaga himself had taken up the brush to write his name, he offered the prayer to the shrine, together with a humming-bulb arrow drawn from the top of his quiver. His younger brother, Tadayoshi no Ason, also offered an arrow from the top of his quiver, and quickly many warriors did the same: Kira, Ishidō, Nikki, Hosokawa, Imagawa, Arakawa, Kō, Uesugi, and others there with this lord, until the shrine was filled with their arrows, piled up in a mound.

When the night lightened, the foremost of these warriors moved onward slowly, awaiting the coming of those behind. As they crossed the pass of Ōe Mountain, Lord Ashikaga beheld a pair of doves, flying and fluttering above his white banner. He commanded the army:

"The Great Bodhisattva Hachiman has sent forth these doves, which are a symbol of his divine protection. We shall follow where they fly."

The standard-bearer spurred his horse after the doves, which flew quietly until they came to rest in a sandalwood tree before the Office of Shrines in the ruins of the great palace enclosure. Then the imperial army galloped forward toward Uchino, their hearts stirred up to valor by this auspicious omen, and in parties of five and ten, enemy horsemen rolled up their banners and stripped off their helmets to surrender. Wherefore, when Lord Ashikaga passed beside the racecourse of the Proximate Guards of the Right, he led fifty thousand horsemen, although he had gone forth from Shinomura with but twenty thousand.

Chapter 9

The Attack on Rokuhara

Now the lords of Rokuhara divided their sixty thousand horsemen into three parties. One was set before the Office of Shrines to oppose Lord Ashikaga, one was sent toward the Eastern Temple to oppose Akamatsu, and one was sent toward Fushimi-no-ue to render aid to Takeda and Fushimi, where Lord Chigusa drew near.

At the beginning of the hour of the snake, the attackers set the battle in array in the front and the rear, both at the same time. Dust from their horses' feet rose up on the north and the south; heaven and earth echoed with the sound of their battle cries.

The defenders at Uchino were Suyama and Kōno, sent there with twenty thousand valiant chiefs. The imperial hosts could not gallop in easily, yet neither might the defenders gallop out easily. Wherefore both of these abode in their places, passing the time with shooting arrows. But soon from within the imperial army there emerged a single rider, wearing a lavender mantle over reddish-yellow armor shading to white toward the skirt. He galloped in front of the enemy, naming his name with a mighty shouting:

"Since I am a person of no consequence, it may be that no man of you will know my name. A retainer of Lord Ashikaga am I, Shidara Gorō Saemon-no-jō! If there is a retainer of the lords of Rokuhara that will fight against me, let him gallop forth to behold the degree of my skill."

So he spoke, and drew a sword three and a half feet long, raising it up in front of his helmet as a protection against arrows. And the two armies left off their fighting to gaze upon this man, whose warlike spirit was as that of one worthy to stand against a thousand.

Thereupon an old warrior of around fifty years advanced slowly from the army of Rokuhara, clad in black-threaded armor and a helmet with five flaps. He rode a pale chestnut horse, decked with blue tassels. And with a mighty shouting he named his name:

"Though I am a stupid man, for many years I served as a commissioner of the military government. And though I am of low degree, and may not be a worthy enemy in your eyes (for perhaps you scorn me, thinking, 'He is but a monk'), yet am I sprung from the house of the general Toshihito, a family that for many generations has followed the way of the warrior. Of the seventeenth of those generations am I, Saitō Genki the monk of Iyo! Why should I cherish life in today's battle, which decides the fate of our two armies? If there be those who are spared, let them speak to their sons and grandsons of my loyal fighting!"

As he spoke, these two galloped forward, and with clashing armor-sleeves grappled together furiously until they fell down. Being the stronger, Shidara got on top of Saitō and set about to cut off his head, but Saitō, nimble of limb, thrust upward and stabbed Shidara three times. Truly these were mighty men, that even in death did not relax their gripping hands, but pierced each one the other with their swords, and laid themselves down on the same pillow.

Again from among the Genji lines there came forth a warrior, clad in armor threaded with blue Chinese damask, with a helmet whereon arrowhead leaves were wrought. He drew out a sword five feet long, put it on his shoulder, and galloped his horse for fifty yards in front of the enemy. And with a mighty shout he named his name:

"Not unknown is the glory of my family, who since the days of Lord Hachiman have served the generations of the Genji, yet today I cannot meet a worthy enemy, by reason that men are unacquainted with my name in this place. Daikō Jirō Shigenari am I, a personal retainer of Lord Ashikaga! Is not Suyama the governor of Bitchū here, or Kōno the governor of Tsushima, of whom men say that they have won honor in past battles? Come forth to meet me, and let us fight with forged weapons to make a show for the eyes of others!"

So he spoke, pulling at his bridle until his horse blew out white foam.

Suyama was not there in that place, since he had gone away in haste toward the Eighth Ward to aid the defenders at the Eastern Temple. But Kōno Michiharu the governor of Tsushima was in the foremost ranks, a mighty man of valor, such as would not hesitate even slightly before Daikō's challenge.

"Here is Michiharu."

So he spoke, and drew near to grapple with Daikō. But there-

Warrior in Armor

Ashikaga Takauji

upon Kōno's foster son Shichirō Michitō galloped in front of him to block his way (for perhaps he thought, "I must not allow my father to be killed"). A young warrior fifteen years old that year, he came up beside Daikō and laid hands on him furiously.

Daikō held Kōno Shichirō in the air by his armor-braid, saying, "I will not grapple with a servant like you!" Yet when he pushed this youth away, he beheld the crest upon his badge, a double-lined square with the word "Three" written inside.

"Assuredly is this Kōno's son or nephew," he said.

And with one hand he brought down his sword, easily cut off Shichirō's legs at the knees, and cast him three bow-lengths away.

Then with flapping stirrups the governor of Tsushima galloped forward to lay hands on Daikō. How might he cherish life, when his beloved foster son was slain before his eyes?

Beholding Kōno, his three hundred retainers arose, shouting, "Do not allow our lord to be struck down!" Likewise a thousand Genji arose, shouting, "Do not allow Daikō to be struck down!" And Minamoto and Taira came together in disorder, attacking and fighting with a mighty raising of dust.

Now many of the imperial army being smitten, they drew away, scattering toward Uchino, but thereupon the Genji sent forward fresh warriors to fight in their stead. And many of the men of Rokuhara being struck down, they hastened to draw away toward the Kamo River, but thereupon the Heike sent forward fresh warriors in their stead, who fought desperately, not to lose that place. Eastward and westward in the First and Second Wards the opposing sides shoved and pushed, seven or eight times giving way and coming back again. Nor was one army more brave than the other, since neither Minamoto nor Taira cherished life. But at last the Heishi drew away toward Rokuhara, beaten down by the greater numbers of the Genji.

Meanwhile the lay monk Akamatsu Enshin went forth toward the Eastern Temple with three thousand horsemen. When these drew near to the temple's storied gate, Norisuke the governor of Shinano stood up in his stirrups, gazed to the left and right, and commanded, "Do some among you tear apart the obstacles at that gate."

More than three hundred eager warriors got down from their horses and ran forward: men of Uno, Kashiwabara, Sayo, and Majima. But when these looked upon the castle, they beheld a wall stretching from the foundation of Rashōmon Gate on the west to the Eighth Ward river bed on the east, made of timbers from Yoshino and Yasu-no-kōri, six, seven, ten, and eleven inches thick, plastered abundantly with mud. Stakes were strewn in the front thereof, and obstacles of other kinds, and there was a water-filled moat ten yards wide.

The hearts of Akamatsu's warriors were troubled. How might they plunge their bodies into the water, not knowing its depth? Or how might they cross over when the bridge was drawn back?

Then flying down from his horse, Mega Magosaburō Nagamune of Harima lowered his bow to try the deepness of the water. And the upper tip remained dry, where the bowstring was attached.

"I am tall enough," thought Nagamune.

He laid his five-foot sword across his shoulder, put off his leather shoes, and plunged his body into the moat. Behold! The water did not rise above his breastplate.

There was one Takebe Shichirō following after Nagamune, a small man not five feet tall. With tranquil heart this Shichirō leaped down, thinking, "It is a shallow moat indeed," yet the water passed over his helmet.

Looking back Nagamune said, "Take hold of my armor-braid and raise up your body." And Takebe Shichirō stood on the belt of Mega's armor, climbed onto his shoulders, and jumped to the other side of the moat.

Mega laughed mightily thereat, saying:

"You have used me for a bridge! Come, let us break down the wall!"

He leaped up from the bank to pull furiously at a support of the wall that looked to be five or six inches thick, whereupon the wall collapsed for fifteen or twenty yards, and with it the dirt from the moat piled like a mountain on top. And the moat became as flat land.

Then there came arrows thicker than falling rain, shot one after another from more than three hundred towers above the roofed wall of the temple. Nagamune did not draw out those arrows, standing in the cross-stitched flaps of his armor and the wings of his helmet, but only bent them back and ran quickly to the base of a high tower, where he leaned on the hilt of his sword before the Two Thunderbolts.[28] Not easily might one know which were the Two Kings and which was Magosaburō grinding his teeth!

Now all the ten thousand warriors of Rokuhara joined together, they who stood at the Eastern Temple, and in the western part of the Eighth Ward, and at Hari and Karahashi.

"The battle rages fiercely at the entrance to the gate!" they clamored, hastening forth from the east gate of the temple like rain-filled clouds billowing from the hills at dusk.

Warriors of the imperial armies galloped against them, lest Mega and Takebe be struck down: Sayo Hyōgo-no-suke, Tokuhira Genta, Bessho Rokurō Saemon, and Gorō Saemon, who looked neither to the left nor to the right, but gave battle furiously. Then the other three thousand attackers, saying, "Do not let them be killed, my lords," drew their swords and galloped forward: the lay monk Akamatsu Enshin, his eldest son Norisuke the governor of Shinano, his second son Sadanori the governor of Chikuzen, his third son Sokuyū the teacher of discipline, and the warriors of Majima, Kōzuki, Kanke, and Kinugasa. And they beat down the ten thousand men of Rokuhara in every direction, chasing them away toward the Seventh Ward river bed.

Likewise the armies of Rokuhara were vanquished in the fighting at Takeda, and also at Kohata and Fushimi, for those that were left could not succeed where the foremost warriors had failed. They fled in disorder to the shelter of Rokuhara castle, pursued by the victorious attackers on the four sides, fifty thousand horsemen, who came together in one place from the Fifth Ward bridge to the Seventh Ward river bed, surrounding Rokuhara with untold thousands and myriads of men. The eastward side alone they suffered to remain open, that they might divide the hearts of the enemy and bring them down easily.

Soon Tadaaki no Ason the Chigusa Middle Marshal spoke to his warriors, commanding:

[28] The Two Deva Kings. See note 16, Chapter Eight.

"Assuredly will the besiegers of Chihaya come forth from thence to smite our rear, if we attack this castle with idle spirits after the usual manner of men. You must unite to bring it down quickly."

Thereupon, warriors of Izumo and Hōki gathered together two or three hundred carts and tied the shaft of one to the shaft of another. They demolished houses, piled up the pieces onto those carts high as a mountain, and brought them to the enemy towers. And in this way they burnt the gate on one side.

Then three hundred followers of the Kajii Prince, monks of the Jōrimbō House and the Shōgyōbō House, clad in armor and helmets, went forth toward the Fifth Ward bridge from the north gate of the Jizō Hall. And by these few monks of Mount Hiei more than three thousand of the attackers were driven back, warriors of the Bōmon Lesser Marshal and the Tono Sign of the Law. But when the monks had pursued the enemy along the river bed for three hundred and fifty yards, they turned back into the castle, by reason that their numbers were few and they thought, "It will not be well to pursue them over a long distance."

Now the wavering of the attackers' hearts was such that perhaps they must have fled, had all the hosts of Rokuhara come forth against them with united hearts. For although the defenders were not so many as the attackers, yet were they twenty or thirty thousand horsemen. But may it not be that the good fortune of the military was ended, and their destruction was ordained? Even mighty men of valor among them were lacking in bravery, those who always had been honored by others; even cunning archers did not bend back their bows, those who had been called matchless warriors. Vainly they gathered together in divers places, without spirit in all things save in making ready to fly.

Those that behaved in this wise were all warriors, men covetous of glory and mindful of family. What of the supreme highness, the ex-emperors, the imperial nun, the empress, the regent's wife, the great nobles, the page boys, the page girls, and the ladies in waiting, whose eyes never before had gazed on a battle? Stricken with terror by the sound of the battle cries, they despaired utterly, saying, "What is to be done now?" And beholding their distress, the two lords of Rokuhara thought, "It is entirely natural," and were as though dazed, their spirits fainting within them.

When the night came down, the warriors within the castle opened the gates, passed over the obstacles, and fled eagerly, even those of whom it had been said, "They are not two-hearted." (Perhaps they thought that the castle could not stand, since the hearts of the defenders were thus timorous.) And at last fewer than a thousand warriors remained behind, mindful of duty and holding their lives as nothing.

The Flight of the Supreme Highness and the Former Emperors

Now Kasuya Saburō Muneaki spoke a word to the lords of Rokuhara, saying:

"One by one have our warriors fled away, until we are not a thousand horsemen, nor in any wise may we stand against the mighty host of the enemy. Since the enemy has not yet encompassed us about on the east, you must go forth toward the Kantō with the supreme highness and the former emperors, that again you may raise a mighty army to attack the capital. Your numbers will not be too few if you are accompanied by Sasaki Hōgan Tokinobu, he who now guards the bridge of Seta, nor will any in the land of Ōmi raise his hand against you while Tokinobu is there. Assuredly will your road be safe, since I have not heard that there are enemies in Mino, Owari, Mikawa, or Tōtōmi. And if once you come to Kamakura, you may strike down the rebels easily. Pray consider whether it be not regrettable that the supreme highness and the former emperors must be shut up in this poor flatland castle, where great generals will die dishonorably by the swords of common fellows!"

So he spoke strongly, two or three times. Perhaps the two lords of Rokuhara thought that it ought to be so, for they resolved:

"If it be thus, we shall send forth the imperial nun secretly, and the empress, and the regent's wife, and the other women and children. When they are gone, with tranquil hearts we shall break through in one place to escape."

And they sent Kogushi Gorō Hyōe-no-jō to bear these tidings to the imperial personages.

Thereupon, the emperor's mother went forth blindly with naked feet, and likewise the empress, the imperial nun, the regent's wife, and ladies in waiting of all degrees. Each strove to be the first to go, thinking nothing of the sadness of sudden parting or the uncertain future, but only shrinking back from the horror of being shut up inside the castle. It was quite like a dream of the past, as though spring blossoms in the Golden Valley Garden[29] were scattering in the mists of the four directions, seduced by the morning wind.

Now to his wife Nakatoki the governor of Echigo spoke a word, saying:

"Heretofore I had thought to keep you with me always, even were I perchance to go forth from the capital. Yet I do not believe that it will be easy to escape to the Kantō, since men say that the enemy block up the roads on all sides. No harm will come to you who are a woman, and likewise Matsuji[30] is still an infant, so that the enemy will not know his lineage, even should they find him. You must go forth secretly in the darkness, hide yourself in a remote place, and wait awhile until the world is quiet. If I come to the Kantō in safety, I shall send men to fetch you quickly. If you should hear that I have perished on the way, you must find another husband, raise up Matsuji, and make him a monk when he reaches the age of understanding, that he may offer prayers on my behalf."

So he spoke with fainting spirit, weeping where he stood.

The lady held his armor-sleeve, lamenting and weeping.

"Why do you speak these heartless words?" she said. "If I wandered in strange places today with the child, would not all men think, 'She is the kinswoman of one who has fled'? And if I were to ask for shelter among our past acquaintance, I would be sought out and put to shame by the enemy, while the child would perish. How bitter that would be! If there is to be an undreamt-of happening on the way, let me die with you there. Even for a time fleeting as a

---

[29] A famous Chinese garden of the Chin dynasty (A.D. 265–419).
[30] His son.

drop of dew in an autumnal gale, I do not wish to linger abandoned beneath a tree which offers no shelter."

So she spoke, nor could the governor of Echigo bear the grievous parting. Though his heart was the heart of a warrior, he was not made of stone or wood. So for a long time he tarried in that place.

[*There follows a famous parallel from Chinese history.*]

In ancient days Kao Tsu of Han and Hsiang Yü of Ch'u strove together more than seventy times, until at last Hsiang Yü, encompassed about by Kao Tsu, resolved to die at dawn. Hearing the warriors of Han on all sides, how they sang songs of Ch'u,[31] Hsiang Yü went into his tent to recite a verse to his consort Lady Yü, afflicted in his heart by the sorrow of parting.

> My strength plucked up mountains;
> My spirit encompassed the world.
> The times are against me; Chiu[32] will not run.
> If Chiu will not run, what can I do?
> Yü, Yü—what will become of you?

As Hsiang Yü lamented and wept, Lady Yü fell on a sword and died before him, unable to endure her grief.

In the fighting on the next day, with twenty-eight riders Hsiang Yü beat down the four hundred thousand riders of Han, and himself took the heads of three generals. Then he spoke a word to those of his warriors who yet lived, saying:

"Not through want of skill in battle have I been destroyed by Kao Tsu of Han. Heaven has destroyed me."

So he spoke, knowing his fate, and at last took his life by Wu-chiang.

[*End of parallel*]

Because the warriors of Rokuhara held these things in their minds, there was none of them but wept, thinking, "It is even so today."

Soon the lord of the south compound of Rokuhara, Sakon Shōgen Tokimasu, went forth to attend in front of the emperor. He rode

---

[31] A Han stratagem designed to make Hsiang Yü believe that there was a major rebellion against him in Ch'u, and to undermine the morale of his soldiers.
[32] His horse.

his horse up to the middle gate of the lord of the north, Nakatoki the governor of Echigo, saying:

"The supreme highness has mounted a horse from the imperial stables. Why is it that you linger here?"

And speaking he rode away.

Nakatoki could not but put away the wife and child clinging to his armor-sleeve. Mounting his horse from the veranda, he went out eastward through the north gate, while tearfully these who were left behind made their farewells, and wandered forth through the east gate. From afar the sound of their lamenting fell grievously upon his ears as they departed weeping, so that the road grew dark before him and he suffered the horse to take its own way. Though Nakatoki and his lady knew it not, it was their last farewell. How sad it was!

Looking back when they were seventeen or eighteen hundred yards distant, those who fled with the emperor beheld flames and a great cloud of smoke, where already the enemy burned the houses of Rokuhara. Moreover when they came to Kuzumeji in the impenetrable darkness (it being a night of the fifth-month rainy season), outlaws waited there in great numbers to shoot arrows from the ten directions. Sakon Shōgen Tokimasu fell down from off his horse headfirst, smitten in the neck bone. And when Kasuya Shichirō got down and pulled out the arrow, Tokimasu perished instantly.

"We cannot gallop to meet the enemy without knowing where they lie," thought Kasuya, "nor may we summon aid to defend against them, since we flee in stealth. I can but take my life in this place, that even unto the afterworld I may preserve the bond between lord and vassal."

Weeping, he hid Tokimasu's head deep in a rice field by the side of the road, wrapped in the sleeve of his brocade coat. And he ripped open his belly and fell down onto his lord's body, embracing it where he lay.

When the imperial personages had fled far away to Shinomiya beach, there came voices in front and behind, saying, "Here are men seeking to run away! Stop them and strip off their armor!"

While arrows flew like falling rain, the imperial attendants scattered in every direction, the crown prince and the great nobles, thinking, "If it be thus, who can say what lies ahead?" And at last none remained but the Hino Great Counselor Sukena, the Kanjuji Middle Counselor Tsuneaki, the Aya no Jōji Middle Counselor Shigesuke, and the Zenrinji magistrate Arimitsu, serving before and behind the dragon carriage.

When the capital lay behind the clouds of dawn, the fugitives turned their thoughts to the road ahead, running eastward for a myriad leagues. Nor might the supreme highness hold back his tears, nor the former sovereigns, through remembrance of the ancient days when the Emperor Hsüan Tsung fled to Chien-ko.[33] Sadly they thought, "Surely the disordered world of Juei was even thus!" [34]

Now in the shelter of cryptomeria trees these stopped their horses to rest awhile, since the short night of the fifth month was not yet done, and darkness lay over Ōsaka barrier. But thereupon a straying arrow smote the supreme highness's left elbow, shot from an unknown place. And the Suyama governor of Bitchū made speed to fly down from his horse, to pull out the arrow and suck the wound, where flowing blood dyed the snowy skin. Truly it was a sight such as men's eyes could not bear to look upon! As the divine dragon entrapped in a fisherman's net,[35] so was this gracious lord of a myriad chariots, wounded by a base fellow's arrowhead. These were shocking times!

At last the sky showed forth its light through the fading morning mists. Yet when those who fled gazed across to the northern hills, sorely affrighted they beheld five or six hundred men resembling outlaws in appearance, who waited eagerly with shields and arrowheads in readiness.

Now there was one Nakagiri Yahachi serving in the front of the imperial party, a resident of the province of Bizen. Nakagiri galloped his horse close to the enemy, saying:

---

[33] After the rebellion of An Lu-shan.
[34] During the Juei era (1182-1185), the infant emperor Antoku fled from the capital with his Taira kinsmen, who were unable to stand against the Minamoto.
[35] This refers to a Chinese story about a whimsical dragon who turned himself into a fish. Bereft of his supernatural powers, he ended by falling victim to a fisherman.

"Who are you that commit this violence where the gracious master of the realm goes forth to the Kantō? If you are right-minded men, turn down your bows, strip off your helmets, and suffer us to pass. If you are fellows who know nothing of manners, we shall arrest you all, cut off your heads, and so pass by."

The outlaws laughed loudly, saying:

"We cannot suffer any man to pass who flees in distress, whatever master of the realm he may be. If he would go on his way without hindrance, let him leave behind the horses and armor of his warriors, whereupon he may flee with a tranquil heart."

So they spoke, and shouted a battle cry all together.

Hearing them, Nakagiri Yahachi said:

"These are indeed the actions of wicked men! Very well! Take the armor you desire!"

And his six retainers galloped forward neck by neck. Like scattered spiderlings the rapacious outlaws ran away on all sides, while in six directions the six pursued them for several thousand yards.

Perhaps because Yahachi himself pursued too far, it came about that more than twenty outlaws turned to surround him. In no wise discomfited, Yahachi galloped alongside the chief of the enemies to grapple with him furiously, so that abruptly they two fell between their horses and tumbled down forty or fifty feet from the top of a high bank, rolling over and over. Into a deep rice field they rolled; yet neither man let go his hold. Being on the bottom, Nakagiri sought his dagger to strike an upward blow, but only the scabbard met his hand (since doubtless the dagger had slipped away as he fell). The outlaw mounted up onto Nakagiri's breastplate and caught hold of his side hair, ready to cut off his head; yet firmly Nakagiri gripped his weapon and held his forearm, saying:

"Listen a moment while I speak a word. Do not fear me now that my dagger is gone, though did it but remain to me I would certainly overturn you and fight to win a victory. Likewise do not think that any man will help me by falling upon you from above, for no friend follows me. Beyond doubt you may strike me down. Yet by no means would it test your skill to take my head, nor would you gain renown therefrom. I am not a famous warrior. All men know that I am merely an underservant of the Rokuhara lords, Rokutarō by name. Spare my life instead of sinfully taking the head of a poor servant! A place is known to me where six thousand *kan* of the Rokuhara lords' money lies buried. Joyfully will I lead you there to make it your own."

May it not be that the outlaw believed his words? He put back his sword into its scabbard, raised up Nakagiri from underneath him, and spared his life. Moreover he gave him presents of divers kinds and offered him wine to drink.

When the outlaw had brought Yahachi to the capital, Yahachi went with him to the burned ruins of Rokuhara. But thereupon Yahachi said:

"Assuredly someone before us has dug up the money buried in this place. I sought to profit you, but your earlobes are too thin!" [36]

So he mocked at him, and went back laughing loudly.

Now the way having been cleared by Nakagiri's cunning, the supreme highness's party came to Shinohara post station on that day. There they sought out a shabby litter of plaited bamboo, and as litter-bearers the warriors on foot served before and behind His Majesty.

Thus far the Tendai abbot, the Kajii Prince of the Blood of second rank, had journeyed together with the emperor. But in his heart this prince thought:

"The road ahead is by no means safe. I would that I might hide awhile in any place whatever!"

"Who among my disciples are present?" he asked. And one answered him, saying:

"No monk of consequence is here, save only the Middle Counselor and monk governor Kyōchō and the abbot Jōshō of second rank. Perhaps the others have remained behind, wounded in last night's fighting on the way, or perhaps they have changed their hearts and run away."

Thereupon the prince made his farewells and went forth toward Ise, thinking, "Indeed, it will be impossible to travel the long distance to the Kantō."

Now this prince bestowed his horses upon the stationmaster of Shinohara, resolved to take his way toward Ise on foot.

---

[36] A sign of bad luck.

"Even were things not as they are," he thought, "assuredly would I fare ill, if with well-fed horses and silver-mounted saddles I sought to cross over Suzuka Mountain, where robbers consort together in great numbers."

Yet none who saw him could fail to think, "Aha! He is certainly a fugitive!" He moved forward with uncertain steps, clad in a long robe of strong silk and unlined footgear made of the leaves of the betel palm, while beside him walked the monk governor Kyōchō, wearing a black robe over garments of figured damask, with a crystal rosary in his hand. But may it not be that the King of the Mountain[37] protected him? For he came upon woodcutters on mountain trails, and encountered grass mowers on field paths, who brought him over Suzuka Mountain by pulling his hands and pushing his hips. In this way he came to Ise Shrine, to place all his faith in the sympathetic priests thereof, who hid him away for more than thirty days, heedless of their bodies' danger. When the capital was become a little more peaceful, he returned and lived in retirement for three or four years at a place called the Byakugōin Cloister.

The Suicide of Nakatoki and His Warriors

Now it was proclaimed abroad that the lords of Rokuhara were fleeing toward the Kantō, beaten down in the fighting at the capital. Wherefore in a single night two or three thousand mountain brigands, robbers, and outlaws galloped together, men from Ataka, Shinohara, Hinatsu, Oiso, Echigawa, Ono, Yonjūkyūnoin, Suribari, Bamba, Kinugasa, and Kashiwabara, and from the base of Ibuki Mountain and the reaches of the Suzuka River. They made the fifth princely son of the former emperor their grand marshal (he who had renounced the world to live in seclusion at the foot of Ibuki), raised a banner of brocade, and waited eagerly at the most advantageous place on the Tōsandō Road, climbing to the tops of hills on both sides of the narrow track.

When the night lightened, Nakatoki the governor of Echigo brought the emperor deep into the mountains beyond Shinohara

[37] The god of the Hiyoshi Shrine on Mount Hiei, where the prince was the abbot.

Chapter 9

station. Although more than two thousand warriors had gone forth yesterday from the capital, those who accompanied the supreme highness now were fewer than seven hundred men. (May it not be that those others had fled away?) Nakatoki commanded Sasaki Hōgan Tokinobu to guard behind, saying, "You must shoot defensive arrows if any pursue after us." He commanded Kasuya Saburō to guard in front, saying, "If rebels seek to block our way, you must open the road by dispersing them." And he himself followed in back of the imperial litter.

As Kasuya made to go through Bamba pass, the thousands of the enemy waited eagerly with the road between them, their shields lined up in a continuous surface and their arrowheads in readiness.

"Assuredly they are evil men from this and other provinces," said Kasuya, "come together to strip away the armor of those who flee. In no wise will they fight with determination if we smite them furiously to drive them back. Let us gallop forward and chase them away!"

So he spoke, and his thirty-six riders galloped forward neck by neck. They chased back the foremost outlaws to the peaks beyond, five hundred men, who ran away to join the second line. And thus Kasuya won a victory.

"Doubtless there will be no further trouble," he thought.

But when the morning mists faded, on the road ahead Kasuya beheld a brocade banner fluttering in the wind from the peaks, where five or six thousand warriors waited eagerly behind steep places. He stood without moving, his spirit fainting before the sight of the great host of the enemy's second line. He could not gallop forward again to break them down, since men and horses were wearied, and the enemy were lodged among cliffs. Nor might he draw near to fight with arrows, since his arrows were shot away, and the enemy were very many. Truly in no wise did it seem that he might prevail! And therefore he and his warriors got down from off their horses beside a crossroads temple at the foot of a mountain to wait for those who came behind.

Now to the governor of Echigo came men saying, "There is fighting ahead." And Nakatoki galloped thither, spurring his mount.

Then Kasuya Saburō spoke a word to Nakatoki, saying:

"Well is it said, 'It is shameful for a wielder of bow and arrow not to die when death is proper.' Though it had been fitting for us to perish in the capital, we fled away to this place, cherishing a day of life. Now we are fallen into the hands of contemptible rustics and bumpkins, who will expose our corpses to the dew on the road. How regrettable it is!

"If the enemy were in no other place than this, by fierce fighting we might drive them back and pass on. But by no means will the rebellious Toki family fail to block our way in the province of Mino. Nor will the Kira forbear to come forth against us, since men say that they have refused many calls to duty, and have built a stronghold in the province of Tōtōmi. Not with a host of a myriad riders might we strike down such enemies as those! Yet we are not a great host, but only a few men running away. We and our horses are wearied, nor is our strength such as might shoot a single arrow truly. How far may we hope to flee? When Sasaki comes up from behind, you must go back into the province of Ōmi, shut yourself up for a time in a suitable castle, and wait for an army to come to the capital from the Kantō."

So he spoke, and Nakatoki the governor of Echigo said:

"Even such is my belief. Yet I place but little trust in Sasaki, who perchance devises a treacherous thing. Therefore I would know the minds of all who are here, since we can neither go forward nor retreat. Howbeit, let us stop awhile at this temple, that before deciding we may see if Tokinobu will come."

So he spoke, and all his five hundred warriors got down from their horses in the temple compound.

Now with three hundred riders Sasaki Hōgan Tokinobu was following a league behind the governor of Echigo. Perhaps because of the intervention of an evil spirit, there came one to Tokinobu, saying, "The lord of Rokuhara was encompassed about by outlaws at Bamba pass, where every man was slain." And thereupon Tokinobu turned back at the Echi River, thinking, "Nothing more can be done." He surrendered himself, and went up to the capital.

For awhile Nakatoki the governor of Echigo waited eagerly for Tokinobu's coming. But when the time for waiting was past, and they were long in that place, he resolved firmly:

"Indeed, even Tokinobu has become an enemy. There is no place whereto we may retreat, no place whereto we may flee. I shall cut my belly as befits a man of honor."

How valiant was his aspect! These were his words, spoken to his warriors at that time:

"I have no words to speak of your loyal hearts, who have cleaved to me thus far, not unmindful of your honor as warriors nor forgetful of past kindnesses, though it is known to you that the prosperity of the military is ended and my family is soon to be destroyed utterly. Profound indeed is my gratitude! How may I reward you, now that adversity overwhelms my house? I shall kill myself for your sakes, requiting in death the favors received in life.

"Even though I am a person of no consequence, I bear the name of Taira. The enemy will certainly offer the lordship of a thousand households for my head. Do you take it quickly and deliver it into the hands of the Genji, that you may atone for your transgressions and prove your loyalty to them."

He stripped off his armor, laid bare his body to the waist, slashed his belly, and fell down dead.

Kasuya Saburō Muneaki held back the tears dropping onto his armor-sleeve.

"How bitter it is that you have gone before me!" he said. "I thought to take my life first, to prepare a way for you in the nether regions. With all my heart I have served you in this world, nor will I break the bond now, saying, 'It must be so, since he has gone to the nether regions.' Wait a bit! I shall go with you to Mount Shide." [38]

Laying hold of the governor of Echigo's dagger, which was driven in to the hilt, he stabbed his own belly and fell on his face embracing Nakatoki's knees. And thereafter four hundred and thirty-two men ripped open their bellies all at once. As the flowing of the Yellow River was the blood soaking their bodies; as meats in a slaughterhouse were the corpses filling the compound! In no wise more pitiable was the barbarians' destruction of five thousand courtiers in the Year of the Earth and Boar, or the drowning of a million soldiers in the river waters during the battle of

---

[38] A mountain in hades.

T'ung-kuan.[39] The supreme highness fainted with terror and distress when he beheld these dead men, and the former emperors did the same.

The Fifth Prince Captures the Supreme Highness and the Former Emperors; the Minister Sukena Renounces the World

Laying hands on the supreme highness and the former emperors, the army of the fifth prince brought them to the Chōkōji Temple on that day. The emperor himself delivered over the three imperial symbols to the prince, as well as the imperial lutes Genjō and Susogo and the sacred image of Kannon from the Second Chamber of the Seiryōden. In no wise was it different from the fall of Ch'in, when Tzu Ying of Ch'in, defeated by the ancestor of Han, mounted up into an unpainted chariot of white wood drawn by a white horse, put the seal of the Son of Heaven around his neck, and surrendered by the side of the Chih-tao pavilion.

Now because he was a favorite minister of this emperor, the Hino Great Counselor Sukena trembled for his life, thinking, "What affliction will be visited upon me?" He went in to a wandering holy man in the crossroads temple at that place, saying, "I desire to renounce the world"; and the holy man, acting as a teacher of the commandments, quickly made ready to cut off his hair.

"When a man renounces the world, is not a certain four-line hymn chanted?" asked Sukena.

Perhaps the holy man did not know the words of that hymn, for he chanted, " 'Let ye who are beasts attain enlightenment.' "[40] And thereupon Tomotoshi the governor of Mikawa made merry, who likewise was washing his hair to renounce the world there.

"How regrettable it is that he calls you an animal," he said, "simply because you renounce the world through love of life!"

In this manner the courtiers of the imperial retinue fled to divers places, or scattered to live in retirement as monks, until no man remained to attend upon the supreme highness, the crown prince, or the two former emperors, save only Tsuneaki and the minister

---

[39] Famous disasters of Chinese history.
[40] From the *Bommōkyō* (*Brahmajāla Sūtra*).

Arimitsu. For the rest, these imperial personages were encompassed about by strange enemy warriors, who brought them back to the capital in coarse litters of plaited bamboo. Men of high degree and low stood in the streets to see them, saying:

"Ah! How strange! In the last year but one the former sovereign was captured at Kasagi and sent away to the province of Oki; yet within three years retribution has come. Truly of such things as these is it said, 'Though they believed yesterday that it was others who were unfortunate, today the sorrow has become their own.' To what place of exile will this emperor be sent to grieve?"

So they spoke, nor was there any of those onlookers, either wise or foolish, but wept into his sleeve, aware of the manifest truth of cause and effect.

The Defeat of the Chihaya Attackers

At the hour of the horse on the morrow, there came men bearing tidings to Chihaya, saying, "Rokuhara was beaten down last night, and the emperor flees toward the Kantō with the former sovereigns." Those within the castle were gladdened and made valiant, rejoicing even as caged birds going forth to sport in the woods. But the hearts of the attackers were as the hearts of sheep going to a sacrifice when, urged forward, they draw near to the temple.

"If we delay to retreat for a single day," these said, "we shall be troubled to pass over the mountain roads, since outlaws will come here in very great numbers." And they drew back early in the morning of the tenth day, more than a hundred thousand riders, seeking to take their way toward the southern capital.

Now before this time outlaws had filled up all the land in front of those who retreated. And likewise the enemy came pursuing them swiftly from the rear. As the besiegers fled in confusion, each striving to be first, they threw away bows and arrows and deserted fathers, sons, and brothers (for such is the way of a mighty host when it gives back). In countless thousands of myriads they cut open their bellies at the edges of trackless crags, or smashed their bones to bits at the bottoms of chasms fifteen thousand feet deep. Moreover, there were barriers and obstacles in the ravines, put up earlier by the attackers themselves lest some among their numbers seek to go away, wherefore many warriors flew off their horses and perished beneath the feet of others, for there was none that took them away.

For two or three leagues the besiegers fled over the mountain paths with the myriads of the enemy following after, nor did they give battle even once. Although they had numbered a hundred thousand warriors until that morning, few indeed were not struck down, and none of the saved but lost his horse and armor. Still do their white bones lie in piles at the foot of Mount Kongō and along the Tōjō valley road, covered with moss and scarred by arrows and swords, for no man has gathered them up.

None of the foremost grand marshals was smitten on the road, but all came to the southern capital midway through that night. Indeed it was useless for them to live on!

10

Master Senjuō Flees from Ōkura Valley

AT KAMAKURA NONE KNEW that Ashikaga Jibu-no-tayū Takauji was become an enemy, since by reason of the long distance no messenger had come there. But it happened that Master Senjuō, the second son of Lord Ashikaga, fled from Ōkura Valley to an unknown place, deep in the night of the second day of the fifth month of the third year of Genkō. And thereupon the high and the low in Kamakura raised a great clamor, saying, "Aha! An important thing has happened!"

Then the Hōjō sent forth two messengers, the lay monk Nagasaki Saemon and the lay monk Suwa Saemon, saying, "In no wise may our hearts be at ease. We are very far from the capital, and have not received trustworthy tidings concerning what passes there." But at Takahashi in Suruga these two messengers fell in with one hastening from Rokuhara, who said, "Lord Nagoya is dead and Lord Ashikaga is become an enemy." And they turned back toward the Kantō, thinking, "Indeed, Kamakura itself is in danger."

Now Takauji's oldest son Master Takewaka abode at Oyama in Izu as the disciple of his uncle, the Magistrate Sign of the Law Ryōhen. Perhaps fearful lest warriors come against him from Kamakura, Takewaka went forth in secret toward the capital with his uncle and thirteen youths of his monastery, who all assumed the guise of wandering monks. Yet Nagasaki Saemon came full upon them at Ukishima-ga-hara, and made to strike them down. And without speaking a word, the Magistrate Sign of the Law cut his belly where he sat on his horse, so that he fell down to the side of the road.

"Truly, those who devise treacherous things on the inside let no word escape on the outside," said Nagasaki.

Laying hands on Master Takewaka, he secretly stabbed him to death in the night, and in full daylight he cut off the heads of the thirteen to hang them up at Ukishima-ga-hara.

The Revolt of Nitta Yoshisada; How a Goblin Summoned the Armies of Echigo

Nitta Tarō Yoshisada had come back to his own province from Chihaya, feigning to be afflicted of a disease, but the reason thereof was the former emperor's mandate which he had received on the eleventh day of the third month. Wherefore secretly he gathered together trustworthy kinsmen to devise plans for making a revolt.

Meanwhile, the Sagami lay monk, knowing nothing of Nitta's planning, summoned the armies of the six provinces of Musashi, Kōzuke, Awa, Kazusa, Hitachi, and Shimotsuke, that with a hundred thousand riders he might send his brother, the lay monk Shirō Sakon-no-taifu, to the capital, to quiet the disturbances in the home provinces and western lands. Likewise, the lay monk levied an urgent tax upon the estates of nearby provinces, saying, "It is to supply the armies." In particular he sent two men, Izumo-no-suke Chikatsura and the lay monk Kuronuma Hikoshirō, to Nitta's estate of Serada, to hand down strict orders, saying, "You must deliver up sixty thousand *kan* of money within five days." (For it was said that there were many rich men in that estate.) And when the two messengers came to the estate, they sent a great host of warriors into the overseer's house, pressing him beyond reason.

On hearing tidings thereof, Nitta Yoshisada said:

"How mortifying it is, that hard by my castle men of low degree trample the ground with their horses' feet! I cannot forbear while my eyes behold this thing."

So he spoke, and sent forth many men to quickly lay hands on the messengers. Izumo-no-suke he bound with bonds, but he cut off the head of the Kuronuma lay monk and hung it up in Serada village on the evening of the same day.

Hearing of this, the Sagami lay monk was greatly angered.

"During the nine generations of my family's power in the land, none within the seas has failed to bow before its mandate," he said. "Yet insolently in these years men of distant places reject our commands, while men of near places mock at our orders. And now our messenger has been struck down by one who is a stay of the house of Hōjō! There must be no remissness, lest a mighty rebellion be raised up."

So he spoke, and sent word to the armies of Musashi and Kōzuke, commanding, "Strike down Nitta Tarō Yoshisada and his younger brother Wakiya Jirō Yoshisuke."

Hearing of this, Yoshisada gathered together the chief of his kinsmen, saying, "What ought to be done in the matter?"

Then these proposed divers things, and their counsels were divided. There were some who said, "Let us make the Numada estate a stronghold, put the Tone River before us, and await the enemy's coming," while others said, "Let us defend ourselves against them by crossing over into Tsubari district, stopping up the Ueda pass, and raising an army, for our kinsmen dwell in many places throughout the land of Echigo." But when Yoshisada's brother Wakiya Jirō Yoshisuke had considered for a time, he came forward and spoke a word, saying:

"For those who follow the warrior's way, it is proper to despise death and esteem honor. Unless fortune is with us, we cannot prevail against the governor of Sagami by standing behind the Tone River. His house, which has ruled the realm for more than a hundred and sixty years, is still so mighty that no man counts its orders as nothing. Nor can we endure for long by trusting to kinsmen in the province of Echigo, if perchance there be those who are out of harmony with us. How mortifying it would be were the men of the realm to say, 'They have fled to this place and that, unable to do great things,' or 'Having killed a messenger from the governor of Sagami, a person called Nitta ran away to another province and was struck down there!' Rather let us be called rebels, and for the court's sake give up these lives that must be forfeited soon. For then our valor will bring honor to our descendants after we are dead, and our fame will cleanse our corpses lying by the side of the road. Why else have we received an imperial mandate before others? Let each of us entrust his fate to heaven with the mandate pressed to his forehead. Though he be but a single rider, let each go out into the provinces to win the hearts of others. If warriors will join themselves to us, we shall soon conquer Kamakura; if they will not, we must die with Kamakura as our pillow."

So he spoke, placing honor above all and thinking first of valor. And the more than thirty kinsmen in that place agreed that it ought to be so.

Now Yoshisada thought, "If it is thus, we must arise quickly before tidings of our plans are spread abroad." At the hour of the hare on the eighth day of the fifth month, he raised his banner in front of the shrine of the Bright Divinity of Ikushina, opened the imperial mandate, bowed to it three times, and went forth toward Kasagakeno.

Of those who rode together with Yoshisada, the chief were these kinsmen: Ōdachi Jirō Muneuji, his son Magojirō Nariuji, his second son Yajirō Ujiakira, and his third son Jirō Ujikane; Horiguchi Saburō Sadamitsu and his younger brother Shirō Yukiyoshi; Iwamatsu Saburō Tsuneie; Satomi Gorō Yoshitane; Wakiya Jirō Yoshisuke; Eda Saburō Mitsuyoshi; and Momonoi Jirō Naoyoshi. All their number did not exceed one hundred and fifty horsemen.

In his heart Yoshisada thought, "How may I prevail with such a force as this?" But in the evening of that day he beheld two thousand warriors with goodly horses and armor galloping forward in a cloud of dust from the Tone River. Although he thought, "They are enemies!" they were not enemies, but kinsmen from the province of Echigo: men of Satomi, Toriyama, Tanaka, Ōida, and Hanekawa.

Rejoicing exceedingly, Yoshisada held his horse, saying:

"I did not think to do this thing yesterday or today (though it has been in my mind for long); yet now suddenly I have stirred up my spirit to go forth. How is it that you know of it, since I have sent no tidings?"

So he questioned them, and the Ōida governor of Tōtōmi bowed in his saddle, saying:

"How should we have galloped here in this wise, had we not heard that you devised a great thing according to the command of His Majesty? On the fifth day there came a goblin in the guise of a wandering monk, calling himself your messenger, who in a single day proclaimed these tidings throughout the province of Echigo. Therefore have we hastened here, joining night to day, and assuredly those that dwell in far places will come before tomorrow. If you think to go forth to another province, please wait awhile for their warriors."

Then all together got down from their horses, greeted each one the other, and rested their bodies and the bodies of their horses. As they abode in that place, there came a mighty host of more than five thousand riders, galloping to join them with family banners held high: the rearmost of the men of Echigo, and the Genji of Kai and Shinano. And Yoshisada and Yoshisuke rejoiced exceedingly, saying, "Solely through the protection of the Great Bodhisattva Hachiman have these things come to pass! We must not remain here even for a little while."

On the ninth day these crossed over into the province of Musashi, whereupon with two hundred riders Ki no Gozaemon galloped to join himself to them, bringing Master Senjuō, the son of Lord Ashikaga. Thereafter warriors of Kōzuke, Shimotsuke, Kazusa, Hitachi, and Musashi gathered together without being awaited and galloped forward without being summoned, until in a single day their number became more than two hundred thousand riders. The warriors and horses of their crowding hosts filled up all the plain of Musashino, that extends for more than eight hundred leagues in the four directions,[1] not leaving a single open space whereon a man might stand. Not a bird could fly, of those that soar through the heavens, nor an animal find refuge, of those that run over the earth. The moon rising from the herb-strewn

---

[1] Not to be taken literally.

moor glimmered above horses and saddles and shone aslant on armored sleeves; the wind cleaving the pampas grass set banners to fluttering and fretted billowing mantles.

Since it was thus, the fast horses of many provinces bore tidings of alarm to Kamakura, one following upon another as closely as the teeth of a comb.

Those who knew nothing of change in the world laughed together scornfully, saying:

"Too much is made of this matter. What can happen? Were attackers to come against us from India or the land of T'ang, it would be a serious thing, but as for those that rise up within our land of Akitsushima[2] to smite the lord of Kamakura—are they not as the praying mantis that sought to block a carriage, or the *ching-wei* bird that sought to fill up the sea?" [3]

But men of understanding spoke together fearfully, saying:

"Alas! A terrible thing has come to pass! A mighty enemy has risen up within our very walls while yet the fighting continues in the western lands and home provinces. Truly it is as when Wu Tzu-hsü advised Fu-ch'ai King of Wu, saying, 'Chin is a wound, but Yüeh is a disease of the vitals.'" [4]

Thenceforward the men of Kamakura no longer made ready to send an army against the capital, but thought only of striking down Lord Nitta. On the ninth day they consulted together concerning the battle to come, and at the hour of the snake on the tenth day they sent forth Kanazawa Sadamasa the governor of Musashi to Shimokōbe with fifty thousand horsemen, that he might assemble warriors in Kazusa and Shimōsa to fall upon the enemy from behind. Likewise, they gave sixty thousand men of Musashi and Kōzuke to the grand marshal Sakurada Jibu-no-tayū Sadakuni, and to Nagasaki Jirō Takashige, and Nagasaki Magoshirō Saemon and the lay monk Kaji Jirō Saemon, all of whom they sent from Kamiji to the Iruma River, to stand behind the river and smite the enemy where they sought to cross.

Now since Shōkyū the storm winds of the east had sunk into

---

[2] A poetic name for Japan.

[3] Classic Chinese examples of futile effort.

[4] Because Chin was a distant enemy and Yüeh was close at hand. (Chin here is a mistake for Ch'i.)

slumber, and men were as though forgetful of the uses of bow and arrow. Wherefore were these sixty thousand warriors stirred up by the marvel of going forth to give battle, and rode out with haughty mien and splendid accoutrements. How glorious was the spectacle of their horses and armor and swords, all glittering and sparkling!

When these had passed two days on the way, they came to Kotesashi Moor in Musashi, it being the hour of the dragon on the eleventh day. From there they gazed upon the distant camp of the Genji, where stood the enemy hosts like clouds or mist, untold thousands and myriads of riders. And Sakurada and the Nagasaki held their horses in that place, forbearing to go forward (since perhaps the enemy was not as they had thought).

Quickly then Yoshisada's armies crossed the Iruma River, moved forward raising a battle cry, and shot humming-bulb arrows to begin the fighting, whereupon the Heike too raised a battle cry, and moved their banners up. First the Genji sent forth a hundred archers to shoot, and the Heike sent forth two hundred; again the Heike sent forth a thousand riders to attack, and the Genji sent forth two thousand. So more than thirty times in one day did Minamoto and Taira strive together, each sending forth more warriors.

The Genji lost three hundred slain, and suffered their horses to draw breath for awhile; likewise, the Heike lost five hundred slain, and rested their horses' feet for awhile. And the night having fallen, both sides said, "Assuredly shall we contend in battle again on the morrow."

The Genji drew away three leagues to camp by the Iruma River, while the Heike drew away three leagues to camp by the Kume River. Nor was the one camp so much as thirty-five hundred yards distant from the other, but through the night both burned watch fires, waiting eagerly for the coming of day.

When the night lightened, the Genji rode forth against the camp by the Kume River, saying, "We must not be second to the Heike!" Meanwhile, the Heike tightened their saddle girths, tied their helmet strings, and made ready for the coming of the enemy, saying, "Assuredly will the Genji advance against us at dawn.

It will be well to await them and set the battle in array at this place." And so these two armies drew together.

The sixty thousand warriors of Kamakura made themselves into one body, that spread out and strove valiantly to encompass the enemy about. But beholding them, the warriors of Yoshisada formed themselves into a wedge, that their center might not be smashed. And the two armies mingled together in disorder, since all men know of Huang Shih Kung's method of binding a tiger, and all are acquainted with Chang Tzu-fang's way of defeating a devil.[5] The one was not smashed, nor was the other surrounded, but the warriors of both offered up their lives in competition to die on this field. Until but one rider in a thousand remained, even so long did these resolute foes strive together.

Now although few of the Genji were slain, the Heike perished in great numbers. (Perhaps it was the fortune of the occasion that it should be so.) And Kaji and the Nagasaki gave back toward Bumbai, thinking, "We have been beaten down in this second battle." The Genji determined to attack as before, yet they rested their horses' feet for a night in their camp beside the Kume River, since horses and riders were wearied by many battles on two successive days.

Meanwhile to Kamakura came men saying, "Sakurada Jibu-no-tayū Sadakuni is giving back, likewise Kaji and the Nagasaki, all of whom were beaten down in battle on the twelfth day." And thereupon the Sagami lay monk named his younger brother to be a general, the lay monk Shirō Sakon-no-taifu, making him the leader of the lay monk Shioda of Mutsu, the lay monk Abu Saemon, the Jō governor of Echigo, Nagasaki Tokimitsu the governor of Suruga, the lay monk Satō Saemon, Andō Saemon-no-jō Takasada, the lay monk Yokomizo Gorō, Nambu Magojirō, the lay monk Shingai Saemon, and Miura Wakasa no Gorō Ujiakira, whom he dispatched with a hundred thousand horsemen. When these came to Bumbai midway in the night of the fourteenth day, then indeed the spirit of the vanquished army returned, and it was valiant to go forth!

Before the end of that night Yoshisada advanced against Bumbai

[5] Traditional Chinese military tactics.

Chapter 10

with a battle shout, all unaware of the great host of fresh warriors come to join themselves to the enemy. But the men of Kamakura chose out three thousand mighty archers, that went forward, shot arrows as thick and fast as falling rain, and smote the Genji so sorely that they could not attack. And then the Heike encompassed Yoshisada's army about, attacking furiously.

In no wise discomfited, the Genji galloped into the center of the Heike host, broke them down fiercely in every direction, and attacked seven or eight times like flashing bolts of lightning. But the enemy were exceedingly numerous, their warriors were fresh, and they fought with high regard for honor, saying, "We must wipe out the shame of defeat!" Wherefore, at last Yoshisada drew away vanquished toward Horigane. Very many of his warriors were struck down, nor could any man tell the number of those who were grievously wounded.

Had the men of Kamakura pursued after Yoshisada quickly on that day to attack him, then must Yoshisada have been destroyed. But foolishly they allowed the hours to pass, thinking, "What can the enemy do now? Assuredly will the men of Musashi and Kōzuke attack Nitta and drive him forth." This was a sign that the luck of the Heike was ended.

Miura Ōtawa Speaks of Warfare

Now there was a warrior who had long inclined his heart toward Yoshisada, one Miura Ōtawa Heiroku Saemon Yoshikatsu, who galloped into the camp of the Genji on the evening of the fifteenth day with six thousand riders from the province of Sagami: men of Matsuda, Kawamura, Doi, Tsuchiya, Homma, and Shibuya. Joyfully Yoshisada hastened to receive him. He dealt with him most courteously, caused him to sit close, and asked him concerning the fighting.

Respectfully Heiroku Saemon said:

"In these days the realm is divided into two camps, whereof neither may abide in peace, save only through victory over the other in warfare. It may be that ten or twelve battles will be contested, yet assuredly we shall know peace in the end, since the last issue must accord with the will of heaven. Now when my armies are joined to yours, we are a hundred thousand riders. Ought we not to give battle again, though we be fewer than the enemy?"

"Not so!" said Yoshisada. "How can our weary warriors attack a greater enemy, one that is exultant and stirred up to valor?"

Yoshikatsu spoke again, saying:

"Assuredly will you win the battle to come. In ancient times, when Ch'in and Ch'u contended together, the Ch'u general Wu Hsin-chün defeated eight hundred thousand men of the Ch'in general Li Yu with but eighty thousand men, and cut off more than four hundred thousand heads. Thereafter Wu Hsin-chün was proud and remiss in fighting, thinking, 'There is nothing to fear from the warriors of Ch'in.' Sung I the assistant general of Ch'u saw this and said, 'It is said, "When a victorious general is proud and his soldiers are negligent, most certainly will they be destroyed." Now it is even thus with Wu Hsin-chün. When else should he be destroyed?' At last in a later battle Wu Hsin-chün was killed by Chang Han, the Left General of Ch'in, who destroyed him in an instant in a single battle.

"Yesterday I sent forth men secretly to gaze upon the enemy's camp. Truly the pride of their generals is even as that of Wu Hsin-chün! It is entirely as Sung I said. Since my men are fresh, let me be the first to contend against the enemy in tomorrow's battle."

So he spoke, and Yoshisada bowed before what was wise, accepted what was correct, and gave over the government of the coming battle to Miura Heiroku Saemon.

At the hour of the tiger on the morrow, which is to say the sixteenth day of the fifth month, Miura advanced from the center of the one hundred thousand riders toward the Bumbai river bed. But though he came very near to the enemy camp, his warriors did not unfurl their banners or utter war cries, for he sought to attack the Heike unaware.

Now even as Miura had said, the bodies of the Heike men and horses were wearied from fighting again and again on the day before, nor was there any that dreamt of the enemy's coming. Their horses were not saddled, nor was their armor gathered together. Some of them had loosened their girdle strings and set their pillows by the side of courtesans, while others lay down drunken with wine, knowing nothing of what passed. Truly because of the evil deeds of a previous life did these invite their own destruction!

Those who were encamped at the river bed proclaimed the coming of the attackers, saying:

"A great host rides toward us quietly with furled banners. Take care lest they be enemies!"

So they spoke, but no man's heart was disquieted. The grand marshal and all the rest said:

"Can such a thing be! Assuredly it is Miura Ōtawa coming. We have heard that he has raised an army in the province of Sagami and hastens to join himself to us. Nothing could be more auspicious!"

Most amazingly had fortune deserted them!

Following after Miura, Yoshisada had divided his one hundred thousand horsemen into three parties. As these drew near from three directions, they raised a battle cry all at once.

"Horses! Armor!" clamored the Heike, seized with amazement by the sound of their shouting.

But the warriors of Yoshisada and Yoshisuke galloped against them from the front, attacking furiously on every side, while Miura Heiroku smote them from the rear with men of Edo, Toshima, Kasai, and Kawagoe, the Eight Heishi of Bandō,[6] and the Seven Bands of Musashi, beating them back in every direction. And by this single stratagem of the Genji were the tens of myriads of the Heike host vanquished, so that they fled in disorder toward Kamakura.

The lay monk Shirō Sakon-no-taifu was hard pressed near Sekido, he who was the grand marshal of the Heike. But Yokomizo Hachirō stood in that place until he had shot down twenty-three approaching enemy riders, and when his arrows were exhausted he drew forth his sword and gave his life for his lord, leaving a name for generations to come. His two retainers did the same, and the lay monk Abu Dōkan with his two sons. Also more than three hundred men turned back to die there, hereditary retainers of the

[6] Bandō is another name for the Kantō. The Eight Heishi were families of Taira descent.

Hōjō or warriors grateful for a word of kindness. And so the grand marshal drew away safely to Yamanouchi.

Now Nagasaki Jirō Takashige caused soldiers of low degree to carry the heads of two enemies that he had grappled with and slain in the battle of the Kume River, as well as the heads of thirteen others killed with arrows. And he came to the mansion of the Lord of Kamakura with arrows still standing in his armor, whereof the white threads were dyed red with blood from the mouths of his wounds.

Takashige's grandfather the lay monk came forth to greet him joyfully. He sucked his wounds, held the blood in his mouth, and wept, saying:

"Although the old proverb says, 'None knows the child so well as its father,' I thought of you as a person who would be of no service to our lord, wherefore constantly I reproached you for your lack of filial piety. Most grievously did I err! You have passed alive through ten thousand deaths, and in smashing the strong and crushing the enemy you have attained to things regarded as impossible by Ch'en P'ing and Chang Liang.[7] Take heed that in the days to come you continue to fight with all your heart, for thereby will you do honor to your ancestors' names and requite the boons of His Lordship the governor."

So he spoke, not admonishing as was his wont, but praising Takashige's valor. And in tears Takashige touched his head to the ground.

Soon men came to Kamakura saying, "Rokuhara is beaten down, and all of our warriors are slain by their own hands at Bamba in Ōmi."

Hearing these things while they were engaged against a great enemy, the chieftains of Kamakura were perplexed utterly, even as men fighting vainly to stop a mighty fire, nor can anything be compared to the wailing and lamenting of their retainers and kinsmen. Even fierce and warlike men were as though benumbed in their feet and hands, unable to distinguish east from west.

Although the men of Kamakura thought to withhold these things from the enemy, in a short time they became known (for truly

---

[7] Chinese heroes of the Former Han period (202 B.C.–A.D. 9).

they were not things such as might be hidden). And no enemy but rejoiced with stirred-up spirit, saying, "Better and better!"

The Battle of Kamakura

When tidings of Yoshisada's victories were proclaimed abroad, like clouds or mist the warriors of the eight eastern provinces joined themselves to him. Tarrying for a day at Sekido to write the names of those who came, he indeed recorded eight hundred thousand riders, a most mighty host, whereof he fashioned three armies, with two grand marshals in charge of each. The general of the left of the first army was Ōdachi Jirō Muneuji and the general of the right was Eda Saburō Yukiyoshi, and with more than a hundred thousand riders these went forth toward the Gokurakuji Passage. The supreme general of the second army was Horiguchi Saburō Sadamitsu and the assistant general was Ōshima Moriyuki the governor of Sanuki, and with more than a hundred thousand riders these went forth toward Kobukurozaka. The generals of the third army were Nitta Kotarō Yoshisada and his brother Wakiya Jirō Yoshisuke, and their kinsmen compassed them about: the Horiguchi, the Yamana, the Iwamatsu, the Oida, the Momonoi, the Satomi, the Toriyama, the Nukada, the Ichinoi, the Ugawa, and the others, and with six hundred thousand horsemen they drew near to Kamakura from Kewaizaka.

Now to those in Kamakura had come men saying, "Even yesterday and the day before were battles set in array at Bumbai and Sekido, wherein our warriors were beaten down." But their hearts were not discomfited thereat, nor their countenances disordered.

"Of little consequence is this enemy!" they thought scornfully.

Yet with few remaining men the lay monk Shirō Sakon-no-taifu, the grand marshal sent forth to attack in front, had retreated toward Yamanouchi on the evening of the past day. Moreover, Kanazawa Sadamasa, the grand marshal sent forth to Shimokōbe to fall upon the enemy from behind, now drew back toward Kamakura from Shimomichi, vanquished by Koyama Hōgan and Chiba-no-suke. And then the hearts of all were dismayed.

"An undreamt-of thing has come to pass!" they said.

Even as these spoke, the enemy fell upon them from three directions, lighting fires in fifty places at Muraoka, Fujisawa, Katase, Koshigoe, and Jikkenzaka at the hour of the hare on the eighteenth day of the fifth month. The warriors of Kamakura ran around in every direction; the high and the low fled away blindly to mountains and fields. Most sorely did they lament, saying:

"While the emperor listened to the song of 'Rainbow Skirts,' the war drums of Yü-yang came shaking the earth. After the king lighted false signal fires, the banners of Jung and Ti barbarians came hiding the sky. Surely even as this was the destruction of Yu Wang of Chou, or the ruin of Hsüan Tsung of T'ang!" [8]

Since the Genji attacked from three directions, the Heike also divided their warriors into three armies. The general of the first army was Kanazawa Aritoki the governor of Echigo, who defended Kewaizaka with thirty thousand men of Awa, Kōzuke, and Shimotsuke. The grand marshal of the second army was Daibutsu Sadanao the governor of Mutsu, who defended the Gokurakuji Passage with fifty thousand men of Kai, Shinano, Izu, and Suruga. The grand marshal of the third army was Akahashi Moritoki the governor of Sagami, who defended Susaki with sixty thousand men of Musashi, Sagami, Dewa, and Ōshū. And eight Heishi of low degree were held behind in Kamakura with a hundred thousand warriors of divers provinces, to go forth to such places as might be weakened.

At the hour of the snake on that day, the two sides set the battle in array, and through the day and through the night they contended together. The attackers pressed forward with fresh men, time after time, so great were their numbers; the defenders held stubbornly in many engagements, so vital were their strongholds. Thunderously their battle cries and shouts on the three sides jarred the heavens and made the earth to tremble. Now attacking in fish

[8] In Po Chü-i's "Song of Everlasting Sorrow," the Emperor Hsüan Tsung is depicted as listening to "Rainbow Skirts" with his beautiful concubine Yang Kuei-fei, heedless of the approaching danger of rebellion. The Chou ruler Yu Wang was in love with a lady named Pao Szu, who could seldom be made to smile. On one occasion, a false war alarm caused the capital's signal fires to be lit, and the lady was much amused by the resulting confusion. Yu Wang later deliberately ordered the fires to be lit in order to divert her. When at last barbarians attacked the capital, the Chinese warriors ignored the king's summons.

scale wedges, now opening out like the wings of a fowl, both armies smote the enemy before and behind, stood fast on the right and left, gloried in honor, and despised life.

Assuredly was this a battle to decide great things, one such as would make it known to generations to come whether those who contended together were brave or cowardly. When a son was stricken, his father did not minister to him, but rode over his body to attack the enemy in front; when a lord was shot down from his horse by an arrow, his retainer did not raise him up, but mounted onto the horse and galloped forward. Some grappled with enemies to the end; some exchanged sword-thrusts and died together with their foes. It was impossible to know when the battle might cease, so valiant was the spirit of those warriors, who were resolved to fight even though a million men perished and became one, or a hundred positions fell and became one.

The Suicide of the Akahashi Governor of Sagami; Homma's Suicide

Now the fighting waxed furious at Susaki, whither the Akahashi governor of Sagami had taken his way in the morning. Sixty-five times during the day and night did warriors contend together with forged weapons, until all save three hundred of the myriads of Akahashi's followers had fallen or fled. At last Akahashi spoke a word to Nanjō Saemon Takanao, who served there as the warrior grand marshal, saying:

"In eight years of warfare between Han and Ch'u, forever was Kao Tsu defeated, yet by a single victory at the battle of Wu-chiang he destroyed Hsiang Yü. In seventy battles between Ch'i and Chin, never was Chung-erh successful, yet at last through the victory of Ch'i-ching he became the protector of the land.[9] It is the way of warfare that one emerges alive from a myriad deaths or wins a victory after a hundred defeats. I do not believe that today will end the prosperity of the Hōjō, even though the enemy is like to win a trifling advantage in the fighting. Nevertheless, I shall cut

[9] I.e., Chung-erh, who was the duke of Chin, became the head of the league of military rulers (note 32, Chapter Four). The title was disputed by the state of Ch'i. See also note 35, Chapter Two.

open my belly in this place without waiting to know the fate of our house, lest the Lord of Sagami and others of my kinsmen shame me by looking upon me with distrustful eyes, by reason that I am kin to Lord Ashikaga through a woman.[10] For when Yen Tan spoke to the teacher T'ien Kuang of a grave matter, saying to him, 'Do not allow it to become known,' T'ien Kuang took his own life in front of Yen Tan, that he might not eye him.[11] Now the bodies of our warriors are tired, since we and the enemy have raged together furiously here, yet not without dishonor may I draw back from the place I defend. Nor do I wish to live on, suspected of men."

Thereupon he stripped off his armor inside his curtain while the battle continued, cut open his belly crosswise, and fell down with his head to the north.[12]

Beholding him, Nanjō likewise cut open his belly, saying:

"For whose sake shall a warrior cherish life after his grand marshal has perished by his own hand? Indeed, if it is thus I shall accompany him!"

And more than ninety other warriors laid bare their upper bodies and died by their own hands, piling up on top of one another.

So on the evening of the eighteenth day Susaki was beaten down first of all, and Yoshisada's army went in as far as Yamanouchi.

For many years a certain Homma Yamashiro no Saemon had found favor in the eyes of Daibutsu Ōshū no Sadanao as his close attendant. This Homma had remained in his lodging place at the beginning of the battle, prohibited from going forth to serve because of a trifling offense. But early in the morning of the nineteenth day there came to his ears a loud clamor of men saying, "The battle waxes furious at the Gokurakuji Passage, where the enemy breaks through." And then Homma Yamashiro no Saemon went toward Gokurakuji-zaka with his hundred retainers and soldiers, who all resolved, "We shall make this our end."

Homma's warriors galloped into the center of the thirty thousand riders of Ōdachi Jirō Muneuji, a grand marshal of the enemy. Seeking to grapple with the grand marshal Muneuji, they chased

---

[10] His sister was Ashikaga's wife.
[11] From the *Shih chi*.
[12] In imitation of the Buddha, who died with his head to the north.

and scattered the exultant host in eight directions, pressing hard upon them until the thirty thousand split and drew back quickly to Koshigoe. And Ōdachi Jirō Muneuji himself fell down dead onto the white sand, cut by the sword of a Homma retainer (doubtless one who grappled with him in the disorder of the flight).

Rejoicing greatly, Homma flew down from his horse to take Ōdachi's head. He pierced it with the end of his sword, galloped to Sadanao's camp, and bowed in front of his curtain, saying:

"By means of this battle, I requite the boons of many years. Likewise I ask leave to go before you tranquilly to the nether regions. If your uncertain life were to end, my mind would hold a wrong thought in this world and the next." [13]

Nor did he finish his words, but held back the flowing tears and cut his belly, so that he died. There was no man but marveled thereat, saying, "Of such a man as this was it said, 'You may rob a three-corps army of its general.' [14] Of such a deed as this was it said, 'Anger is requited with virtue.' " [15]

A Beach Appears at Inamura Cape

Now to Nitta Yoshisada came men saying, "Ōdachi Jirō Muneuji, who went forth to the Gokurakuji Passage, is slain by Homma, and his warriors are drawn back to Katase and Koshigoe." Wherefore, Yoshisada went around by Katase and Koshigoe with twenty thousand mighty men of valor, took his way toward Gokurakuji-zaka deep in the night of the twenty-first day, and observed the enemy camp by the light of the setting moon. Northward he beheld a steep path over high mountains which extended all the way to the passage, as well as a gate where fifty or sixty thousand warriors were lined up together behind rows of shields. Southward at Inamura Cape the road was a narrow beach, strewn abundantly with obstacles to the waves' edge. Moreover, there

---

[13] The regret he would feel because of his lord's death would be a worldly tie interfering with his attainment of enlightenment.

[14] From the *Analects*: "You may rob a three-corps army of its general, but you cannot take away the free will of a common man." The meaning here is that nothing could deprive Homma of his honor.

[15] An allusion to a passage in the *Tao-te-ching*.

were ships lined up on the water five or six hundred yards distant, ready to shoot flanking arrows from towers.

"It was entirely natural that those who attacked these positions drew back unable to prevail," thought Yoshisada. He dismounted from his horse, stripped off his helmet, and fell down and worshiped the sea, praying to the dragon-gods with all his might.

"I have heard that the Sun Goddess of Ise, the founder of the land of Japan, conceals her true being in the august image of Vairocana Buddha, and that she has appeared in this world in the guise of a dragon-god of the blue ocean. Now her descendant our emperor drifts on the waves of the western seas, oppressed by rebellious subjects. I have come against the enemy camp with my battle-ax to do a subject's duty, that I may render aid to His Majesty and restore peace to the people. Let the eight dragon-gods of the inner and outer seas look upon my loyalty; let them roll back the tides a myriad leagues distant to open a way for my hosts."

So he prayed, and cast his gold-mounted sword into the sea. May it not be that the dragon-gods accepted it? At the setting of the moon that night, suddenly for more than two thousand yards the waters ebbed away from Inamura Cape, where for the first time a broad flat beach appeared. Likewise, the thousands of warships deployed to shoot flanking arrows were carried away with the running tide, until they floated far out on the sea. How strange it was! Never was there such a thing as this!

Now Yoshisada spoke a word, saying:

"It is said of the General of the Second Host of Later Han[16] that he drew out his sword and smote a rock when those within his castle thirsted, whereupon suddenly a fountain of water burst forth. Likewise is it said of the Empress Jingū of our court, that going forth against Silla[17] she caused the waters to recede by casting a tide-ebbing pearl upon the surface of the sea, wherefore at last she was enabled to win a victory in the fighting. These are auspicious precedents from Japan and China, and marvelous things for all times. Warriors, advance!"

---

[16] Li Kuang-li.

[17] An ancient Korean kingdom. According to the traditional account, the empress conquered it in A.D. 200.

Chapter 10

So he commanded them, and the warriors of Echigo, Kōzuke, Musashi, and Sagami all came together in one place: the Eda, the Ōdachi, the Satomi, the Toriyama, the Tanaka, the Ugawa, the Yamana, the Momonoi, and the others. And when they had galloped across the wide beach at Inamura Cape in a straight line, they entered riotously into Kamakura.

Then in perplexity the Heike wavered between two courses, instead of facing the enemy resolutely to give battle. If they were to fall upon this enemy in their rear, the attackers in front would follow after them and break through; if they were to defend against the enemy in front, these hosts in the rear would block the roads and strike them down.

Now there was a certain Shimazu Shirō, a person renowned for his great strength, superior to others in body and build, of whom from early times the Nagasaki lay monk[18] had thought, "He is one who will be of service to our lord in time of need." The lay monk himself had placed the cap of manhood upon Shirō's head, and had looked to him as one worthy of a thousand men. Therefore Shirō had not been sent forth to defend a gateway, but had been commanded to stand hard by the mansion of the Sagami lay monk, that he might fight in the last battle. When men raised a clamor, saying, "The warriors at the beach are beaten down, and the Genji have pressed in to Wakamiya Road," the Sagami lay monk called Shimazu to him and personally filled his cup with wine. And after Shimazu had drunk three times, the lay monk brought forward his horse Shiranami for him, saddled with a silver-trimmed saddle, the finest horse of the Kantō, kept in a stable three bays long on every side. Of those who watched, not one but was envious in his heart.

Quickly Shimazu mounted this horse in front of the gate, his great crimson badge fluttering in the sea breeze from Yui-no-hama. And he took up his weapons and galloped forward impressively. Of the many Heike warriors looking on, not one but thought, "Truly he is a warrior equal to a thousand! It is only natural that he has been favored by the steward, and has behaved himself as though other men were of no consequence."

Beholding Shimazu, Yoshisada's warriors shouted, "An excellent

[18] Nagasaki Enki.

enemy indeed!" Fierce fighters galloped toward him, each striving to be first, men renowned for great strength, who thought, "I will grapple with this warrior to the end": Kuriu, Shinozuka, Hata, Yabe, Horiguchi, Yura, Nagahama, and the others. And Genji and Heike clamored loudly, saying, "Famous strong men of the two sides are going to fight alone. Let us watch them!" Anxiously they held their breath and sweated, and stood ready to look.

But thereupon Shimazu leapt down from his horse, stripped off his helmet, and declared his allegiance to the Genji host. Noble and base took back their words of praise, and high and low abhorred him.

Now when Shimazu had become the first of the Heike to surrender himself, favored retainers of many years likewise abandoned their lords to become prisoners, or deserted their fathers to become enemies, and vassals of many generations did the same. Truly did it seem that no longer after today would Minamoto and Taira contend together to rule the realm!

War Fires in Kamakura; the Bravery of Nagasaki and His Son

Fires were lighted among the commoners' houses along the beach, and also east and west of the Inase River, wherefrom flames like carriage wheels flew and scattered in black smoke, blazing up in more than twenty places a thousand or two thousand yards distant (for just at that time the sea wind blew furiously). Entering clamorously beneath the fierce flames, the warriors of the Genji everywhere shot the bewildered enemy with their arrows, cut them down with their swords, grappled with them, and stabbed them. They captured prisoners, took spoils, and chased women and children wandering lost in the smoke, causing them to flee into fires or tumble down to the bottoms of ditches. Surely even thus was the battle of Indra's palace, when the asuras fell onto the swords and halberds, punished by the ruler of heaven! [19] Even thus is the

---

[19] The demonic asuras of Hindu tradition constantly endeavor to conquer **Indra**, the ruler of the heaven on top of Mount Sumeru.

plight of the sinners in the Hell of Constant Scorching,[20] who sink to the bottom of the molten iron, driven by jailers' whips!

As spreading flames blew mightily from the four directions, a fire started up beside the mansion of His Lordship the Sagami lay monk. And thereupon His Lordship took refuge in Kasai Valley with a thousand riders, warriors of the various grand marshals, who filled the precincts of the Tōshōji Temple.[21] This was in order that he might perish tranquilly by his own hand in the burial place of the generations of his ancestors, while the warriors shot defensive arrows.

Now two men of the Heike force had gone to the Gokurakuji Passage to stand against the enemy there: the lay monk Nagasaki Saburō Saemon Shigen and his son Kageyu Saemon Tamemoto. When these heard the enemy battle cries at Komachiguchi[22] and beheld the fire at the mansion of the Lord of Kamakura, they left the seven thousand warriors of their party and went toward Komachiguchi with none but their own six hundred retainers.

Yoshisada's warriors thought to surround and destroy these two, yet drawing together the father and son broke through with fish scale wedges, and drawing apart they chased and subdued the enemy by means of the tiger strategy. And after the two sides had contended together seven or eight times, Yoshisada's scattered warriors drew back quickly to Wakamiya Road to rest their men and horses.

Thereupon the father and son resolved to part to the left and right, that the one might take his way to the Tengudō Temple and the other to Ōgi Valley, where they beheld dust from horses' feet rising in great abundance, as though men fought in those places. May not the son Kageyu Saemon have thought, "We shall not meet again"? He gazed back toward his father with the aspect of one stricken with the grief of parting. But Shigen shamed him loudly, saying:

"Why do you grieve because of our parting? Were one of us to die while the other remained alive, truly it would be long until

[20] Avīci, one of the Buddhist eight hot hells.
[21] The Hōjō family temple in Kasai Valley.
[22] The center of the city.

we met again. But both of us will fall today, and tomorrow we will meet in the nether regions. What is so regrettable about parting for a single night?"

So he spoke in a loud voice.

Tamemoto dried his tears, saying:

"If that is the case, hasten to make the journey to hades! I shall await you at the mountain road of Shide."

And speaking, he galloped into the middle of the great host.

Although the three thousand horsemen of the enemy eagerly surrounded Tamemoto when they saw that the warriors with him were a mere twenty men, the sword at Tamemoto's waist was called Omokage, a three-foot blade made by Raitarō Kuniyuki, who purified himself for a hundred days beforehand. Omokage smashed to pieces the helmet-bowls of those that came within its compass, or cut off their breastplates as though they had been monks' scarves, until at last the enemy no longer dared to draw near to that sword, but only sought to strike down Tamemoto by shooting arrows furiously from distant places.

When seven arrows stood in the flesh of his horse, Tamemoto thought, "Since it is thus, I cannot draw close to a suitable enemy to grapple with him." Lightly he leapt down from the horse in front of the great torii of Yui-no-hama, where he stood alone with his sword turned up to make a staff, most like to the Two Kings. Yet as before, the warriors of Yoshisada were content to shoot distant arrows from the ten directions without seeking to draw near.

To deceive the enemy, Tamemoto feigned to suffer a wound, cutting his knee with a small cut and laying his body down. And then fifty unknown warriors came forward all together, wearing badges emblazoned with a hand drum and two lines; and each thought to cut off Kageyu Saemon's head. But Tamemoto made speed to rise up with his sword in readiness, saying, "Who are these that awaken a man where he naps wearied from fighting? Come! I shall let you have the head you desire!"

Speaking, he waved his sword, covered with blood to the guard, and like a falling thunderbolt pursued them with outstretched arms. And the fifty fled with all their might.

Loudly Kageyu Saemon abused them, saying:

"How far do you think to flee? Come back, contemptible wretches!"

When he shouted, it was as though all of those horses leapt up in one place, that had seemed to be running swiftly before.

Now all alone Tamemoto broke in and broke out, retreated and attacked, and fought desperately. But may it not be that he was slain at last? For although he beat down the great host of the enemy at Yui-no-hama in the battle of the twenty-first day, amazing the eyes of foes and friends alike, thereafter he was not seen again.

Daibutsu Sadanao and Kanazawa Sadamasa Die in Battle

Until the day before, Daibutsu Sadanao the governor of Mutsu had fought a defensive fight with twenty thousand men at the Gokurakuji Passage. But in the battle of the beach that morning he had been brought down to three hundred riders; likewise, he was cut off behind by the enemy, so that he could not go forward or backward. And even then did the fire blaze forth at the mansion of the Lord of Kamakura.

Thereupon, thirty of the chief of Sadanao's retainers cast off their armor onto the white sand and cut open their bellies, lined up together in a row. Perhaps they thought, "This is the end for this world," or perhaps they sought to arouse their lord to kill himself. But beholding them, Sadanao said:

"This is indeed the behavior of the most dishonorable men in Japan! The true warriors are those who leave their names from generation to generation by smiting the enemy until a thousand riders become one. Come! Let us fight a last battle with cheerful hearts, that we may quicken the spirit of righteousness in men of the future!"

With his two hundred and fifty warriors, he broke into the center of the six thousand riders of Ōshima, Satomi, Nukata, and Momonoi, struck down enemies in abundance, and galloped away quickly, yet now the two hundred and fifty were but sixty.

"It is of no more avail to attack lesser men among the enemy!" Sadanao called out. He rode into the middle of Wakiya Yoshisuke's host, where it waited like clouds or mist, and with all his men left his corpse in the dirt of the battlefield.

Likewise, in the fighting at Yamanouchi the eight hundred followers of Kanazawa Sadamasa the governor of Musashi were slain. Sadamasa himself, wounded in seven places, went back to the abiding place of the Sagami lay monk at the Tōshōji, whereupon in gratitude the lay monk made haste to hand down an order naming him one of the two lords of Rokuhara, and appointed him to be the governor of Sagami instead of the governor of Musashi.

"Our family will be destroyed before this day is done," thought Sadamasa. But he accepted the order, saying, "It is an office I have desired for many years, one that does honor to my house. I would like to have it as a keepsake in the nether regions." And he turned back again to the battlefield.

On the back of that order Sadamasa wrote in large characters, "I give up my life of a hundred years to requite one day's favor from my lord." He put it into the place where the front and back of his armor joined together. And he indeed galloped into the middle of the enemy host to die at last in battle. How sad it was!

Shinnin Dies by His Own Hand

In the beginning the lay monk Fuonji Shinnin of Sagami went forth to Kewaizaka with three thousand men, yet in five days and nights of fighting his retainers were beaten down utterly, until but thirty-six remained. And when at last men came saying, "All the places of attack are breached, and the enemy has broken into the valley," Shinnin and his thirty-six warriors ran into the Fuonji Temple to kill themselves, all at the same time.

In a later day men beheld a verse that Shinnin had written with blood on a pillar of the hall, saying, "Wait awhile—traversing together the travel-road of Shide Mountain, let us speak of the transient world." (Surely he thought of his son, Nakatoki the Governor of Echigo, how he took his life at Bamba.) Not even at the end did Shinnin forget his many years' love of elegant pursuits, but wrote of the grief in his heart and left this verse to be praised by the realm. How refined were his tastes!

Chapter 10

The Suicide of Shioda and His Son

There was one Mimbu-no-tayū Toshitoki, a son of the lay monk Shioda Dōyū of Mutsu, who cut open his belly and fell down in front of his father Dōyū to stir him up to slay himself. Darkness seized Dōyū's eyes by reason of this sudden parting, and his spirit was disordered, nor could he stop his falling tears. Perhaps he thought to intercede for the enlightenment of the son who had died before him, or it may be that he desired to pray for himself, soon to perish. For he turned his face toward the dead body of his son, untied the strings of a sutra kept beside him for many years, and recited tranquilly, calling out passages of note in a loud voice.

Now it came about that enemies shouted battles cries hard by that place, wherefore Dōyū spoke a word to his two hundred retainers, waiting in the courtyard to die with him.

"Do you shoot defensive arrows until I shall have finished the reading of this sutra," he said.

And he divided them into three parties to go forth in three directions. But there was one among them called Kano Gorō Shigemitsu, a man advanced in years, whom the lay monk held there, saying, "Set fire to the house when I shall have cut open my belly, so that the enemy may not take my head."

When Dōyū was about to finish the Deva Chapter of the fifth scroll, Shigemitsu went forth in front of the gate to look in the four directions. At once he returned, saying:

"Assuredly are all of those slain that shot defensive arrows, for the enemy battle shouts are very near. Quickly resolve to die! Soon I too shall go with you to the nether regions."

Thereupon, the lay monk of Mutsu grasped the sutra in his left hand, drew forth his dagger with his right hand, and cut open his belly. And the father and the son lay on the same pillow.

Shigemitsu did not cut open his belly or light a fire in the house, but stripped off the armor from his two lords, and the swords and daggers, and gave them to servants to bear away, together with the precious things in the house: damask, gauze, gold, and silver. Then for a time he hid himself at the archive office of the Engakuji

Temple, saying, "Never shall I want, with these treasures!" But it came to pass that the Funada lay monk laid hands on him, and in the end his head was hung up at Yui-no-hama. Doubtless it was the punishment of heaven that it should be so.

The Suicide of the Shiaku Lay Monk

The lay monk Shiaku Shōon called forth his eldest son Saburō Saemon Tadayori, saying:

"I have heard that all the places of attack are brought down, and that Hōjō kinsmen cut open their bellies in great numbers. I too desire to make known my loyalty by dying in advance of His Lordship the governor. But none would look upon you as lacking in honor if you were to refrain from giving up your life here, since being as yet under my care you have not enjoyed favors from our lord. I hope that you will hide yourself in some place for awhile, become a monk to pray for me in the afterlife, and live out your days in peace."

So he spoke weeping, and tears filled the eyes of Saburō Saemon Tadayori.

For a time Tadayori spoke no word, but soon he said:

"Although I myself have received no favors from our lord, the life of our family has been supported wholly by the boons of the military. Moreover, if I had been a disciple of the Buddha from the beginning, then fittingly might I turn away from duty to enter the way of non-action. But would it not be a dishonor if one born of a warrior clan were to forsake the world, thinking only to flee the troubles of the times? How might such a one's ears endure the words of the men of the realm?"

Nor did he finish, but drew forth his dagger from beneath his sleeve, secretly plunged it into his belly, and died where he knelt.

Beholding this, Tadayori's younger brother Shiaku Shirō thought to cut his belly after him. But his father admonished him sternly, saying:

"Let me go before you, as is fitting in a filial son. You may take your life when I have done."

Thereupon, Shiaku Shirō put away his dagger to kneel before

his father the lay monk. The lay monk caused a monk's chair to be brought to the middle gate, whereon he sat with legs crossed and soles upturned, as on his widemouthed trousers he wrote a death song in praise of the Buddhist Law.

> Holding the trenchant hair-splitter,
> He severs emptiness.
> Within the mighty flames—
> A pure cool breeze.

He folded his hands, stretched out his neck, and commanded his son Shirō, "Strike!" And when Shirō had laid bare the upper half of his own body, he struck off his father's head. After he had made the sword right again, he thrust it into his body up to the hilt and fell on his face. Moreover, three retainers ran forward to be pierced by the same sword, falling down with their heads in a row like fish on a skewer.

The Suicide of the Andō Lay Monk; the Matter of Wang Ling of Han

Among the Heike warriors there was an uncle of the wife of Nitta Yoshisada, the lay monk Andō Saemon Shūshu. In the beginning, this Andō went to the Inase River with three thousand riders, but the men of Serada Tarō beat him back, coming around behind him from Inamura Cape, and thereafter he was surrounded by the armies of Yura and Nagahama, who slew all but one hundred of his warriors. Andō returned to his house, wounded in many places, but the house had been consumed utterly by flames at the hour of the snake in the morning. His wife, children, and kinsmen were fled away to unknown places, nor was there any to ask concerning them. Moreover men came saying, "The mansion of the Lord of Kamakura is burned down, and His Lordship the lay monk has fled to the Tōshōji."

"Can it be seen in the ruins of His Lordship's house that warriors have cut their bellies and perished there?" Andō asked.

"No person can be seen," they replied.

"How regrettable a thing is this!" said Andō. "What a dishonor it would be, were men of the future to say contemptuously, 'The warriors of the Heike suffered the feet of enemy horses to fall upon the place where for many years dwelt the Lord of Kamakura, the ruler of the land of Japan, nor did so many as a thousand or two thousand of them die there.' Come, warriors! On the ruins of that august dwelling let us tranquilly take the lives we are about to lose, that we may cleanse the Lord of Kamakura of shame."

So he spoke, and went forth toward Komachiguchi with the hundred retainers left to him. At Tōnotsuji he got down from off his horse to look upon the dead ruins, where until the morning had stood the stately mansion with its towering walls. Swiftly were these turned to ashes; instantly was all swept away, save only the smoke of change. Of the kinsmen and friends who had made merry there until yesterday, how many lay stricken on the field of battle, their dead bodies telling of the decline which follows prosperity! Truly this was unbearable sorrow in the midst of sorrow!

Now to Andō where he stood weeping there came one calling himself a messenger from the wife of Lord Nitta, bearing a letter written on thin paper. Taken with surprise, Andō opened it.

"I have heard that the end is at hand in Kamakura," it said. "By all means come to this place. Since it is a matter of this kind, I will intercede for you though I die for it."

Such were the words written therein. But Andō waxed exceeding wroth, saying:

"It is said, 'The robes of one who enters a sandalwood grove will become fragrant of themselves, without being dyed.' [23] When a warrior's wife is of steadfast heart, then will that family endure, and its descendants will have a name in the land. So when Kao Tsu of Han and Hsiang Yü of Ch'u contended together in ancient times, a person called Wang Ling built a castle and shut himself up therein, and though Ch'u attacked it, it did not fall. The warriors of Ch'u consulted together, saying, 'By no means is Wang Ling lacking in filial piety toward his mother. If we were to lay hands upon his mother and put her in front of our shields when we attacked the castle, assuredly Wang Ling would not be able to shoot an arrow, but would come out to surrender.' And thereupon by stealth they seized Wang Ling's mother.

[23] From a Buddhist sutra. Andō means that when a woman marries into the warrior class she is expected to adopt its code.

"In her heart this lady thought:

"'Wang Ling's devotion to me exceeds the filial conduct of the great Shun and Tseng Ts'an.[24] If I go before his castle bound in front of a shield, he will suffer the castle to be beaten down, overmastered by his affliction. I would not have it thus. Rather would I give up this fleeting life for the sake of my descendants.'

"So she thought, and indeed brought honor to Wang Ling's name by dying on a sword.

"Now until this time I have enjoyed the favors of the Hōjō family, and have become a person known to others. If I were to surrender myself in the hour of their extremity, would any man believe that I knew the meaning of shame? If Yoshisada understood a warrior's duty, never would he suffer his wife to write such a letter, though her woman's heart stirred her up to speak. Likewise, if Yoshisada were to seek in this way to know the enemy's mind, then would it be fitting that his wife should turn away from it with all her might, thinking, 'My kinsmen must not be put to shame.' Well is it said that like seeks out like! For the sake of my descendants I will refuse to call upon them."

So he spoke, now weeping and now waxing angry. And while the eyes of the messenger gazed upon him, he took up the letter with his dagger, cut open his belly, and died.

Master Kameju Flees to Shinano; Sakon-no-taifu Escapes in Disguise to Ōshū

In many battles on one day and the next, the attackers slew all the retainers of Suwa Saburō Moritaka, he who was the son of the lay monk Suwa Sama-no-suke. With but a single follower, Moritaka came to the camp of the lay monk Shirō Sakon-no-taifu, saying:

"I believe that the battle in Kamakura has become hopeless, so I have come to wait upon you at the end. Quickly make your resolution!"

---

[24] Shun was a mythical Chinese sage-emperor. Tseng Ts'an was a disciple of Confucius noted for his filial piety.

When Moritaka pressed him in this manner, the lay monk sent away his people and spoke secretly in Moritaka's ears, saying:

"Because of the disturbance which has arisen unexpectedly, our house must surely be destroyed. Truly the cause thereof lies solely in the comportment of the Lord of Sagami, who has turned his back on the minds of men and transgressed against the will of the gods. But although heaven detests the proud and diminishes the full, yet if it be that our family has not used up all the good karma of its generations of virtuous acts, may not one among its sons pick up the thing that is broken off and revive the thing that is ended? So in ancient times there was a minister of the state of Ch'i, Pao Shu-ya by name. Understanding that Ch'i would be destroyed by the unrighteousness of Duke Hsiang, Pao fled to another country with Duke Hsiang's son Hsiao-po. And it came to pass that Duke Hsiang was destroyed by Wu-chih, and forfeited the land of Ch'i. Thereupon, Pao Shu-ya raised up Hsiao-po, went forth against the land of Ch'i, killed Wu-chih, and at last protected the land of Ch'i. This Hsiao-po was Duke Huan of Ch'i.[25]

"Therefore is it meet that I should consider carefully instead of hastening to take my life. It is in my mind to flee, that I may wipe out this 'shame of K'uai-chi.' Do you likewise think well concerning the days to come. Prolong your life by hiding your body in such a place as you may find, or by surrendering to the enemy. Conceal my nephew Kameju,[26] raise a great host again when the time is right, and bring about the thing desired of our hearts. As regards Manju the elder brother of Kameju, my heart is at ease, for I have given him into the keeping of Godaiin Uemon."

Holding back his tears, Moritaka said:

"Before this, it was not fitting that life should be precious in my eyes, since the fate of my body was determined by the fortunes of your house. I came here to make known my loyalty by taking my life in your presence, yet now I shall bow before your words. It is said, 'To resolve hastily to die is easy; to leave a stratagem for a myriad generations is hard.'"

Moritaka went forth from thence to Ōgi Valley, where abode

---

[25] The most famous leader of the league of military rulers.
[26] Takatoki's son.

Chapter 10

the Lady Niidono, beloved of the Lord of Sagami. The lady rejoiced greatly at his coming, saying:

"Alas! What is happening in the world? There is no hiding place for me, that am a woman. And what is to be done with Kameju? My heart is at ease touching Manju his brother, for this morning Godaiin Uemon fetched him away, saying, 'There is a place wherein he may be concealed.' But I am troubled for Kameju; likewise I tremble for this dew life of mine."

So she spoke, and lifted up her voice and wept.

In his heart Moritaka thought, "I would that I might speak truthfully to her to comfort her spirit." But again he considered, "Women are untrustworthy. It may be that she will let others know of it hereafter." And therefore with tears he spoke to her, saying:

"Assuredly have we come to the end in this world. Of the house of Hōjō, all have perished by their own hands, save only His Lordship the governor, who lingers at Kasai Valley. His Lordship has said, 'I wish to look once upon the young lords my sons before I cut my belly.' Wherefore am I come to fetch them."

Then the lady was cast down utterly, who had looked upon him joyfully before. With tears choking her throat, she said:

"My heart is at ease concerning Manju, since he is in Muneshige's care. Will you not find a good place of concealment for this child?"

So she spoke, and Moritaka sorrowed in his heart, his body not being made of stone or wood. Yet strengthening his spirit, he said to her:

"Although Lord Manju was fetched away by Godaiin Uemon Muneshige, the enemy found them out and pursued them. Muneshige ran into a house at Komachiguchi, where he stabbed the child to death, cut open his belly, and died in the flames. Likewise, as regards Kameju, you must think that you are parting from him for the last time in this world. There is no place wherein he may be concealed. Would it not be regrettable, were he to be sought out by the enemy, where like a hunted pheasant he hid in the grass, and with his young corpse dishonored the family name? Let him rather fall by the hand of His Lordship, and go together with him to the nether regions, that his filial piety may be remembered in generations to come. Please deliver him up quickly!"

"Most terrible are these your words!" said the lady. "If the enemy lay hands upon him, there is no hope, but how may I endure to have him struck down by those who have reared him and his brother? Do as you will, but take my life first!"

So she spoke, and the nurses said the same. Holding fast to the child before and behind, they lifted up their voices and wept.

Darkness covered Moritaka's eyes, and his spirit fainted within him. Yet he thought, "Assuredly will I not prevail against her if my heart be weak." He raised his voice angrily and glared at the lady with changed color, saying:

"Do you not know that such may be the lot of any person born into a warrior family, even from the age of swaddling clothes? Assuredly does His Lordship grow impatient. Deliver the child quickly, that he may go together with His Lordship the governor."

He ran forward, put Master Kameju on his shoulder over his armor, and hastened out through the gate.

In a single voice the laments of those ladies assailed Moritaka's ears beyond the gate where, powerless to restrain tears, he suffered the horse to take its way. Heedless of men's eyes, the weeping nurse called Osai ran after him barefooted for five or six hundred yards, falling down to the ground again and again, until resolutely he caused the horse to run, that she might not find him out. And when her eyes beheld him no longer, the nurse Osai cast her body into a deep well and perished.

Thereafter, Moritaka fled with this young lord to Shinano, placing his trust in the priests of Suwa. Kameju was that Sagami Jirō called the Twenty-Day General, who took the Kantō for awhile in the spring of the first year of Kemmu and raised a great host in the realm.

Now the lay monk Shirō Sakon-no-taifu summoned trustworthy retainers, saying:

"It is in my mind to flee to Ōshū, where I will lay plans to overturn the realm again. Nambu Tarō and Date Rokurō will go together with me, since they are acquainted with the road. Let all others kill themselves after lighting a fire in the mansion, so that the enemy may believe I have cut my belly and perished in the flames."

So he spoke, and none of his twenty retainers said him nay, but all said, "Even as our lord commands, so shall it be done."

Then Date and Nambu assumed the guise of commoners, such as might have been impressed for service. They gave their armor and horses to two soldiers of low degree, causing them to wear badges depicting a black bar in a circle.[27] And they placed the lay monk Shirō on a stretcher, covered over with a bloody robe, that he might appear as a wounded warrior of the Genji returning to his province. So indeed they fled to Musashi.

The retainers who were left behind ran out to the middle gate, crying aloud, "Our lord has killed himself! Let all loyal men accompany him!"

Then these twenty lighted a fire in the mansion, quickly lined up together in the smoke, and cut their bellies. And not willing to be outdone, three hundred other warriors cut their bellies and leapt into the consuming flames, men who had been standing with joined sleeves inside the court and outside the gate.

So none knew of the flight of the lay monk Shirō Sakon-no-taifu, but all believed that he had taken his life. This lay monk was that very Tokioki who served the house of Saionji in a later day, and became a grand marshal of the capital around the time of Kemmu.

The Last Battle of Nagasaki Jirō Takashige

Since the battle of Musashino, in more than eighty contests by day and by night had Nagasaki Jirō Takashige fought in the foremost lines. Times beyond number had he broken encirclements and personally contended against enemy warriors. And therefore great numbers of his retainers were struck down, until they became but a hundred and fifty riders.

At last on the twenty-second day of the fifth month, there came men saying, "The Genji have poured into the valleys, and few of the family's grand marshals remain unslain."

[27] The Nitta crest.

Thereupon Takashige galloped to meet the enemy wherever they drew near, not asking the names of the defenders in any place, but driving back the attackers in every direction and breaking them down on every side. When his horse was wearied, he mounted a new one; when his sword was broken, he put a new one at his waist. But after he himself had cut down thirty-one enemies and broken the Genji lines eight times, he went back to the abiding place of the Sagami lay monk at Kasai Valley, where he bowed tearfully at the middle gate, saying:

"Never again after today shall I greet my lord in this world, whose face I have beheld morning and evening, honored even as my ancestors in the service of his house. Singlehanded have I put the enemy to flight in many places; ever have I been victorious in many battles. Yet on every side the gateways are breached by enemy warriors who fill all of Kamakura, nor longer can the most valiant prevail against them. My lord must resolve with all his heart not to be seized by enemy hands. Yet let him not take his life quickly, but await the time of my return, for I shall gallop joyfully into the center of the enemy to fight a worthy battle while he lives, that I may have a tale to tell when I go with him to the nether regions."

So he spoke, and went forth again from the Tōshōji. And with tears in his eyes, the Sagami lay monk looked after him until he had gone a long distance, thinking sorrowfully, "Never shall we meet again."

First Takashige took his way to the abiding place of the abbot of the Sōjuji Temple, the Harmonious Reverence of the Southern Mountain, since it was his last battle. And that teacher of Zen sat down in his seat of honor to receive him. Takashige did not make obeisance before him, being in great haste, and likewise being clad in armor and helmet, but he bowed a little to the left and right and asked him, saying, "Who is the valiant man?"

"Even he who takes up a sword swiftly and goes forward," answered the Harmonious Reverence.

There was no word more that Takashige might say when he heard this.

Then before the gate Takashige mounted his horse, with his

hundred and fifty warriors before and behind him. Casting away his badge, he rode quietly into the camp of the enemy, thinking only to draw near to Yoshisada to grapple with him to the end. With tranquil hearts the warriors of the Genji opened a way for him, until he came to a place not fifty yards distant from Yoshisada. (Doubtless these failed to understand that he was an enemy, since his men bore no banner aloft, nor drew forth the swords from their scabbards.) Yet how strong was the luck of the Genji! Even as the moment was at hand, there was one who saw Takashige and knew him: Yura Shinsaemon, standing in front of Yoshisada. Yura raised a mighty shout, saying:

"It is Nagasaki Jirō drawing near without raising a banner! Assuredly does he come here with a design, for he is a mighty man of valor. Let none remain! Let none escape!"

Thereupon, three thousand warriors came crowding forward from the east and west to encompass Takashige's riders about: men of the Seven Bands of Musashi from the foremost ranks.

"That which I devised has gone amiss," thought Takashige.

He gathered together his hundred and fifty warriors tightly into one place and sent them galloping into the center of the three thousand riders with a mighty shout. Sweeping forward to give battle, they mingled here, appeared there, and fought with flying sparks of fire. Most swiftly did they come together and disperse! Suddenly they were in back while yet it seemed that they were in front, and assuredly many warriors were enemies who looked to the Genji to be friends. Each of them was in ten places at once, and they were equal to ten thousand men. Nor could the warriors of Yoshisada find out Takashige, but struck down their fellows in great numbers.

Beholding these things, Nagahama Rokurō commanded:

"The enemy are all without badges. Let that be a sign to you to grapple with them and kill them."

Thereupon Genji warriors rode up beside the enemy and grappled with them fiercely: men of Kai, Shinano, Musashi, and Sagami. Those who grappled fell down together to the ground, where some took heads and the heads of some were taken. The sky was darkened with rising dust; the earth was clotted with sweat and blood. Surely it was not otherwise when Hsiang Yü humbled the three generals of Han,[28] or when the Duke of Lu-yang caused the sun to move backward through three constellations! [29]

As before, Nagasaki Jirō contended against the enemy with his seven remaining men. He drove back the warriors who drew near to him, still thinking to grapple with a grand marshal of the Genji (for truly his eyes were set on Yoshisada and his brother), yet there was one foe who galloped close to cut him off and grapple with him: Yokoyama Tarō Shigesane, a resident of the province of Musashi. Nagasaki rode to meet him, thinking, "If he be a worthy enemy I shall engage him," but when he saw that it was Yokoyama Tarō Shigesane he thought, "Indeed, he is not a suitable adversary." He put Shigesane on his left side and split his helmet-bowl down to the cross-stitched bottom flap, so that Shigesane was cleft in two and perished. Likewise Shigesane's horse, its knee cut, was knocked over backward in a heap.

There was one Shō Saburō Tamehisa that beheld these things, a resident of the same province. He galloped forward in his turn to grapple with Nagasaki, thinking, "Here is a worthy enemy." But Nagasaki laughed loudly, saying:

"If it had been meet for me to grapple with a member of your band, I would not have disdained Yokoyama. Come, come! I shall show you how an unworthy foe is killed!"

He laid hold of the braid of Tamehisa's armor, held him in the air, and tossed him away easily for a distance of five bow-lengths; whereupon two warriors fell down from off their horses head over heels, struck by this man flying like a cast stone, and died spitting blood.

Then in a mighty voice Nagasaki proclaimed his name, saying:

"Now I shall die in battle to requite the favors of the military: Jirō Takashige the eldest son of the eldest son of the lay monk Nagasaki Enki, who is steward to Takatoki the former governor of Sagami, who is descended in the thirteenth generation from Sadamori the general of the Taira, who was descended in the third

---

[28] In his final battle at Wu-chiang.
[29] It is said that when darkness began to fall while the duke was fighting a battle, he prevailed upon the sun to move backward by gesturing at it with a spear.

generation from Katsurabara the fifth princely son of the Emperor Kammu. If one among you thirsts after fame, let him draw near to grapple with me!"

He cut off his armor sleeves and skirt and made ready to cleave into the middle of the enemy with his hair falling down around his face.

Thereupon Takashige's retainers galloped in front of his horse to hold him, saying:

"What is it that you do? You must go back now to press the Lord of Sagami to take his life. Already the enemy enter the valleys in disorder."

"Truly!" said Takashige. "Too well have I amused myself with cutting down enemies, so that I forgot my promise to our lord. Come! If it be thus, let us return!"

So he spoke, and drew back from Yamanouchi with his seven retainers.

Now five hundred riders of the Kodama band abused Takashige and his men, saying, "Despicable fellows, come back!" as they raced their horses in pursuit (for doubtless they thought that Takashige fled). But whenever these enemies drew near, the eight turned back to contend against them, seventeen times, from Yamanouchi to Kasai Valley. Wherefore Takashige came to the abiding place of the Sagami lay monk with twenty-three arrows in his armor, hanging down even as the head feathers of the snowy heron.

Takashige's grandfather the lay monk awaited him, asking, "How is it that you come so late?" And respectfully Takashige answered:

"It was in my mind to draw near to the grand marshal Yoshisada to grapple with him to the end. More than twenty times I galloped among the enemy, yet I could not draw near to him, nor did I behold any man worthy to be my foe. I smote and drove away four or five hundred warriors of no consequence, men of Musashi and Sagami, and thought to pursue them to the beach, cutting them into round slices and circles, and cleaving them in two. But my mind was ill at ease concerning our lord, and therefore I came back."

So valiantly he told his tale, cheering the spirits of those who were near to death.

Takatoki and His Kinsmen Kill Themselves at the Tōshōji Temple

Now Takashige ran around to this place and that, saying, "Kill yourselves quickly! I shall go before you as your example!"

He stripped off the stomach armor which alone remained on his body, caused his younger brother Shin'uemon to serve him wine in a cup that had been placed before the Lord of Sagami, drank three times, and put down the cup in front of the lay monk Dōjun of Settsu, saying, "To you do I give the cup, with this relish!"[30] And he cut his body with a long cut from left to right and fell down, pulling out his inwards in front of Dōjun.

Dōjun took up the cup, jesting, "Ah, what a relish! However abstemious a man might be, he would not refuse to drink this!" He drank the half of the wine therein, put down the cup in front of the Suwa lay monk, and in the same way cut his belly and died.

When with tranquil spirit the lay monk Suwa Jikishō had tipped the cup three times, he put it down in front of His Lordship the Sagami lay monk, saying:

"Most fully have the young men displayed their loyalty. It will not do for others to be idle, or to say, 'I am ripe in years.' From this time forth, let all eat of this repast!"

He cut open his belly in a cross, drew forth the dagger again, and laid it down before His Lordship the lay monk.

Now the lay monk Nagasaki Enki had delayed to cut his belly, by reason that he looked with anxious eyes upon the Sagami lay monk.[31] But Nagasaki Shin'uemon, a young boy fifteen years old that year, bowed before his grandfather, saying:

"Assuredly will the buddhas and gods give sanction to this deed. The filial descendant is he who brings honor to the name of his fathers."

With two thrusts of his dagger he slashed the veins of his aged

---

[30] *Sakana*, food eaten with sake.
[31] He was afraid that Takatoki might behave in a cowardly manner.

grandfather's arms. He cut his own belly, pushed his grandfather down, and fell on top of him.

Thereupon the Sagami lay monk also cut his belly, urged to duty by this youth newly come of age, and the castle lay monk did the same,[32] while in the hall Hōjō kinsmen and men of other houses bared their snowy skins to the waist, some cutting open their bellies and some striking off their own heads. Truly two hundred and eighty-three men of the Hōjō took their lives, each striving to be first.

Thereafter, a fire was lighted in the hall, wherefrom fierce flames leapt up and black smoke darkened the sky. When the warriors in the courtyard and before the gate beheld that fire, some among them cut their bellies and ran into the flames, while others smote one another with their swords and fell down together in a heap, fathers, sons, and brothers. As a great river was the rushing of their blood; as on a burial field were their dead bodies laid everywhere in piles!

Although the bodies of these disappeared in the flames, later it was known that more than eight hundred and seventy men perished in this one place. And in untold numbers others who heard of these things requited their obligations in the after-life: those sprung of Heike stock and those who had received favors from the family, whether monk or layman, man or woman. Truly it is said that in Kamakura alone they were more than six thousand persons.

Ah! What a day was that! On the twenty-second day of the fifth month of the third year of Genkō, the prosperity of the Heike was destroyed utterly, after enduring for nine generations. The discontent of the Genji was dispelled in a morning, that had been nurtured for many long years.

[32] Takatoki's maternal grandfather.

11

Godaiin Uemon Muneshige Deceives Sagami Tarō

WHEN YOSHISADA HAD CHASTENED Kamakura and extended his domination near and far, none among the great lords and mighty houses of the eight eastern provinces made bold to oppose him, not even those who had gained his trust through many years of friendship. And men that until now had sought after the favors of the Heishi as adherents of the enemy camp, these indeed surrendered themselves up to such of the Genji as were bound to them by any ties whatever, seeking thereby to preserve their wretched lives. From temples they fetched out Heishi kinsmen who had forsaken the transient world to become monks, and stained their holy robes with blood. Likewise in divers places they violated the chasteness of the widows of the dead, who had cut off their hair to become nuns, resolved never to wed again. For in their hearts they thought, "We must atone for our misdeeds, though it be by breathing the dust of the fat horses of the Genji,[1] or by sweeping the ground outside their high gates."

Those of the Heike who cherished honor and died quickly—they became wretched asuras, doomed to suffer for many ages.[2] How regrettable it was! And those who subjected themselves to humiliation by remaining alive—they fell into destitution at once, and were mocked at by all men. How pitiful it was!

[1] An allusion to a poem by Tu Fu.
[2] Warriors who died in battle were reborn in the world of asuras, where warfare never ceased.

Chapter 11

Now Godaiin Uemon-no-jō Muneshige was a warrior who had been most kindly treated by the Sagami lay monk. Moreover, Muneshige's younger sister had given birth to the lay monk's heir, Sagami Tarō Kunitoki. Doubtless the lay monk thought with certain faith, "My son is both his nephew and his lord. By no means will he be false." For he spoke to Muneshige, saying:

"I shall entrust Kunitoki to your keeping. Devise a means of concealing him, and raise him up when the time is right, so that he may wipe out the bitterness afflicting my spirit."

Muneshige agreed, saying, "There will be no difficulty." And in the battle of Kamakura he gave himself up to the enemy.

Within two or three days thereafter, the Heishi were destroyed utterly. By reason that all the Kantō bowed under the Genji dominion, in great numbers Heishi kinsmen were sought out, where they hid in divers places. Those who captured them received properties, but those who concealed them were struck down swiftly. Wherefore Godaiin Uemon thought:

"No, no! Merely to protect a luckless person, shall I lose this life, preserved by chance? Rather let me say to the Genji warriors that I have learned of Sagami Tarō's abiding place, so that I may show my loyalty and receive a piece of land."

On a certain night he spoke a word to Sagami Tarō, saying:

"Although I had believed that none might learn of your staying here, it seems that it is noised abroad. Even now I have received a warning that the Funada lay monk prepares to come tomorrow to search for you. You must by all means change your lodging tonight and make speed toward the mountains of Izu in the darkness. It is in my heart to go with you, but I will not do so. If all my family flees, the Funada lay monk will suspect, 'It is as I have thought,' and will never leave off searching for you."

So he spoke, honest-seeming, and Sagami Tarō thought, "Truly!" And Sagami Tarō fled from Kamakura secretly, deep in the night of the twenty-seventh day of the fifth month.

How shocking were the changes recent time had brought! Until yesterday, it had been possible that if Sagami Tarō had so much as gone forth on a trifling pilgrimage or sought to avoid an inauspicious direction, he would have been encompassed about by three hundred or five hundred close retainers and great lords, mounted on goodly horses chewing at their bits. Yet now his sword was carried by a single shabby soldier, nor was there so much as a post horse for him to ride. Blindly he journeyed forth, trusting to his feet; weeping he sought the mountains of Izu, clad in broken straw sandals and a braided hat. How pitiful were the feelings in his heart!

Now Godaiin Uemon thought:

"Through a stratagem I have caused this person to go forth from hence. Yet if I were to smite him and fetch him out, men would point their fingers at me, saying, 'He has forgotten the ties formed in the years of service to his lord.' I would that I might cause a suitable Genji warrior to kill him, and myself receive a property as a reward."

He hastened to the abiding place of the Funada lay monk, saying:

"Most fully have I found out the abiding place of His Lordship Sagami Tarō. If you were to go forth alone to slay him, would not the merit thereof exceed comparison? I place my trust in you, that in return for these loyal tidings you will obtain a piece of land for me, such as will sustain my life."

"These are the words of a wicked man," thought the Funada lay monk. Yet he promised him, saying, "It shall be done." And together with Godaiin Uemon-no-jō he lay in wait on the road where Sagami Tarō fled.

In no wise believing that enemies were before him on the road, Sagami Tarō sought to cross the Sagami River at dawn on the twenty-eighth day, shabby and weary. But while he attended the coming of the ferry on the river bank, standing aside Godaiin Uemon instructed Funada, saying, "There indeed is the person of whom we spoke."

Thereupon, three of Funada's retainers flew down from their horses. They laid hands on Sagami Tarō straitly, put him onto a horse, bound him tightly with rope from the boat, and caused two soldiers of low degree to pull the horse's mouth (for there was no litter, it being a sudden affair). And in full daylight they brought him into Kamakura. Of those who saw or heard of this thing, there was not one but wrung his sleeves.

Now the Genji said:

"There is nothing to fear from Sagami Tarō, since he is but a child. Yet we must not spare the life of the eldest son of an enemy of the throne."

And secretly they struck off his head at dawn on the next day.

How inferior was Godaiin Uemon to Ch'eng Ying, who killed his child in ancient times, to exchange its life for the life of his infant lord,[3] or to Yü Jang, who requited his old lord's favors by assuming unfamiliar guises![4] For he caused enemies to strike down his lord of many years, forgetting duty for the sake of greed. All who looked upon him shunned and detested him, saying, "Most marvelously unrighteous is his heart!"

Hearing of this thing, Yoshisada said, "Truly!" and thought in secret to strike Muneshige down. But tidings thereof came to Muneshige's ears, so that he went forth and hid himself in divers places. Broad were the Three Worlds,[5] yet there was no place wherein Muneshige's heart might be at ease. Many were Muneshige's friends of old, yet there was no man who would give him food to eat. It is said that in the end he became as a beggar and starved to death on the highroad. Was not this a punishment for the wickedness of his sin?

The Generals Send Couriers to Funanoe

On the twelfth day of the fifth month in the capital, fast messengers were sent forth to Funanoe with tidings of the fall of Rokuhara, the one after the other, coming from the Chigusa Middle Marshal Tadaaki no Ason, Ashikaga Jibu-no-tayū, and the lay monk Akamatsu Enshin. The courtiers at Funanoe consulted together, offering each his own judgment, whether it was meet that

---

[3] A story from the Era of Warring States.
[4] Disguising himself in various ways, Yü Jang tried repeatedly to gain access to the man who had overthrown his lord. He finally succeeded in killing him, after which he committed suicide.
[5] The world of desire, the world of form, and the world of formlessness.

the emperor should return to the capital. And it came to pass that Mitsumori the assistant chief of the audit office spoke words of admonition, saying:

"Although the two Rokuharas are beaten down, the home provinces are filled with the besiegers of Chihaya, whose strength is such as may swallow up the capital. The proverb says, 'The strength of the eight eastern provinces is a match for all Japan; the strength of Kamakura is a match for the eight eastern provinces.' Iga Hōgan Mitsusue[6] was driven back easily in the war of Shōkyū, but when the hosts from east of the Hakone Pass came up to the capital the imperial armies were beaten down, and for long the realm lay beneath the hand of the military. Now if we consider the outcome of this single battle, our side has but gained one or two of a possible ten. Let His Majesty tarry awhile in this place, send commands to the provinces, and observe the changes in the eastern lands. For it is said, 'The upright man does not draw near to criminals.'"[7]

So he spoke, and all the ministers approved his words.

Then the supreme highness opened the *Book of Changes* to divine concerning the auspiciousness of a return to the capital, thinking, "It is difficult to decide fittingly." The august divination came out upon the *shih* hexagram, that said:

"When an army is sent forth with righteousness, and with a worthy leader, then it will be auspicious, and there will be no fault. In the first Six, the sovereign has his command, opens the country, and governs the families. But small men must not be used."

In Wang Pi's commentary it was written:

"'The sovereign has his command' means that the sovereign has not lost his power. 'Opens the country and governs the families' means pacifying the state. And it is because small men are unrighteous that it is said, 'small men must not be used.'"

"When the divination is thus, what more is there to doubt?" said the supreme highness. And he went forth from Funanoe in Hōki on the twenty-third day, taking his august litter eastward on the San'indō Road.

[6] The Kamakura representative in the capital.
[7] See note 24, Chapter Four.

Not as in former times were the traveling costumes on that journey! Two persons alone served in high-crowned caps and robes: Yukifusa the chief archivist and Mitsumori the assistant chief of the audit office. All the others rode before and behind in warlike attire: the great nobles and courtiers, the officers of the imperial guards, and the assistants of the civil offices, while for thirty leagues on either side rode men of war in helmets and armor, carrying bows and arrows. En'ya Hōgan Takasada served in the foremost place with a thousand riders, a day in advance of the supreme highness; Asayama Tarō served in the rearmost place with five hundred riders, a day's journey behind. The Kanaji governor of Yamato raised up a brocade banner on the left side of the emperor, and Nagatoshi the governor of Hōki guarded him on the right side. The rain god cleansed the roads; the wind god swept away the dust. How majestic it was! Surely even thus is the Pole Star, encompassed about by the stars of the heavens! The emperor rejoiced to behold the very mountains, clouds, sea, and moon that had afflicted his spirit and called forth his tears in the spring of the past year, when he journeyed to the land of Oki. The wind blowing in the pines seemed to call "Banzai!" and even the smoke from salt fires on the coast became the cookstoves of a prosperous folk.[8]

The Emperor Visits Shosha Mountain; Nitta's Report

On the twenty-seventh day of the fifth month, the supreme highness took his way to Shosha Mountain in Harima,[9] a place he had desired to look upon for many years. Worshiping at each building in its turn, he caused men to open a hall wherein was preserved the image of the Most Holy Shōkū, the founder of that temple. And in the hall he beheld precious treasures in abundance, such as had been kept secret through many years. He summoned a venerable monk of the temple to ask concerning those things, whereupon respectfully the aged man spoke of them one by one.

[8] The benevolent emperor Nintoku (traditional dates A.D. 313–399) considered the nation prosperous when he could look down from a tower and see the smoke from many cookstoves, even though his palace was in ruins.
[9] The site of a temple called the Enkyōji.

First there was a folded sheet of Sugihara paper,[10] whereon were inscribed in minute characters the eight scrolls of the *Lotus Sutra*, and also the sutras called *Muryōgi* and *Samanthabhadra bodhisattva dhyāna caryādharma*, all written in an instant by the Eighth Ruler of Darkness[11] in human form, when the holy man recited the sacred text of the *Lotus* inside the door of his retreat.

There was a pair of cryptomeria rain clogs with their stilts eaten away to stumps, worn by the holy man when he went forth daily from this mountain to the halls of Mount Hiei, walking over thirty-five leagues of coastal road in a single moment. Also there was a sacred scarf of a light red hue tinged with yellow, that had covered the holy man's body daily. When the holy man had worn that scarf for a very long time, he saw that it was blackened from the smoke of incense.

"Ah, would that I might wash it!" he said.

Thereupon, there was one who said, "I will wash it": the Protector of the Law Oto, his faithful attendant. Oto flew far away toward the western heavens with the scarf, and when a little time was past he hung it in the sky to dry, like a single cloud lit up by the evening sun. The holy man called to the Protector of the Law, saying, "What was the water wherewith you washed that scarf?" And the Protector of the Law answered, "I rinsed it in Mānasarovara Lake in India, because the water of Japan was not fittingly pure." This was that very scarf.

There was an image of Kanzeon carved from a tree that was a buddha,[12] and there were five great bodhisattvas made by Viśvakarman.[13] Nor were these all the marvels whereof the old monk spoke. For when the holy man recited the *Lotus Sutra,* Fudō and Bishamon appeared in the guise of two youths to wait upon him.[14] And on the day of the dedication of the Śākyamuni Hall of the Enryakuji, the holy man but intoned hymns, seated on this

[10] A type of thick paper originally produced at Sugihara village in Harima.
[11] The eighth of the ten kings who rule in hades.
[12] The Tendai and Amida schools of Buddhism hold that trees and grasses are capable of attaining buddhahood.
[13] An artisan in Indra's heaven.
[14] For Fudō and Bishamon, see note 20, Chapter Two, and note 4, Chapter 3, respectively.

Chapter 11

mountain, yet miraculously his praise of the Buddha echoed in the distant clouds of Mount Hiei.

When the old monk had spoken of these things fully, the faith of the supreme highness was so fervent within him that he offered up the rural district of Yamamuro in that province as a recompense for the perpetual copying of sutras according to the Law. Never until today has there been remissness in this holy work, which follows the sacred Law and conforms to the teachings of the Buddha. Auspicious indeed were the imperial petitions whereby the supreme highness sought the destruction of evil and the preservation of good!

On the twenty-eighth day the emperor went to worship at the halls of Hokke Mountain. Then swiftly the august litter took its way forward, until on the last day of the month it came to a temple of Hyōgo called the Fukugonji. And while the supreme highness rested there on that day, the Akamatsu lay monk and his three sons came to him with five hundred horsemen.

Joyfully the emperor praised these, saying:

"It is because of your loyal fighting that We have prevailed in the realm. To each shall be given the reward desired of his heart."

And he commanded them to guard his palace gates.

Now the emperor was pleased to abide for a day in the Fukugonji, thinking to make ready the procession of his attendants and prepare the ceremony of his return. But at the hour of the horse on the day of his coming there (which is to say the last day of the month), there came three messengers on fast horses, bearing urgent letters hanging down from their necks. And these rode up before the gate and presented their letters in the courtyard.

With affrighted hearts, the ministers of state made speed to open those letters. Behold! they were sent from Nitta Kotarō Yoshisada, saying, "Swiftly have I brought peace to the eastern provinces by subduing the Sagami lay monk and all his kinsmen and vassals."

Until this time the supreme highness had thought, "Though the imperial armies have won victories in the fighting in the western provinces and the capital, such as have brought down the two Rokuharas, yet it is a most grave matter to attack the Kantō."

But with the coming of Nitta's report, the supreme highness and all the ministers gave over doubting, praising Nitta joyfully. The emperor decreed, "His reward shall be as he desires," and as a beginning he gave a reward for meritorious service to each of the three messengers.

Masashige Comes to Hyōgo; the Emperor Returns to the Capital

When the emperor had sojourned for a day at Hyōgo, he went forward again in his litter (it being the second day of the sixth month). And then Kusunoki Tamon Hyōe Masashige came to meet him with seven thousand horsemen. Valiant indeed was Masashige's appearance! The supreme highness raised his screens high, summoned Masashige close, and spoke to him gratefully, saying, "To none other than your loyal fighting is it due, that thus swiftly Our great work is done."

Respectfully Masashige refused the honor, and made himself humble, saying, "Had not His Majesty been sage, spiritual, and rich in civil and military attainments,[15] how might his poor servant's insignificant devisings have broken through the encirclement of a mighty enemy?"

From the day when the emperor went forth from Hyōgo, Masashige was sent ahead to ride in the foremost ranks with seven thousand horsemen of the home provinces. Peacefully the supreme highness traversed the eighteen leagues of the road to the capital, where halberds, shields, and battle-axes stood tight together, where ministers of state lined up on the left and on the right, and the imperial hosts advanced in goodly order. And on the evening of the fifth day of the sixth month, he indeed arrived at the Eastern Temple.

All men hastened to assemble at that temple: not alone the warriors of the capital, but also regents, great subjects of the grand preceptorate, grand marshals of the left and right, great counselors and middle counselors, the eight consultants and seven controllers, men of fifth and sixth rank, officials of the court and of the

---

[15] Qualities attributed to the sage-emperor Yao in the *Book of History*.

provinces, and even physicians and doctors of divination, whose carriages and horses stood before the gates in a great multitude. As trailing clouds were the ranks of those waiting together on the ground;[16] as stars in the heavens were the colored robes of the great nobles, lighting up the halls.

The next day was the day of the emperor's going forth from the Eastern Temple to the Palace of the Second Ward.[17] On that day by an extraordinary decree the office of minister of civil affairs was conferred upon Ashikaga Jibu-no-tayū Takauji, and the office of master of the stables of the left was conferred upon his younger brother Hyōbu-no-tayū Tadayoshi.

Now this was the order of the going forth: Serving before the phoenix carriage to guard the august person, the Chigusa Middle Marshal Tadaaki no Ason caused five hundred warriors with swords to walk in two rows, saying, "It is still a time when prudence is required, lest there be an untoward occurrence." Takauji and Tadayoshi followed after on horseback, spurring their mounts behind the hundred officials, with more than five thousand armored warriors (since they said, "Tadayoshi is now an officer of the imperial guards"). Thereafter followed Utsunomiya with five hundred horsemen, Sasaki Hōgan with seven hundred horsemen, and Doi and Tokunō with two thousand horsemen. Also in parties of three hundred and five hundred the great lords of the provinces followed, each behind his own banner, riding through the streets quietly with the imperial carriage in their midst: Masashige, Nagatoshi, Enshin, Yūki, Naganuma, En'ya and the others. In no wise like to that journey of a former day[18] was the nature of the procession on the way, or the ceremony thereof, but most straitly the hundred officials guarded the supreme highness. The high and the low filled the streets to look, praising the imperial virtue with fervent voices.

[16] They remained there because their status was too low for them to be permitted to enter the halls.
[17] A former nobleman's mansion which had come to be used as an imperial residence.
[18] The journey to Oki.

The Battle of Tsukushi

Now the emperor said:

"By the valiant deeds of Takauji and Yoshisada are the capital and Kamakura pacified. Next we must send forth an army to Tsukushi to attack Hōjō Hidetoki the military governor of Kyushu."

He named the Nijō Great Counselor Lord Moromoto to be the head of the Dazaifu,[19] and made ready to send him forth. But then there came fast messengers to the capital, all at the same time on the seventh day of the sixth month, sent by Kikuchi, Shōni, and Ōtomo,[20] who reported to the throne, saying, "The enemies of the court in Kyushu are beaten down utterly."

Later when men inquired fully concerning the fighting in Kyushu, it was known that three persons concerted together while the emperor sojourned at Funanoe: the lay monk Shōni Myōe, the lay monk Ōtomo Gukan, and the lay monk Kikuchi Jakua, who sent to the emperor, saying, "It is in our minds to join ourselves to the august cause." And the emperor gave them a mandate and a brocade banner.

These three hid their devisings in their hearts, nor showed any sign in their faces. But because such a matter could not remain secret, soon tidings thereof were borne to the military governor Hidetoki. And Hidetoki sent one to summon the lay monk Kikuchi Jakua to Hakata, that he might examine closely whether their hearts were false.

Kikuchi was sore amazed by the coming of the messenger, thinking:

"In some way our plot has been uncovered. He calls us to destroy us. If it is thus, we must not suffer him to overreach us, but must ourselves cut the ties binding us to him, and go against Hakata to contend with him in battle."

So he thought, and sent tidings to Shōni and Ōtomo according to their agreement. But Ōtomo forbore to answer clearly, thinking doubtfully, "Not yet may one foretell the fate of the realm." Also

---

[19] The Kyushu Government Office.
[20] Prominent Kyushu families.

it may be that Shōni sought to atone for his fault, having heard that the men of Rokuhara were victorious in every battle in the capital. For he slew Kikuchi's messenger Yahata Yashirō Muneyasu, turning his back on the promise of a former day, and sent the head to the military governor.

Then, sorely angered, the Kikuchi lay monk said:

"It was indeed a mistake to trust the two most dishonorable men in Japan in such a grave matter as this. Very well! Let us see whether I cannot fight a battle without their aid!"

And with but a hundred and fifty horsemen he took his way toward the dwelling place of the governor, it being the hour of the hare on the thirteenth day of the third month of the third year of Genkō.

As Kikuchi passed before Kushida Shrine, suddenly his horse was stricken of a palsy, so that it could not advance even a step. (Perhaps it was a portent of evil in the battle to come, or perhaps it was a punishment, since he sought to ride past the shrine without dismounting to worship as was meet.) The lay monk was greatly angered, saying:

"Whatever shrine you may be, ought you to blame me for riding past when I go to set a battle in array? If it is thus, I shall present you with an arrow. Try receiving it!"

He drew humming-bulb arrows from the top of his quiver, whereof he shot two through the door of the god hall. And his horse's palsy was healed when he had released those arrows, so that he rode forward with a laugh, saying, "This is as it should be!"

Later, when men looked at that shrine, they beheld a great snake more than six feet long, slain by Kikuchi's arrows. How strange it was!

Now the military governor dispatched a great host to fight beyond his castle gate, having put all in readiness beforehand. But although Kikuchi's army was small, every man attacked with a regard for duty that was as firm as iron and stone, and every man held his life as lightly as dust. Wherefore in great numbers the defenders fell before them, until at last they drew away to the uttermost defenses of the castle, while Kikuchi's warriors scaled the walls victoriously, destroyed the obstacles, and broke into every part of the castle. Nor could Hidetoki himself stand against them, but made ready to take his life.

Yet just at that time Shōni and Ōtomo fell upon Kikuchi from the rear with six thousand horsemen. And therefore Kikuchi called his eldest son, Takeshige, the governor of Higo, saying:

"Deceived by Shōni and Ōtomo, I am like to die on this battlefield. Not unwillingly do I take leave of life, since such is my duty. I shall perish here, making Hidetoki's castle my pillow. Do you hasten back to our dwelling place, build a strong fortress, and bring together warriors to avenge me when I am dead."

So he spoke, and gave Takeshige fifty of his retainers, bidding him go back to the land of Higo. Likewise he wrote a poem on his sleeve badge to send home: "Now all at home await my coming, not knowing that my life must end tonight." For his heart was grieved because of the wife and children in his native place who waited eagerly for his return, not knowing that theirs had been a final parting.

Over and over Takeshige the governor of Higo said, "By all means let me remain here where my father of more than forty years resolves to die in battle against a greater foe." But sternly his father admonished him, saying, "I leave you behind for the sake of the realm." Takeshige could do no other than leave him forever and return weeping toward Higo. How pitiful were the feelings in his heart!

Thereafter, with his second son Higo Saburō and his hundred retainers, the Kikuchi lay monk advanced against the governor's house, heedless of the attackers in the rear. Nor did any of his men give back a step, but all perished smiting the enemy with their swords. Even thus were Chuan Chu and Ching K'o,[21] zealous to requite boons, and Hou Sheng[22] and Yü Jang,[23] who cherished honor above life.

[21] Chuan Chu and Ching K'o were heroes whose stories appear in the *Shih chi*. Both tried to kill the enemies of men to whom they were under obligation. Chuan Chu succeeded; Ching K'o died in the attempt.

[22] Hou Sheng was under obligation to a man named Hsin Ling-chün. Because he was too old to accompany Hsin when the latter set out on a military campaign, he killed himself on the day when Hsin was scheduled to begin to fight.

[23] See note 4 above.

Chapter 11

Now the people of the realm censured Shōni and Ōtomo, saying, "They are no better than wild beasts," yet, feigning innocence, these waited to hear of what passed in the world. When men came saying, "The two Rokuharas were beaten down on the seventh day of the fifth month, and all the attackers at Chihaya castle have drawn away toward the southern capital," the heart of the Shōni lay monk was sore amazed.

"What shall I do?" he thought. "If it be thus, should I not kill the governor to escape blame?"

Secretly he sent messengers to speak thereof to the Kikuchi governor of Higo, and to the Ōtomo lay monk. Kikuchi would not listen, being warned by what had passed before, but Ōtomo agreed firmly, saying, "I will aid you," because he too was guilty.

Tidings of Shōni's plotting were borne to Hidetoki while yet these two selected an auspicious day, saying, "Shall it be today? Shall it be tomorrow?" And Hidetoki sent Nagaoka Rokurō to Shōni's dwelling place, saying, "Learn whether there be truth in it."

Nagaoka sought to call upon Shōni, but Shōni would not meet him, saying, "Just now I am afflicted of a disease." Thereupon, Nagaoka went to the home of the lay monk's son, Chikugo no Shin Shōni, to ask for a meeting, and when as though by chance he gazed upon this place and that, he beheld men joining together the boards of shields and sharpening arrowheads, as if to go forth to battle at once. Moreover, he observed a flagstaff of green bamboo with a white top, standing at the guards' quarters beside the middle gate.

"It is even as we have heard," he thought. "Has not Shōni received a brocade banner from Funanoe? When I meet his son I will cut him down at once!"

With guileless seeming Shin Shōni came forth to his reception hall to meet Nagaoka Rokurō. But even as Nagaoka entered the room, he drew the sword at his waist and flew against Shin Shōni, crying, "Wicked men, to plot a rebellion!"

Agile of limb, Shin Shōni received the sharp blade with a chess board by his side, grappled with Nagaoka fiercely, and rolled over and over fighting him. And soon many Shōni retainers came running in, who stabbed the enemy on top three times to rescue their master on the bottom. Nor did Nagaoka Rokurō satisfy his desire, but perished instantly.

Now thereupon the Shōni lay monk of Chikugo said:

"It is known to the military governor that we devise a rebellion. There is no more help for it."

Together with the Ōtomo lay monk, he led forward an army of more than seven thousand horsemen, that drew near to the castle of the governor Hidetoki at the hour of the horse on the twenty-fifth day of the fifth month. And in a single day's fighting Hidetoki was forced to take his life, together with three hundred and forty of his kinsmen and retainers.

Few are the men who cherish duty in this age of degeneration, but many are the seekers after gain. Although the warriors of the nine provinces of Tsukushi had sworn allegiance to the military, they forgot their obligations and ran away. Caring nothing for honor, they transferred their loyalty. How regrettable it was! Yesterday Shōni and Ōtomo served Hidetoki and slew Kikuchi; today the same Shōni and Ōtomo joined themselves to the imperial cause to slay Hidetoki. Truly indeed did Po Chü-i write, "Not from mountains or rivers arise the sorrows of life's journeying, but from the fickleness of human hearts"!

The Surrender of the Military Governor of Nagato

Now to Hōjō Tokinao the governor of Tōtōmi, the military governor of Nagato, men came saying, "The battle of the capital goes hard against us." And Tokinao went northward over the sea with more than a hundred great vessels to render aid to Rokuhara.

When Tokinao had come to Naruto Strait in Awa, there were men that said, "The capital and Kamakura are beaten down by the Genji, and all the realm bows before the imperial virtue." Wherefore Tokinao rowed his boats back from Naruto toward wearisome Tsukushi, thinking to join himself to the military governor of Kyushu. Yet when at Akama-ga-seki he sought tidings of Kyushu, men said, "Yesterday Shōni and Ōtomo destroyed Hidetoki the military governor of Tsukushi. All within the nine

Chapter 11

provinces and two islands[24] have joined themselves to the emperor's cause."

Then quickly the warriors changed their hearts, those who had followed Tokinao obediently in the past. Each fled away as he willed, until but fifty men remained, drifting on the waves of Yanagi-ga-ura. When Tokinao sought to lower his sails in an inlet, enemies waited with arrowheads ready; when he sought to tie up his ropes on an island, imperial armies aligned their shields to smite him. The men with him longed for their loved ones, riding on the white waves far out on the sea, yet there was no means whereby they might return home, nor any place to which they might draw near. Miserable indeed were the hearts of these who suddenly floated before the wind like boats with severed oar-ropes!

"With tranquil heart would I perish," thought Tokinao, "could I first but learn the fate of my wife and children left behind."

Seeking to prolong his life awhile, he landed a retainer from one of the boats, bidding him say to Shōni and Shimazu, "It is in Tokinao's mind to surrender himself." And perhaps the hearts of Shōni and Shimazu were stirred to pity by these tidings of Tokinao's estate, since they were his friends of many years. For quickly they came to fetch him to their abiding place.

Now there was a person called the monk reformer Shunga of Mine, a kinsman of the emperor's mother, sent away to the land of Chikuzen after the battle of Kasagi. Around this time all the men of the land advanced respectfully to serve Shunga on the left and right, since he had come to be favored by fortune. And the government of Kyushu lay for a time with this monk reformer, because no imperial orders had yet been received.

Shōni and Shimazu went up to Shunga's abiding place with Tokinao, to pray that Tokinao might be suffered to surrender. And the monk reformer agreed, calling Tokinao into his presence. Tokinao entered on his knees, knocked his head against the floor, and prostrated himself far away in the last seat, not venturing to look up.

Then weeping the monk reformer spoke a word to Tokinao, saying:

[24] The nine provinces of Kyushu and the islands of Oki and Tsushima.

"When without reason I was exiled to this place in the beginning of Genkō, I was as an enemy in your sight. Before undeserved words I lowered my face and wiped away tears; by discourtesy and arrogance I was oppressed and put to shame. Now heaven has blessed the humble, and the world has turned about most amazingly. Good has taken the place of evil; prosperity has replaced decline. Is it a dream or reality that yesterday my plight was piteous and today another person suffers? I will do my utmost to save your life. It is said, 'Requite enmity with kindness.'"

So he spoke, and Tokinao touched his head to the floor with tears in his eyes.

Soon Shunga reported this matter to the throne by a fast messenger, whereupon the emperor pardoned Tokinao and granted him a piece of land to sustain his life.

So Tokinao preserved his worthless life, suffering the jeers of the men of the realm, against the time when the Hōjō might rise again. But very soon the fog of sickness came down upon his body, and he passed away like the evening dew.

The Suicide of the Steward of Ushi-ga-hara in Echizen

During the fighting in the capital, Aikawa Ukyō-no-suke Tokiharu went down to the province of Echizen to subdue risings in the northern land, sojourning at the place called Ushi-ga-hara in the district of Ōno. But when very soon there came men with tidings of the fall of Rokuhara, the armies of the province who had previously followed Tokiharu fled away in haste, until none remained to him save his wife, children, and personal retainers.

Then swiftly the monks of the Heisenji Temple urged rebellion upon the warriors of that province and others, hopeful of receiving Tokiharu's lands as a reward. And with seven thousand horsemen they indeed advanced against Ushi-ga-hara in full daylight on the twelfth day of the fifth month.

Beholding the enemy host like clouds or mist, Tokiharu thought, "Though I were to fight against them, how long might I endure?"

While his twenty retainers opposed the approaching enemy, he caused his hair to be cut off with a razor by a monk of the

Chapter 11

neighborhood, of whom he received the Buddhist commandments. His wife and small children did the same, and weeping performed rites to attain buddhahood in the life to come.

When the monk was gone back, Tokiharu spoke a word to his wife, saying:

"Since our two children are boys, I think that the enemy will not suffer them to live, even though they are young. It will be best for me to take them along with me on my journey to the nether regions. But since you are a woman, the enemy will not go so far as to kill you, even if they find you out. If you survive in this world, form an attachment to some man who will comfort your grief. If your heart is at ease, I shall rejoice beneath the grass and moss."

So he spoke to her urgently, weeping. But sorely grieved, his wife said:

"Not even the mandarin ducks dwelling in the water forget their conjugal vows, nor the swallows nesting among the beams. Have not you and I brought forth two children together, reared beneath the sleeves of ten swiftly passing years of intimacy? Was it a vain thing that we prayed to be united for a thousand years? Indeed my grief cannot be endured, nor can I live even for a little while, if now you fall beneath the frost of autumn[25] and our babies perish sooner than the morning dew. I cannot bear to think of it at all, so I shall not remain alive. I shall perish with my beloved, mindful of our vow to share a single grave."

So she spoke, weeping bitterly.

Soon there came one saying, "The retainers who shot defensive arrows are all slain, and the monks have come across the valley toward the mountain behind us."

Then Tokiharu put his two young sons of four and five years into a Chinese armor chest with legs, bidding their two nurses carry it before and behind.

"Let them be drowned in the Kamakura River," he said, and watched where they went. But the lady their mother walked holding to the cord of the box, thinking to drown her body in the same pool. How pitiful were the feelings in her heart!

[25] Beneath a sword. The shining blade was thought to resemble sparkling frost.

When the nurses put down the chest on the riverbank and opened the lid, the two babies raised their faces, jesting innocently:

"Where are we going, mama? Come and ride in the box so that your feet won't hurt."

Holding back her tears, their mother told them:

"This river is one of the eight waters of meritorious deeds of the Pure Land paradise, where children are born to play. Say the name of Amida Buddha with me before you submerge your bodies."

The babies joined their hands to the hands of their nurses, sat down facing the west,[26] and chanted the name of Amida Buddha loudly. Then each of the two nurses leaped to the bottom of the green water with one of them in her arms, and the mother cast her body after them into the same depths.

Afterward Tokiharu too slew himself and became a heap of ashes.

Though it is said that the things of life are forgotten after death, yet does the karma of a fleeting thought endure for five hundred lives, while the effect of fixing the mind on a thing endures through worlds without end. Wherefore it may be that Tokiharu's thoughts became flames consuming him at the bottom of a limitless hell.[27] How pitiful it was!

The Suicide of the Protector of Etchū; the Matter of the Unquiet Spirits

Now to the protector of Etchū came men saying, "Armies friendly to the emperor seek to travel over the Hokurikudō Road from Dewa and Echigo, thinking to attack the capital." The protector, Nagoya Tokiari the governor of Tōtōmi, resolved to stop them on the way, with his younger brother Shuri-no-suke Aritomo and his nephew Hyōgo-no-suke Sadamochi. And these three encamped at a place called Futatsuzuka in Etchū, where they called together the warriors of nearby places.

Just at that time men came, saying, "Rokuhara is beaten down, and armies rise up in the eastern provinces to go forth against Kamakura." The warriors of Noto and Etchū, they who had

---

[26] The direction of the Pure Land.

[27] He would have to suffer because of his inability to rid his mind of worldly attachments.

Chapter 11 331

galloped forward according to the protector's orders, fell back to Hōshōnotsu, where they concerted together to advance against the protector's camp. And then even the protector's retainers fled away instantly to join the enemy, although previously they had thought dutifully and loyally, "We will exchange our bodies for the body of our lord; we will exchange our lives for the life of our lord!" Those who came in the morning departed in the evening, and swiftly Tokiaki's friends bore malice toward him, they who had cleaved to him and loved him. At last but seventy-nine persons remained, close kinsmen who refused to leave, or hereditary retainers grateful for many boons.

At the hour of the horse on the seventeenth day of the fifth month, there came one to Tokiari, saying, "The enemy advance to give battle with more than ten thousand horsemen." And thereupon Tokiari and his brother and nephew said:

"To what avail may we fight when our numbers are thus few? We would be mocked by men of generations to come, if through rash fighting we fell into the hands of the enemy to suffer the shame of imprisonment."

They left their camps, thinking in their hearts, "We shall send out our wives and children in a boat to sink in the sea before the enemy draw near, and we shall take our lives inside our castle."

Now the lady of the governor of Tōtōmi had married him twenty-one years before, and there were two sons of their love, eight years old and six years old. Shuri-no-suke Aritomo's wife of more than three years was great with child, while the wife of Hyōgo-no-suke Sadamochi was a lady of high degree, come from the capital four or five days earlier to be Sadamochi's bride.

Long ago when Sadamochi had first gazed for a moment upon the peerless countenance and curving painted brows of this lady, he had yearned after her, thinking, "Were there but a crack in her screen!" And when he had loved her for more than three years, by devising various means he had stolen her away. Since the days of their intimacy were but yesterday and today, death was indeed bitter to him, though previously he had lamented to her, "'I would give up life for the happiness of communion with you.'" [28] Longer

---
[28] From a poem by Ariwara no Narihira (827–880) in the *Shinkokinshū*.

were the months and days of his sad yearning than the life of the rock rubbed by the heavenly robe of feathers;[29] shorter than a spring night's dream was their love after they were joined together. How pitiful were the vows that instantly met with this affliction! Grievously did they two weep, and sorrowed to part, saying, "We have heard of the sadness of death which early or late is visited upon all men, even as the passing of the dew on the branches of a tree and the drops on its trunk;[30] yet never did we believe that we would part thus miserably, the one to sink beneath the waves and the other to burn to death in a fire."

Soon it seemed that the enemy drew near, for men clamored, "Behold the dust raised by horses on the east and west!" And thereupon all the wives and small children entered weeping into a boat.

As the boat rowed out toward the distant sea, the favorable wind did not leave off blowing even a little, but spitefully blew these travelers far out on the water. Nor did the ebbing tide turn back, but heartlessly drew the rowing vessel beyond the bay. Even such was the sorrow of Lady Sayo of Matsuura, who waved her scarf from Tamatsushima Mountain to the boat going out to sea![31]

Now working the oar the boatman stopped the boat among the waves. The one lady pressed the two children against her sides, the two ladies joined their hands together, and all alike cast their bodies into the water. For a time their crimson skirts and red trousers floated on the surface of the sea, which became as river waters of Yoshino or Tatsuta, dyed with fallen cherry blossoms or scattered maple leaves, but at last they sank into the depths.

When the warriors at the castle had witnessed these things, they cut their bellies all together and burned to death at the bottom of a war fire: seventy-nine men of high estate and low.

May it not be that the spirits of the dead remained there, still thinking wrong thoughts of attachment to husbands and wives? Of late a boatman coming up from Echigo suddenly met with an

[29] According to one explanation, the length of a kalpa is the time required to destroy a rock forty leagues long on every side by rubbing it once every three years with an angel's robe.

[30] An allusion to a poem in the *Shinkokinshū*. Though the dew on the branches may vanish before the drops on the trunk, the same fate awaits both in the end.

[31] Her husband was in the boat, going to fight against Silla. She is said to have stayed there until she died.

ill wind and rough waves at that bay, wherefore he let fall his anchor. Deep in the night when the waves had quieted, all the aspect of that travel lodging became fearful: the wind from the pine trees, the moon shining on the reed flowers. Far out on the water there came a sound of women weeping and grieving, and even as the boatman listened, sorely amazed, men's voices called, "Come hither, boat!" from the beach.

The boatman could do no other, but took his craft to the shore, where three men entered its cabin, most valiant in appearance.

"We will ride with you to the offing," they said.

When the boatman had taken them out to the place where the tidal currents joined together, these three got down from the boat and stood upon the boundless waves. And soon three ladies of about fifteen, sixteen, or nineteen years floated up weeping from below the waves, clad in red trousers and many skirts.[32] The men looked upon them with loving eyes, as though to draw near to them, but a fierce fire burned up suddenly, coming between the men and the women with its flames. The yearning figures of the three ladies sank to the bottom of the waves, while the men swam back weeping on top of the water toward Futatsuzuka.

Sorely perplexed, the boatman pulled at the sleeve of one of those men, asking, "In the past, what men were you?" And he answered, naming each of them, "We were the Nagoya governor of Tōtōmi, Nagoya Shuri-no-suke, and Nagoya Hyōgo-no-suke." Whereupon the three vanished as though wiped out.

Śubhakara[33] of India yearned after a queen so uncontrollably that his body was consumed by the flames of his passion, while through love of her husband the Maiden of Uji Bridge[34] in our country moistened her sleeve with tears where she slept alone. These were both strange happenings of antiquity, recorded in old chronicles. But sinful indeed was the love of the dead that caused such things to appear in the world before men's eyes!

[32] These were the ghosts of the ladies as they had appeared in their girlhood.
[33] A fisherman who loved a queen so intensely that his body burst into flames.
[34] She was so jealous of her husband's other wife that she drowned herself in the Uji River.

The Punishment of the Besiegers of Mount Kongō; the Matter of Sakai Sadatoshi

Although there was peace in the capital, men said, "Still do the Heishi from Mount Kongō remain in the southern capital, where they make ready to attack the capital." Wherefore an army of fifty thousand horsemen was sent forth toward the Yamato Road, with the Naka-no-in Middle Marshal Sadahira as its general; likewise, Kusunoki Hyōe Masashige was sent from the province of Kawachi to attack from the rear with twenty thousand horsemen of the home provinces.

Although the Heishi warriors had scattered in the ten directions, those who remained in the southern capital were more than fifty thousand horsemen.

"We will fight one fierce battle," they thought.

But their ardor of a former day was used up utterly, so that they passed the days vainly, even as fish dying in the foam of a small bit of water.

First of all, by imperial command, Utsunomiya went up to the capital with the Ki and Kiyowara: seven hundred riders, who had been the guards of the outer gateway of the southern capital at the Hannyaji Temple. Afterward others of those warriors hastened to surrender in parties of one or two hundred, or of five or ten, until no man remained who was not a Taira kinsman or a member of a family of hereditary retainers, grateful for many boons.

It had been fitting for all of these to win fame by dying in battle, since there was nothing to hope for, such as might cause them to cherish life. Yet such was the baseness of their karma that thirteen of the great Taira captains became monks of the Ritsu faith at the Hannyaji, putting on the three garments of religion over their shoulders, taking up bowls in their hands, and coming forth as prisoners. The chief thereof were Aso no Danjō Shōhitsu Tokiharu, Daibutsu Uma-no-suke Takanao, the Ema governor of Tōtōmi, and the Sakai governor of Aki. Likewise more than fifty powerful warriors of the Kantō did the same: Nagasaki Shirō Saemon-no-jō, the lay monk Nikaidō Dōun of Dewa, and others.

Chapter 11   335

Sadahira no Ason received these, bound their arms behind them tightly, tied them across the saddle seats of relay horses, and brought them to the capital in full daylight in front of the myriads of the imperial armies.

Now in the era of Heiji, Akugenta Yoshihira[35] was taken prisoner and beheaded by the Heike, while in Genryaku Lord Munemori the Great Subject of the Interior was captured by the Genji and made to travel over the highroads.[36] Even today these are mocked by men's mouths, and after a hundred years the descendants of their two houses are shamed when others speak of them. Yet sore against their wishes were they delivered into the enemy's hands on the day of battle, whether by being outwitted or by having no leisure to take their lives. How much the worse were those of whom we speak now, that were not outwitted by the enemy nor lacked an occasion to take their lives! Never was such dishonor! They willingly put on the black garments of religion before their vigor was exhausted, and faced ahead with their hands tied behind their backs, so reluctant were they to give up their doomed lives.

When the prisoners came to the capital, the black robes were stripped off their bodies, their religious names were changed back to their former names, and each man of them was given into the charge of a powerful chief. As they waited to be punished, they rose up and lay down in heavy bonds, nor was there a time when their tears did not fall by reason of the grievous affliction of their spirits. To their ears came uncertain tidings of Kamakura: of chaste wives, pledged to eternal fidelity, who were carried off by wretched countrymen to taste the sorrow of Wang Chao-chün,[37] or noble sons, reared tenderly in rich halls, who became the slaves of rankless men, such as never before had been permitted to draw near

---

[35] Minamoto no Yoshihira, a brother of Yoritomo. He escaped death during the initial fighting in the Disturbance of Heiji, but was later discovered in hiding by a greatly superior force, which succeeded in wounding him severely and capturing him alive.

[36] Taira no Munemori, the son and heir of Kiyomori. After losing the crucial battle of Dan-no-ura, he leaped into the sea, but was pulled out and captured by the Minamoto, who executed him in the vicinity of the capital after taking him to Kamakura and back.

[37] A Chinese court lady who was forced to marry a barbarian chief during the Han dynasty.

to them, and suffered a fate similar to that of Teng T'ung.[38] Yet that these still lived made their adversity as nothing. For faintly they heard the talk of wayfarers, who yesterday had passed over the roads and today rested beside their gates, saying:

"How sad it is! Whose mother was that lady who spread her sleeve in the street as she begged for food, and now is fallen down dead? Whose father was that traveler who disguised his person in a short cotton robe as he went around seeking his family, and now is captured and killed?"

And they lamented, saying, "Alas, that we have lived so long!"

On the ninth day of the seventh month fifteen men were struck down at Amida Peak: Aso no Danjō Shōhitsu, Daibutsu Uma-no-suke, the Ema governor of Tōtōmi, the Sakai governor of Aki, Nagasaki Shirō Saemon, and others. Their heads were cut off secretly, and were not paraded, for it was said, "It is unseemly to think of punishments alone, when even now the emperor is returned to his throne and divers matters of government are not yet looked to." And their dead bodies were sent to fitting temples, wherein prayers were said for their enlightenment in the life to come.

Now notwithstanding that the lay monk Nikaidō Dōun of Dewa, a counselor to the Hōjō, was one of the foremost among the enemies of the court, the emperor thought to take him into his service, since for many years the fame of Dōun's talents had reached his hearing. He lessened his sentence of death by one degree and suffered him to hold his former lands, yet after all Dōun was struck down late in the autumn of that year, for it was said that he had again plotted rebelliously.

Sakai Sakyō-no-suke Sadatoshi was a person who esteemed himself highly, thinking, "Assuredly is it meet that I become a grand marshal, for not only am I of the house of Taira but also I am a mighty warrior, a man of superior ability." Because the appreciation of the Sagami lay monk did not extend so far, Sadatoshi joined the besiegers of Mount Kongō with a resentful and angry heart. And

[38] A famous Chinese of the Han dynasty who died of starvation after having been wealthy for a time.

Chapter 11

when the Chigusa Middle Marshal sent him an imperial command to join the armies of the court, he came down submissively from Chihaya early in the fifth month, and took his way back to the capital.

Now when the Heishi had taken religious vows and become prisoners, all those in their service were spoiled of their lands and driven forth from their houses, sore distressed to find a lodging place. Likewise, Sadatoshi was sent away toward the province of Awa, with not even a low-ranking retainer or soldier to accompany him. Yesterday's happiness became today's grief, and more and more his suffering increased.

"Though it is true that the prosperous must decline," he thought, "still the world is a heartless place. Would that I might hide my body deep in the mountains!"

When Sadatoshi asked concerning the Kantō, people said, "His Lordship the Sagami lay monk and all his kinsmen have perished. No man knows the abiding places of their women, children, and retainers."

Then indeed there was none in whom Sadatoshi could place his trust, nor any hope for a time to come. And he was worried and affrighted by all that he saw and heard.

At this time it was said:

"Although those who served the Kantō have come forth as prisoners to save their lives, in the end they will be treacherous. They must all be struck down."

So it was said, and Sadatoshi too was seized.

Sadatoshi no longer cherished life, so wearied was his spirit by this transient world. Nonetheless it was grievous to him to die without knowing the fate of the wife and children left behind in his native place. He begged his dagger of his guardian, a weapon that for many years had not left his body, and gave it to a holy man who had come to urge him to recite the name of Amida Buddha ten times at the last, praying him to take it to his wife. And the holy man received it, saying, "I will seek her out."

Then Sadatoshi rejoiced exceedingly. Seated straight on an animal skin, he composed a poem, saying, "Though I counted as nothing in the days of my lords' prosperity, still must I share their affliction." He chanted the name of Amida Buddha loudly ten times, and tranquilly suffered his head to be stricken off.

The holy man took the dagger, together with the narrow-sleeved jacket that Sadatoshi had worn at the last, and made speed to go down to Kamakura, where he sought out Sadatoshi's wife to give those things to her. The lady could not listen to his words, but wept cruelly, as one helpless to contain her sorrow. Drawing forward the inkstone by her side, she wrote on the bottom of Sadatoshi's jacket, "For whose eyes did he send these keepsakes? I cannot bear to live." She put on that garment over her head, thrust the dagger into her breast, and perished instantly.

Also there were wives who cast their bodies into deep waters, unwilling to marry anew when the loss of their husbands made their vows as vain things. And there were aged mothers, lingering on after their sons were dead, who fell over into chasms by their own will, since they had no more means of living and could not find a day's food.

Now it was more than a hundred and sixty years that the nine generations of the Taira ruled the realm after Shōkyū. Their house prospered exceedingly under heaven, so that more than eight hundred men thereof brought glory to its name, showing their might as military governors and protectors of divers places and provinces, and wielding power as they willed. Nor can any say how many myriads of hundreds of millions of men of divers families were their retainers. Wherefore assuredly did it seem that not in ten years might Tsukushi and Kamakura be conquered, nor in twenty, even though Rokuhara were to be attacked and brought down. Yet as though by joined tallies the armies of the more than sixty provinces rose up together, until within forty-three days all was destroyed. A shameful karma!

How foolish were the warriors of the Kantō, who for many years governed everything under heaven, compassed the seas with their power, and yet ruled without justice! Because of this their strong armor and sharp weapons were beaten down by canes and whips,[39]

---

[39] I.e., by greatly inferior military strength.

and they were destroyed in an instant. From ancient times until today, the proud have been cast down and the humble have prevailed. Yet the men of the world know not that heaven diminishes the full, but give themselves over to boundless avarice. How can they fail to go astray?

12

The Court Governs Alone

WHEN THE FORMER SOVEREIGN had returned to the throne, the name of the era was changed back again to Genkō, and Shōgyō was rejected, by reason that it was a name newly adopted by the deposed emperor. In the summer of this third year the ministers of state consulted together concerning the affairs of the realm, and rewards, punishments, laws, and edicts sprang from the government of the court alone. The hearts of all men bowed before the imperial virtue, even as frost melted by the spring sun; their trembling before the court's laws was as that of one treading on a sword with thunder overhead.

Now on the third day of the sixth month, men said, "The Prince of the Great Pagoda is come to the Bishamon Hall on Mount Shigi." The armies of the home provinces and nearby places galloped to join themselves to him, each striving to be first, and even warriors from the capital did the same, and men of distant provinces. Wherefore the prince's host waxed exceeding great, so that men said, "Truly more than half the realm have joined themselves to him."

Although it was appointed that the prince should enter the capital on the thirteenth day, after all he delayed to go forth. Then there were those that said, "The prince summons the warriors of the provinces, by whom he causes shields to be made and arrowheads to be sharpened in preparation for battle." And the hearts of the

Chapter 12   341

warriors in the capital were disquieted, though none knew the enemy's name.

Thereupon the supreme highness sent forth an imperial messenger, the Controller of the Right Kiyotada, to say to the prince:

"The realm is returned to tranquillity, the lingering might of the seven military virtues[1] is brought down, and We work a great revolution in affairs of state. Wherefore is it needful that you should take up weapons and gather together warriors? While the four seas were disturbed, you returned for a time to the world to defend against the enemy, but in this era of peace it is meet that you should cut off your hair quickly, resume your black-dyed garments, and go back again to the abbacy of the Tendai faith."

So the emperor spoke through the mouth of his messenger Kiyotada. But the prince called Kiyotada close and answered him, saying:

"It is because of His Majesty's marvelous virtue that now for a time the four seas are quiet and the myriad folk live in safety; likewise it is because of his humble subject's devisings. But now that Ashikaga Jibu-no-tayū has won a victory in one battle, he seeks to place himself above ten thousand men. If we fail to strike while his strength is weak, assuredly will the warlike might of Takauji be joined to the treasonable heart of the monk Takatoki.[2] So I gather together warriors and make weapons ready, but in no wise do I do a blameworthy thing.

"As regards cutting off my hair, it may be that men will censure me, such as know a thing not in advance of its coming. Although peace has been returned to the realm by means of the sudden destruction of the rebels, there are enemies hiding their bodies, men who seek an opening and await an auspicious hour. If those above are weak, those below will certainly become insolent. Wherefore those who govern in today's world must esteem warlike prowess equally with the arts of peace. Were I to return to my clerical state, giving up the dignity of a mighty general, who would sustain the military strength of the court?

---

[1] An allusion to the *Tso chuan*, which lists seven useful functions of the military.

[2] I.e., Takauji will use his military strength to establish himself in the position formerly occupied by Takatoki.

"Truly there are two ways whereby buddhas and bodhisattvas benefit living beings. They are called receiving good and subduing evil. Receiving good means being mild and forbearing, and thinking first of all of mercy, but subduing evil means being powerful and angry, and thinking first of all of punishment. Many times in China and Japan, when there was need of a virtuous sovereign, a wise counselor, or a man skilled in making war, a monk was returned to the world or a retired monarch was set upon the throne. So Chia Tao the Hermit of the Waves[3] left the cloister to be a servant of the court, and Temmu and Kōken of our country gave up their holy retirement to sit upon the throne.[4] Which is best for the sake of the state: that as an abbot I should dwell in a retired valley on Mount Hiei, or that as the chief of His Majesty's military government I should keep peace in all the realm? Do you petition His Majesty, that quickly he may grant me these two things." [5]

So he spoke, and bade Kiyotada return again to the court.

When Lord Kiyotada returned bearing these tidings to the throne, the supreme highness considered carefully and made a decision, saying:

"Assuredly does it seem that the prince is resolved to endure men's jeers for the sake of the court, since he seeks to strengthen Our readiness for war by becoming Our shogun. But wherein has Takauji shown disloyalty, that he must be punished? The warriors of the realm are still fearful in their hearts after the coming of peace. If We chastise a blameless man, how may their minds be at ease? Although We shall not refuse to make the prince Our shogun, he must by all means lay aside his plan for chastising Takauji."

And he made the prince his barbarian-subduing shogun.

Now perhaps the anger left the prince's heart because of this, for he went forth from Shigi on the seventeenth day of the sixth month and entered the capital on the twenty-third day, after tarrying for a week at Yahata.

---

[3] A T'ang poet. At first a monk, he returned to lay life, took a high degree in the civil service examination system, and became an official.
[4] Temmu (reigned 673–686) was a monk before he became emperor. Kōken (reigned 749–758) abdicated and became a nun, but returned to the throne later as the Empress Shōtoku (reigned 764–770).
[5] Permission to attack Takauji and appointment to the office of shogun.

Chapter 12

Never was there such a glorious sight as that procession! The lay monk Akamatsu Enshin served in the foremost rank with a thousand horsemen, the Tono Sign of the Law Ryōchū rode in the second place with seven hundred horsemen, and the Naka-no-in Middle Marshal Sadahira rode in the third place with eight hundred horsemen. Next there came five hundred mighty men of valor in splendid armor, walking in two lines to guard the prince. Behind these rode the prince himself, clad in garments of red brocade under scarlet-threaded armor with metal fittings, whereon lions sported beneath peony bushes, chasing and meeting each other on all sides. His tassets were exceedingly long, and he wore a gold-handled sword in a golden scabbard, attached to a belt of silver chain made by the Imperial Munitions Bureau, and encased in a tiger-skin bag tied to the middle of a leather strip high on the left side of his armor skirt. On his back he carried a quiver of thirty-six arrows feathered with swan's feathers, with plain bamboo shafts lacquered lightly below the knots. His bow was bound with rattan in two places, and again in two places, over all its length, with a silver hook above the leather grip to stop the arrow from slipping. Most thick and vigorous were the tail and mane of his light bay horse, whereon he had placed a saddle lacquered over all its surface with gold dust, as well as freshly dyed cords with thick tassels hanging to the ground. Truly the street was narrow where he advanced, surrounded by twelve mounted warriors on his left and right, with a sound of horses' feet as of the beating of plovers' wings!

Behind the prince's horse, Tadaaki no Ason the Chigusa Middle Marshal accompanied him with more than a thousand riders, while three thousand armed warriors from divers provinces rode quietly through the streets. For it was thought, "We must guard against untoward happenings with trustworthy warriors, since it is still a time for using caution."

As a rearguard three days later came all the warriors of the home provinces and nearby lands: two hundred and seven thousand riders of Yuasa Gon-no-tayū, Yamamoto Shirōjirō Tadayuki, Itō Saburō Yukitaka, Katō Tarō Mitsunao and others.

Although it is true that all things are transient in this changing world, still it was a most rare and dazzling sight, this entry of the Tendai abbot who had suddenly become the emperor's shogun, wearing armor and followed by warriors.

Thereafter the Prince of the Myōhōin Cloister came back to the capital from the land of Sanuki with an army of warriors from Shikoku. And Lord Fujifusa the Madenokōji Middle Counselor came back from the province of Hitachi with his guardian, Oda Mimbu-no-tayū. Suefusa the senior secretary of the crown prince's office had died in exile, wherefore his father Lord Nobufusa lamented in the midst of rejoicing, and in his old age moistened his sleeve with tears. The Most Holy Enkan of the Hosshōji was brought to the capital by his guardian, the Yūki lay monk of Kōzuke, whereupon, rejoicing that no harm had come to this holy man, the emperor hastened to grant Yūki the holding of his former properties. The Most Holy Monkan came up to the capital from Iō-ga-shima, and the monk reformer Chūen returned from the land of Echigo.

The men who had been deprived of office when the emperor fled to Kasagi, or who had been forced to leave off attending to their duties, these were called forth from divers places, with their offspring who had been sentenced to death or exile, and all their sorrow was dispelled at once.

But the powerful warriors who had exulted in their warlike prowess and despised the owners of landed estates,[6] these became servants in the mansions of court nobles, running after their swift perfumed carriages and kneeling before their junior samurai and watchmen. Wherefore many of them thought:

"Though we know that it is useless to bewail the vicissitudes of life and the changes brought by time, still if the court is to govern the realm in this wise, all the provincial stewards and housemen of the Hōjō will be as the most humble of servants. Alas! How unexpected it is! Would that the military again controlled the four seas!"

Now it was said, "Beginning on the third day of the eighth month, rewards will be given to the armies." And Lord Saneyo, the Tōin Commander of the Left Gate Guards, was given the charge thereof.

---

[6] The courtiers who were the absentee owners of the estates had been too weak to defend their rights.

Chapter 12

Thereupon untold thousands and myriads of men from the hosts of the provinces held up proofs of their loyal fighting, and presented papers, and sought after rewards. In truth those who were loyal trusted to their merits instead of seeking favor, but those who were lacking in loyalty courted the god of the hearth, sought out the god of the hall,[7] and deceived the imperial ears. In five or six months but twenty men were rewarded, and soon even these grants were taken back, it being said that they were wrongfully bestowed.

"If it be thus," said the emperor, "let us have a new president."

He gave the charge of the petitions to Lord Fujifusa the Madenokōji Middle Counselor, whereupon Fujifusa engaged himself thereto, distinguishing between the loyal and the disloyal, separating the shallow from the deep, and seeking to give to each according to his desert. But those close to the throne spoke privately to the emperor, prevailing upon him to confirm the holdings of former enemies of the court, or to grant five or ten pieces of land to disloyal men. And Fujifusa resigned his office on the pretext of illness, since in no wise might he utter words of reproof.

Next Kujō Mitsutsune the minister of popular affairs was made the president (for it was thought, "Matters cannot be left thus"). Lord Mitsutsune enquired closely of the grand marshals concerning the loyal deeds of their followers, and sought to give to each according to his desert. But all the lands of the Sagami lay monk were named to furnish revenues for the palace, the lands of Takatoki's brother Shirō Sakon-no-taifu were granted to the princely minister of war,[8] and the lands of the Daibutsu governor of Mutsu were granted to the lady who was an empress's peer.[9] Likewise, through the speaking of private words to the emperor, by ones and by twos the estates of Takatoki's kinsmen and Kantō vassals were given away to undeserving persons: singing girls, kick ball players, officials of the guards headquarters and offices, court ladies, and monks. In all of the sixty-six provinces there was no estate that could be given to a warrior, not even a place big enough to drill a

---

[7] An allusion to a passage in the *Analects*. The god of the hall was the most honored god; the god of the hearth was obscure but powerful. Important and influential men.

[8] Prince Morinaga, the Prince of the Great Pagoda.

[9] Lady Sammi.

hole. Wherefore Lord Mitsutsune passed the days vainly, though in his heart he desired to grant rewards fairly.

Likewise, courts were established on the left and right sides of Ikuhōmon Gate[10] to decide suits of divers kinds. The judges were erudite and wise nobles and courtiers, and officials and secretaries of the Grand Preceptorate learned in literature and the law. They were divided into three parties, that took six days of every month to be their days of business. Yet not even by these solemn and imposing bodies was the realm put in order or the state made secure. When a suitor gained sanction for a petition through private words, the court found righteousness in the defendant; when the court confirmed a man in his holdings, the emperor bestowed those lands upon another because of words spoken privately. And there being confusion in this wise, for one piece of land there were four or five owners, nor was there any end to the disturbances in the provinces.

Moreover, in the beginning of the seventh month the Inner Princess was afflicted of an illness, whereof she died on the second day of the eighth month; likewise, the crown prince died on the third day of the eleventh month.

"These are not commonplace occurrences," men said. "Assuredly they are the doing of the angry spirits of the dead." [11]

To stop the evil-doing of those spirits and send them to the Pure Land, the emperor caused fifty-three hundred scrolls of the Tripitaka to be copied in one day at the four great monasteries,[12] and a dedicatory mass to be held at the Hosshōji.

The Building of the Great Palace Enclosure; The Matter of the Shrine of Sugawara no Michizane

The nobles reported to the throne on the twelfth day of the first month of the next year, saying:

"His Majesty's affairs have become exceedingly numerous, and the hundred offices are out of order. The bounds of this palace are narrow, nor is it a place where ceremonies can be made ready, since its length is but four hundred and seventy-five yards on the four

---
[10] One of the palace gates.
[11] The warriors killed in the recent fighting.
[12] The Tōdaiji, the Kōfukuji, the Enryakuji, and the Onjōji.

Chapter 12   347

sides. But though it were to be made greater on every side by a hundred and twenty yards, and though halls and buildings were to be built, still it would not equal the imperial residence of antiquity. A great palace enclosure ought to be built."

So they spoke, and thereupon the emperor commanded the provinces of Aki and Suō to bear the expense thereof, and set aside the twentieth part of the yearly yield of taxes of all the stewards and housemen of the land of Japan.

[*There follows a description of the original palace enclosure, which in turn leads to a lengthy biography of Sugawara no Michizane (845–903), the exiled minister whose angry spirit was believed to have caused the palace's destruction by fire.*]

Now the great palace enclosure of old was modeled after the palace at Hsien Yang, the capital of Ch'in Shih Huang Ti.[13] It was four thousand two hundred and eighty yards long from north to south and two thousand three hundred and eight yards long from east to west; likewise the stones of the Dragon Tail [14] were laid down. On the four sides were twelve gates: on the east, the gates called Yōmeimon, Taikemmon, and Yūhōmon; on the south, the gates called Bifukumon, Suzakumon, and Kōkamon; on the west, the gates called Dattemmon, Sōhekimon, and Imbumon; and on the north the gates called Ankamon, Ikammon, and Tatchimon. Moreover, there were an Upper East Gate and an Upper West Gate, where armed warriors guarded constantly against untoward happenings. In thirty-six rear apartments three thousand virtuous ladies made their toilettes,[15] and in seventy-two front halls military and civil officials awaited the imperial pleasure. East and west of the Shishinden[16] stood the Seiryōden[17] and Ummeiden,[18] and on the

---

[13] Founder of the Ch'in dynasty in China (221–207 B.C.).
[14] A raised stone platform at the end of the audience courts (Chōdōin), where the Great Hall of State, or Daigokuden, was situated. The author seems to conceive of it as jutting out beyond the enclosure proper, but it was actually well inside. (The *Taiheiki* exaggerates the size of the enclosure, which was about four-fifths of a mile north and south and three-fourths of a mile east and west.)
[15] See note 1, Chapter Six.
[16] The main building of the residential section of the enclosure, the site of such major ceremonies as were not important enough to be held in the Daigokuden.
[17] The emperor's regular place of residence.
[18] The hall where the sacred mirror was enshrined.

north stood the Jōneiden and Jōkanden.¹⁹ The Jōkanden, also called the Hall of the August Comb Boxes, stood northward of the empress's apartments. And there was the Kōshōden,²⁰ that was also called the Archery Hall, and stood south of the Seiryōden. The Shōyōsha was the same as the Pear Court; the Shikeisha was the same as the Paulownia Court; the Hikyōsha was the same as the Wisteria Court; the Gyōkasha was the same as the Plum Court; and the Shūhōsha was the same as the Thunder Court.²¹

Also there were the Lespedeza Room,²² the Jin-no-za,²³ the Takiguchi-no-to,²⁴ the Imperial Falcon-Yard, and the Needlework Office. The offices of the Military Guards of the Left were at Sen'yōmon Gate, and the offices of the Military Guards of the Right were at Immeimon Gate.²⁵ The Sunflower and Moonflower Gates faced the guards' offices on the left and right.²⁶ And there were the Daigokuden,²⁷ with the Koan-dono waiting hall and the Green Dragon and White Tiger Towers;²⁸ and the Burakuin,²⁹ with the Seishodō waiting hall, where the Gosechi banquet³⁰ and Great Food Offering ceremony³¹ were held. The Chūwa-in was the same as the Naka-no-in,³² and the Naikyōbō was the same as the Ceremonial Music Office.³³ Buddhist prayers for the protection of the

---

¹⁹ Two halls of the women's quarters.
²⁰ Used mostly for storage. It faced an archery field.
²¹ The uses of these buildings are not entirely clear, but some at least were at the disposal of court ladies. Their alternate names came from the trees in their courtyards, except in the case of the Shūhōsha, which was called the Thunder Court because it was once struck by lightning during a storm.
²² One of the rooms of the Seiryōden.
²³ Used for appointments and promotions, certain Shinto rituals, etc.
²⁴ Quarters of the warriors who guarded the palace.
²⁵ These were gates in the inner wall enclosing the buildings of the emperor's living quarters.
²⁶ Two gates leading to the emperor's garden.
²⁷ The main building of the entire enclosure, where coronations, New Year's levees, and other functions of supreme importance took place.
²⁸ These faced one another across the courtyard in front of the Daigokuden.
²⁹ A group of buildings west of the Chōdōin group.
³⁰ A court banquet held annually in the eleventh month after the Gosechi dances, which were performed by five girls of noble birth called the Gosechi dancers. (The literal meaning of *gosechi* is five rhythms.)
³¹ A Shinto ritual performed by a new emperor after his enthronement.
³² A group of buildings in the southwest corner of the residential quarters, where the emperor went to worship the gods.
³³ A place where dancing girls were kept and various kinds of singing and dancing were rehearsed.

Chapter 12

state were offered up at the Shingon Cloister,[34] and the rice-offering ceremony was held at the Shinkaden.[35] At the Hall of Military Virtues the emperor watched shooting on horseback and horse races.[36] And the Chōdōin was a place that held the offices of the eight ministries of state.[37]

Now there was an orange tree, presented to His Majesty by the Proximate Guards of the Right,[38] which still preserved its ancient fragrance, and there were two clusters of bamboo, growing thickly at the garden steps,[39] which had borne the frosts of many generations. Truly the Hall of the Eight Deities of the Office of Shrines[40] was the desolate building where the Ariwara Middle Marshal remained through a night of thunder with bow and quiver at his side,[41] and likewise, a small room of the Kōkiden was the place wherein the Grand Marshal Hikaru Genji admired the "misty moonlit night," while a voice recited, "There is nothing so beautiful." [42] And when long ago the consultant of the house of Ōe went down to the province of Echigo, it was the Kōrokuden,[43] south of Rashōmon Gate, whereof he wrote sadly, "Not soon shall we meet again—O tears that drench the cherry trees in the dawn at Kōroku!"

Now the Chamber of the Demon was in the Seiryōden, and likewise the regent's reception room, the bell-rope to announce the

[34] Just west of the emperor's living quarters.
[35] The rice-offering ceremony (*jingonjiki*) was performed by the emperor in honor of Amaterasu twice a year. The Shinkaden was the main building of the Chūwa-in.
[36] The Butokuden, opposite Imbumon Gate.
[37] The halls in this group of buildings included the Daigokuden and halls for the use of the great nobles when ceremonies were being held. They were not the offices of the ministries, which were located elsewhere.
[38] In front of the Shishinden, where there was also a famous cherry tree.
[39] In the east courtyard of the Seiryōden.
[40] The buildings of the Office of Shrines were concentrated in the southeast corner of the palace enclosure.
[41] According to the *Ise monogatari* (*Tales of Ise*), Ariwara no Narihira and a lady took shelter from a storm in a ruined building late one night. A demon devoured the lady in an inner room, while Narihira, unable to hear her cries because of the thunder, stood guard in the outer doorway.
[42] From the *Tale of Genji*. The "misty moonlit night" (*oborozukiyo*) was a lady with whom Genji had an affair. The line of verse is from a ninth-century poem which she was reciting when they met for the first time: "There is nothing so beautiful as a misty moonlit night."
[43] A building for the reception of foreign envoys.

coming of ministers of state, and the screens whereon wild waves were depicted. But the screens of the sages were in the Shishinden. In the first bay on the east there were Ma Chou, Fang Hsüan-ling, Tu Ju-hui, and Wei Cheng; in the second bay there were Chu-ko Liang, Ch'ü Po-yü, Chang Tzu-fang, and Ti-wu Lun; in the third bay there were Kuan Chung, Teng Yü, Tzu-ch'an, and Hsiao Ho; and in the fourth bay there were I Yin, Fu Yüeh, T'ai-kung Wang, and Chung-shan-fu. In the first bay on the west there were Li Chi, Yü Shih-nan, Tu Yü, and Chang Hua; and in the second bay there were Yang Hu, Yang Hsiung, Ch'en Shih, and Pan Ku; and in the third bay there were Huan Jung, Cheng Hsüan, Su Wu, and Ni K'uan; and in the fourth bay there were Tung Chung-shu, Wen Weng, Chia I, and Shu-sun T'ung. It is said that the paintings were made by the brush of Kanaoka,[44] and that Ono no Tōfū[45] wrote the words of praise.

Marvelously wrought as were the buildings of this great palace enclosure, they could not prevail against the acts of heaven, though their phoenix roof tiles soared to the sky and their rainbow beams stood among the clouds. They were destroyed utterly by many visitations of the fire god, so that nothing but the ancient foundation stones remained.

If we enquire concerning the reason for these fires, it is said that Yao, Yü, and Shun, the rulers of the four hundred regions of China, were virtuous in the sight of heaven and earth, yet they forbore to cut off the ends of the reeds and thorny plants wherewith they thatched their roofs, nor scraped the bark from their oaken rafters. It was indeed improper that the rulers of a small foreign country should have built such a great palace enclosure!

The great teacher of Kōya[46] understood this, thinking in his heart, "If rulers to come are lacking in virtue and think only to live in comfort, the wealth of the land will be expended wholly." When he wrote the name tablets for the buildings and gates,[47] he

[44] Kose no Kanaoka, a renowned painter of the early Heian period (fl. *ca.* 885–900).
[45] Ono no Tōfū (d. 966) was a master calligrapher of the tenth century.
[46] Kōbō Daishi.
[47] His calligraphy was famous.

took out the middle of the *dai* of Daigokuden, so that it became *hi*, which is to say fire, and instead of the *su* of Suzakumon he wrote *kome*, which is to say rice.

When Ono no Tōfū saw the tablets, he blamed the teacher of Kōya. But thereafter when Tōfū took up his brush his hand shook and his characters lacked correctness (perhaps it was a punishment for censuring the things prophetically written by a living buddha and great sage, and calling him ignorant). Yet because Tōfū was a person skilled in cursive writing, soon his brush became strong, though he wrote with a shaking hand.

But it came to pass that a fire broke out in the Daigokuden and burnt up all the offices and ministries. And it is said that, though they were rebuilt swiftly, they burnt again when the malevolent spirit of fire and thunder, a lesser god of the Shrine of Kitano Temman Tenjin, came down on the southwest pillar of the Seiryōden.

He that is called Temman Tenjin is the master of elegant accomplishments and the great preceptor of men of letters. In heaven he shows his brilliance to the sun and moon and illumines the land; on earth he became a minister of state and made the people flourish. To speak of his beginnings: Once on a time a little boy of four or five years stood alone in the south garden of Lord Zezen, the Sugawara consultant, a child most fair to behold, reciting a poem touching on the flowers of the garden.

Seized with amazement, Lord Zezen spoke a word to him, asking, "Whence are you come, and of whose family are you a son?"

"I have no father or mother," he said. "Will you not be my father?"

And rejoicing in his heart, Lord Zezen carried him on his shoulder, held him in his arms, and reared him lovingly inside doors of brocade. This was he who is known to men as the Kan minister of state.[48]

Now this child understood the way of things without being taught, unequaled in wit and learning. In his tenth year, his

---

[48] Sugawara no Michizane. See note 2, Chapter Six. Kan is the Sino-Japanese pronunciation of the Suga- of Sugawara.

father the Kan consultant smoothed his hair, asking, "Can you not compose a Chinese poem?" Whereupon tranquilly the boy spoke of the coldness of that night, and in clear words made a poem of five-word lines.

> Bright is the moonlight, as on new-fallen snow;
> Like shining stars are the blossoms of the plum.
> Alas! The golden mirror[49] runs its course,
> But in the courtyard there is a fragrant smell.

Thereafter his Chinese poems were abundantly inspired, their brilliance even as that of the poems of the great days of T'ang. His prose was as skillful as the prose of Han and Wei, and he committed a myriad scrolls of books to memory. Wherefore he succeeded beyond all others in the examinations on the twenty-third day of the third month of the twelfth year of Jōgan.

In the spring of the same year, it came to pass that men gathered together at the house of Miyako no Yoshika to shoot at archery. And the Kan minister of state likewise came to that place. Miyako no Yoshika thought in his heart:

"This lord is a person who is always studying, even by the light of fireflies. Surely he is unable to distinguish one part of a bow from another, since he can have no leisure to practice. Let us amuse ourselves by making him shoot."

So he thought, and put a bow and practice arrows in front of the Kan minister of state, saying, "Since it is the beginning of spring, amuse yourself for awhile."

The Kan minister of state did not draw back, but joined himself to a side. He bared his snowy skin to the waist, raised up and pulled down, steadied the bow for awhile, and let go an arrow. The five virtues of the skilled archer were displayed abundantly in the flight of that arrow, and in the twang of the bowstring and the turning over of the bow. Nor was his aim at all mistaken, but in five turns of two arrows each, he struck the mark ten times. And Miyako no Yoshika's heart was moved thereby, so that he came down, drew him by the hand, feasted him for many hours, and gave him presents of divers kinds.

On the twenty-sixth day of the second month of the same year,

[49] The moon.

the emperor of Engi⁵⁰ (being yet the crown prince), summoned the Kan minister of state and said to him:

"Surely you are as talented as Li Ch'iao of the court of Han, who wrote a hundred poems in one night. Compose ten Chinese verses within two hours, that the emperor may look upon them."

When the Kan minister of state received the ten subjects, in an hour he composed ten poems. Doubtless one of those ten was his poem speaking of the last days of spring:

> In sending off the spring
> I use no boat or carriage,
> But only say goodbye to the last bush warbler,
> And to the falling blossoms;
> And lodge tonight in a poet's house,⁵¹
> So that the spring may know my heart.

There was nothing lacking at all, not in men's praise of his wit and intelligence, nor in his following of the way of benevolence and righteousness. The emperor looked upon him with unbounded approbation, thinking, "Through this man alone will the sovereign's virtue become as that of the sage-rulers of Chinese antiquity, and the land will be ruled as by Confucius and the Duke of Chou." He rose from middle counselor to great counselor in the sixth month of the ninth year of Kampyō, and soon he became a grand marshal. When the emperor of Engi came to the throne in the tenth month of that year, all affairs of state were in his hands, and all military matters. No man could stand alongside him, not even a regent or a member of a ministerial family. And in the second month of the second year of Shōtai he became a great subject and grand marshal.

In those days there was a person called the Great Subject of the Main Cloister,⁵² a descendant of Fujiwara no Kamatari in the ninth generation, and the first son of Lord Shōsen. Because he was the elder brother of the empress and the uncle of Murakami Tenno, he thought, "By no means is any man my equal, whether he be of a regent family or of the highest lineage." It was most hateful to his

---

⁵⁰ Daigo Tenno (reigned 897–930). Engi was the era name given to the years 901–923.
⁵¹ Spend the night writing verses.
⁵² Fujiwara no Tokihira (871–909), who became the most powerful figure of his day.

heart that he was overreached by the Kan minister of state in office and rank, and in emoluments and rewards.[53] Plotting secretly with Lord Hikaru, Lord Tadakuni, and Sugane no Ason, he summoned the chief of the Bureau of Divination, buried dolls in the eight corners of the imperial dwelling place, and laid a curse on the Kan minister of state by worshiping the invisible powers. But because it is not the way of heaven to be unjust, no harm came to the august person of the minister.

Then the Great Subject of the Main Cloister thought, "If it be thus, I will speak evil words against him, that he may be punished and destroyed." Many times he spoke, saying, "The Kan minister of state governs the realm with a selfish heart, cares nothing for the people's misery, and makes wrong right." And thereupon the emperor thought:

"He is a treacherous minister, causing disorders and harming the people. He is not a loyal minister who censures what is wrong and prohibits what is unjust."

How unfortunate it was! "What man is this, who tells lies as smoothly as a piper plays? If he would prevail upon you to cover your nose, cover it not, lest husband and wife be made as two stars that never meet. If he would prevail upon you to pick up a bee, take it not, lest mother and son be made as wild beasts." [54] By a slanderer's false words may husband and wife be set apart, and parent and son, who ought to cherish one another as their own souls. How then might it be otherwise with sovereign and minister?

On the twentieth day of the first month of the fourth year of Shōtai, the emperor decreed, "The Kan minister of state shall be demoted to be deputy chief of the Dazaifu, and shall be sent forth in exile to Tsukushi."

Unable to bear the sorrow of being sent away, the Kan minister of state sent the former emperor a poem filled with a thousand

---

[53] This is incorrect, as becomes apparent later in the story.

[54] From a poem by Po Chü-i. A Chinese queen told a beautiful rival that the king disliked her nose, advising her to cover it. Then the queen told the king that the lady covered her nose because his smell was displeasing to her, whereupon the king cut off the offending member. Another woman put a bee into her clothing after first removing its sting. When her son tried to capture the insect, she screamed to her husband that he was assaulting her. The husband became suspicious of the son, who finally killed himself.

griefs: "Will not His Majesty become a weir to stop me where I float away?" The former emperor wept into his sleeve and took his way to the palace to prevail upon the sovereign to take back the punishment of exile, yet in the end he returned vainly, swallowing his anger, for the emperor would not come out to meet him.

Thereafter a sentence of banishment was handed down quickly, commanding the Kan minister of state to go forth to the Dazaifu. Among his twenty-three children, the four that were sons were set apart utterly, banished to provinces in every direction. His eldest daughter alone was suffered to remain in the capital, but eighteen daughters departed from the city weeping, to go to wearisome Tsukushi. How pitiful it was!

Then from the Red Plum Hall, his study for many years, the Kan minister of state went forth into the pale moonlight of dawn. Smelling the lingering fragrance of plum blossoms in his sleeve, he thought, "This alone is my memento of spring at home!" Tearfully he recited, "If an east wind blow, send me your fragrance, O blossoms of the plum; forget not the spring because your master is gone!"

He got up into his carriage, sped on his way by officials named to stop him from lingering on the journey, who said, "You must go as far as Yodo Crossing by nightfall."

May it not be that the minister's trees and plants grieved to part from him, albeit no hearts beat within them? For his plum tree flew away on a wind from the east and let down its roots in the garden of his exile dwelling. This is the very flying plum tree of the Dazaifu which spoke to a man in his dream, lamenting, "How cruel are you who break my branches!"

In the time of Ninna, when the Kan minister of state went down to be an official in the land of Sanuki, even as Kan Ning[55] he rode in a boat furnished with ropes of brocade, while poles of yew and oars of cassia wood struck against the sides beneath the moon of the southern seas. But when he went forth to exile in Shōtai, between waves and rush roofing he spread out the sleeve of a robe given him by the emperor in a bygone day, and thought on the

[55] An ostentatious rich man who lived during the Three Kingdoms period in China (220–280).

clouds of the Dazaifu with his heart in sorrow. Mourning for his wife and daughter left behind in the capital, he thought, "Yesterday's parting was the end"; grieving sorely to remember his eighteen sons[56] sent away to unknown lands, he thought tearfully, "Indeed, they must suffer in body and spirit as they go forth on these unexpected journeys."

In a Chinese poem he spoke of his feelings on that trip:

> Driven forth by the imperial commissioners,
> Father and sons are set apart in five places.
> My mouth cannot speak; there is blood in my eye.
> I bow myself down before the gods of heaven and earth.

When the messenger sent with him by his wife turned back on the way, he wrote, "Until they disappeared I looked back as I journeyed—the treetops beside your dwelling place."

Quickly the days and nights passed, until he came to the place of his exile at the Dazaifu. And the officials from the capital set him inside a wretched hut and went away home.

As the Kan minister of state gazed sadly upon the colored roof tiles of the Dazaifu tower and listened to the bell of the Temple of Kannon, the autumn became the autumn of his life. Morning and evening he thought of home, his tears growing thicker with every word that was spoken, so that the sleeves of his garments were never dry. Nor might it have been otherwise, even had he not yearned after his home, since he had been thus grievously and unjustly accused!

Now beyond endurance his bitterness entered into the marrow of his bones, that by false slanders he was condemned to be exiled. After purifying his body for seven days, he wrote a prayer to the gods, climbed up onto a high mountain, put up the prayer on the front of a pole, and for seven days stood on the tips of his toes. May it be that Brahma and Indra pitied him because of those slanders? For a black cloud came down from the sky, and took up the petition, and raised it to the distant heavens.

At last the Kan minister of state perished from the sorrow of his banishment, on the twenty-fifth day of the second month of the third year of Engi, and men made his grave in the place that is now

---

[56] The author is confusing Michizane's sons with his daughters.

the Anrakuji Temple. How sad it was that this spring flower of the imperial palace floated away, following the never-returning waters! How sad it was that this moon of the night of the western government[57] was obscured, entering the clouds of a false name! The noble and the base shed tears, longing for a world where honesty and sincerity might flourish; the far and the near were silent, sorrowing to live in an era of degeneracy.

Late in the summer of that same year, a certain Hosshōbō was sojourning on top of the Hill of the Four Brightnesses, purifying the waters of his mind in the moonlight shining before the floor of the Ten Ways to Buddhahood: Hosshōbō the thirteenth abbot of the Enryakuji, who was also called Son'i, and received the title of monk reformer after his death. Suddenly there came a noise of someone knocking at the Personal Buddha Hall.[58] And when Hosshōbō opened the door he beheld the Kan minister of state, even he of whom men said, "Assuredly he died last spring in Tsukushi."

Seized with amazement Hosshōbō invited the minister to enter, saying, "Please come in." Again he said:

"Truly did I hear that you died in Tsukushi on the twenty-fifth day of the second month, wherefore I wept into my sleeve bitterly, and constantly performed pious works to pray for your enlightenment in the afterlife. Do I wake or dream, that now you come here looking exactly as before?"

So he spoke, and the Kan minister of state wiped away the tears falling one after another onto his face. He spoke a word to Hosshōbō, saying:

"For a time I descended among men to bring tranquility to the realm by acting as a minister of the court. Yet because His Majesty believed in the slanders of Lord Tokihira, at last I sank beneath an unjust punishment. More fierce than the flames of a kalpa-fire[59] is the heat of my wrath! Though my body is destroyed, that was made up of the five skandhas, assuredly my spirit lives on in heaven. Having obtained leave to wreak my vengeance from the

---

[57] The government of Kyushu.
[58] See note 31, Chapter Two.
[59] See note 3, Chapter Eight.

great and small divinities, and from Brahma, Indra, and the Four Kings, I am resolved to draw near to the ninefold imperial palace to kick to death the crafty courtiers and slanderers who used me ill, the one after the other. The court will certainly call upon the Mountain Gate to perform the mystic rites of absolute control,[60] but do you refrain utterly from going forth to the palace, though the emperor himself send a command."

"My debt is not small to you who were my teacher," said the monk reformer, "yet neither is my duty to the emperor an inconsequential thing. Though I turn away once, must I not go to the palace if His Majesty summons me a second or third time?"

Then suddenly the face of the Kan minister of state grew wroth. He took up a pomegranate from before him, crunched it with his teeth, and spit it out against the door of the hall. And the seeds became a violent fire, burning the door. Yet the monk reformer was in no wise affrighted, but turned his face toward the burning fire, made the water-sprinkling sign with his hands, and extinguished the fierce flames in an instant, so that the door was but half burnt. Men say that this very door stands today at the Mountain Gate.

Thereafter, the Kan minister of state stood up and ascended into the heavens. Soon thunder rolled high and low above the imperial palace, as though high heaven itself were like to fall down to earth, and the great earth itself were to be rent in twain, and the emperor and the hundred officials made their bodies small, their spirits fainting within them. For seven days and seven nights the rain came down mightily, while a tempest blew and darkness covered the earth. Even as the suffering in the Hell of Crying and Wailing, or in the Hell of Great Crying,[61] even so were the crying voices of the high and low of the capital and Shirakawa, and of the men and women, for the people's houses were swept away in the flooding waters.

At last a thunderbolt fell down onto the Seiryōden in the great palace enclosure, lighting a fire in the outer robes of the Great Counselor Lord Kiyotsura such as would not be put out, though

---

[60] Over all influences, whether good or evil.
[61] The Hell of Crying and Wailing and the Hell of Great Crying are the fourth and fifth of the eight hot hells of Buddhism.

Chapter 12

he laid his body down and rolled over and over. Mareyo no Ason arranged an arrow along his bowstring and turned his face toward the thunder (a brave man, a Controller of the Right). And he spoke a word to it, saying, "Whatever kind of thunder you may be, do you not tremble before the imperial authority?" But a palsy seized Mareyo's five members, and he fell down on his face. Next the side hair of Konoe no Tadakane caught fire, so that he burned to death, and Ki no Kagetsura perished choking in the smoke.

Now the Great Subject of the Main Cloister thought in his heart, "Alas! A divine punishment is visited upon me!" Standing near the emperor's side, he drew forth his sword, saying:

"When you served at the court, you were not lacking in propriety toward me.[62] Though you are become a god, do you no longer owe a duty to the emperor? If you revere the Son of Heaven and have not refused to be a protecting divinity, then be quiet awhile, and tranquilly make your virtue felt."

So he spoke to him with reasonable words. Perhaps the thunder god became quiet because of his logic, for he climbed up to heaven, not striking down the Great Subject Tokihira or harming the emperor.

The rain and wind continued upon the earth until the world was like to wash away, with all the lands thereof. And therefore the emperor called upon Hosshōbō, saying, "Let Us appease the wrath of the god through the power of the Buddhist Law." Hosshōbō excused himself once and twice, yet the emperor summoned him a third time. Whereupon indeed he went down to the capital, for he could do no other.

The Kamo River was swollen so greatly that none might cross over it save in a boat. But the monk reformer commanded, "Let my carriage enter the water." And when the ox driver hastened to take the carriage into the overflowing river according to his command, the flood waters parted to the left and right, so that the carriage passed over the ground.

From the time that this monk reformer went to the palace,

---

[62] Tokihira outranked Michizane in the official hierarchy, and therefore was entitled to respectful treatment from him. (Tokihira had actually been dead for twenty-two years when lightning struck the Seiryōden.)

the rain stopped and the wind was stilled, as though the wrath of the god had been appeased instantly. The emperor looked graciously upon him, and he climbed back up to the mountain. Men say that it is because of this that all the realm praises the miraculous powers of the Mountain Gate.

Thereafter it came to pass that the Great Subject of the Main Cloister was taken of a sickness whereby his body and spirit were tormented everlastingly. And he begged the reverend father Jōzō to pray for him. But then a small blue snake thrust out its head from the left ear of the Great Subject, and likewise from the right ear, and spoke to the reverend father Jōzō, saying:

"It is in my heart to kill this minister to be avenged of his false slanders. Your prayers and healing will be of no avail. If you wish to know who it is that speaks in this way, I am the god Temman Daijizai Tenjin, even he who was once the Kan minister of state."

The reverend father Jōzō left off praying and went away, affrighted by the strangeness of the revelation, and at once the Great Subject of the Main Cloister died. Likewise, his daughter died very soon, she who was an imperial handmaiden, and his grandson the crown prince.

In the same way the second son of the Great Subject of the Main Cloister was smitten of a grievous disease, the grand marshal Yasutada of the Eighth Ward. And a monk attended on him, reciting the *Sutra of the Healing Buddha.* When this monk read loudly, "the general Kumbhīra," [63] it came to Yasutada's ears as the voice of one saying, *"kubi kiran,"* which is to say, "I will cut off your head," and he died. Also Tokihira's third son, Atsutada the Middle Counselor, died in the early years of his life. Awe-inspiring indeed was the divine punishment that instantly destroyed this man, his children and his grandchildren!

Around that time there was a cousin of the emperor of Engi who died suddenly for no reason, a person called Kintada the Great Controller of the Right. Three days later this Kintada came alive with a great sigh, saying:

"I have a thing to tell to the throne. Help me up, for I would go to the palace."

---

[63] One of the twelve divine generals of Yakushi, the Healing Buddha.

And he went forth to the palace with his sons Nobuaki and Nobutaka supporting him on the left and right.

When the emperor asked Kintada, "What is your business?" Kintada trembled exceedingly, saying:

"To a most terrible place have I been, called the court of the judges of hell. There I beheld a man more than ten feet tall, correctly attired in robes and a high-crowned cap. He offered up a memorial rolled on a golden roller, that said:

"'There is a ruler of a small country who has sinned most grievously, one known to men as the emperor of Engi. For he believed in the slander of the Great Subject Tokihira, and sent a blameless minister into exile. Let the court quickly decree that he be dropped into the Hell of Constant Scorching.'

"So he spoke, and the thirty judges of hell were greatly angered, agreeing, 'He shall be condemned at once.' Then the second of those judges said, 'What if he shall apologize for his fault by changing the name of the era?' And all were as though troubled in their hearts. Thereafter, I came alive again."

So he spoke, and the emperor, sorely affrighted, changed the name of the era from Engi to Enchō. He burned the imperial decree commanding the Kan minister of state to go forth into exile, made him a Great Subject again, and promoted him a grade to senior second rank.

Thereafter in the ninth year of Tengyō, a commission was given to Mibu no Yoshitane, a priest of Hirano Shrine in the land of Ōmi, to build a shrine at Kitano hard by the great palace enclosure, even on the spot where the thousand pine trees grew up miraculously in one night.[64] And men worshiped the Kan minister of state therein, calling him Temman Daijizai Tenjin.

Although it was so, perhaps the one hundred and sixty-eight thousand gods were not yet tranquil, those who owed allegiance to that divinity. For three times the divers offices and eight ministries burnt down in the twenty-five years between the second year of Tentoku and the fifth year of Tengen.

After one of these burnings, there was a certain pillar, newly erected by the cunning builders wielding their axes to build the

[64] See note 2, Chapter Six.

buildings of the great palace enclosure, whereon a verse appeared, saying, "Though it be built, again will it burn, till Sugawara's heart be set at ease."

Fearfully the Emperor Ichijō thought, "From this verse may we know that the god's heart is not yet satisfied." He gave the Kan minister of state the title of Great Subject of the Grand Preceptorate, honored him with the senior grade of the first rank, and sent an imperial messenger to the Anrakuji to read the decree aloud.

Then indeed a voice was heard in the sky, reciting a Chinese poem:

> Yesterday I was made wretched by the court;
> Today in the City of the West
> Honor is restored to my dead body.
> What are these things to me—
> This sorrow in life and joy in death?
> Now I shall be content
> To guard the imperial throne.

Thereafter, the god's wrath was appeased, and the land was at peace. How awesome it was!

If you would know the true being of this god, he is the greatly benevolent and greatly compassionate Kanzeon, through whose vows vast as the sea all living things reach the opposite shore of salvation. If we speak of his manifestation as a god, he is Temman Daijizai Tenjin, who every day anew helps all living things, and fulfills the desires of all who come to him. There is none but bows his head in deep reverence before him, from the emperor on high to the myriad folk below. Truly his is a praiseworthy and unequaled shrine!

[*End of biography*]

In the past there was a rebuilding of the palace that began on the fourteenth day of the eighth month of the fourth year of Jiryaku, and the emperor removed thereto on the fifteenth day of the fourth month of the fourth year of Enkyū, in the august reign of Go-Sanjō-in. It was a most auspicious occasion, with Chinese verses presented by men of letters, and music offered up by

Chapter 12

musicians. Yet very soon all of the buildings in the great palace enclosure burned down again, in the second year of Angen, because of a curse of the Hiyoshi King of the Mountain. Thereafter, the strength of the nation waned, and until this time of Go-Daigo Tenno none among the generations of sage rulers set his hand to the work of rebuilding.

But now it was said, "The great palace enclosure must be rebuilt," though truly the world was disordered from war, the nation was wearied, and the people suffered. (For not yet were the horses sent back south of Flower Mountain, nor the oxen released in the fields of Peace Grove.) [65] Paper money was made, such as was not used in our country from ancient times until the present; and taxes and requisitions of labor were laid on the lands of the stewards and housemen of all the provinces. Wherefore, many men of understanding knit their eyebrows, saying, "It is contrary to the will of the gods, and extremely arrogant."

The Rites for the Pacification of the State, and the Rewards Given to the Grand Marshals

Around the spring of the third year of Genkō, kinsmen of the Heike rose in Tsukushi: Kiku Kamon-no-suke Takamasa and Itoda Sakon-no-taifu Sadayoshi. These gathered together men remaining from those who had been destroyed before, and invited traitors in divers places to join them in disordering the nation. Likewise, rebels in the province of Kawachi built a fortress on Iimori Mountain, raising up a person called the Sasame monk reformer Kembō to be their general. Moreover, in the province of Iyo there was a person called Suruga Tarō Shigetoki, a son of the Akahashi governor of Suruga, who built a castle on Tate-eboshi Peak, whence he spoiled and conquered the estates on all sides.

The courtiers made haste to raise up an altar in the imperial chamber of the Shishinden, whereto they summoned the Take-

---

[65] When Wu Wang, the founder of the Chou dynasty, conquered the last ruler of Shang, he sent away his war horses south of Flower Mountain and released his oxen in the fields of Peace Grove, since they were no longer needed for military campaigns.

nouchi monk reformer Jigon to pray for peace in the land. For they said, "We must add the power of the Buddhist Law to our warlike might, if we would bring down the rebels quickly."

When Jigon offered these prayers, armed warriors guarded the four gates, while the ministers in charge of arrangements stood below the steps with the members of the proximate guards. And before the musicians began to play, warriors lined up on the left and right in the South Garden to pacify the four directions with drawn swords.

Those who guarded the four gates were Yūki Shichirō Saemon Chikamitsu, Kusunoki Masashige the governor of Kawachi, En'ya Hōgan Takasada, and Nawa Nagatoshi the governor of Hōki. Those who were summoned to duty in the South Garden were Miura no Suke on the right and Chiba Ōsuke Sadatane on the left. At first Miura and Chiba consented to serve, but at the last they held back and would not come. For it was hateful to Chiba's heart to be Miura's partner, and likewise Miura was wroth that he was commanded to stand on the right of Chiba. Even thus by the interference of evil spirits was a holy gathering disordered! When one thinks about it afterward, this was a sign that the realm would not be at peace for long.

Perhaps because of the efficacy of Jigon's prayers, Iimori castle was brought down by Masashige, Tate-eboshi castle was conquered by Doi and Tokunō, and the rebels in Tsukushi were defeated by Ōtomo and Shōni. The heads of the court's enemies were sent to the capital to be paraded through the avenues and hung up before men's eyes.

Then the eastern and western provinces being quiet, in more than seven hundred great boats Shōni and Ōtomo came to the capital from Tsukushi, with Kikuchi and Matsuura; with more than seven thousand riders came Nitta Sama-no-suke Yoshisada and his brother Hyōgo-no-suke. All the warriors of the provinces came up and gathered together, filling the capital and Shirakawa, until the wealth and dignity of the imperial city increased a hundredfold.

Now it was thought, "Though for a time we may delay to reward the armies, we must make amends swiftly to those who have done the greatest deeds." To Ashikaga Jibu-no-tayū Takauji were given

Chapter 12

the three provinces of Musashi, Hitachi, and Shimōsa; to his younger brother Sama-no-kami Tadayoshi was given the province of Tōtōmi; to Nitta Sama-no-suke Yoshisada were given the two provinces of Kōzuke and Harima, to his son Yoshiaki the province of Echigo, and to his younger brother Hyōgo-no-suke Yoshisuke the province of Suruga; to Kusunoki Hōgan Masashige were given Settsu and Kawachi; and to Nawa Nagatoshi the governor of Hōki were given the two provinces of Inaba and Hōki. Likewise were two or three provinces given to other nobles and warriors. But to the lay monk Akamatsu Enshin was given only the single estate of Sayo, though his military exploits had not been slight; moreover, his appointment to be protector of the province of Harima was soon taken back. It is said that it was because of this that Enshin quickly changed his heart and became an enemy of the court in the Disturbance of Kemmu.

For the rest, the offices of protector and governor in more than fifty provinces were received by nobles and court officials; likewise, confiscated lands and great estates were given them, until they became as rich and powerful as T'ao Chu[66] and were as satiated with food and clothing as those who benefited from the labors of Cheng and Po.[67]

The Extravagance of Lord Chigusa and the Monk Reformer Monkan; the Matter of the Most Holy Gedatsu

It had been fitting that the Chigusa Middle Marshal Tadaaki should look joyfully upon learning as his calling, since he was a grandson of Lord Arifusa, the Great Subject of the Interior of the Sixth Ward. Yet from the age of nineteen Tadaaki's taste was for such unseemly things as hat shooting and dog chasing, and he gave himself over so completely to gaming and lechery that his father Lord Aritada broke the tie between father and child, unwilling to call him son. But perhaps it was Tadaaki's karma from the past that he should prosper for a time. For because he accompanied the su-

---

[66] The name adopted by Fan Li (Chapter Four), who became very wealthy in later life.

[67] Two Chinese engineers of the Era of Warring States (403–221 B.C.). They constructed canals which greatly increased the yield of the fields.

preme highness to Oki and attacked the men of Rokuhara, he was rewarded most amazingly beyond his station with three large provinces and several tens of seized estates. Daily he prepared drinking banquets for favored housemen and gathered together more than three hundred warriors of fifth rank in his halls. Not ten thousand pieces of money would be enough to pay even once for the wines, fishes, and choice foods that he served up! Likewise, he built stables a hundred yards long, wherein he stabled fifty or sixty horses satiated with food. When he left off drinking, he went out toward Uchino or the Northern Hills with several hundred riders in search of diversion, passing the day in sending out dogs or hunting small birds with falcons. He wore leg guards made of leopard skin or tiger skin, and trousers and coats of gold brocade or spotted white cloth. How shocking it was that he was not shamed by the admonition of Kung An-kuo, who said, "For the base to wear the clothes of the noble is called arrogance. Those who are arrogant and lacking in propriety are a nation's treacherous men"!

After all, these were not things to be remarked greatly, since Tadaaki was of the laity. But truly it is strange to hear of the behavior of the monk reformer Monkan! In vain had Monkan left the world of renown and profit to meditate on the three mystic things,[68] for he thought only of gain and reputation, caring nothing for holy contemplation. Beyond all need he piled up goods and treasures in storehouses, instead of rendering aid to those who were poor and in want. He gathered together arms of war, kept soldiers in very great numbers, and gave presents for nothing to people who flattered him and formed a tie with him, so that the city was filled with men who said, "We are retainers of the monk reformer Monkan," and banded together with outspread elbows, five or six hundred of them. Even when he traveled the short distance to the palace, several hundred warriors on horseback encompassed his litter about, behaving as they pleased on the way. Quickly were his holy garments soiled by the dust from horses' feet; quickly his lack of propriety called forth words of censure from men's mouths.

[68] The body, voice, and mind of the Buddha.

Chapter 12

Now the teacher of the law Hui-yüan[69] of Lu Mountain vowed never to forsake his mountain, even from the time when he left the realm of worldly annoyances to seat himself in the chamber of solitude. He joined together the Eighteen Wise and Holy Ones,[70] and for many years exerted himself in worship and praise six times a day. Likewise, the Harmonious Reverence Fa-ch'ang[71] of Ta-hai moved his thatched abode far from the ways of men, thinking, "By no means will I allow my dwelling place to be known." He recited poems that sang of the pleasure of living in the mountains, and his master affirmed that he achieved enlightenment.

So right-thinking monks of ancient and recent times have ever wrapped up their light and wiped out their tracks. All their lives, they have followed the clouds hanging over the mountains at dusk, taken pond lotuses as garments, practiced virtue, and purified their hearts. Wherefore it was no common thing that in this wise the monk reformer Monkan was tied by the bonds of renown and profit. May it not be that demons and heretics took possession of his heart, causing him to behave in that way?

[*There follows a digression designed to illustrate the conduct becoming to a monk.*]

If you would know why I say this: Around the time of Bunji there was a certain monk of the capital called the Most Holy Gedatsu. This Gedatsu's mother thought in her heart, "My son is not as other men," for she bore him after she dreamed of swallowing a hand bell, in the seventeenth year of her life. When he was in his third year, she sent him to a monastery to become a holy saint. And because Gedatsu was compassionate and wise, he did not regret the rents in his three garments; because he was good and virtuous in thought, word, and deed, he did not lament the emptiness of his single bowl. He walked in the dust of the impure world (for the man who truly lives apart does not reject the haunts

---

[69] The famous founder of the Pure Land sect in China (333–416). He stayed on Lu Mountain for thirty years without leaving it.
[70] Members of his religious community.
[71] A Chinese monk of the T'ang period.

of men), yet his mind was not invaded by the fog of the three poisons.[72] Trusting to fate, he passed the months and years; helping living things, he went on foot across mountains and rivers.

Once this holy man went to the Grand Shrine of Ise to worship at the Outer and Inner Shrines and speak secretly of the delights of complete response to the teachings of Buddhism.[73] These shrines are not as other shrines, for their bargeboards are not curved, nor do their pointed boards bend backward. Wherefore it seemed to Gedatsu that they were as "the straight way that rejects what is roundabout." [74] And beholding the ancient pines lowering their branches and the old trees spreading out their leaves, he likened them to bodhisattvas descending from heaven to save living things here below.

"Although the names of the Three Treasures of Buddhism may not be spoken here," he thought weeping, "yet in this way too men may reach salvation."

When the day was done, the holy man began to pass the hours of the night reciting the name of Amida Buddha in front of the Outer Shrine, for it was in his heart that he would not lodge in a house. He turned aside sleep with the pine wind from Kamiji Mountain and purified his spirit in the moonlight on the Mimosuso River. But suddenly the sky grew cloudy, rain and wind blew violently, and there came a noise of galloping horses above the clouds, pulling thunderous carriages from the east and west.

"Alas, how terrible! What can it be?" Gedatsu said, fainting with fright.

As he watched, palace buildings appeared in the heavens, and towers and pavilions, with curtains in the courtyards and hangings before the gates. It seemed that there were two or three thousand guests come thither in horse-drawn carriages from the ten directions, who sat in two long lines on the left and right. To the place of honor there came a giant, most extraordinary to behold, borne by eight dragons. He was two hundred or three hun-

---

[72] Wrong desire, hatred, and stupidity.
[73] Buddhist preaching was not permitted at these most revered of Shinto shrines.
[74] The One Vehicle doctrine of the Tendai sect. The quotation is from the *Lotus Sutra*.

Chapter 12

dred feet tall, with twelve demon heads and forty-two arms on the left and right, grasping the sun and moon and holding up weapons. Nor were his followers ordinary men. There were some among them with eight arms and six legs, who pressed iron shields to their sides, and others with three heads, who wore metal armor on their bodies.

When all had sat down, each in his appointed place, the giant spoke to those on the left and right, saying:

"Because I have won a victory in battle against Indra, I have laid hands on the sun and moon, taken up my abode on the summit of Mount Sumeru, and trod on the great sea with one foot, yet daily are many myriads of my followers destroyed. The cause thereof is a saint called Gedatsu, who has come forth in the neighborhood of the capital of the Country of the Extreme East in the world of men. By reason of his instruction and guidance and his assistance to living things, the power of the Buddhist Law has waxed great and Indra the King of Heaven has become strong. The demons have been made weak; the asuras have lost their power. While Gedatsu is thus, we cannot prevail in battle against the King of Heaven. In some way we must work upon his spirit which seeks enlightenment, so that his heart will become arrogant and lazy."

Thereupon one came forward into the middle of the assembly with his name writ in golden letters on the front of his helmet: Māra the King of the Sixth Heaven.[75] Māra spoke a word, saying:

"It will be easy to work upon his heart which seeks enlightenment. First we shall put it into the mind of Go-Toba-in to destroy the Hōjō family, so that he will go forth against Rokuhara. Yoshitoki will certainly fight against the imperial armies, whereupon we shall lend him strength to defeat them. When Go-Toba-in is sent away to a distant land, Yoshitoki will rule the realm and look to the government of the state. And will he not place the second princely son of Hirose-no-in[76] upon the throne? Then Gedatsu will be made a court monk, since he is the sage to whom that prince

---

[75] A wicked god, the enemy of Buddhist saints.
[76] A son of Takakura Tenno (reigned 1168–1180). Hirose-no-in's second son was Go-Horikawa (reigned 1221–1232), the emperor selected by the Hōjō after the Disturbance of Shōkyū.

turns in matters of religion. Attending closely upon the emperor, he will concern himself with the ceremony of serving at court. Daily from that time he will become more neglectful in thought, word, and deed, and his pride will increase constantly until he becomes a rule-breaking, shameless monk. Likewise, in this way we shall gain new followers."

The demons and heretics lined up in two rows all agreed, "What he says is entirely correct." And they flew away to the east and west.

Hearing these things the holy man wept tears of joy, thinking, "This is a kindness to me from Amaterasu,[77] who encourages me to seek enlightenment."

Thereafter he did not return to the capital, but abode in a cave in the mountain called Kasagi in the land of Yamashiro, gathering fallen leaves to make his robes and picking up fruits, nuts, and berries to be his food. For long he sought to leave this impure world, and prayed constantly with all his might to go to the Pure Land.

When Gedatsu had passed three or four years in this manner, men strove together in the Disturbance of Shōkyū. Yoshitoki ruled the realm, Go-Toba-in was banished, and the princely son of Hirose-no-in sat upon the throne. When the new emperor heard that the Most Holy Gedatsu abode in the cave at Kasagi, again and again he sent imperial messengers to summon him, that he might make him a monk of the court.

"Indeed, it is as Māra the King of the Sixth Heaven said," thought the holy man.

Nor did he obey the command, but zealously practiced austerities to purify his heart. And his wisdom and virtue grew so great that at last he became the founder of a temple where even today the Buddhist Law flourishes and spreads.

[*End of digression*]

If we think of this person in the light of that one, how dreadful was the behavior of the Most Holy Monkan, who thus foolishly suffered his eyes to be blinded! When very soon the Disturbance of Kemmu began, he became a solitary beggar with no disciple to

---
[77] The Sun Goddess, enshrined at Ise.

Chapter 12 371

inherit his teachings, and wandered around in the neighborhood of Yoshino until he died. Or so we have heard.

Hiroari Shoots a Strange Bird

In the seventh month of the third year of Genkō, the court changed the name of the era to Kemmu. (It may be that they imitated an era name of the Han court, saying, "It is an auspicious precedent that Kuang Wu of Later Han put down the disturbance of Wang Mang, and again continued the rule of Han.") [78] There was a pestilence in that year, and the numbers of those who sickened and died were exceedingly great. Moreover, from around autumn a strange bird came out above the Shishinden, crying, "How long? How long?" with a voice that echoed in the clouds and awoke men from their sleep. All who heard it detested it and feared it.

The courtiers consulted together, saying:

"Long ago in a different land ten suns came forth, even in the days of Yao. And a person named I shot down nine of those suns, according to the command of Yao. Likewise in ancient days in our country, when Horikawa-in sat upon the throne, there was an apparition distressful to the emperor, and Yoshiie[79] the former governor of Mutsu stood at the lower entrance to the hall, where three times he twanged his bowstring to quiet it, according to the imperial command. Likewise, when Konoe-in sat upon the throne, by imperial command did Yorimasa the Minamoto minister of third rank shoot down a bird called the *nue,* that flew and cried in the clouds. Since there are these precedents, let someone from among the Genji shoot at this bird."

But although they asked, none said, "I will do it," for perhaps every man thought in his heart, "I shall be dishonored in my lifetime, should I fail to hit it."

"If it is thus," said the emperor, "let a worthy man be chosen

[78] Wang Mang ruled China briefly between the Former Han (202 B.C.–A.D. 9) and Later Han (A.D. 25–220) dynasties. Kuang Wu, the first emperor of the Later Han, adopted Chien-wu (Japanese Kemmu) as an era name.

[79] See note 7, Chapter Seven.

from among the senior members of the former emperor's palace guards." [80]

Then there was one who said, "Oki no Jirō Saemon Hiroari is a worthy man, he who is in the service of His Lordship the Nijō regent."

"Let him be summoned immediately," said the emperor.

And they called Hiroari forth.

Hiroari answered the summons, standing near the Bell Chamber of the Seiryōden. Nor was he unwilling, but assented respectfully, thinking, "If this bird is as small as a mite nesting in a mosquito's eyelash, an arrow cannot strike it, or if it flies far away in the air, I cannot kill it. But if it is a bird visible to a man's eye, and if it flies within the compass of an arrow, come what may I shall not fail to hit it." He drew up the bow and arrows that a servant fetched for him, hid in the shadow of the outer veranda, and spied out the situation of the bird.

The air was pure and clear, and the shining of the moon was exceedingly bright, it being the seventeenth night of the eighth month. Yet above the palace there hung a black cloud, whence unceasingly the bird cried out. When it called, did it not vomit flames from its mouth? For there were flashes of lightning coming together with the sound of its voice, such as pierced the august screens with their brightness.

When Hiroari had made sure of the bird's abiding place, he strung his bow, moistened the string with his mouth, fitted in a humming-bulb arrow and took his aim. The supreme highness came out to the South Hall to watch, and men stood sleeve to sleeve above the stairs and below: His Highness the regent, grand marshals of the left and right, great counselors and middle counselors, the eight consultants and seven controllers, ministers and assistant ministers of the eight ministries, and warriors in the service of divers houses. And all the civil and military officials looked on, holding their breath and clenching their fists.

Hiroari turned his face toward the bird, ready to pull back the bowstring. First he took off the two-pronged arrowhead fitted to

---

[80] An elite corps of warriors.

his humming-bulb arrow and cast it away, as though a thought of some kind had entered his mind. Then strongly and fully in the great bow he drew back his arrow, one that measured twelve hands and the breadth of two fingers. Yet not lightly did he suffer it to fly on its way, but awaited the crying voice of the bird.

The bird flew down beyond his wont, crying out two hundred feet above the Shishinden. And listening attentively, Hiroari released the arrow with a mighty twang.

The humming-bulb sang and echoed above the Shishinden until it found its mark within the cloud, whereupon at once a thing dropped down from the eaves of the Jijuden with a sound as of the falling of a large stone, and lay doubled up in front of one of the clusters of bamboo.

All the men above the stairs and below called out together, "Ah, he has hit it! He has hit it!" For an hour their admiring voices clamored, nor was there any time when they were quiet.

The emperor caused men of the imperial guard to hold pine torches on high, that he might gaze upon the bird. And he saw that the head was as the head of a man, and the body as that of a snake. The bill was crooked in front, with saw teeth, and there were long spurs on the legs, as sharp as swords. When the wing tips were stretched out, its length was sixteen feet from end to end.

"When Hiroari shot, why did he take off the two-pronged arrowhead and cast it away?" asked the emperor.

Respectfully Hiroari answered:

"Because the bird called above the palace, therefore I took off the two-pronged arrowhead and cast it away. It would have been a vexatious thing had my arrow fallen down and stood on top of the august building."

By these words Hiroari found increased favor in the sight of the supreme highness. Quickly that night he was invested with the fifth rank, and the next day he received two large estates in the province of Inaba. Surely his fame as an archer will endure for all time!

The Matter of the Garden of Divine Waters

Soon the emperor set his hand to restore the Garden of Divine Waters, thinking:

"Although the war is ended, strange portents continue to tell of evil to come. For turning away calamity, what can be more efficacious than the mysteries of the True Word?"

[*The remainder of this section is devoted to a history of the garden.*]

Now this Garden of Divine Waters was a garden twenty yards long on the four sides, modelled after the Divine Park of King Wen of Chou, that was laid out when first the great palace enclosure was built.[81] Thereafter, in the august reign of the Emperor Kammu two temples were established on the east and west of Suzakumon Gate. The one on the left was called the Eastern Temple, and the one on the right was called the Western Temple. In the Eastern Temple Kōbō Daishi of Mount Kōya enshrined the more than seven hundred images of the Womb Treasury[82] to guard the throne, while in the Western Temple the monk reformer Shubin of the southern capital displayed the more than five hundred images of the Diamond Realm[83] to pray for the long life of the emperor.

Around the spring of the twenty-third year of Enryaku, in the august reign of Kammu Tennō, it came to pass that Kōbō Daishi crossed the seas to T'ang in search of the Law. And Kōbō Daishi being thus absent, the monk reformer Shubin alone attended closely upon the dragon countenance, reciting prayers in the morning and evening.

Once when the emperor had called for water wherewith to wash his hands, the water that was brought him was exceedingly cold, so that he put it aside for awhile (for indeed it was frozen). Shubin

---

[81] As the story told below suggests, the lake which was to give the garden its name was not added until later.

[82] The images were in a mandala depicting the deities of the Womb Treasury, or material world. There are usually 414 figures in such a mandala, but the number varies.

[83] I.e., he displayed a mandala depicting the deities of the Diamond Realm, or eternal world.

made the fire sign in front of that water, and behold: the ice melted instantly, becoming as boiling water. And the emperor marveled exceedingly.

Thereupon the emperor caused an abundance of charcoal to be burned in a brazier and commanded sliding doors to be placed around it, so that the heat might remain inside. When the air in the cold chamber had become as in the third month of spring, wiping away the sweat from his face, the emperor said, "Try to put out this fire." Shubin made the water sign in front of the fire, and behold: the blazing flames were extinguished instantly, becoming as cold ashes. And a chill pierced men's flesh, as though water had been poured over their bodies.

Thereafter, many strange and miraculous things of this kind were wrought by Shubin, until the emperor's trust and admiration waxed exceeding great.

Now Kōbō Daishi returned to Japan and came to the palace. And when the emperor had inquired concerning other lands, he spoke to Kōbō Daishi concerning the marvels wrought by the monk reformer Shubin. But Kōbō Daishi spoke derisive words, saying:

"When Aśvaghoṣa raised the curtain, the evil spirit fled with closed lips;[84] when Candana worshiped the heretical stupa, it fell apart.[85] I do not believe that Shubin will perform such miracles when I am present."

So he spoke, and the emperor thought, "If it is thus, We shall cause these two men to work miracles, that We may see whose virtue is the stronger." And on a certain occasion when Kōbō Daishi had come to the palace, he hid him by his side and commanded Shubin to serve before him.

Just at that time His Majesty was making ready to drink a

---

[84] A certain brahman covenanted with an evil spirit, through whose power he was able to overcome all the learned men of his day in disputations. In order to conceal the fact that he was receiving such assistance, he invariably sat behind a curtain when confronting an adversary. He was discredited by the celebrated Buddhist teacher Aśvaghoṣa (first century A.D.?), who outargued the demon and raised the curtain.

[85] Candana, a Buddhist king of Central Asia, bowed before a stupa without knowing that it had been erected by the followers of another religion. The stupa fell apart, unable to stand before the king's virtue.

medicinal brew. He set the bowl aside, saying to Shubin, "This liquid is too cold. Please perform rites as usual to make it warm."

"There will be no difficulty about it," thought Shubin.

He prayed with the fire sign, facing the bowl, yet the liquid would not grow hot. The emperor winked at his attendants, saying, "This is very odd." And a lady in waiting poured in some water, boiled for this purpose.

Again the emperor raised the hot liquid to drink, and again he laid the bowl down, saying, "This is too hot to hold." Not profiting from previous experience, Shubin again faced the bowl and made the cold water sign. Yet the hot liquid did not cool, but boiled within the bowl as before. And because of these two failures, Shubin lost color and was sore at heart.

Thereupon Kōbō Daishi came out laughing from behind a sliding door, saying:

"How now, Shubin? Did you not know of my presence? The radiance of the stars pales before the morning sun; the fireflies grow dark before the dawn moon."

So he spoke, and Shubin went away in chagrin, suppressing dejection and concealing anger.

Now Shubin's resentment against the emperor entered deep into the marrow of his bones.

"I will cause a great drought to afflict the realm, that all men within the four seas may suffer from hunger and thirst," he thought.

Capturing the dragon-gods who dwell in the vast universe of the three kinds of thousands of worlds, he shut them up in a tiny water jar, wherefore no rain fell for three months, even from the beginning of summer.[86] The farmers forbore to go forth to toil in the fields, and all the realm suffered because of the emperor's transgression.

Grieved that this calamity afflicted the folk, the emperor summoned Kōbō Daishi to pray for rain. And according to the imperial command, Kōbō Daishi composed his mind in a trance for seven days, looking clearly into the three kinds of thousands of worlds. He saw that the dragon-gods of near and distant seas were all shut

---

[86] Because the dragon-gods are rain-bringers.

Chapter 12

up in a water jar by the power of Shubin's spell, wherefore there were no dragon spirits to cause rain to fall. But there was one dragon king called Zennyo, dwelling in Heatless Lake northward from the Great Snowy Mountains on the border of northern India. Because he was a higher bodhisattva than Shubin, he alone had not responded to Shubin's summons, but had stayed in Heatless Lake.

When Kōbō Daishi awoke from his trance, he told these things to the emperor, who at once caused a lake to be dug in front of the palace enclosure, filled it with fresh cool water, and prayed the dragon king to come there. The dragon king Zennyo indeed came to the lake in the guise of a golden dragon ten inches long, riding on a nine-foot snake. And when his coming was reported to the throne, all the court marveled exceedingly.

Then as the emperor's representative, Wake no Matsuna worshiped the dragon king with paper strips[87] and offerings of divers kinds, whereupon moist clouds welled up, rain fell upon all the land for three days without ceasing, and the calamity of the drought was ended utterly. From this time on, the emperor's reverence for the teachings of the True Word [88] waxed stronger and stronger.

Shubin's heart was angered within him.

"If it is thus," he thought, "I shall lay a curse upon Kōbō Daishi."

He shut himself up in the Western Temple, made a three-cornered altar, and established an image facing northward, where he did honor to demon-quelling Amrta.[89] But hearing tidings thereof, Kōbō Daishi built a fire altar at the Eastern Temple to do honor to the Bright Monarch Yamāntaka.[90]

Since both of these two were venerable and revered monks, rich in virtue and well practiced in austerities, their humming-bulb arrows came together in the air and fell down, nor was there a time when their sound was not heard.

At last Kōbō Daishi noised it abroad that he had entered Nirvana

---
[87] *Gohei;* traditional Shinto offerings.
[88] Shingon; Kōbō Daishi's sect.
[89] One of the Five Bright Monarchs.
[90] A protective divinity.

suddenly, thinking, "I shall make Shubin careless." Monks and laymen shed bitter tears; noble and base swallowed their voices mourning. And Shubin destroyed his altar, thinking joyfully, "The power of my rituals has prevailed."

Thereupon, Shubin's eyes were blinded, blood dripped from his nose, and his mind and body were stricken with anguish, so that he fell down dead in front of his Buddha altar. Truly was this a most awesome miracle, a revelation of the truth of the golden teaching,"Spells and poisonous medicines return to their makers." [91]

Thenceforward the Eastern Temple prospered, but the Western Temple was destroyed.

Kōbō Daishi bound together grasses of the kind called *chigaya* in the semblance of a dragon, which he put up above his altar. When his rites were done, he sent off the divine hosts that he had summoned, but Zennyo the dragon king he kept in the Garden of Divine Waters. Even today that dragon king dwells therein, because of a promise that he made, saying, "Until the dawn when Maitreya comes to preach the three sermons under the dragon flower tree, even so long will I guard this land and govern the workings of the Buddhist Law."

Some say that the grass image turned into a great dragon and flew back toward Heatless Lake, while others believe that it mounted up into the sky with the divine hosts and flew away eastward to Atsuta Shrine in the land of Owari. Was this perhaps an omen of the eastward spread of the Buddhist Law, or an auspicious portent signifying the pacification and protection of the eastern seas?

Now Kōbō Daishi said, "If this dragon king moves to another realm, the waters of the lake will become shallow and the land will be laid waste. At such a time, let my disciples petition the dragon king, that he may be kept here to save the nation."

Truly there were times when the waters of the lake were shallow, as though the dragon king had gone away to another place. But whenever the rituals of the rain-beseeching sutra were performed, then most marvelous indeed was the response thereto, so

---

[91] From the *Lotus Sutra*.

Chapter 12

that it seemed that he had not yet cast the nation away. To be sure, this was a praiseworthy and miraculous lake, bringing wind and rain as the season required. Wherefore the generations of emperors worshiped it, and the great nobles of every family reverenced it. When there was a drought, this lake was purified first of all.

Yet this place fell into ruin after the abdication of the priestly retired emperor Go-Toba, and brambles closed its paths after the years of Kempō. Boar and deer roamed therein, as well as poisonous snakes. The sound of hunters' humming-bulbs affrighted the hearing of the Protectors of the Law; the noise of galloping horses startled the hearts of the invisible spirits. Men of good sense lamented because of these things, and were sore afraid.

After the Disturbance of Shōkyū, the Zen monk of Musashi,[92] regretting in his heart that it should be so, raised up a high mud wall with a roof and strong gates to stop the defilement. But again, with the passing of many seasons of cold and heat, the gates and walls failed of their design, leaving nothing to prevent impure and defiled men and women from entering therein, nor did cattle and horses fear to go back and forth in search of water and grass.

[*End of history*]

Truly it was because of these things that now the supreme highness said, "Assuredly is this displeasing to the dragon king! We must bring peace to the land by restoring the garden with all speed and worshiping him respectfully."

The Banishment of the Princely Minister of Military Affairs; the Matter of Lady Li

It could not be helped that the princely minister of military affairs had put off his holy robes while the realm was disturbed, for in no other way might he have escaped calamity. But now that the four seas were tranquil, it was the desire of the buddhas that he should return to be the abbot of the three thousand as before, to receive and foster the Buddhist Law and the imperial way. Nor was the will of the supreme highness otherwise. Yet he asked to

---
[92] Hōjō Yasutoki.

govern the military affairs of the realm as the barbarian-subduing shogun. And at last the emperor commanded that it should be so, although his august heart was troubled within him.

Since it was thus, it had been fitting for the prince to conduct himself circumspectly, with esteem for the high estate wherein the four seas placed their trust, yet he was exceedingly arrogant, cared nothing for men's censure, and thirsted mightily after pleasures of the flesh. Wherefore indeed were the men of the realm put in fear of new perils to come.

It is said, "After a great disturbance, men wrap up their bows and arrows and put their shields and battle-axes in bags." [93] Yet if this prince but heard that men were wielders of strong bows and long swords, he rewarded them beyond all reason, ordering them to serve him closely (though to be sure there was no need for it). Furthermore, these fellows found no amusement save with weapons of war, but went around in the capital and Shirakawa by night, fell upon men at crossroads, and in this place and that cut down passersby: youths, monks, women, and children. Truly there was no end to their murdering! But after all, it was only to strike down the Ashikaga minister of civil affairs that in this wise the prince gathered together warriors and practiced the military arts.

"Would you know why the anger of the princely minister of military affairs raged thus furiously against the minister Takauji (though until this time Takauji had behaved loyally and with due regard for his station—nor was there any report of his having committed an impropriety)? Learn then that in the fifth month of the past year, when the imperial armies brought down Rokuhara, followers of the Tono Sign of the Law destroyed earthen storehouses in the capital, and carried off goods and precious things. Lord Ashikaga arrested these to put an end to their violence, cut off the heads of more than twenty, and hung them up at the Sixth Ward river bed with high placards whereon was written: "Followers of the Tono Sign of the Law, the priestly servant of the Prince of the Great Pagoda, executed for committing robberies in full daylight in many places."

Angered thereat, the Tono Sign of the Law complained to the

[93] From the *Book of Odes*.

Chapter 12

prince, devising slanders and schemes of various kinds. And such things were repeated many times, until tidings concerning them reached the ears of the emperor. The prince too grew angry, thinking constantly, "Would that I could strike down the minister Takauji," even from the time of his abiding at Shigi, yet could he do no other than abide in silence, since the supreme highness would not agree. But may it not be that slanderous words were still being spoken? For secretly for a secret purpose the prince sent orders to all the provinces to summon warriors.

Hearing tidings of these orders, the minister Takauji went in stealth to the prince's stepmother, she who was an empress's peer.

"It is clearly proven that the princely minister of war summons warriors from the provinces to seize the throne," he said, and offered up orders for the emperor to behold, sent by the prince to divers provinces.

Now thereupon the emperor waxed exceeding wroth, saying, "This prince must be banished." And he summoned the prince, telling him that there would be a poetry meeting in the Central Hall.[94]

Not thinking at all that it was such a matter, the prince went to the palace privately, with but two forerunners and fifteen or sixteen attendants. Yet two men made ready to receive him near the Bell Chamber, according to the emperor's command: Yūki Hōgan and the governor of Hōki, who laid hands upon him and shut him up in the Race Track Hall.

Thenceforth the prince rose up and lay down tearfully in a tiny room far from the paths of men, barred with boards like a spider's web.

"Alas! What karma is mine?" he thought. "When the military caused me to conceal my person in the beginning of Genkō, ever were my sleeves moistened by dew under trees and between rocks. Now that I am come back to the capital, I suffer punishment because of the words of a slanderous minister before a day of my lifetime of happiness is spent."

Truly there was nothing of which he did not think, not even the karma of his unknown former lives.

---

[94] Another name for the Seiryōden, the emperor's living quarters.

"Since it is said that unjust dishonor does not endure forever, will not His Majesty alter his design?" he thought.

But there were those that said, "The court has agreed to banish the prince." And his spirit was eaten up with sorrow.

Secretly the prince wrote a letter setting forth all that was in his heart, and handed it to a lady in waiting with whom he had dealt kindly in a past day, bidding her give it to such an official as was appointed to present communications to the throne from exalted personages, and to take care that it reached the emperor quickly. In the letter he said:

"Now would I declare my innocence to the throne, I who am struck down by the imperial displeasure, yet my tears fall and my spirit faints in darkness. Despair encompasses me about; my words are lacking in wit. Great indeed will be my thankfulness for all the days of my life if His Majesty will but deign to 'understand ten thousand things from one,' if he will but add to my words and look upon me with compassion.

"After the time of Shōkyū, the military took power into their hands, causing the court to leave off its governing. And it was so for many years. Because this thing was hateful to my heart, I put away the holy garments of compassion and humility to clothe my body in the strong armor that subdues enemies in an instant. Within myself I trembled at the sin of disobeying the Buddhist commandments; before the eyes of men I bore the censure of those who called me shameless. But although it was thus, for His Majesty's sake I forgot selfish things, nor did I fear death, but thought only to smite the enemy.

"At that time there were many local ministers and filial sons at the court, yet some were lacking in resolution, while others waited vainly, saying, 'Let the will of heaven be done.' I alone roused up valiant men without the help of arms of war, spied out the doings of the enemy hosts, and hid my body in steep and cramped places. The traitors looked on me as the chief of the imperial cause, commanded the four seas to lay hands upon me, and posted rewards on a myriad doors. Truly, though I lived, there was no place wherein my body might rest. By day I lay in hidden valleys and deep mountains where moss overspread the rocks; by night I went forth to desolate hamlets and remote villages, walking with bare feet over the frost. How many thousands and tens of thousands of times my spirit fainted as I stroked the dragon's beard! How many times my heart froze as I trod on the tiger's tail!

"At last by my devisings the enemy was crushed beneath an iron battle-ax. For was it any other man than myself, who by his loyal deeds brought back the imperial carriage to the capital and made the phoenix calendar to govern the heavens for all time? Yet now my warlike successes are held as nothing, and suddenly I am blamed for wicked things. I have heard men speak of the sins that are held against me, but not one thing thereof is a thing done by me. Most bitterly do I grieve that His Majesty does not enquire concerning the place whence these false slanders have issued.

"Though I look up to sue to heaven, the sun and moon forbear to shine on an unfilial son; though I look down to cry out to earth, the mountains and rivers will not support a subject lacking in propriety. The bond between parent and child is severed. Heaven and earth alike cast me away. Can there be another sorrow equal to this? No longer do I seek to hold office, for henceforth there is none on whose behalf I may devise meritorious actions. If His Majesty will deign to lighten my sentence of death, I will give up the name of prince forever and assume the robes of a monk at once.

"Does His Majesty not see it? When Shen-sheng died, the land of Chin became disordered.[95] When Fu-su was struck down, the days of Ch'in were ended.[96] 'Slanders that soak in slowly and accusations that wound directly'[97] arise from small things and grow into big things. Why does His Majesty not look at the present, though his gaze extends to antiquity? With all my heart I beg to be heard."

[95] This allusion is explained in the story which follows below.
[96] Fu-su, the eldest son of the First Emperor of the Ch'in dynasty (221–207 B.C.), had been sent into exile on the northern frontier. When the emperor became mortally ill in 210 B.C., he ordered that Fu-su be recalled, but a younger son and two ambitious courtiers substituted a forged letter commanding Fu-su to commit suicide. Although the success of this ruse enabled the younger son to ascend the throne, the dynasty collapsed within three years.
[97] A tag from the *Analects*.

"Written with fear and awe on the fifth day of the third month.

"Morinaga, to His Lordship the Former Great Subject of the Left."

Perhaps the supreme highness would have pardoned the prince, had this letter but reached his ears, but in the end the official spoke no word thereof, fearful lest the wrath of certain persons descend upon him. Heaven did not hear the prince, nor was his plea of loyalty made known.

Moreover, it came to pass at this time that in stealth the court struck down thirty personal followers of the prince, men who for two or three years had stayed by his side faithfully, and now awaited their rewards. Truly this was beyond words!

Finally on the third day of the fifth month, they took the prince to the abiding place of Tadayoshi no Ason, who sent him down to Kamakura with an army of five or six hundred guards, to put him into a cave prison in Nikaidō Valley. None accompanied him save a palace lady of high degree called the Lady of the South. Slanting rain drenched his sleeves in the dark cell far from the rays of the sun and moon; ever was his pillow damp with water dripping from the rocks. And for half a year he abode in that place. How pitiful were the feelings in his heart!

Although the emperor had sent the prince away to Kamakura in sudden anger, assuredly was it contrary to the imperial will that he should be dealt with thus harshly. But Tadayoshi no Ason locked him up in a prison because he bore an old hatred against him. How shameful it was!

[*In the following anecdote, a Chinese parallel for Lady Sammi's behavior is recalled.*]

Since ancient days, many times has a stepmother's slander of a filial child brought ruin to a nation or family. Long ago in a different land, there was a man called Duke Hsien of Chin, who had three sons of his consort Ch'i Chiang. The eldest son was called Shen-sheng, the second son was called Chung-erh, and the third son was called I-wu. When these three were grown to manhood, their mother Ch'i Chiang fell ill and died suddenly.

Although Duke Hsien mourned Ch'i Chiang tenderly, truly is

Chapter 12

it said, "The flower of the heart of man fades and changes." [98] For when the time since her death had become long, unmindful of his ancient vows he took to wife a beautiful woman called Lady Li, who bewitched the eye with her rosy cheeks and curving painted brows, and rejoiced the heart of a man with her adroit words and complaisant manners. Duke Hsien loved this lady so deeply that he never saw the face of the person who had died, not even in a dream.

When some time had passed in this wise, Lady Li also gave birth to a son, whose name was Hsi-ch'i. Although Hsi-ch'i was very young, his father favored him above his three older sons because of his love for the mother Lady Li, thinking always, "I would that I might set aside the three sons of my former consort Ch'i Chiang, and yield the state of Chin to the child of the womb of Lady Li."

In her heart Lady Li rejoiced thereat, but deceitfully she spoke aloud, saying:

"Hsi-ch'i is still too young to distinguish good from evil. It would be hateful to the hearts of the men of the realm were he to succeed to the rule of the state before the three older sons, not knowing the wise from the foolish."

So she admonished him many times. Duke Hsien looked with increased favor upon Lady Li because of her unselfish spirit, her concern for the censure of men, and her thought for the safety of the state. He entrusted all affairs of government to her, until her power waxed exceedingly great, and the whole realm bowed before her.

Now it came to pass on a certain occasion that the eldest son Shen-sheng made an offering for a memorial service for his mother, worshiping with an ox, a sheep, and a swine at Ch'i Chiang's tomb in Ch'ü-wo. That which remained from the offering he brought to his father Duke Hsien, and Duke Hsien being gone out to his hunting ground just then, he wrapped up the offering and left it. Yet secretly Lady Li added a deadly poison thereto, such as men call *chen*.

When Duke Hsien came back from the hunting ground, he

[98] From a famous verse by Ono no Komachi (834–900).

made to eat of this sacrificial meat, but Lady Li said, "When a thing is sent from without, let the master not eat of it until another has been given thereof." She gave of it to a person that was there, and immediately the man died spitting blood. Lady Li cried out and gave of the meat to the fowls and dogs in the courtyard, whereupon all the fowls and dogs died. Then, greatly astonished, Duke Hsien threw the remaining pieces down to the ground, and the ground where he threw them was bored through, and all the plants thereabout were shriveled up.

With feigned tears, Lady Li said:

"When you sought to make Hsi-ch'i your heir, I admonished you and would not suffer it to be so, because I loved your heir Shen-sheng equally with Hsi-ch'i. How heartless it is that with this poison Shen-sheng sought to kill his father and me, thinking to seize the land of Chin! Truly when Duke Hsien is gone, Shen-sheng will not allow Hsi-ch'i and me to live for a single day. Please put me away and kill Hsi-ch'i, that the heart of Shen-sheng may be set at ease."

So she spoke to Duke Hsien, and lifted up her voice and wept. And Duke Hsien, greatly angered, commanded his jailers to kill his heir Shen-sheng, since by nature he was a man of shallow wit, credulous of slanders.

All the courtiers regretted that Shen-sheng should be struck down without having done any evil.

"Flee quickly to another land," they warned.

But Shen-sheng said:

"Long ago in the days of my youth I lost a mother, and now in the days of my manhood I have found a stepmother. Indeed, I have added bad fortune to unhappiness! But is there any country between heaven and earth that does not have fathers and sons? If I were to go to another land to escape death, all who saw me would hate and dishonor me, saying, 'Behold the unfilial monster who gave his father poison to kill him.' Heaven knows that I have done no wrong. It will be best to die of this false accusation, that my father's wrath may be appeased."

So he spoke, and died on his sword before the coming of the executioners.

Chapter 12

Hearing of this, Shen-sheng's brothers Chung-erh and I-wu fled to another country, fearful of the slanders of Lady Li. Hsi-ch'i was enabled to succeed to the dukedom of the state of Chin, but because they flouted the mandate of heaven, very soon Duke Hsien and Hsi-ch'i were both killed by a minister named Li K'o, and the state of Chin was destroyed in an instant.

[*End of anecdote*]

Now the men of Japan spoke together, saying:

"Is it not entirely because of the martial accomplishments of the Prince of the Great Pagoda that the war is ended and the deposed emperor sits upon the throne again? It had been meet that His Majesty admonish and forgive the prince when he erred in trifling matters, yet he has banished him into the hands of his enemies. Is this not a sign that the court will again bow before the power of the military?"

So they spoke, and at last when the life of the Prince of the Great Pagoda was ended, all the realm entered swiftly upon the age of the generals' rule.

Character List

This list includes bibliographical references and the principal Chinese characters which figure in the narrative.

Azuma kagami	吾妻鏡
Bunka Daigaku	文科大學
Bunka Daigaku shishi sōsho	文科大學史誌叢書
Dai	大
Gempei seisuiki	源平盛衰記
Genkō	元弘
Genkyō	元亨
Gyokuyō	玉葉
Hanazono tennō shinki	花園天皇宸記
Hi	火
Hō	方
Imai Kōsai	今井弘濟
Ishida Kichisada	石田吉貞

Kandabon taiheiki	神田本太平記
Kokubun chūshaku zensho	國文註釋全書
Kokusho Kankōkai	國書刊行會
Kome	米
Kume Kunitake	久米邦武
Kusunoki	楠
Man	万
Mozume Takakazu	物集高量
Muromatsu Iwao	室松岩雄
Nagazumi Yasuaki	永積安明
Nihon bunkashi taikei	日本文化史大系
Nisshō	日性
Ressei zenshū	列聖全集
Ressei Zenshū Hensankai	列聖全集編纂會
Ryōgon'in	楞嚴院
Saigen'inbon taiheiki	西源院本太平記
Sankō taiheiki	參考太平記
Shigaku zasshi	史學雜誌
Shigeno An'eki	重野安繹
Shinshaku Nihon bungaku sōsho	新釋日本文學叢書

Character List

Sō	相
Su	朱
Taiheiki shinshaku	太平記新釋
"Taiheiki wa shigaku ni eki nashi"	太平記は史學に益なし
Taiheikishō	太平記鈔
Tanaka Kazuhiko	田中一彦
Teikoku Bunkō	帝國文庫
Tōin Kinsada nikki	洞院公定日記
Tōkyō Teikoku Daigaku	東京帝國大學
Washio Junkei	鷲尾順敬
Zoku kokushi taikei	續國史大系
Zoku Nihon koten tokuhon	續日本古典讀本

Index

Adachi Tokiaki, xxxvii, 132
Aikawa Tokiharu, 328–30
Akahashi Moritoki (Sōshū), 239, 286–88
Akahashi Shigetoki, 363
Akamatsu Enshin, 213, 242, 255; advance to Rokuhara, 190–91; at Battle of Maya, 201; at Sakabe and Segawa, 203–4; attack on the capital, 222–28; at the Katsura River, 206–7; at Yamazaki, 229; joins imperial cause, 162–63; retreat from capital, 215–16; reward for aid, 365
Akamatsu, governor of Chikuzen, see Akamatsu Sadanori
Akamatsu Noriie, 243–44
Akamatsu Norisuke, 202, 208, 255, 257
Akamatsu Sadanori, 191, 202, 204, 208, 211–12, 257
Akamatsu Sokuyū, 137, 143–44, 163, 202, 205; in attack on capital, 206–7, 211–13, 257
Akasaka, xliii, xliv; battle of, 85–91, 166–73 *passim*
Akuma Mitsuyasu, 202, 204, 207
Andō Shūshu, 299–301
Arao Kurō, 73
Arao Yagorō, 73
Ariwara no Narihira, 331*n*, 349*n*
Armor, xxxiv, 73, 165, 242–43, 343
Ashikaga Hyōbu-no-tayū, see Ashikaga Tadayoshi
Ashikaga Tadayoshi, 239, 321, 365, 384
Ashikaga Takauji, 364–65; and Prince Morinaga, xlvii–xlviii, 341, 380–81; comes to Shinomura, 246; defection to Go-Daigo, xlv–xlvi, 241; fate of sons, 273–74; goes to capital, 237–40; march from Shinomura to Rokuhara, 250–52
Ashikaga Takewaka, 273–74
Ashikaga Yoshiakira (Senjuō), xlvi, 239, 273, 277
Aso Tokiharu, 164, 166, 170–71, 334, 336
Asuke Shigenori, 13, 14, 72–74, 93
Audience courts (*Chōdōin*), 347*n*, 349
Awa no Ogasawara, 203

Bandō, Eight Heishi of, 283
Barriers, abolition of, 6–7
Battles, three stages of xxxiv–xxxv; see also specific battles, e.g., Tsukushi, battle of; *and* disturbances, e.g., Genkō, disturbance of
Bōmon Kiyotada, 341–42

Castle lay monk, see Adachi Tokiaki
Castles, xxxv–xxxvi; see also specific castles, e.g., Chihaya castle
Ch'ang-li, 15–17
Chang Liang, 30*n*, 86, 284
Ch'ao Fu, 129
Ch'eng Ying, 315
Ch'en P'ing, 86, 145*n*, 284
Chiang-tu, 30
Chia Tao, 342
Chiba Sadatane, 364
Chieh Fei, 121
Chigusa, Lord, see Minamoto no Tadaaki
Chihaya Castle, xliv, xlvi, 271; battle of 181–88, 190

394

Chi Hsin, 65
Chikyō, 31, 32
Chin, state of, Fu-ch'ai's war against, 123
Ching-ch'i, 11
Ching K'o, 324
Chōgosonshiji Temple, 68n
Chōkōdō Hall, 84
Chronicle of Antiquity (Shōtoku Taishi), 161
Ch'u, prince of, 7
Chuan Chu, 324
Chūen, 31, 33–36, 344
Chūgū, see Inner Princess
Chu-ko Liang (K'ung-ming), 147n
Chung-erh, 56, 117, 287, 384
Chung-ta, 147
Chün Ming-chi, 103–4
Cinnabar Courtyard, 119
Consort, imperial, see Inner Princess

Daibutsu Sadanao, 286, 295–96
Daibutsu Takanao, 334, 336
Daigokuden (Great Hall of State), xxiv, 347n, 348, 351
Daijoin Cloister, 54
Daikakuji line, xxxix, xln, 10
Daikō Shigenari, 254–55
Date Rokurō, 304–5
Date Yūga, 14
Dengaku (field music), 131n
Dengyō Daishi (Saichō), xxviii, 30
Divine Waters, Garden of, 374–79
Dogfights, 133
Doi Jirō, 192, 321, 364
Dragon Tail, 347
Dress, 57, 62, 165, 343; see also Armor

Enkan, 12, 31, 33–37, 344
Enryakuji, xxvii–xxix, 13; partial destruction by fire, 54; extinction of perpetual lamp, 130; Go-Daigo dedicates Great Lecture Hall, 29; Morinaga becomes a monk of, xl; Nashimoto Monastery as subsidiary of, 11n; soldier monks invade capital, 217–221
Enshin, see Akamatsu Enshin
En'ya Takasada, 193–94, 317, 321, 364
Era names, xlix

Fan K'uai, 112, 178n
Fan Li, 108–25 *passim*

Index

Field music (*dengaku*), 131
Fifth Prince (son of Go-Daigo), 270
First Prince (son of Go-Daigo); see Sonryō
Forecast of the Future of Japan (Shōtoku Taishi), 132, 161
Forty-eight places, the, 20
Fourth Prince (son of Go-Daigo), 11, 99
Fu-ch'ai, 109–25
Fu-chiao-hsien, 111
Fujifusa, see Madenokōji Fujifusa
Fujiwara no Fubito, 28n
Fujiwara no Kanezane, xxiiin
Fujiwara no Kinkado, 9
Fujiwara no Mitsuchika, 40
Fujiwara no Nakanori, 132
Fujiwara no Nobuakira, 100–1
Fujiwara no Takasuke, 13, 14, 57, 63
Fujiwara no Tameakira (Tameaki), 32–33, 57, 63, 81
Fujiwara no Tameko, 10
Fujiwara no Teika, xxvin
Fujiwara no Tokihira, 353n
Fukakusa, Emperor, 29
Fukugonji Temple, 319
Funada lay monk, 298, 313–14
Funada Yoshimasa, 188–89
Funanoe, battle of, 198–99
Fuonji Shinnin, 296
Fu-su, 383

Garden of Divine Waters, 374–79
Gedatsu, 367–70
Gempei seisuiki (Rise and Fall of the Minamoto and Taira), xvi, xxviii
Gen'e, 15
Genjitsu, 57
Genki, 14
Genkō, disturbance of, xliii
Genson, see Kōrimbō Genson
Go-Daigo, Emperor, xvii; abdication of, 82–84; appoints Morinaga shogun, 342; banishment of Morinaga, 379–84; character, xxxvii–xxxix; consort of, 8; dethronement of, by Takauji, xlvii; disagreement with Morinaga, 341; dreams of Kusunoki, 67–69; fear of military, 13; flight, capture, exile, and return of, xlii–xlvi, 55–57, 79–80, 105–7, 125–26, 192–97; Kamakura shoguns and, xxvi, xxxix–xliii; mandate to Nitta Kotarō Yo-

Index

shisada, 189; message to Takatoki, 26; parting from Inner Princess, 104–5; performs Golden Wheel rites, 228–29; receives Chün Ming-chi, 103–4; reign of, 3–82; rejection of holy orders, 103; religious offerings, xli, 28–31; restoration of, xlvi; returns to capital, 320–21; soldier-monks and, xl–xlii, 63–64; sons of, 10–11; visits temples, 316–20; Yoshida Fuyufusa's advice to, 25–26
Godaiin Muneshige, 312–15
Go-Fukakusa, Emperor, xxxix
Go-Fushimi, Emperor, 62n, 127–28
Gōkan, 220–21
Golden Chamber, 121
Golden rats, 251
Go-Saga, Emperor, xxxix
Gōsen, 220–21
Go-Shirakawa, ex-emperor, 3
Go-Toba, ex-emperor, xxiii, xxiv, xxxiii, 4
Gotō Sukemitsu, 51–54
Go-Uda, Emperor, xxxvii, xxxviiin, 6
Gōyo Jōrimbō, 58, 63
Great Hall of State (Daigokuden) xxiv, 347n, 348, 351
Great Pagoda, Prince of; see Morinaga
Gunki monogatari (war tales), xv–xvi, xxv
Gyokuyō (Fujiwara no Kanezane), xxiiin

Hachiman Shrine (Iwashimizu), 105
Hachiman Shrine (Shinomura), 250
Hachiman Tarō Yoshiie, see Minamoto no Yoshiie
Hanazono, ex-emperor, xxxviii–xxxix, xliin, 62n
Han Ch'ang-li, 15–17
Han Hsiang, 15–17
Hannyaji Temple, 135, 334
Han Yü, 15n
Hatano Nobumichi, 58, 96
Hayami Magosaburō, 224–26
Hayami Matajirō, 224–26
Heiji, disturbance of, xxiin
Heiji monogatari (Tale of Heiji), xvi, xxiin
Heike monogatari (Tale of the Heike), xv, xvi, xxv
Hiei, Mount, xviii, xxviii–xxix, xl, xlii; see also Enryakuji

Hikaru Genji, 349
Hikida Myōgen, 250, 252
Hino Kunimitsu, see Kumawaka, Master
Hino Sukeakira, 128–30, 209
Hino Sukena, 127, 209, 270
Hino Suketomo, xxxviii, xl, xli, 13; Band of Roisterers and, 14–15; banishment of, 27; execution of, 46–47; goes to the Kantō, 24–25
Hino Toshimoto, xxxviii, xl–xlii passim, 13; execution of, 51–53; feigned seclusion of, 13–14; goes to the Kanto, 24–25, 27; journey to Kamakura (michiyuki), 38–42
Hiraga Saburō, 137, 144
Hirano Shōgen, 172–73
Hiroari, see Oki no Jirō Saemon Hiroari
Hitomi On'a, 166–70
Hōgen, disturbance of, xxiin
Hōgen monogatari (Tale of Hōgen), xvi, xxiin
Hōjō Hidetoki, xlv, 322–26
Hōjō Kunitoki, 312–15
Hōjō Manju, 302
Hōjō Masako, xxiiin, 240
Hōjō Nakatoki, 95n, 152, 206, 260–62, 266–9, 296
Hōjō Shirō Sakon-no-taifu, see Hōjō Tokioki (Yasuie)
Hōjō Takatoki, xxxvi–xxxvii, 3, 26n, 134–35; amused by field music and dogfights, 131–33; assembles army, 163–64; Ashikaga Takauji and, 237–40; fate of family, 303–4; Go-Daigo's message to, 26–27; orders arrest of monks, 31; praises Nagasaki Takashige, 284; and resistance of Kasagi castle, 75; suicide of, 310–11
Hōjō Tokifusa, 5n
Hōjō Tokimasa, xxii, xxiiin, 134
Hōjō Tokimasu, 152, 261–62
Hōjō Tokinao, 192, 326–28
Hōjō Tokioki (Shirō Sakon-no-taifu Yasuie), 280, 283, 285, 301-2, 304–5, 345
Hōjō Tokiyori, xxxi, 4
Hōjō Tokiyuki (Kameju), 302–4
Hōjō Yasutoki, 4, 5n, 44n, 379
Hōjō Yoshitoki, xxiii, 4, 44n
Hokke Mountain, 319
Homma, Yamashiro lay monk, 44–46

Homma Saburō, 48
Homma Sukesada, 166–69
Homma Suketada, 168–70
Homma Yamashirō no Saemon, 288–89
Honjōbō, 74
Hōshu, 127–28
Hosshōbō, 357–60
Hosshōji Temple, 218, 219
Hours of the day, Oriental names of, xlviii
Hou Sheng, 324
Hsiang Chuang, 178n
Hsiang Po, 178n
Hsiang Yü of Ch'u, 64–66, 112, 178n, 261
Hsiao-po, 302
Hsi-ch'i, 385–87
Hsien, duke of Chin, 384–87
Hsi-po, 117
Hsi Shih, 119–23
Hsüan-tsang, 136
Hsü Yu, 129
Huan, duke of Ch'i, 7, 129
Hui-yüan, 367
Hung Yen, 107

I, duke of Wei, 5, 6n, 107
Ichijō Yukifusa, 105, 126
Iimori Mountain, 363, 364
Ikan, 57n
Ikuhōmon Gate, 346
Imose, bailiff of, 143
Inamura Cape, 289–90
Inner Princess (imperial consort), 8, 9, 12, 104–5, 346
Ise monogatori (*Tales of Ise*), 349n
Itō Hikojirō, 22
Itō Yamato no Jirō, 191
Iwagikumaro, 176

Jigon, 364
Jimyōin line, xxxix, xln, 10, 42, 62, 84; see also Kōgon, Emperor
Jingonjiki (rice-offering ceremony), 349
Jiyū of Uratsuji, 215
Jobu, Mount, xlii, 57
Jōdoji Temple, 31
Jōhen, 141, 142
Jōjōji Temple, 236
Jōjubō, 68

Journey (*michiyuki*), 38n, 137
Juntoku, ex-emperor, xxiv

Kaijitsu, 59
Kaitō Kōwakamaru, 60
Kaitō Sakon Shōgen, 58, 59
Kajii Prince (Son'in), 127, 209–14, 247, 265–66
Kaji no Genjirō Saemon, 191
Kalmasada-pada, king, 190n
Kalpa, 332n
Kalpa-fire, 208
Kamakura: army of, defeated at Bumbai, 282–85; army routs Nitta Yoshisada, 278–81; banishment of Morinaga to, 384; battle of, 285–311 *passim*; capture of, xlv; field music popular in, 131; monks questioned and punished at, 35–36; shogunate established at, xxiii; way of life in, xxix, xxxi–xxxii; see also Kantō; Shogunate
Kameju, see Hōjō Tokiyuki
Kameyama, Emperor, xxxviiin, xxxix
Kanazawa Aritoki, 286
Kanazawa Sadamasa, 278, 285, 296
Kanazawa Uma-no-suke, 164, 176, 182
Kandabon Taiheiki, xiv
Kanke family, 226
Kano Shigemitsu, 297–98
Kantō, the, xxii, xliii; messages of uprisings from Rokuhara to, 163; order from, regarding Morinaga, 142; rites of exorcism against, 12–13; three monks at, 33–36; see also Kamakura
Kao Tsu of Han, 64–66, 112n, 178n, 261
Karasaki Beach, battle of, 58–62
Kariginu, 62n
Kasagi Castle: battle of xliii, 70–74; capture of, 75–79; treatment of captives, 93–99
Kasagi Temple, xlii, 67
Kasuya Muneaki, 70, 84, 259, 267–69
Kataoka Hachirō, 137, 141, 146
Katsura River, 206
Katte-no-myōjin Shrine, 177
Kazan'in Morokata, 13, 14, 55; banishment and death, 97; capture of, 81; disguises self as Go-Daigo, 57–58, 63
Kazuragi Mountain, 188
Kembō, 363

Index

Kemmu, disturbance of, 365
Kidera Sagami, 137, 141, 177–78, 207
Ki family, 158, 160, 90, 334
Kikuchi Jakua, 322–24
Kikuchi Takeshige, 324
Kimpu, Mount, 176–77
Kimpusan Temple, 149n
Ki no Tsurayuki, 33
Kintoshi, see Tōin Kintoshi
Kinuzuri Sukefusa, 22
Kitabatake Chikafusa, xxxviii
Kitsune River, 217
Kiyotada, see Bōmon Kiyotada
Kiyowara family, 158, 160, 190, 334
Kobayakawa, 71, 231
Kōbō Daishi (Kūkai), 374–78
Kōfukuji Temple, xxvii, 28, 54
Kōgon, Emperor, xln, xliin, xlvi; blames self for wars, 247; enthronement of, 127–28; flees with family, 260–63; goes to Rokuhara, 62, 209, 247; orders prayers for peace, 214; surrenders imperial symbols, 270
Kogushi Gorō Hyōemon-no-jō, 95, 260
Kogushi Noriyuki, 20, 21
Kojima Hōshi, xvii–xviii
Kojima Takanori, 107–8, 125, 232–34
Kōken, Empress, 342
Kōkiden, 8
Kokinshū (Tsurayuki), 33n
Komiyama Jirō, 76–78
Kō Moronao, 246
Kongōbuji Temple, 180n
Kōno Michiharu, 210–11, 213–14, 223, 231, 232, 253, 254–55
Kōno Michitō, 255
Kōrimbō Genson, 59, 64, 137, 139–40
Kōsen, 135
Kose no Kanaoka, 350n
Kotesashi Moor, battle of, 279
Kou-chien, 81n, 108, 109–25
Kōya, Mount, 180
Kōzuki, 208
K'uai-chi Mountain, 80; battle of, 111–14
Kuan I-wu, 129
Kudō Saemon-no-jō Jirō, 52, 53, 93, 238
Kuge Tokishige, 246
Kugyo, 4
Kujō Mitsutsune, 345
Kumawaka, Master, 44–51
Kume Kunitake, xviii

K'ung-ming, 147
Ku-su Castle, 116, 117
Kusunoki Masashige, xl, xlii–xliii, xliv; at Chihaya Castle, 181–85; at Tennōji, 160–62; battles at Tennōji and Watanabe Bridge won by, 154–56; defense of Akasaka Castle by, 85–91; destruction of Iimori Castle by, 364; distrust of Ashikaga Takauji, xlviii; Go-Daigo dreams of and meets, 68–69; Go-Daigo praises, 320; intimidation of Utsunomiya, 156–60; retakes Akasaka Castle, 153; sees *Forecast* of Tennōji, 160–62; to Tennōji, 153–60
Kusunoki Shichirō, 86
Kyōen, 31, 32

Lespedeza Room, 126, 348
Li, Lady, 385–87
Li Ch'iao, 353
Li Ssu, 6
Lung-po, Lord of, 190
Lu Pan, 186

Madenokōji Fujifusa, 28, 55–56, 69, 79–80, 83, 84, 97–99, 344, 345
Madenokōji Nobufusa, xxxviii, xli, 344; captivity of, 81, 84, 93–94; mission of, to Kamakura, 26–27; serves two masters, 128–30
Madenokōji Suefusa, 55–56, 79–81, 97, 344
Makino Shōken, 149
Manju, 302
Masashige, see Kusunoki Masashige
Maya, battle of, 201–2
Maya Castle, 191
Mega Magosaburō Nagamune, 227–28, 256–57
Meng Shih-she, 145
Michiyuki (journey), 38n, 137
Miidera Temple (Onjōji), xxvii, 11n
Military rulers, league of, 125
Mimbukyō, Lady, 10, 150–52
Minamoto no Sadahira, 57, 215, 222, 334, 335, 343
Minamoto no Sanetomo, xxiii, 3–4
Minamoto no Tadaaki (Lord Chigusa), 56, 84, 105, 126, 242, 257–58, 343; accompanies Go-Daigo to Hōki, 194–

Minamoto no Tadaaki (*Cont.*) 97; attacks the capital, 229–33; extravagance of, 365–67
Minamoto no Tomoyuki, 44, 56, 81, 84, 94–95
Minamoto no Yoriie, xxiii, 3–4
Minamoto no Yoritomo, xxii–xxiii, xxix, xxxi, 3
Minamoto no Yoshihira, 335*n*
Minamoto no Yoshiie, 188*n*, 235, 371
Minamoto no Yoshisada, 81
Minamoto no Yoshitomo, xxii
Mine-no-dō Temple, 229, 232, 233, 235
Misu lay monk, 80
Mitsuishi Mountain, 191
Miura no Suke, 364
Miura Yoshikatsu, 281–83
Monkan of Ono: arrest and exile of by Sagami lay monk, 31, 33–36; disregards holy vows, 366–67, 370–71; prays for Inner Princess, 12; return from exile, 344
Monks, xix, xxvi, 141*n;* arrested and punished by Sagami lay monk, 31–36; rewarded and bribed by military, 215, 222; proper conduct of illustrated, 367–70; *see also* Soldier-monks
Mononobe no Moriya, 161*n*
Morinaga, prince: Ashikaga Takauji and, xlvii–xlviii, 341, 380–81; banishment to Kamakura, 379–84; becomes military leader, 58–59; birth of, 10; flees to Kumano, 137–38; flees to Nara, 64; flight from Yoshino Castle, 177–79; head of Tendai sect, xl; hides in Hannyaji Buddha Hall, 135–37; Imose bailiff and, 143–45; issues command to Akamatsu Enshin, 162–63; journey to Totsugawa, 138–43; at Kimpusan Temple, 149; plan to save Go-Daigo, 55; replaced as Tendai abbot, xli; restores Go-Daigo to throne, xliii–xlv; Tamaki bailiff and, 145–48; trains for war, 30–21
Morokata, *see* Kazan'in Morokata
Mountain Gate, *see* Enryakuji
Mu, duke of Ch'in, 129
Mukai-no-myōjin Shrine, 216, 217
Munenaga, Prince, *see* Sonchō
Murakami Yoshitaka, 180
Murakami Yoshiteru, 137, 178–79

Mutsu Uma-no-suke, *see* Kanazawa Uma-no-suke
Myōhōin, Prince of, *see* Sonchō
Myōkōbō, *see* Kōrimbō Genson

Nagai Munehira, 58
Nagai Takahiro, 84, 101
Nagaoka Rokurō, 325–26
Nagasaki Enki, xxxvii, 238, 284, 291, 309–11
Nagasaki Kurō Saemon-no-jō, 173, 184
Nagasaki Shigen, 273, 293–94
Nagasaki Shin'ueon, 310–11
Nagasaki Takashige, 278, 284, 305–10
Nagasaki Takasuke, xxxvii, 42–44
Nagasaki Tamemoto, 293–95
Nagasaki Yasumitsu (Shirō Saemon), 24, 165, 181, 184, 334, 336
Nagoya Aritomo, 330–33
Nagoya governor of Echizen, 182–83
Nagoya Hyōgo-no-suke, 186
Nagoya Sadamochi, 330–33
Nagoya Takaie, 240, 241, 242–44
Nagoya Tokiari, 330–33
Nakagiri Jūrō, 244–45
Nakagiri Yahachi, 263–65
Naka-no-in Sadahira, *see* Minamoto no Sadahira
Nakatoki, *see* Hōjō Nakatoki
Nakatsugawa, battle at, 147–48
Nakayama Mitsuyoshi, 204
Nambu Tarō, 304–5
Nanjō Munenao, 24
Nashimoto monastery, 11, 127
Nawa Nagashige, 197–99
Nawa Nagataka, 199, 232
Nawa Nagatoshi, xlv, xlviii, 197–98, 317, 321, 364–65
Nawa Shichirō, 198
Niidono, Lady, 303–4
Nikaidō Dōun: advises against removal of Go-Daigo, 43–44; becomes Ritsu monk, 334; death of, 336; warns Sagami lay monk, 26; at Yoshino Castle, 164, 175, 180–81
Nikaidō Kōchin, 93
Nikaidō Shimotsuke Hōgan (Tokimoto), 31
Nimmyō, Emperor, 29*n*
Ninth Prince (son of Go-Daigo), 100–1
Nishigori Hōgandai, 13, 79

Nitta Yoshisada: captures Kamakura, xlv; distrust of Ashikaga Takauji, xlviii; prays for aid at Inamura Cape, 289–90; receives mandate of Go-Daigo, 188–90; reports to Go-Daigo on victories, 319; revolt of, 274–81
Nonagase Rokurō, 148–49
Nonagase Shichirō, 148–49
Nuka Shirō, 244–45

Ōdachi Muneuji, 276, 285, 288–89
Ogasawara Magoroku, 21–22
Ogino Tomotaka, 231–32, 234
Oki no Hōgan, see Sasaki Kiyotaka
Oki no Jirō Saemon Hiroari, 371–73
Onjōji Temple, xxvii, 11n
Ono no Tōfū, 350
Ōta Saburō Saemon-no-jō, 99, 229, 231
Ōtomo family, xlvn
Ōtomo Gukan, 322, 324–26

Pagoda, Prince of the Great, see Morinaga
Palace, imperial, xxiv; lightning strikes, 358–59; rebuilding of, 362–63; rooms and halls of, 347–50; see also specific halls or rooms, e.g., Daigokuden
Pao Shu-ya, 302
Pao Szu, 121, 286n
Pei-kung Yu, 145
Po-i, 129
Po-li Hsi, 129
Prince of the Great Pagoda, see Morinaga
Prisoners, captured at fall of Kasagi, 81–82

Raizen of Sasame, 35
Renshi, see Sammi, Lady
Rice-offering ceremony (Jingonjiki), 349
Rise and Fall of the Minamoto and Taira (Gempei seisuiki), xvi, xxviii
Roisterers, Band of, 14
Rokuhara, xlii, xliii; attack on, 253–58; and battle at Yamazaki, 215–17; defeat of soldier-monks, 219–21; defense of, 205–8, 222–28, 249; Kōgon goes to, 62, 209, 247; Kōgon's family flees from, 260–63; learns of Ashikaga's defection, 245; monks taken to, 31–32; origins of, 5n; repulse of Tadaaki, 230–32
Rokuhara of the North, 5n
Rokuhara of the South, 5n
Rokujō Tadaaki, see Minamoto no Tadaaki
Ryōchū, 95–96, 222, 229, 343, 380

Sadahira, see Minamoto no Sadahira
Sado-no-zenji, 199
Saemon-no-suke, Lady, 98–99
Sagami Jirō, see Hōjō Tokiyuki
Sagami lay monk, see Hōjō Takatoki
Sagami Tarō, see Hōjō Kunitoki
Saichō (Dengyō Daishi), xxviii, 30
Saiga Hayato-no-suke, 31
Saigen' inbon Taiheiki, xiv
Saigyō, 40
Saionji, house of, 8
Saionji Kimmune, 62
Saionji Sanekane, 8
Saitō Genki, 253–54
Saitō Toshiyuki, 18, 19, 26–27
Saji Magoro, 220
Sakabe, battle of, 203
Sakai Sadatoshi, 336–38
Sakurada Sadakuni, 278, 280
Sakurayama Shirō, 91–92
Sammi, Lady, 9, 105, 126, 194, 345, 381
Sanju jōkai, 34n
Sankō taiheiki, xiv
Sansom, Sir George, xx
Sasaki Danjō Saemon-no-jō, 198–99
Sasaki Dōyo, 94–95, 105
Sasaki Kiyotaka (Oki no Hōgan), 85, 126, 192, 196, 198–200
Sasaki Sadakiyo, see Sasaki Kiyotaka
Sasaki Tokinobu, 23, 58, 61, 62, 70, 84, 101, 201, 222, 231, 259 267–68, 321
Sasaki Yoshitsuna (Fujina no Hōgan), 192–94
Sayo Noriie, 204, 243–44
Secret Waters of the Five Places, 182
Segawa, battle of, 203–4
Seiryōden, xxiv, 103, 126, 347, 351
Senjuō, Master, see Ashikago Yoshiakira
Shen-sheng, 384–86
Shiaku Shirō, 298–99
Shiaku Shōon, 298–99
Shiaku Tadayori, 298

Shibuya Jūrō, 173
Shichijō Bridge, 233
Shidara Gorō Saemon-no-jō, 253–54
Shih-yü, 113, 119
Shimazu Aki-no-zenji, 223–25
Shimazu Shirō, 291–92
Shingon Cloister, 349
Shinkaden, 349
Shinkokinshū, 331n, 332n
Shinshaku Nihon bungaku sōsho, xiv
Shintaikemmon'in, *see* Sammi, Lady
Shioda Dōyū, 297
Shioda Toshitoki, 297
Shirakawa barrier, 100
Shirō Sakon-no-taifu, *see* Hōjō Tokioki
Shishinden, xxiv, 67, 347
Shōgoin Cloister, 11
Shogunate, xxxi–xxxiii; Go-Daigo plots against, xl–xliii; Hōjō Takatoki and, xxxvii; origins of, xxii–xxiii; *see also* Warrior class
Shōjin, xlii, 81, 84
Shōkyū, disturbance of, xxiv, 4
Shōni family, xlvn
Shōni Myōe, 322, 324–26
Shosha Mountain, 317
Shōtoku, Empress, 342n
Shōtoku Taishi, 132, 159, 161
Shubin, 374–78
Shunga of Mine, 99, 327–28
Sokutai, 57n
Sokuyū, *see* Akamatsu Sokuyū
Soldier-monks, xxvii–xxviii; in battle of Karasaki Beach, 58–62; Go-Daigo and, xl–xlii, 63–64; invasion of capital, 217–21; of Yoshino, 149
Sompi bummyaku (Tōin Kinsada), xvii
Sonchō (Prince of Myōhōin), xli, 10, 29, 64, 81, 84, 101–2, 344
Son'in, *see* Kajii Prince
Sonryō, Prince, 10, 81, 84, 101–2
Son'un, *see* Morinaga
Ssu-ma I (Chung-ta), 147n
Subhakara, 333
Suda, Saemon, 70, 154–56, 206, 211, 214, 231
Sugawara no Michizane, 151, 347–57, 351n, 361
Sugawara no Zezen, 351
Suketomo, *see* Hino Suketomo
Susaki, battle at, 287–88
Suwa Moritaka, 301–4

Suyama Jirō, 210–11, 213–14, 223, 231, 232, 253, 254, 263
Suyama Yoshitaka, 76–78

Tadaaki, *see* Minamoto no Tadaaki
Ta-fu Chung, 113–16
Taiheiki: authorship, xvii–xviii; date of, xviii; as history, xviii–xix; length, xvi–xvii; meaning of title, xvii; as war tale, xv
Taiheiki shinshaku, xiv
Taiheiki (*Zoku Nihon koten tokuhon*), xiv
T'ai-kung, 205, 207
Taira no Kiyomori, xxii, 106
Taira no Munemori, 335n
Taira no Narisuke, 13, 81, 96
Taira no Shigehira, 39
Taira no Takatoki, *see* Hōjō Takatoki
T'ai-tsai P'i, 113–16
Tajima, 231
Tajimi Kuninaga, xl–xli, 14, 19, 21–23
Takada Hyōgo-no-suke, 191
Takahashi Matashirō, 70, 84, 154–56, 206, 211, 214, 231
Takasuke, *see* Fujiwara no Takasuke
Takatoki, *see* Hōjō Takatoki
Takauji, *see* Ashikaga Takauji
Takebe Shichirō, 256, 257
Takehara Hachirō, 138, 142
Tale of Heiji (*Heiji monogatari*), xvi, xxiin
Tale of the Heike (*Heike monogatari*), xv, xvi, xxv
Tale of Hōgen (*Hōgen monogatari*), xvi, xxiin
Tales of Ise (*Ise monogotari*), 349n
Tamaki, bailiff of, 145–48
Tameakira, *see* Fujiwara no Tameakira
Tanaka Morikane, 224–26
Tanaka Moriyasu, 224–26
Tani-no-dō Temple, 235–36
T'ao Chu, 365
T'ao Chu-kung (Fan Li), 125
Tate-eboshi castle, 363–64
Ta Wang, 56
Temmu, Emperor, 342
Teng T'ung, 336
Tennōji Temple, 131, 154, 155, 160
Tōdaiji Temple, xxvii, xlii, 28
Tōfukuji Temple, xlvi
Tōin Kinsada, xvii

Index

Tōin Kintoshi, 56, 99
Tōin Saneyo, 14, 96, 344
Tōji Temple, xlvi
Tokihito, Prince, see Kōgon
Tokiwa Norisada, 32n, 153
Toki Yorikazu, 18–19
Toki Yorisada, xl–xli, 14, 19–21
Tokunō Yasaburō, 192, 321, 364
Tomoyuki, see Minamoto no Tomoyuki
Tono Hyōe, 139–42
Tono Sign of the Law, see Ryōchū
Tōshōji Temple, 293
Totsugawa, 138, 139
Ts'ao Chih, 29n
Ts'ao Tzu-chien, 130
Tseng Ts'an, 301
Tsuchimikado, Emperor, xxiv
Tsukushi, battle of, 322–26
Tsumori no Kuninatsu, 30
Tzu-fang, 30

Uji Bridge, Maiden of, 333
Ummeiden, 347
Uno Kuniyori, 204, 207
Urabe no Sukune, 54
Utsunomiya Jibu-no-tayū, xxx, 156–60, 190, 321, 334

Vārānsī, 36
Viśvakarman, 318
Vulture Peak, 29

Wada Magosaburō, 157–59
Wada Masatō, 86
Wakiya Yoshisuke, 275–76, 285, 364, 365
Wang Chao-chün, 335
Wang Ling, 300–1
Warrior class, xix, xxix–xxxvi, xliii– xliv; Go-Daigo's fear of, 13; low morale of, 258; mood of, after Go-Daigo's restoration, xlvii, 344; Nikaidō Dōun sums up, 43; prosperity of, 3–27; rewards for loyalty to emperor, xlvi; rewards to monks, 215; rise of Taira and Minamoto, xxi– xxii, xxviii, see also Shogunate
Warrior monks, see Soldier-monks
War tales (*gunki monogatari*), xv–xvi, xxv
Watanabe Bridge, 154–56
Wei Pao, 144
Wen T'ing-yün, 107n
Wen Wang, 44
Wu, State of, 108–25
Wu-tzu, 223
Wu Tzu-hsü, 109–10, 118, 120–23

Yahata, battle at, 241–44
Yamamoto Tokitsuna, 20–21
Yamazaki, 215–16, 241–44
Yata Hikoshichi, 137, 141, 146
Yoshida Fuyufusa, 25–26
Yoshida Sadafusa, xxxviii
Yoshikawa Hachirō, 171
Yoshino Castle, battle of, 175–80
Yoshisada, see Nitta Yoshisada
Yoshisuke, see Wakiya Yoshisuke
Yü, Lady, 261
Yuasa Magoro, 153, 158
Yü-ch'üan, 11
Yüeh, 108–25
Yü Jang, 315, 324
Yūki Chikamitsu, 240, 242, 321, 364
Yü-shan, 29
Yu Wang, 286

Zennyo, 377–78